Praise for the Marta's Legacy series

"Writers like Rivers are why people buy Christian fiction: it's dramatic, engaging . . . [and] this well-told tale will have readers eagerly awaiting the story's resolution."

PUBLISHERS WEEKLY

"An emotionally rich exploration . . . Rivers's novel will appeal to readers who enjoy historical fiction and sweeping family sagas with exotic settings. As her compelling characters seek to do what they feel their faith demands, Rivers sets their resonant struggles against dusty streets, windswept Canadian plains, and California vineyards in vivid scenes readers will not soon forget."

BOOKLIST
Starred Review

"*Her Mother's Hope* has all the meaty elements of a blockbuster. . . . It's a solid novel of family relationships, a page-turner that appeals far beyond both the romance and the Christian categories."

DENVER POST

"This long-awaited novel is every bit as engrossing and stunning as Rivers's previous books. The prose is elegant and life changing, and the characters are memorable. This sweeping family saga will touch both the heart and soul."

ROMANTIC TIMES
Top Pick

"Best-selling author Rivers delivers another captivating novel in *Her Mother's Hope*. . . . Rivers proves once more that she can keep readers transfixed and wanting more."

CHRISTIAN RETAILING
Top Pick

"Top-notch writing and storytelling . . . make *Her Mother's Hope* quite the saga and an exceptional work of historical fiction."
BOOKREPORTER.COM

"The conclusion to Rivers's two-book saga featuring mothers and daughters is both engrossing and emotionally satisfying. . . . The sweeping time period from the 1950s through the present day allows the reader to engage personally in the amazing narrative."
ROMANTIC TIMES
4½ Star Review

"Rivers has written another page-turner. . . . This heartfelt and sweeping saga is as ambitious as its central matriarch."
PUBLISHERS WEEKLY

"*Her Daughter's Dream* . . . is a not-to-be-missed novel for anyone who enjoys good writing. Spanning the 1950s to the present, Rivers stays true to each generation."
CHRISTIAN RETAILING

"Hauntingly beautiful, *Her Daughter's Dream* explores the bonds of love between four generations of mothers and daughters. Francine Rivers holds nothing back in often fragile, always emotional, and sometimes explosive relationships. . . . Like an exquisite melody, *Her Daughter's Dream* will stay with you long after you turn the last page."
NOVEL JOURNEY

HER
MOTHER'S
HOPE

HER MOTHER'S HOPE

FRANCINE RIVERS

Tyndale House Publishers, Inc., Carol Stream, Illinois

Visit Tyndale's exciting Web site at www.tyndale.com.

Check out the latest about Francine Rivers at www.francinerivers.com.

TYNDALE and Tyndale's quill logo are registered trademarks of Tyndale House Publishers, Inc.

Her Mother's Hope

Designed by Beth Sparkman

Edited by Kathryn S. Olson

Published in association with Browne and Miller Literary Associates, LLC, 410 Michigan Avenue, Suite 460, Chicago, IL 60605

This novel is a work of fiction. Names, characters, places, and incidents either are the product of the author's imagination or are used fictitiously. Any resemblance to actual events, locales, organizations, or persons living or dead is entirely coincidental and beyond the intent of either the author or the publisher.

Library of Congress Cataloging-in-Publication Data

Rivers, Francine, date.
  Her mother's hope / Francine Rivers.
    p. cm. — (Marta's legacy ; 1)
  ISBN 978-1-4143-1863-9 (hc)
  ISBN 978-1-4143-1864-6 (sc)
    1. Mothers and daughters—Fiction.   2. Self-actualization (Psychology) in women—Fiction.   I. Title.
PS3568.I83165H47 2010
813'.54—dc22   2009042434

ISBN 978-1-4143-3679-4 (International Trade Paper Edition)

Printed in the United States of America

17 16 15 14 13 12 11
7   6   5   4   3   2   1

For Shannon and Andrea

Acknowledgments

Most of the novel you are about to read is purely fictional, though there are bits and pieces of personal family history woven throughout. The manuscript has taken various forms over the last two years, and in the end morphed into a saga. Many people have helped me in the process of writing the stories of Marta and Hildemara in this first volume and Carolyn and May Flower Dawn in the second. I want to thank each and every one of them.

First of all my husband, Rick, has ridden the storm through this one, listening to every variation of the stories as the characters took form in my imagination and acting as my first editor.

Every family needs a historian, and my brother, Everett, has played that role to perfection. He sent me hundreds of family pictures that helped flesh out the story. I also received invaluable help from my cousin Maureen Rosiere, who described in detail our grandparents' almond and wine-grape ranch, a pattern I used in this novel. Both my husband and my brother shared their Vietnam experiences with me.

Kitty Briggs, Shannon Coibion (our daughter), and Holly Harder shared their experiences as military wives. Holly has been a constant help to me. I know of no other person on the planet who can find information on the Internet faster! Whenever I ran into a wall, Holly tore it down. Thanks, Holly!

Holly's son, U.S. Army Lieutenant Daniel Harder, gave me information on the engineering and ROTC programs at Cal Poly. He is now on active duty. Our prayers are with him.

Ila Vorderbrueggen, a nurse and personal friend of my mother's, helped me fill in information about long-term patient care in the Arroyo del Valle Sanatorium. I've enjoyed our correspondence.

Kurt Thiel and Robert Schwinn answered questions about Inter-Varsity Christian Fellowship. Keep up the good work, gentlemen!

Globus tour guide Joppy Wissink rerouted a bus so that Rick and I had the opportunity to walk around my grandmother's hometown of Steffisburg, Switzerland.

All along the course of this project, I have had brainstorming partners when I needed them. Colleen Phillips raised questions and encouraged me from the beginning. Robin Lee Hatcher and Sunni Jeffers jumped in with ideas and questions when I didn't know which way to go. My agent, Danielle Egan-Miller, and her associate, Joanna MacKenzie, helped me see how to restructure the novel to show the story I wanted to tell.

I would also like to thank Karen Watson of Tyndale House Publishers for her insights and encouraging support. She helped me see my characters more clearly. And, of course, every writer needs a good editor. I am blessed with one of the best, Kathy Olson. She makes revision work exciting and challenging rather than painful.

Finally, I thank the Lord for my mother and grandmother. Their lives and Mom's journals first inspired the idea of writing about mother-daughter relationships. They were both hardworking women of faith. They both passed on some years ago, but I cling to the promise that they are still very much alive and undoubtedly enjoying one another's company. One day I will see them again.

Marta

Marta usually loved Sundays. It was the only day Papa closed the tailor shop and Mama had a rest. The family dressed in their finest clothes and walked to church, Papa and Mama ahead, Marta's older brother, Hermann, behind them, and Marta and her younger sister, Elise, bringing up the rear. Usually other families joined them along the way. Marta would watch eagerly for her best friend, Rosie Gilgan, who'd run down the hill to join her and walk the rest of the way to the old Romanesque church with its arches mortared shut and the white clock tower.

Today, Marta hung her head, wishing she could run away and hide among the pines and alders while the townsfolk gathered for services. She could sit on her favorite fallen tree and ask God why Papa despised her so much and seemed so set on making her suffer. Today, she wouldn't have complained if Papa had told her to stay home and work in the shop alone and not step foot outside the door for a week, though it would take longer than that for the bruises to fade.

Despite evidence of the beating he had given her, Papa insisted everyone attend services. She wore a knitted cap and kept her chin down, hoping no one would notice. It wasn't the first time she had borne the marks of his anger. When people came close, Marta shifted the woolen scarf or turned her face away.

When they came into the churchyard, Papa sent Mama ahead with Elise and Hermann. He caught Marta by the elbow and spoke into her ear. "You'll sit in back."

"People will want to know why."

"And I'll tell them the truth. You're being punished for defying me." His fingers dug in painfully, but she refused to utter a sound of pain. "Keep your head down. No one wants to see your ugly face." He let go of her and went inside.

Fighting tears, Marta went in alone and stepped into the last row of straight-backed chairs.

She watched her father join Mama. When he glanced back, she tucked her chin quickly, looking up again only after he had seated himself. Her sister, Elise, looked back over her shoulder, face far too pale and strained for a child. Mama leaned close, whispering, and Elise turned face-forward again. Hermann sat between Mama and Papa, his head turning to the right and left. No doubt he was looking for friends and would disappear as soon as the services ended.

Rosie passed by and sat near the front. The Gilgans had eight children and took up an entire row. Rosie glanced toward Marta's mother and father, then back. Marta hid behind Herr Becker, sitting in front of her. She waited briefly and peered around the baker again.

All the murmuring stopped when the minister stepped into the pulpit. He opened the service with prayer. Joining with the congregation, Marta said the prayer of confession, and she heard the minister's assurance of God's mercy and forgiveness. As the creed and Scriptures were read, Marta let her mind drift like the snow blowing across the Alpine meadows above Steffisburg. She imagined herself spreading her arms like wings and letting the white swirling flakes lift and carry her wherever God willed.

And where would that be? she wondered.

The minister's voice rose as he preached. He always said the same thing, but used different words, different examples from the Bible. *"Strive harder. Faith is dead without good works. Do not become complacent. Those who turn their backs on God are destined for hell."*

Was God like Papa, never satisfied no matter how hard she tried? Papa believed in God, but when had he ever shown her mercy? And if he believed God created everyone, then what right had Papa to complain over how tall she was, how thin, how white her skin, how large her hands and feet? Her father cursed her because she passed the school examinations "and made Hermann look a fool!"

She'd tried to defend herself. She should have known better. "Hermann doesn't apply himself. He'd rather hike in the hills than do his studies."

Papa came after her. Mama tried to get between, but he shoved her roughly aside. "You think you can talk to me like that and get away with it?" Marta raised her arm to protect herself, but it did no good.

"Johann, don't!" Mama cried out.

Still gripping Marta's arm, he turned on Mama. "Don't you tell me—"

"How many times must we turn the other cheek, Papa?" Something white-hot rose up inside Marta when he threatened Mama.

That's when he used his fist on her. He let go of her abruptly and stood over her. "She made me do it. You heard her! A father can't tolerate insolence in his own home!"

Marta didn't know she'd fainted until Mama stroked the hair back from her face. "Be still, Marta. Elise is getting a wet cloth." Marta could hear Elise crying. "Papa's gone to the tanner. He won't be back for a while." Mama took the cloth Elise held out. Marta sucked in her breath when Mama dabbed her split lip. "You shouldn't provoke your father."

"So it's my fault."

"I didn't say that."

"I pass the examination with the highest marks in school and get a beating for it. Where's Hermann? Strolling along on some mountain trail?"

Mama cupped her cheek. "You must forgive your father. He lost his temper. He didn't know what he was doing."

Mama always made excuses for him, just as Papa made excuses for Hermann. No one made excuses for her.

"Forgive," Mama said. *"Seventy times seven. Forgive!"*

Marta's mouth twisted as the minister spoke of God the Father. She wished God was like Mama instead.

When the service ended, Marta waited until Papa motioned her to join the family. Head down, she fell into step beside Elise.

"Johann Schneider!"

Papa turned at Herr Gilgan's voice. The two men shook hands and talked. Hermann took advantage of the distraction to join some friends heading up the hill. Mama took Elise's hand when Frau Gilgan joined them.

"Where have you been all week?" Rosie spoke softly and Marta turned. Rosie gasped softly. "Oh, Marta." She moaned in sympathy. "Again? What was his reason this time?"

"School."

"But you passed the examination!"

"Hermann didn't."

"But that's not fair."

Marta lifted one shoulder and gave Rosie a bleak smile. "It does no good to tell him so." Rosie would never be able to understand. *Her* father adored her. Herr Gilgan adored all his children. They all worked together in the running of *Hotel Edelweiss*, encouraging one another in everything. They teased one another with good-natured humor, but never mocked or belittled anyone. If one of them had a difficulty, the others lovingly closed ranks around him and helped.

Sometimes Marta envied her friend. Every member of the Gilgan family would finish school. The boys would serve their two years in the Swiss Army and then go off to university in Bern or Zurich. Rosie and her sisters would learn fine cuisine and the art of running a large household that embraced up to thirty outsiders. She would be tutored in French, English, and Italian. If Rosie had further aspirations, her father wouldn't deny her simply because she was a girl. He would send her to university along with her brothers.

"You've been in school long enough," Papa had declared when he came back from the tanner. "You're old enough to carry your share of the financial burden."

Begging him for one more year of school had done no good at all.

Tears filled Marta's eyes. "Papa said it's enough that I can read, write, and do arithmetic."

"But you're only twelve, and if anyone in our class should make it to the university, it would be you."

"There will be no university for me. Papa said I'm done with school."

"But why?"

"Papa says too much school fills a girl's head with nonsense." By *nonsense* Papa meant ambition. Marta burned with it. Marta had hoped that with enough schooling, she would have choices about what to do with her life. Papa said school had puffed her up and she needed to be brought down to where she belonged.

Rosie took Marta's hand. "Maybe he'll change his mind and let you come back to school. I'm sure Herr Scholz will want to talk to him about it."

Herr Scholz might try, but her father wouldn't listen. Once he made up his mind, not even an avalanche would change it. "It'll do no good, Rosie."

"What will you do now?"

"Papa plans to hire me out."

"Marta!"

Marta jumped at Papa's bellowing voice. Scowling, he motioned sharply for her to come. Rosie didn't let go of her hand as they joined their families.

Frau Gilgan stared at Marta. "What happened to your face?" She cast an angry look at Papa.

Papa stared back at her. "She fell down the stairs." Papa gave Marta a look of warning. "She's always been clumsy. Just look at those big hands and feet."

Frau Gilgan's dark eyes snapped. "She'll grow into them." Her husband put his hand beneath her elbow.

Mama held out her hand to Marta. "Come along. Elise is cold. We need to go home." Elise huddled close to Mama's side, not looking at anyone.

Rosie hugged Marta and whispered, "I'll ask Papa to hire you!"

Marta didn't dare hope her father would agree—he knew how much she would enjoy working for the Gilgans.

Papa went out that afternoon and didn't return home until late in the evening. He smelled of beer and seemed quite pleased with himself. "Marta!" He slapped his hand on the table. "I have found work for you."

She would work for the Beckers at the bakery every morning. "You must be there by four in the morning." She would spend three afternoons a week working for the Zimmers. The doctor thought his wife would welcome some freedom from tending their fractious new baby. "And Frau Fuchs says she can use you to tend her hives. It's getting colder, and she'll be ready to harvest the honey soon. You'll work nights as long as she needs you." He leaned back in his chair. "And you'll work at *Hotel Edelweiss* two days a week." He watched her face closely. "Don't think you're going to have tea and cookies with your little friend anymore. You're there to work. Do you understand?"

"Yes, Papa." Marta clasped her hands in front of her, trying not to show her pleasure.

"And don't ask for anything. Not from any of them. Herr Becker will pay in bread, Frau Fuchs in honey when the time comes. As to the others, they will settle with me and not you."

Heat spread through Marta's limbs, surging up her neck into her cheeks and burning there like lava beneath pale earth. "Am I to receive nothing, Papa? nothing at all?"

"You receive a roof over your head and food on your plate. You receive clothes on your back. As long as you live in my house, whatever you make rightfully belongs to me." He turned his head away. "Anna!" he shouted at Mama. "Are you done with that dress for Frau Keller yet?"

"I'm working on it now, Johann."

Scowling, Papa shouted again. "She expects delivery by the end of the week! If you don't have it ready by then, she'll take her business to another dressmaker!" Papa jerked his head. "Go help your mother."

Marta joined Mama by the fire. She had a box of colored threads on the table at her side and black wool partially embroidered spread across her lap. She coughed violently into a cloth, folded and tucked it in her apron pocket before taking up her sewing again. Anyone could see by her pallor and the dark circles under her eyes that Mama wasn't well again. Mama had weak lungs. Tonight, her lips had a faint bluish tint. "Help your sister, Marta. She's developing another headache."

Elise had spent all evening on her sampler, brow furrowed over every stitch in pained concentration. Marta had helped her until Papa returned. About the only thing Elise could do well was hem, leaving Mama and Marta to do the fine embroidery work. Elise struggled as much as Hermann in school, though not for the same reasons. At ten, Elise could barely read and write. However, what she lacked in intellect and dexterity was overlooked because of her rare and delicate beauty. Mama's greatest pleasure took place every morning when she brushed and braided Elise's waist-length white-blonde hair. She had flawless alabaster skin and wide, angelic blue eyes. Papa asked nothing of her, taking pride in her beauty, acting sometimes as though he owned a priceless piece of art.

Marta worried about her sister. Papa might be right about suitors, but he didn't understand Elise's deep-seated fears. She had an almost-desperate dependence upon Mama and became hysterical when Papa went into one of his rages, though never in Elise's life had a hand been laid on her in anger. Papa would have an eye out for a settled man with money and position for Elise.

Marta prayed nightly that God would bless her sister with a husband who would cherish and protect her—and be rich enough to hire others to cook, clean, and raise the children! Elise would never be able to carry out such responsibilities.

Marta lifted a stool and set it beside her mother's chair. "Frau Keller always wants things done yesterday."

"She's a good customer." Mama laid a section of skirt carefully over Marta's lap so they could work on it together.

"*Good* is not a word I would use, Mama. The woman is a tyrant."

"It's not wrong to know what you want."

"If you're willing to pay for it." Marta fumed. Yes, Papa would ask Frau Keller to pay for the additional work, but Frau Keller would refuse. If Papa pressed, Frau Keller would become indignant "at such treatment" and threaten to take her business "to someone more appreciative of my generosity." She would remind Papa that she ordered six dresses a year, and he should be thankful for her business in these hard times. Papa would apologize profusely, then add what he could to the amount Herr Keller owed for the suits Papa made him. And Papa often had to wait six months for even partial payment. No wonder the Kellers were rich. They clung to their money like lichen to rock. "If I were Papa, I'd demand a portion of the money before beginning the work, and full payment before any garment left the shop."

Mama laughed softly. "So much fire from a twelve-year-old girl."

Marta wondered how Mama would ever finish the skirt on time. She threaded a needle with pink silk and set to work on flower petals. "Papa has hired me out, Mama."

Mama sighed. "I know, *Liebling*." She quickly drew the cloth from her apron pocket to cover her mouth. When the spasm passed, she fought for breath as she pushed the cloth back into its hiding place.

"Your cough is getting worse."

"I know. It comes from the years I worked in the cigar factory. It'll get better when summer comes." In summer, Mama could sit outside and work instead of sitting by a smoking fire.

"It never goes away completely, Mama. You should see the doctor." Perhaps when Marta worked for Frau Zimmer, she might speak with the doctor about what could be done to help Mama.

"Let's not worry about that now. Frau Keller must have her dress!"

❊　❊　❊

Marta quickly became used to her work schedule. She got up while it was still dark, dressed quickly, and went up the street to the bakery. When Frau Becker let her in the front door, the room smelled of fresh baking bread. Marta went into the kitchen and chopped nuts for *Nusstorten* while Frau Becker stirred batter for *Schokoladenkuchen*.

"We're making *Magenbrot* today," Herr Becker announced as he stretched out a long snake of dough and cut it into small pieces. "Marta, dip those in butter and roll them in cinnamon and raisins, and then arrange them in the angel cake tins."

Marta worked quickly, aware that both of the Beckers watched her. Frau Becker poured the dark batter into cake forms and handed the wooden spoon to Marta. "Go ahead. Lick it clean."

Herr Becker laughed. "Ah, see how the girl can smile, Fanny." He punched dough down. "You learn quickly, Marta." He winked at his wife. "We'll have to teach her how to make Epiphany cakes this coming Christmas. *Ja?*"

"And *Lebkuchen*." Frau Becker winked at Marta. Mama loved the spicy gingerbread. "And *Marzipan*." Frau Becker took the spoon and tossed it into the sink. "I'll teach you how to make *Butterplätzchen*." She set butter, flour, and sugar on the worktable. "And tomorrow, I'll teach you how to make anise cookies."

When the bakery opened for business, Frau Becker gave Marta two breakfast loaves as payment. "You're a good worker."

Marta took the bread to Mama and had a bowl of *Müsli*. After doing her chores and eating an early lunch, she headed down the road past the schoolhouses to the doctor's house.

Frau Zimmer looked distressed when she opened the door.

"Here! Take him!" She thrust her screaming baby into Marta's arms and grabbed her shawl. "I'm going to visit a friend." She slipped around Marta and headed off without a backward glance.

Marta went inside and closed the door so people wouldn't hear the baby wailing. She paced, singing hymns. When that didn't calm little Evrard, she tried rocking him. She checked his diaper. Finally, exasperated, she put him down on the rug. "Go ahead and scream your head off."

The baby stopped crying and rolled onto his stomach. Arching his back, he reached his arms out and kicked his feet. Marta laughed. "You just wanted a little freedom, didn't you?" She collected scattered toys and dropped them in front of him. He kicked his legs harder, gurgling in delight. He squealed, his hands opening and closing. "Reach for it! I'm not giving it to you." He managed to scoot a few inches and grasp a rattle. Marta clapped. "Good for you, Evrard!" He rolled onto his back.

When little Evrard wore himself out, Marta picked him up and rocked him to sleep. Frau Zimmer came in an hour later, looking refreshed. She stopped and listened, looking somewhat alarmed. "Is he all right?" She hurried over to the crib and peered in. "He's sleeping! He never sleeps in the afternoon. What did you do?"

"I let him play on the rug. He tried to crawl."

The following afternoon, Marta went up the hill to *Hotel Edelweiss*, where Frau Gilgan put her to work stripping beds and remaking them with fresh mattress sheets and duvets for the feather beds. Fluffing them full of air, she rolled them on the end of the bed, then took the laundry downstairs to the wash room. Frau Gilgan worked with her, sharing amusing stories of past guests. "Of course, you have some who are not pleased with anything you do and others who break their legs skiing."

Two of Rosie's older sisters manned the washtubs and kept great pots of water boiling on the woodstove. Marta's arms ached from stirring linen; pushing sheets and duvets down, around, and over; spreading folds; and stirring again. Kristen, the older girl, hooked a sheet and dragged it up, folding and wringing it into tight ropes,

letting the water cascade back into the washtub. Then she shook
the sheet out into a tub of steaming rinse water.

Snowflakes caught on the window frames, but perspiration
dripped from Marta's face. She blotted it away with her sleeve.

"Oh!" Frau Gilgan came over and held out her hands, strong
and square, reddened and callused from years of washing. "Let me
see your hands, Marta." Frau Gilgan turned Marta's hands palms
up and clucked her tongue. "Blisters. I should not have worked
you so hard on your first day, but you didn't complain. Your hands
will be so sore you won't be able to make a stitch."

"But there's a whole pile of sheets yet to do."

Frau Gilgan put her fists on her ample hips and laughed. "*Ja*,
and that's why I have daughters." She put her arm around Marta.
"Go on upstairs. Rosie will be back from school by now. She'll
want to have tea with you before you leave. And if you've time,
she needs help with geography."

Marta said she'd be delighted.

Rosie jumped from her chair. "Marta! I forgot you started
work today. I'm so glad you're here! I missed you at school. It's not
the same without you. No one to answer Herr Scholz's difficult
questions."

"Your mother says you need help with your geography."

"Oh, not now. I've so much to tell you. Let's go for a walk."

Marta knew she'd have to listen to the latest escapades of Arik
Brechtwald. Rosie had been in love with him since the day he
fished her out of a creek. It did no good to remind her Arik had
caused the fall in the first place. He'd dared her to cross the Zulg.
She'd made it halfway across when she slipped on a rock and slith-
ered down over a small waterfall before Arik could catch hold of
her. He'd lifted her out and carried her to the bank. Ever since
then, Arik had been Rosie's knight in shining armor.

Snow sifted softly from the clouds overhead, adding thickness to
the blanket of white over Steffisburg. Smoke curled up like ghostly
fingers from chimneys, dissipating in the chill afternoon air. While
Rosie chattered on gaily, Marta trudged along beside her. White

drifts covered the Alpine meadow, which would in a few months turn verdant green with splashes of red, yellow, and blue blossoms tempting and nourishing Frau Fuchs's bees. Rosie brushed snow off a log and sat where they could look down on *Hotel Edelweiss* and Steffisburg below. If the day had been clear, they could have seen *Schloss Thun* and the *Thunersee* like a sheet of gray glass.

Today, low clouds made the sun look like a white, blurred ball ready to bounce off the mountains beyond Interlaken.

Marta's breath made steam. Tears welled up as she listened to Rosie's musings about Arik. Her friend didn't have a care in the world other than whether Arik liked her or not. Pressing her mouth tight, Marta tried not to feel jealous. Maybe Papa was right. She and Rosie would be friends for a little while longer, and then their different situations would build a wall between them. Marta worked for the Gilgans now. She wasn't the friend who came to call or have tea or sit and chat while Rosie's mother put out anise cookies on a silver platter and hot chocolate in fine porcelain cups. Everything was about to change, and Marta couldn't bear it.

Now that Papa had removed her from school, she would only be qualified to be a servant or tend someone's fractious baby. She could help Mama with dressmaking, but Mama made so little money when one considered how many hours she worked for women like Frau Keller, who expected perfection for a pittance. And Mama never saw a franc of what she made. Papa held the purse strings and complained bitterly about how little they had, though he always managed to find enough for beer.

Rosie put her arm around Marta's shoulders. "Don't look so sad."

Marta stood abruptly and moved away. "Herr Scholz was going to teach me French. I could've continued with Latin. If I knew even one more language, I might be able to find a decent job someday in a nice shop in Interlaken. If my father has his way, I'll never be more than a servant." As soon as the bitter words poured out, shame filled her. How could she say such things to Rosie? "I'm not ungrateful to your parents. Your mother was so kind to me today. . . ."

"They love you like a daughter."

"Because you've loved me like a sister."

"That's not going to change just because you're not in school. I wish I could quit. I'd rather stay home and help my mother than try to cram facts into my head."

"Oh, Rosie." Marta covered her face. "I would've given anything to stay, through high school at least."

"I could give you books."

"I've no time now. Papa's seen to that." Marta stared off at the cloud-shrouded mountains that stood like prison walls. Her father intended to keep her captive. She was stronger and healthier than Mama. She could learn faster than Hermann or Elise. Hermann would go off to university. Elise would marry. Marta would be kept at home. After all, someone would have to do the work when Mama couldn't.

"I have to go home. I need to help Mama."

As they walked down the hill, Rosie took Marta's hand. "Maybe when Hermann makes it into high school, your father will allow you to come back to school."

"Hermann will fail again. He has no head for books." At least, the next time, Papa would not be able to blame her.

Marta spent two years working for the Beckers, Zimmers, and Gilgans. During the winters, she worked for Frau Fuchs as well, smoking the bees into a stupor so she could rob the hives. Marta cranked the handle to spin the honey from the combs. After days and days of hard work, Frau Fuchs paid her in honey, only two small jars. When Papa saw them, he went into a rage and threw one against the wall.

At least, Mama and Elise appreciated the fresh breakfast loaves Marta brought home from the bakery, and sometimes she brought cookies. At Christmas, the Beckers gave her *Marzipan* and *Schokoladenkuchen*. Dr. Zimmer came to see Mama every few weeks, although Papa preferred francs in his pocket to the poultices and elixirs the doctor gave Mama. All through spring and summer, Frau Zimmer paid in fresh vegetables and flowers from her garden. Mama didn't have to purchase anything from the market.

Only the Gilgans paid in francs, but Marta never saw any of them.

"Herr Gilgan says you're smart enough to run your own hotel someday." Papa gave a derisive laugh as he dipped bread into hot cheese. "Since you're so smart, you can make sure Hermann passes the examinations next time."

"And how can I do that, Papa?" Marta bristled. "Hermann has to want to learn."

His face flushed in anger. "Listen to her, Hermann. She thinks you're stupid. She thinks you can't learn. She still thinks she's better than you."

"I never said I was better!" Marta shoved her chair back. "I was just more interested!"

Papa stood and loomed over her. "Make Hermann interested and maybe I'll send you to school. If he fails again, you'll answer to me!" He leaned across the table and shoved her back into her chair. "Do you understand me?"

Angry tears filled her eyes. "I understand you, Papa." She understood him all too well.

He grabbed his coat and went out the door. Elise didn't raise her head, and Mama didn't ask where he was going.

"I'm sorry, Marta." Hermann spoke glumly from across the table.

❄ ❄ ❄

Marta worked with Hermann every evening to no avail. "It's all so boring!" Hermann groaned. "And it's nice outside."

Marta slapped him across the back of his head. "That's nothing to what I'll get if you don't concentrate."

He pushed his chair back. "As soon as I'm old enough, I'm quitting and going into the Army."

She went to Mama. "Please speak to him, Mama. He won't listen to me." Maybe if Mama pleaded with Hermann, he might try harder. "What hope have I of going back to school when that dolt refuses to use the brain God gave him?"

Dr. Zimmer's poultices and elixirs had done little to help Mama's cough. She looked drawn and pale; her clothes hung loosely on her thin frame. The bones of her wrists looked as fragile as birds' wings.

"There's not a thing I can do, Marta. You can't change a dog into a cat."

Marta flung herself into a chair and put her head in her hands. "Because he's hopeless, I have no hope."

Mama left her needle tucked into an embroidery stitch as she reached over to cover Marta's hand. "You're learning new things every day, from the Beckers and Gilgans. You must wait and see what God will do."

Sighing, Marta threaded a needle to help Mama. "Every franc I earn will be used to pay Hermann's school expenses. And he doesn't care, Mama. Not a bit." Her voice broke. "It's not fair!"

"God has plans for you, too, Marta."

"It's Papa who makes the plans." She stabbed her needle into the wool.

"God says to trust and obey."

"So I must submit to one who despises me and crushes every hope I have?"

"God does not despise you."

"I meant Papa."

Mama didn't disagree. Marta stopped and watched her mother's slender fingers dip the needle in and out of the black wool. A delicate white edelweiss began to take form. Tying off and snipping the white thread, Mama took up another with yellow and made tiny French knots at the center of the flower. When she finished, she smiled at Marta. "You can find pleasure in work well done."

Marta's chest squeezed tight with pain. "I'm not like you, Mama. You see the world through different eyes." Mama found blessings everywhere because she searched diligently for them. How often had Marta seen Mama leaning against the work counter in the kitchen, bent with exhaustion, sweat pouring from her brow as she watched the mountain finches flitting from branch to branch in the linden tree outside the window? A soft word from Papa would bring a tender smile. Despite his cruelty, his selfishness, Mama found something to love in him. Sometimes Marta would see a look of pity come into her mother's face when she looked at Papa.

"Do you know what you want?"

"To make something of my life. To be more than someone's servant." Her eyes grew hot and grainy. "I knew it was too much to dream of going to the university, Mama, but I would've liked to finish high school."

"What about now?"

"Now? I'd like to learn French. I'd like to learn English and Italian, too." She stabbed her needle through the black wool. "Anyone who can speak multiple languages can find a good job." She pulled the thread through too quickly and it tangled. "But I'll never have the—"

"Stop, Marta." Mama reached over and touched her gently. "You're making it worse."

Turning the black wool over, Marta plucked at the loops, loosening them.

"If the opportunity arose for you to learn more . . . ?" Mama looked at her in question.

"I'd find a good job and save money until I had enough to buy a chalet."

"You want a place like *Hotel Edelweiss*, don't you?" Mama began on another flower.

"I'll never dream of having anything as grand as that. I'd be happy with a boardinghouse." She gave a bleak laugh. "I'd be happy to work in a nice shop in Interlaken selling *Dirndln* to tourists!" She yanked the thread through. "But that's not likely, is it? What's the use of dreaming?" She thrust the wool aside and rose. If she sat another minute, she'd suffocate.

"Perhaps God put the dream in your head."

"Why?"

"To teach you patience."

"Oh, Mama . . ." Marta groaned. "Don't I show patience teaching that mulish brother of mine? Haven't I shown patience hoping Papa might change his mind and let me go back to school? It's been two years, Mama! I've done everything he's told me to do. I'm fourteen! Rosie doesn't ask me to help her anymore. I grow more stupid every year! What good is patience when nothing will ever change?"

"Nonsense. Come and sit, *Bärchen*." Mama put her work aside and took Marta's hands firmly. "Look at what you've gained through the Beckers, Frau Fuchs and Frau Zimmer, and the Gilgans. You've learned to bake, tend bees and children, and you've seen what it takes to run a fine hotel. Doesn't that show you God is preparing you—?"

Her hands tightened when Marta opened her mouth to protest.

"Hush, Marta, and listen to me. Listen carefully. It doesn't matter what your father plans, nor what his motives might be. God will prevail. God will use everything to His good purpose if you love and trust Him."

Marta went cold. She saw something in her mother's expression that warned her. "Papa's made plans for me, hasn't he? What plans, Mama?"

Mama's blue eyes grew moist. "You must search out the usefulness in every situation."

Marta snatched her hands from Mama's. "Tell me, Mama."

"I can't. It's for your father to explain." She took up her sewing and said nothing more.

Papa laid out his plans for Marta the next morning. "You will be pleased to know I'm sending you to school. I would've sent you sooner, but *Haushaltungsschule Bern* only takes girls fourteen and older. Count and Countess Saintonge are the instructors. Royalty! You should be happy! I've been assured that any girl who graduates from their housekeeping school will have no difficulty in finding a good position. You'll be in Bern six months. You can pay me back when you come home and find a position."

"Pay you back?"

His eyes cooled. "The tuition cost me 120 francs and another 30 francs for books. You should be pleased. You wanted to go to school." His voice hardened. "You're going!"

"This isn't the kind of school I had in mind, Papa." As well he knew!

"You're so smart; let's see you make the most of the opportunity

I'm giving you. This is my thanks for Hermann passing his examinations. Who knows? If you do well enough in Bern, you might end up working at *Schloss Thun!*" The idea seemed to please him. "That would be something to boast about! You leave in three days."

"But what about the Beckers, Papa? and the Zimmers and Gilgans?"

"I told them yesterday I was sending you to school. They said to wish you well."

School! Marta fumed. Training to be a better servant was more like it.

Mama sat silent at the end of the table, hands in her lap. Angry, Marta looked at her. How could Mama look so serene? She remembered Mama's plea. *"Search out the usefulness . . . Count your blessings. . . ."*

She would be away from home for the first time. She would live in Bern. She wouldn't have to look at Papa or listen to his constant complaints.

"Thank you, Papa. I look forward to it."

Elise gave a soft cry and fled the table.

"What's wrong with that girl now?" Papa muttered.

"Marta's leaving home, Johann."

"She's coming back!" He waved his hand in exasperation. "It's not as though she's leaving for good. She'll only be gone six months and then she'll be home forever."

The hair on the back of Marta's neck rose. *Forever.*

As soon as Papa left the table, Mama asked Marta to find Elise. "She'll probably be down by the creek. You know how she loves to listen to the water."

Marta found her where the creek ran into the Zulg. She sat down beside her. "I have to go sometime, Elise."

Elise clasped her knees against her chest and stared at the shimmering ripples below. "But Bern is so far away." Her blue eyes filled with tears. "Do you want to go?"

"I'd rather be going to the university, but housekeeping school will have to do."

"What will I do without you?" Tears slipped down Elise's pale cheeks.

"What you always do." Marta wiped the tears away. "Help Mama."

"But I'll be alone in our room at night. You know I'm afraid of the dark."

"Let the cat sleep with you."

Elise started to cry. "Why can't things stay as they are? Why can't Papa let you stay here?"

"Things can't stay the same." She pushed a blonde curl behind Elise's ear. "Someday, you'll marry, Elise. You'll have a husband who loves you. You'll have a home of your own. You'll have children." She gave Elise a rueful smile. "When you go, Elise, where will I be?" Papa said no man would ever want such a plain, ill-tempered girl.

Elise blinked, like a child waking to a bad dream. "I thought you'd always be here."

In Steffisburg, in Papa's tailor shop, under Papa's thumb, doing Papa's will. "That's what Papa thinks. Is that what you wish for me, Elise?"

"Aren't you afraid to leave?" Tears slipped down her white cheeks. "I want to stay home with Mama."

"You're not going anywhere, Elise." Marta lay back in the spring grass and flung an arm over her head. "And I'm only going to be away six months."

Elise lay back and rested her head against Marta's shoulder. "I wish you could stay here and not go at all."

Marta put her arm around her sister and stared up at the darkening sky. "Every time you think of me, Elise, pray. Pray I learn something useful. Pray I learn more in Bern than how to be someone's maid."

❄ ❄ ❄

Marta went by to thank the Beckers and Zimmers and to say good-bye. And she went to the Gilgans' the day before she left. Frau Gilgan served tea and cookies. Herr Gilgan gave her twenty francs. "This is for you, Marta." He closed her fingers around it. Marta couldn't speak past the lump in her throat.

Frau Gilgan suggested Marta and Rosie go for a nice walk up to the meadow. Rosie took her hand. "Mama doesn't think you'll come back. She thinks you'll find a job in Bern and stay there, that I'll have to wait until our family goes up there before I see you again." The Gilgans went up every few months to buy things for the hotel. Sometimes Rosie and her sisters came back with ready-made dresses from one of the shops along the *Marktgasse*.

When they sat on their favorite fallen log, Rosie lifted her white apron and dug into the deep pocket of her skirt. "I have something for you."

"A book!" Marta took it with pleasure. Finding no title on the spine, she opened it. "Blank pages."

"So you can write all your adventures." Rosie grinned. "I expect you to let me read it when I see you. I want to know about all the handsome city boys you meet, the places you see, all the wonderful things you're going to do."

Blinking back tears, Marta ran her hand over the fine leather. "I've never had anything so fine."

"I wish I were going with you. There's so much to see and do. What fun we'd have! When you've finished school, you'll be hired by a handsome aristocrat who'll fall in love with you, and—"

"Don't be silly. No one will ever want to marry me."

Rosie took Marta's hand and wove their fingers tightly together. "You may not be as beautiful as Elise, but you have fine qualities. Everyone thinks so. My mother and father think you could do anything you set your mind to."

"Did you tell them about my dream?" Marta pulled her hand away.

"In a weak moment, and go ahead and scowl at me, but I'm not sorry I did. Why do you think Mama told you so much about what it takes to run a hotel?"

As they walked down the hill toward Steffisburg, Rosie took Marta's hand again. "Promise you'll write and tell me everything."

Marta wove her fingers with Rosie's. "Only if you promise to write back and not fill every line with dribble about Arik Brechtwald."

They both laughed.

3

Mama awakened her before dawn the next morning. Papa gave Marta just enough money to buy a one-way train ticket to Bern. "I'll send you enough to get you home when you graduate." He handed her the letter of acceptance, proof of tuition payment, and a map of Bern with the address of the housekeeping school. "You better start now. The train leaves Thun in two hours."

"I thought you might go with me."

"Why? You can make it on your own." He went into the shop to start work early.

"Don't look so worried."

"I've never been on a train, Mama."

Mama gave her a teasing smile. "It goes faster than a coach." Mama hugged her tightly and handed over the knapsack she had packed with a spare skirt, two shirtwaists, undergarments, a hairbrush, and toiletries.

Marta tried not to show how nervous she felt going off on her own. She was thankful Elise hadn't awakened, for if her sister had started crying, Marta would have given in to tears, too. She kissed Mama's cool cheek and thanked her. "Good-bye, Papa!" she called out.

"You'd better hurry!" he shouted back.

Mama went out the door with her. She took a small purse from her pocket and gave it to Marta. "A few francs for paper, envelopes, and postage stamps." She cupped Marta's face and kissed her twice, then whispered in her ear. "And buy yourself a cup of chocolate. Then find the Samson Fountain. It was my favorite." She kept an arm around Marta and walked with her a little ways. "When you get up each morning, you will know I'm praying for you. And every evening when you go to bed, I'll be praying then, too." If God listened to anyone in the family, surely He listened to Mama, who loved Him so much. "In whatever you do, Marta, do it as unto the Lord."

"I will, Mama."

Mama let her go. When Marta looked back, she saw tears in her mother's eyes. She looked so frail. "Don't forget us."

"Never." Marta wanted to run back and hold on to her.

"Go on now." Mama waved.

Afraid she might lose her courage, Marta turned away quickly and started off down the street at a brisk walk.

The farther she went, the more her excitement grew. She ran part of the way and arrived at the train station just as the ticket office opened. Her heart leaped when the train arrived. She watched to see what other passengers did, then handed her ticket to the conductor before climbing aboard. She made her way down the narrow aisle, passing a man in a ready-made business suit shuffling through papers from his case. Another sat two rows behind him, reading a book. A woman told her three children to stop fussing at one another.

Marta took a seat near the back. She put her knapsack between her feet and looked out the window. She jumped in fright when the train jolted. She caught hold of the seat in front of her and hung on, fighting down panic. How fast would this train move? Would it jump the tracks? Could she reach the door and get off before the train left the station? The thought of what Papa would say and do if she showed up at the front door stopped her. She looked at the other passengers and saw that no one else seemed alarmed at the jolting and creaking, or the loud whistle. She leaned back and watched Thun pass by outside her window.

As the train picked up speed, her heart did, too. Every minute took her farther away from Mama and Rosie and Elise. When tears came, silent and hot, she wiped them away.

The Aare River ran alongside the train tracks. She watched out the window as she rode through hills dotted with plump, broad-boxed farmhouses topped with roofs curving almost to the ground. The train stopped at every town, and she leaned this way and that to see as much of the squares and markets as she could. She saw old covered bridges not yet replaced with stone. Every village had a clock tower, even if it didn't have a train station.

The wheels clickity-clicked as the train sped toward Bern. When the outskirts of the city came into view, Marta picked up her knapsack and held it on her lap. She could see great stone buildings and a bridge across the green Aare as it curved around the old city. Houses stood in rows above the river on the other side. She looked at her map and out the window again, not sure which direction she would have to go to find the Saintonges' housekeeping school. She would have to ask directions.

When the train stopped inside the station, Marta followed the others down the steps. She felt as though she had stepped into one of Frau Fuchs's beehives with its constant, churning move-ment of bodies and the hum of voices. Conductors called out train numbers. Steam hissed. Someone bumped into her and excused himself quickly, hurrying on to catch his train. She spotted a tall man in black uniform and red cap and headed toward him. When she showed her map, he pointed out the route she would have to take and told her how much time it would take to ride the short distance. "You can take the tram."

Marta decided to walk. She wanted to see some of the city, and who knew how many days would pass before she had free time to do whatever she pleased. Was the school in session on Saturday?

She didn't know. Knapsack over her shoulder, she hurried from the station and strolled along a cobblestone street, looking up at the high stone buildings with flags flying. She paused to watch the tower clock's animated figures strike the hour. She passed by plazas and wandered in the crisscross of arcades lined with cafés, jewelers, clothiers, pastry shops, and shops with window displays of chocolate.

As the sun dipped, Marta hurried toward the bridge across the River Aare. She climbed the hill and found the street name on the letterhead. By the time she found the right address, she felt tired but exhilarated. No sign told her she'd come to the right place, and the house in front of her looked like a grand mansion rather than a school.

A woman in black dress, white apron, and cap answered the door.

Marta gave an awkward curtsy. "I'm Marta Schneider from Steffisburg." She held out her documents.

"Never curtsy to the staff," the woman said as she took the papers, glanced at them, and beckoned her in. "Welcome to the *Haushaltungsschule Bern.*"

She closed the door behind Marta. "I'm Frau Yoder. You're the last to arrive, Fräulein Schneider. You look tired. You didn't walk, did you?"

"From the train station." Marta gaped at the grand staircase and the walls with portraits in gilded frames, the finely woven rugs, the porcelain figurines. This was a housekeeping school?

"Most people ride back up."

"I wanted to see some of the city." Marta stared up at the ceiling painted with angels. "I wasn't sure when I would have a free day to see the sights."

"You'll have Sundays to yourself. Come. I'll give you an orientation tour. The downstairs holds the parlor, living room, the count's offices, and the countess's conservatory. The kitchen is on the other side, next to the dining room. The second floor has a ballroom and several large bedrooms. The third floor has most of the guest rooms. You and the other girls will be in the fourth-floor dormitory. The classroom is there also."

Frau Yoder walked head high, hands clasped in front of her. She extended her hand as she identified each room and allowed Marta a few seconds to glance around at the rich interiors. "The countess receives guests in this parlor. She had the walls repainted royal yellow after visiting the *Schloss Schönbrunn* in Vienna last year." She lifted a hand before clasping both in front of her again. "That's the countess's portrait over the fireplace. She's lovely, isn't she?"

A young woman with dark eyes and long, flowing black hair over bare shoulders seemed to stare down at her. The countess wore a necklace of diamonds and emeralds around her slender throat, and her dress looked like something from a history book Marta had read. "She looks like Marie Antoinette."

"Let's hope she doesn't end up the same way."

It seemed a surprising thing to say, and especially with such a dry tone. Frau Yoder moved on. Marta followed, growing more curious. "Do the count and countess conduct the classes?"

"They will speak with you on occasion, but I do the teaching."

"Saintonge. Are they French?"

"It's not polite to ask, Fräulein."

Marta blushed. "Oh." *And why not?* she wanted to say, but Frau Yoder moved on down a hall. Marta felt like a duckling racing after its waddling mother. "How many other students are in attendance, Frau Yoder?"

"Seven."

"Only seven?"

Frau Yoder paused and turned. She looked down her nose at Marta. "Only the most promising are accepted." She looked Marta over. "Your coat is custom-made, is it not?"

She had made it herself, but didn't feel inclined to tell the woman. "My mother is a dressmaker and my father is a tailor."

Frau Yoder leaned closer and looked at the embroidery. "Beautiful work." She smiled at Marta. "I'm surprised your parents sent you here. Come along." Frau Yoder turned away again. "I want to show you the rest of the house. If you're hungry, there is cabbage soup and bread in the kitchen. The count and countess are out for the evening. You'll meet them tomorrow morning at ten in the upstairs classroom. However, I expect you there by eight for instructions."

Marta's curiosity grew even more with her first sight of Countess Saintonge standing in the bare-floor hallway outside the classroom door. She was very young to be a headmistress of anything, and she wore less-than-modest clothing. Her brows slanted over a pair of sly, dark eyes. She opened her mouth in a silent laugh, showing small, straight white teeth. She whispered something behind her hand and a man appeared. He had gray hair, pale eyes, and a thin, angular face. He looked old enough to be the lady's father! When he leaned close, Marta thought he meant to kiss Countess Saintonge right there in the hallway. He said something in a low voice and disappeared. The countess looked annoyed, but lifting her head, she entered the room with an air of hauteur. "Good morning, students."

Everyone shot to their feet and curtsied as they had been instructed to do.

"Countess." Frau Yoder gave a graceful curtsy. Each girl curtsied again as her name was mentioned.

The countess clasped her hands delicately at her waist and began to talk about the fine reputation of the *Haushaltungsschule Bern* and the glowing reports she and the count had received from satisfied employers. "We select only the best." Marta wondered at that, having spent the night with the others, most of whom had less schooling than she. *We are the best?*

"Those who make it through the first three months will be fitted for one of our uniforms." When the countess raised one hand, Frau Yoder made a slow turn, showing off the ankle-length black wool skirt, white high-collared shirtwaist with long sleeves and cuffs, full-length white apron with *HB* embroidered on the right pocket, and white lace-trimmed cap. "Only those who graduate receive the honor of wearing our uniform."

As the countess went on talking, Marta studied the translucent linen day dress with its tiny pin tucks, lace insertions, white embroidered flowers and leaves, and swirls of *passementerie*. She knew the hours and cost to make such a dress.

"Fräulein Schneider, stand."

Marta rose, wondering why the countess had singled her out from among the others.

"I expect you to pay attention when I speak."

"Yes, ma'am."

"Yes, *Countess*. And you will curtsy when you rise next time, and curtsy again before speaking."

Marta felt a rush of heat flood her cheeks. One hundred and fifty francs to learn how to be treated like a slave! One hundred and fifty francs Papa would expect to be repaid whether she completed the course or not. Clenching her teeth, Marta curtsied. "Yes, Countess." She curtsied again.

Countess Saintonge's dark eyes surveyed her coolly. "Did you hear anything I said, or must I repeat it all?"

Marta dipped again. "Yes, Countess. I heard." She began to tell her word for word until the countess lifted one of those delicate hands to stop the flow. The countess gave a slight nod for her to sit. Marta remained standing. The countess inclined her head lower this time. Marta stared back at her. The countess's cheeks flushed pink. "Why are you still standing, Fräulein Schneider?"

Marta dipped more slowly this time and a few inches lower. "I awaited your command, Countess Saintonge." She heard the nervous shifting of bodies around her. With another curtsy, Marta took her seat.

When class ended, Countess Saintonge told her to remain behind. "Marta Schneider from Steffisburg, is that correct? What does your father do?"

"My father is a tailor and my mother is a dressmaker."

"Ah!" She smiled. "That's why you were staring. . . ." She looked at Marta's shirtwaist and black skirt. "Did you make what you're wearing?"

Wondering at the woman's change in manner, Marta dipped just to be cautious. "Yes, Countess."

The countess's mouth curved with an odd, pleased smile. "Wonderful. You can make the uniforms."

Marta stiffened. "Will I have spare time?"

"Most of your evenings will be free."

Her evenings might be free, but she wasn't. "If you have the materials, we can discuss wages."

The countess's dark eyes widened in surprise. "What would you demand?"

Marta made a swift mental calculation and named an elevated sum for the uniforms.

"That's outrageous!" The countess named a lower price.

Marta raised it. "And if I am expected to provide the materials, I will require the funds for that in advance, and the rest paid before I hand over the uniforms."

"You've been cheated, haven't you?"

"I haven't, but my father and mother have."

"Is that any reason not to trust me?"

"This is business, Countess."

The countess's eyes lit up with amusement. After several rounds, she agreed on a price slightly above what Marta had decided was fair. When everything had been settled between them, the countess laughed. "Fräulein Schneider, you are not like any girl we've ever had before." She shook her head, eyes sparkling. "I doubt you will ever be a proper servant."

Marta wrote to Rosie and received a swift answer.

What do you mean you doubt the Countess Saintonge is a countess?

Letters flew back and forth with the speed of the trains.

The countess sounds German one day and French the next. I heard C and C speaking English in the parlor yesterday, though they shut up fast enough when they saw me in the doorway. Actors, perhaps? Frau Yoder says it is impolite to ask. The pair of them could even be Swiss! I intend to take Mama's good advice and learn all I can. . . .

Perhaps they are just very good at languages and have absorbed the proper accents. . . .

Did I forget to tell you C and C have parties every Friday and often have overnight guests on the weekend? C and C say everything is planned in order to train us. If that is true, then I am a cheesemaker's daughter. I have said nothing of my suspicions in my letters home, but I will tell you. This house is large enough to need eight full-time maids to keep it clean and neat! C and C have taught us how to wash windows, floors, and chandeliers. Frau Yoder has taught us how to wax and polish banisters and floorboards. We dust figurines, beat dust from the drapes, clean rugs. We change beds. This place turns into a hotel from Friday night through Sunday afternoon. How can I not admire such audacity? C and C found a way to make servant girls pay for the privilege of maintaining their mansion!

Are you writing all this in your journal?

I'm saving the journal for better things.

She had filled only one page, with recipes of the Beckers' best-selling bakery goods.

❋ ❋ ❋

Marta never worked Sundays. She walked down the hill and across the bridge, into the old city to attend services at the *Berner Münster*, the most famous gothic cathedral in Switzerland. She loved to linger at the portal, studying the carved and painted figures. Green devils with red maws fell into hell while white and gilded angels flew to heaven. After church, Marta walked the *Marktgasse*, its arcades lined with shops bustling with customers. She bought chocolate and a pastry and sat near the Samson Fountain, thinking of Mama and Elise. She went to see the *Bundeshaus* and the *Rathaus*. She bought carrots and fed the brown bears at the *Bärengraben*, along with a dozen other visitors to Bern who had come to see the city's mascots. She liked to buy a cup of chocolate and stand beneath the western gate and clock tower, waiting for the show when the hour struck. By the end of two months, Marta knew every cobblestone street and fountain in the old city.

Mama and Elise sent a letter once a week. Nothing changed. Mama was making another dress for Frau Keller. Elise stitched the hem. Papa worked hard in the shop. Everyone was well.

We miss you, Marta, and we count the days until you come home. . . .

Every Sunday, before going back up the hill to the school, Marta sat near the fountain depicting Samson breaking the jaws of a lion and wrote to Mama and Elise. She told them what she was learning about housekeeping, leaving out her suspicions of the so-called count and countess. She described the city.

I love Bern. Standing in the Marktgasse is like being inside one of Frau Fuchs's hives. . . .

Rosie suggested she stay.

Have you thought about living in Bern? Think of living in Zurich! Wherever you go, you must write and tell me everything!

Near the end of her six-month course, Papa wrote.

I expect you to return home as soon as you receive your certificate. Ask the count and countess for a recommendation.

He enclosed enough francs to buy a one-way ticket to Steffisburg and a notice. *Schloss Thun* had an opening for a maid.

4

ON GRADUATION DAY from the *Haushaltungsschule Bern*, Marta
received a fancy diploma, a letter of recommendation signed by
Count and Countess Saintonge, and a uniform with *HB* embroidered in black silk on the pocket of the white apron. She also had
the francs she had earned tucked into the purse Mama had given
her. She boarded the early train home. When she arrived in Thun,
she went straight to the castle and asked to speak to the mistress
of housekeeping.

When Frau Schmidt came into the office, Marta took an immediate, instinctive dislike to the woman as she looked down at Marta
with disdain. "You asked to see me, Fräulein?"

Marta handed over her documents. The woman put on wire
spectacles to read them. "You will have to do." She handed the
documents back to Marta. "You can start right away."

"What pay do you offer?"

Frau Schmidt looked affronted. She took off her spectacles
and tucked them into a small case on a chain around her neck.
"Twenty francs."

"A week?"

"A month."

Marta forgot all the lessons Frau Yoder had taught on diplomacy. "An untrained dishwasher is paid more than twenty francs a month!"

Frau Schmidt harrumphed. "Everyone understands what a great honor it is to work in *Schloss Thun*, Fräulein!"

"As great an honor as working at the *Haushaltungsschule Bern*, I imagine." She tucked her documents back into her knapsack. "No wonder the position is still open. Who but a fool would take it!"

When Marta arrived home, before Mama could reach her, Elise let out a cry of pleasure and flew into her arms. As Marta held Elise, she saw the changes that had occurred in Mama during the six months she had been in Bern. Dismayed, she set Elise aside. Mama patted her cheek rather than embrace Marta, who took her hand and kissed it.

Papa barely raised his head from the garment he fed through his sewing machine. "When do you plan to apply for that job at the castle? You should go now or it'll be gone."

Marta looked over her shoulder. "You could welcome me home, Papa."

He raised his head and gave her a cold glare.

"I went to the castle before coming here. I turned down their offer."

His face reddened. "You did what?"

"I assume you sent me to school so that I would earn more than twenty francs a month, Papa."

"Twenty francs!" He looked taken aback. "That's all the castle pays?"

"Frau Schmidt looked like Frau Keller's twin sister. She seemed to think the great honor of working there is worth the lesser pay."

Papa shook his head and pumped the sewing machine pedals. "The sooner you find work, the sooner you can repay the money you owe me."

She'd hoped he might congratulate her on her graduation, that he might feel some pleasure in having his elder daughter home. She should have known better. "I'll start looking first thing tomorrow morning, Papa." He'd get his tuition and book money, though there had been no books! How she wished she could tell him he'd been duped, but he'd only take it out on her. Nor did she dare take the satisfaction of telling him she'd earned back twice what he paid those two scoundrels by demanding a fair wage.

Mama looked tired, but happy. "It's so good to have you home." She coughed. Unable to stop, she sank into her chair, covering her mouth with a soiled rag. When the spasm finally ended, she looked drained and gray.

Elise looked at Marta. "It's been worse the last month."

"What does the doctor say?"

"She doesn't go to the doctor." Papa pulled the garment carefully from the machine. "Doctors cost money."

Marta got up early the next morning and prepared coffee and *Birchermüsli* so Mama wouldn't have to do it.

Mama came into the kitchen looking drawn and pale. "You're up so early."

"I wanted to talk with you before I go out." She took Mama's hand and folded the francs she'd earned into it.

Mama gasped. "How did you come by so much money?"

"I made the school uniforms." She kissed her mother's cold cheek and whispered. "I did spend a few francs on chocolate and pastries, Mama. I want you to see the doctor. Please . . ."

"It's no use, Marta. I know what's wrong." Mama tried to press the money back into Marta's hand. "I have consumption."

"Oh, Mama." She started to cry. "Surely he can do something."

"They say the mountain air helps. You must put this away for your future."

"No!" Marta tucked them deeply into Mama's apron pocket. "See Dr. Zimmer. Please, Mama."

"And what would Papa say if I went?"

"Papa doesn't have to know everything. And don't worry about his money. He'll get it." *A little at a time.*

❋ ❋ ❋

Marta found a job in the kitchen of the *Hotel auf dem Nissau*, famed for its magnificent view of the mountains. A dining platform had been built above the hotel, and guests made the climb each morning, enjoying a sumptuous breakfast and the sunrise.

After less than a month, Chef Fischer told Marta to report to the supervisor for reassignment. Herr Lang told her she would carry trays of meals up and dirty dishes down the mountain. Her pay would also be lowered, and she would receive only a small share of the servers' tips.

"What did I do wrong, Herr Lang?"

"I don't know, but Chef Fischer was furious. She wanted you dismissed. What did you do yesterday?"

"I measured out the meats and spices for her sausage. I had everything—" She grew indignant. "Why are you laughing?"

"You were too helpful, Fräulein." He snapped his fingers and motioned to a woman in the blue *Dirndl* costume of the restaurant. "Guida will show you what to do. You'll need to change into a *Dirndl* before you can go up to the platform."

As Guida searched through the rack of uniforms in a small dressing room, Marta grumbled about being kicked out of the kitchen. "I could make her sausages if she wanted to take a day off."

"You're a sharp one, aren't you? You're fortunate Chef Fischer didn't stick a fork in your back! The old crone guards her recipes the way a banker guards his vault. No one is allowed to know what she puts in her sausage. She's famous for it."

"I wondered why my questions always annoyed her. I thought she expected me to figure out things for myself." It had taken three weeks of watching before Marta finally figured out all the ingredients and proper portions. She recorded everything in the book Rosie had given her.

On her way home, she ordered beef, pork, and veal from the butcher, asking him to grind them and have everything ready on

Saturday. She purchased the spices she would need, then worked late into the night so the family would have Fischer sausages, *Rösti*—fried potatoes—tomatoes Fribourg-style, and cherry bread pudding for dessert.

She set aside enough for Rosie to sample.

Pleased, she watched her family devour the meal. Mama and Elise complimented her cooking. Even Hermann had something nice to say. Papa paid her no compliments, but when Hermann reached for the last sausage, Papa got his fork into it first.

❄ ❄ ❄

"I hope you like it, Rosie." She bit her lip, watching her friend sample the sausage. "I didn't use all of the spices Frau Fischer does, but I added some allspice."

Rosie raised her head, eyes gleaming. "It's wonderful!" She spoke with cheeks bulging. "Mama would die for this recipe."

"I'll write it out for her." Marta flopped back on the spring grass and put her hands behind her head. "I have others, too, for *Streusel, Jägerschnitzel,* and *Züricher Geschnetzeltes.*"

Rosie licked her fingers. "Are you going to start a restaurant?"

Marta snickered. "And have Frau Fischer coming after me with her meat cleaver?" She looked up at the cloudless blue sky and allowed herself to dream. "No. I'm just collecting the best so that someday, when I have a hotel or boardinghouse, I'll know how to cook well enough to keep my guests happy."

"They'll be happy and fat!" Rosie laughed. She flopped back beside Marta. "It's good to have you home, and not just because you've learned how to make the best sausage I've ever tasted!"

"I'm not going to stay long."

"What do you mean?"

"Every muscle in my body aches. I'm nothing more than a pack mule carrying trays up and down the mountain. I need to find another job where I can learn more. And there are none in Steffisburg or Thun."

Rosie grinned. "Think of the honor of working inside the walls of *Schloss Thun*!"

"Very funny."

"Go to Interlaken, then. It's not so far away you couldn't come home every few weeks to visit. We could still have our walks in the hills. My father could help you. He knows the manager of the *Germania Hotel*."

Herr Gilgan was more than willing. He wrote Marta a letter of recommendation. "Derry Weib always needs good workers. I'll send him a wire." A few days later, he told Marta that Herr Weib needed an assistant cook. "He'll pay fifty francs a month, and you'll have a room off the kitchen."

Mama congratulated Marta on her good fortune. Papa didn't care where she worked as long as she paid him twenty francs a month. Elise took the news poorly. "How long will you be gone this time? And don't tell me to sleep with the cat. She purrs and keeps me awake."

"Grow up, Elise!"

Her sister burst into tears and turned to Mama for comfort, then felt too sick to attend church the next day.

"Mama, you can't keep coddling her."

"She has such a tender heart. She's easily bruised."

When services ended, Papa stood talking with other business owners, discussing hard times. Hermann went off with his friends. Mama tucked Marta's hand into the crook of her arm. "Let's take a walk. It's been a while since I've gone up the hill to the meadow. Remember how we used to walk there when you were a little girl?" They stopped several times along the way. "You've been restless all week, Marta. Something's on your mind."

"I'm worried about you, Mama. You work too hard."

She patted Marta's hand. "I do what needs to be done, and I enjoy it."

She sighed. "So you're going to Interlaken. I think this will be the beginning of a long journey for you." She walked more and more slowly, each breath more difficult. When they came to the bench near the road to *Hotel Edelweiss*, Mama could go no further. "When I was a girl, I walked all day in the hills." Her lips had turned a faint tinge of blue despite the warmth of the afternoon.

"We should go back, Mama."

"Not yet. Let me sit awhile in the sunshine." Mama didn't look down over Steffisburg, but up at the heavens. A dozen finches flew by, chittering as they landed among the branches of a nearby tree. A crow had come too near a nest and smaller birds attacked wildly, driving it away. Mama's eyes shone with tears. "Papa called you a cuckoo bird, once."

"I remember."

She had been five or six at the time, and Papa had flown into one of his drunken rages. He grabbed her by the hair and shoved her across the room to the mirror. "Look at you! You're nothing like your mother! You're nothing like me! Dark hair and muddy eyes. It's like some cuckoo laid her egg in our nest and left us stuck with her ugly chick. Who will be fool enough to take you off my hands?" Papa had let go of her so abruptly, Marta fell against the mirror and cracked it. "And now bad luck on top of everything else!"

Tears slipped down Mama's cheeks. "You cried for hours. I tried to explain he'd been drinking and didn't know what he was saying."

"He knew, Mama. That's what hurt so much."

Mama sighed. She took Marta's hand firmly. "You have my mother's eyes. She didn't like your father. She didn't want me to marry him."

"Maybe you should have listened."

"Then I wouldn't have had Hermann or you or Elise. The three of you are my greatest blessings in life. I've never been sorry."

"Never?"

"God permits suffering. He permits injustice. I know your father can be cruel and selfish at times. But there were tender moments in the beginning. He lives with bitter disappointment. He's never learned to count his blessings. If you are to rise above your circumstances, you must learn that, *Liebling*." She took Marta's hand again. "Don't worry so much about me. I learned a long time ago to take my pain to Christ, who understands suffering so much more than I." She closed her eyes. "I imagine Jesus gathering me in His arms and lifting me onto His lap and holding me there like a child cradled against a mother's heart. His words are full of comfort. He strengthens me in my weakness."

She opened her eyes and smiled at Marta. "You won't welcome this, Marta. But you are more like your father than you are like me. You have his passion and ambition. You want more than life has given you." She sighed deeply. "And I love him. I have always loved him and always will, despite his faults and frailties."

"I know, Mama. I just wish your life could be easier."

"And if it were easier, would I have given my heart so fully to God? Wherever you go, let Christ be your refuge. Put your hope in Him, and you won't be disappointed by what life offers."

Mama lifted her head again. "Look at the birds, *Liebling*." Shivering despite the warm day, Mama drew her shawl more tightly around her shoulders. "Most species fly in a flock." A tear ran down her white cheek. "An eagle flies alone."

Marta felt her throat tighten. Pressing her lips together, she closed her eyes.

Mama put both hands around Marta's. "You have my blessing, Marta. I give it to you wholeheartedly and without reservation. You have my love. And I will pray for you every day of my life. Don't be afraid to leave."

"What about Elise, Mama?"

Mama smiled. "Elise is our lovely little barn swallow. She'll never fly far from home."

They walked down the hill together, Mama leaning into Marta for support. "Don't come home too often. There may come a time when your father won't let you go."

1904

Marta slipped into the small room off the kitchen, momentarily escaping the infernal heat of the stoves. She wilted onto her cot and dabbed the sweat from her face with the towel she kept over her shoulder. Leaning back against the stone wall, she sighed in relief. On the other side flowed the River Aare that ran between the *Thunersee* and *Brienzersee*. Constant moisture seeped through the mortar, making icicles in winter and sprouting with mushrooms through summer.

"Marta!" the chef, Warner Brennholtz, shouted from the kitchen. *"Marta!"*

"Give me a minute or I'll melt faster than your chocolate!" She hadn't had a break all evening, and Herr Weib had brought her a letter from Mama. She took it from her apron pocket, tore it open, and began to read.

My dearest Marta,

I hope you are well and happy. I hold you close to my heart and pray for you unceasingly. I have sad news.

Papa had to go to Bern and fetch Elise home from the housekeeping school. Countess Saintonge said she is unfit for service.

Papa didn't go the first time they wrote. He thought Elise would adjust. But he had to go when the count wired him to come for Elise or pay the expenses of having her escorted home.

The count refused to return a single franc. He said she had taken space that should have been given to another girl, and he would not accept the loss. That was bad enough, but he made it worse by telling Papa a father should know whether his own child could bear separation from her family. I know God has a lesson for all of us in this.

"Oh, Mama." Her mother had unwittingly encouraged Elise's dependence, but the full responsibility couldn't be laid at her feet. Marta blamed herself for giving Papa the money to send Elise to Bern. He had made her feel so guilty when she had said no the first time.

"If you loved your sister . . . if you weren't so grasping and selfish . . . You think nothing of your family. . . . You hoard your francs when they could help. . . ."

She should have told Papa how he'd been duped by those two counterfeits in Bern. Instead, she'd convinced herself Elise might benefit by getting away. Perhaps she would blossom among the other girls her age and enjoy Bern as much as Marta had. Marta had sent extra francs to Elise and told her to walk the *Marktgasse* and buy some chocolate and pastries at the *Café Français*.

Now, all she could do was pray Papa wouldn't take out his anger on Elise.

Marta lifted the letter and continued reading.

Please don't be angry with her. I know it was your money wasted, but Elise did try. She managed to stay three weeks before she wrote the first time. And she suffers now. Papa hasn't spoken a word to her since he brought her home.

Elise helps me as much as she can. Her stitches are as fine as mine now. She will learn to work faster with more experience. She also helps Frau Zimmer with little Evrard. He is so dear, but he's at that age when he's into everything. He got away from her for a few minutes the other day. She is keeping closer watch now.

Write soon, Liebling. Your letters are a great comfort to us all. May the Lord bless you and keep you. May His face shine upon you. I love you.

Mama

Marta folded the letter and tucked it back into her apron pocket. She would write and tell Mama to make Elise go to the market. She needed to learn to talk with people. She could buy the bread from the Beckers and talk with Frau Fuchs about more honey. Elise needed to learn to stand on her own. She wouldn't always have Mama.

The clatter of china went on in the other room. Warner Brennholtz shouted an impatient order to someone. Her door banged open and the chef stepped into her room. She had long since learned not to be surprised or offended when someone barged in. The heat of the kitchen made escape necessary, and her small bedroom was convenient. All day from breakfast through dinner, workers danced around one another, and someone would regularly slide in for a few minutes of cool respite before facing the stoves and ovens again. Only after the last customers had gone and the last dishes had been washed and put away did Marta have any privacy.

Brennholtz stood taller than Papa and several stones heavier.

He liked his beer, too, but became jolly when he overimbibed, rather than moody or violent like her father. "What's the matter with you? You look like you ate bad *Sauerkraut*." The chef wiped perspiration from his red face and neck.

"My sister wasn't able to finish housekeeping school."

"Is she ill?"

"She's fine, now that she's home with our mother."

"Ah. Is she a good worker? She could come here and live in this room with you. We could use another dishwasher."

"You'd frighten her to death." Brennholtz could shout louder than Papa. Even his laughter boomed enough to rattle crockery. Elise would probably break half the dishes before the end of her first week.

"A pity Derry doesn't need another maid."

"He would if he rented rooms to the English."

Warner wiped the towel over his thinning blond hair. "He did a few years ago, but the English and Germans are like oil and water, and Derry doesn't speak enough English to sort things out. When he couldn't bring peace, customers didn't want to pay. So now he caters to Swiss and Germans."

"And makes less money."

"And has fewer headaches." Warner slapped the towel over his shoulder. "Money isn't everything."

"People who have it always say that."

He laughed. "You'd know how to stop a ruckus, *ja*? Bang two heads together. Derry should train you to manage and take a long vacation."

She knew he meant it as a joke, but she pushed herself up and faced him. "If I could speak French and English, I'd figure out a way to fill every room in this hotel."

He laughed. "Then learn, Fräulein."

"In a basement kitchen?" She put her hands on her hips. "Do you speak French?"

"*Nein.*"

"English?"

"Not a word."

"Then I should quit and go to Geneva or London." She brushed past him.

"I don't like your joke!" He followed her.

"Do you think I plan to remain an assistant cook for the rest of my life?"

Warner snatched a pot off a hook and slammed it on the work-table. Everyone jumped except Marta. "This is the thanks I get for training you!"

How many times did she have to say it? Marta bared her teeth in a smile and dipped in an exaggerated curtsy. "*Vielen Dank*, Herr Brennholtz." She spoke with cloying sweetness. "*Danke. Danke. Danke.*"

He laughed. "That's better."

Her anger evaporated. Why take out her frustrations on Warner when he had been nothing but kind? "I told you I wouldn't stay here forever."

"*Ja.* I know. You have big dreams! Too big, if you ask me."

"I didn't."

His hands worked quickly, coating pieces of meat in flour and seasonings. "It takes years to become a chef."

She tossed flour on her work area and grabbed a hunk of dough from a bowl. "I don't have to become a chef, Herr Brennholtz, just a good cook."

"Ha! Then you're not as ambitious as I thought!"

She felt a fierce rush inside her. "I'm more ambitious than you'll ever know."

❄ ❄ ❄

Mama wrote again. Papa had found a position for Elise in Thun.

The family is wealthy. They come from Zurich and spend the summer. Elise has room and board, and she can come home on her day off.

When will we see you? You haven't been home since Elise returned from Bern. Papa told her you're probably upset over the wasted money.

Marta wrote back right away.

Mama, please tell Elise not to be distressed. I work fourteen hours a day, six days a week, and spend Sunday mornings in church. When summer ends, the Germania will have fewer patrons. I'll come home then. In the meantime, give our little barn swallow my love.

Mama's next letter gave Marta some hope that Elise would do better.

Elise seems well settled. She hasn't been home for two weeks. Herr Meyer told a friend what a lovely child she is. Their son Derrick changed his plans to return to Zurich. . . .

Marta wondered if Derrick might be the reason Elise didn't feel the need to come home.

Rosie wrote, too, filling two pages about Arik Brechtwald dancing with her at a summer festival, and wouldn't her father lock her up if he knew she'd received her first kiss! She filled another page with news of her sisters and brothers and mother and father, and town gossip.

Marta wrote back and asked Rosie if her father knew any hotel managers in Geneva.

Warner speaks High German, but not a word of French. . . .

Rosie responded quickly.

Father has only acquaintances in Geneva; unfortunately, no one upon whom he could prevail for a favor. Mama has an older second cousin in Montreux. Luisa von Olman is a widow with six children, only two left at home. Her eldest son is the commander of a fortress, but I've forgotten where. Mama says he married a lovely little Swiss-Italian girl and they have ten children, but since it was too far for the children to go to a valley school, the government built one right there on the mountain where they live. Mama will write Cousin Luisa. . . .

Marta wrote to Frau Gilgan to thank her, and then to Rosie.

I plan to come home for a week the middle of September, then go to Montreux. If Cousin Luisa cannot help, I will haunt the hotels along the lakeshore. I'll find something. I would like to speak some French before my eighteenth birthday! Something more than bonjour and merci beaucoup!

Toward the end of summer, Marta received a letter from Elise. Surprised and pleased, Marta tore it open immediately rather than wait for a quiet moment alone.

Dearest Marta,

Please help me. I'm afraid of Herr Meyer. He won't leave me alone. Papa will be angry if I come home without any money, but I haven't been paid anything at all and

I'm terrified of Frau Meyer. She hates me because of her horrible son. I thanked God when he left for Zurich. I would ask Mama to come, but she is not well enough. Please. I'm begging you. Come and help me get away from here.

Your loving little sister,
Elise

"What's wrong?" Warner was slicing veal. "You look ill."

"My sister needs me." She shoved the letter into her skirt pocket. "I have to go."

"*Now?*"

She raced into her small bedroom and threw a few things into her shoulder bag. "I'll be back as soon as I can."

"Go tomorrow." Warner blocked her way. "I need you here."

"Elise needs me more, and you have Della and Arlene."

"I could dismiss you!"

"Go ahead! That would give me the excuse I need to go to Montreux! Now, get out of my way!"

He caught her by the shoulders when she tried to push past him. "It won't be the last time your sister needs you. When your mother is gone, you'll be the one she leans on. . . ."

"I have to go."

With a sigh, Warner released her.

Marta raced up the stairs and out of the hotel, boarding a hired coach to Thun.

After asking directions, she found her way to the huge chalet at the end of a street on the edge of town. A man trimming roses in the front garden straightened as she approached. "Can I help you, Fräulein?"

"I've come to see my sister, Elise Schneider."

"Go around back to the kitchen. Frau Hoffman will help you."

An old woman with a crown of white braids answered the door.

Marta quickly introduced herself and stated her business. The woman looked relieved. "Come in, Fräulein. I'll fetch Elise for you."

The kitchen smelled of baking bread. Apples, nuts, raisins, and oats had been set out on the worktable. The floors looked freshly washed, the copper pots polished, the counter surfaces clean. Marta paced, agitated.

Elisa flew through the kitchen door. "Marta!" She threw herself into Marta's startled embrace and burst into tears. "You came. I was so afraid you wouldn't. . . ."

Marta could feel how thin she was. "Don't they feed you?"

"She's been too upset to eat." The cook closed the door behind her and went to the worktable.

Marta saw a purple bruise on her sister's cheek. Heat surged through her body. "Who struck you?"

Elise gulped sobs, leaving Frau Hoffman to answer grimly. "Frau Meyer." The cook picked up another apple and sliced through it cleanly. "And she's not the only one in this family who's done harm to your poor sister."

Marta's body went cold. She pressed Elise away, holding her by the arms. "Tell me what's been going on, Elise." She spoke gently, but her sister cried harder, her mouth opening and closing like a dying fish. She seemed incapable of uttering even a single distinguishable word.

Frau Hoffman cut an apple into four pieces and began removing the core from each section with quick gouges. "A father has no business putting a pretty young girl like Elise in this house. Not with the young man and his father. I could've told him!"

Marta stared at her, stomach turning over.

Frau Hoffman sliced apple into the bowl. "I risk losing my job if I say more." She gave Elise a pitying glance before returning to her work. "But you should get her out of this house now if you don't want more harm to come to her."

Marta tipped Elise's chin. "We'll go as soon as we collect your things and what salary is owed you."

"Well, good luck trying, Fräulein." Frau Hoffman snorted.

"The mistress hasn't paid anyone since the beginning of summer. She never does until the last day, and seldom the full amount."

Tears streamed down Elise's white cheeks, making the purple bruise stand out even more. "Can't we go now, Marta?" Her body trembled violently. "Please."

Frau Hoffman tossed the paring knife into the bowl and grabbed a towel. "I'll get your sister's things. You two wait here."

Marta tried to calm Elise. "Tell me what happened, *Liebling*."

"I want to die." Elise covered her face, shoulders shaking. When she swayed, Marta made her sit. Sobbing, Elise pulled her apron up over her head and rocked back and forth. Marta held her tightly, her cheek against the top of her sister's head. Anger grew inside her until she didn't know who shook more. "We'll leave soon, Elise. Here's Frau Hoffman now."

"I got everything."

Everything but Elise's wages. "Where's Frau Meyer?"

"In the parlor, but she won't speak to you."

"You sit right here." She stood.

"Where are you going?" Elise grabbed Marta's skirt. "Don't leave me!"

She cupped Elise's face. "Stay here in the kitchen with Frau Hoffman. I'll be back in a few minutes and we'll go home. Now, let go so I can get your wages."

"I wouldn't go, Fräulein."

"They're not getting away with it!" Marta banged the kitchen door open, strode through the dining room and across the hall. As she entered the parlor, she saw a heavyset woman in a green day dress half-reclined on a settee near the windows overlooking the garden. Startled, the woman dropped her delicate china cup, shattering it on the saucer. Tea splashed down the front of her. Gasping, she rose and brushed frantically at the stain. "I don't know you! What are you doing in my house?"

"I'm Elise's older sister, Marta." She didn't stop in the door. "And I've come to collect her wages."

"Eginhardt!" Frau Meyer cried out angrily. "I'll have you thrown out! How dare you come in here demanding anything!" When Marta kept coming, the woman's pale blue eyes widened, and she moved quickly behind a wide table strewn with books. *"Eginhardt!"* she screamed shrilly, then glared at Marta. "I'll have you arrested."

"Call the constable! I'd like to tell him how you cheat your staff! I wonder how many shop owners are waiting to be paid?"

Paling, Frau Meyer pointed. "Stand over there by the door and I'll get her wages!"

"I'll stand right here!"

Frau Meyer stepped cautiously around the table and hurried to a desk on the other side of the room. Fuming as she sorted through keys she had taken from her pocket, she finally managed to find the one to unlock the desk drawer. She removed some francs and locked the drawer before holding them out. "Take them!" She tossed the coins on the desk. "Take them and get that worthless girl out of my house!"

Marta gathered the coins and counted them. Raising her head, she glared. "Elise has been here three months. This barely covers two."

Frau Meyer's face turned red. She unlocked the drawer, yanked it open, and removed more francs, locking the drawer again. "Here's the money! Now, get out!" She tossed the coins in Marta's direction.

Pride made Marta want to storm out without the money, but fury over the abuse Elise had suffered kept her in the room, collecting each coin, and counting them. Frau Meyer shouted for Eginhardt again. Marta straightened and sneered. "Perhaps your Eginhardt doesn't come because you haven't paid him either."

Stiffening, Frau Meyer lifted her chin, eyes flashing. "Your sister is a worthless slut."

Marta dropped the coins into the pocket of her skirt and came around the desk. "One more thing I need before we leave, Frau Meyer." Marta slapped the woman hard across the face. "That's for the mark you left on my sister." Gasping, Frau Meyer backed into the drapes. Marta slapped her across the other cheek. "And that's for insulting her." When she raised her fist, Frau Meyer shrank from her. "One more word against my sister, and I'll let every father in Thun and Steffisburg know what your son and husband have done to my sister. What I just did to you is nothing compared to what will happen to them!"

❋ ❋ ❋

Marta still shook with rage as she walked alongside Elise, holding her hand as she carried both their bundles. She didn't need to ask any more questions. Elise walked with her head down, her hand clammy with sweat. Marta thanked God her sister had at least managed to stop crying. "Smile and say hello, Elise."

"I can't."

When they came in sight of the house, Elise let go of Marta's hand and ran as though pursued by demons. By the time Marta entered the house, Mama had Elise in her arms and Papa had come in from the workroom in back. He stood in the middle of the room, glowering at Marta. "What's going on here? Why did you bring her home?"

"Because she wrote and begged me to come and get her."

"It was none of your business!"

"You always blame me! But you're right this time, Papa! This is *your* business! You put her there in that house with those wretched people!"

"Come, *Engel*." Mama put her arms around Elise and helped her up. "We'll go upstairs."

"She can't quit a job without notice, Anna!" Papa shouted after them. "She has to go back!"

Marta came all the way inside the house, threw the bundles down, and closed the door firmly behind her. "You are not sending her back, Papa."

He turned on her. "Who are you to say whether she comes or goes? I'm her father! She'll do what I tell her!"

"She's not going back!"

"It's time she grew up!"

"That may be so, Papa, but next time, check her employers'

references! Make sure they pay their servants! They didn't give her a single franc! Worse, they ravished her."

"Ravished her!" he sneered. Waving his hand, he dismissed the accusation. "Elise cries over spilt milk."

Marta hated him in that moment. "Did you see the bruise on her cheek?" She came farther into the room, hands balling into fists. "Frau Meyer called *your daughter* a slut because Herr Meyer can't keep his hands off Elise! And the son did worse before going back to Zurich!"

"Nonsense! It's all nonsense! You ruined everything by taking Elise out of that house!"

"I have ruined nothing. You have helped them ruin *her*!"

"Herr Meyer told me Elise is exactly the kind of girl he wants for his son."

Could her father be such a fool? "And you thought he meant marriage?" Marta cried out in fury. "A tailor's daughter and an aristocrat's son?"

"Her beauty is worth something."

Sickened, Marta swept by him and headed for the stairs.

"Don't you turn your back on me!" Papa raged.

"God forgive you, Papa!" She flew upstairs. A moment later, she heard a door slam below. Mama sat on the bed Marta had shared with Elise. Her sister lay with her head in their mother's lap. Mama stroked her like she would a pet dog. "You're home now, my darling. Everything will be all right."

Marta came into the room and closed the door quietly behind her. "No, it won't, Mama. It'll never be right."

"Hush, Marta!"

Hush? Marta took the coins from her pocket. "This money belongs to Elise."

Elise rose up, eyes wild. "I don't want the money! I don't want anything *he* touched."

Mama looked shocked and frightened. "Who is she talking about?"

"Herr Meyer. And he wasn't the only one." When Marta told her what the cook had said, Mama's face crumpled.

"Oh, God . . ." Mama put her arms around Elise. "Oh, God, oh, God. I'm so sorry, *Engel*." She rocked Elise, sobbing into her hair. "Throw the money away, Marta. It's filthy lucre!"

"It's not mine to dispose of." Marta left the coins on the bed. "Let Elise do it." Maybe it would give her sister some small bit of satisfaction after what had been done to her. "At least, Papa won't profit from his mistake."

Mama raised her head. "Do it for her. She's too distressed."

"Oh, Mama!" Marta wept. "Papa is right about one thing. You've crippled her. She can't even defend herself!"

Mama looked stricken.

Unable to bear more, Marta turned away.

"Where are you going?" Mama spoke in a broken voice.

"Back to Interlaken. I have responsibilities."

"There are no coaches until morning."

"There will be less trouble if I go. I seem to bring out the worst in Papa." With her gone, he might think over what she had told him and regret the part he had played in this tragedy. "I'll ask the Gilgans if I can stay for a night."

"Perhaps you're right." Mama stroked Elise's head, buried in her lap. "I'm sorry, Marta."

"I'm sorry, too, Mama. More sorry than I can express."

Elise sat up. "Please don't leave, Marta. Stay here with me."

"You have Mama to take care of you, Elise. You don't need both of us."

Elise looked at Mama. "Tell her to stay!"

Mama cupped Elise's face. "You can't ask for more than she's done already, Elise. She brought you home, *Engel*. But she doesn't belong here anymore. God has other plans for your sister." Mama gathered Elise close and looked at Marta. "She has to go."

❄ ❄ ❄

The Gilgans welcomed Marta and asked no questions. Perhaps they assumed she had fought with her father again. She couldn't tell them what had happened to Elise, though rumors would spread soon enough. She told Rosie when they went to bed, knowing Elise would have terrible days ahead.

"I can't bear to stay. I can't stand by and watch Papa sulk and grumble about his ruined plans or see Mama coddle her. But Elise will need a friend." She wept.

Rosie put an arm around her. "You needn't say more. I'll offer my friendship, Marta. I'll invite Elise to tea. I'll invite her for walks in the hills. If she wants to talk, I'll listen and never repeat a word. I swear on my life."

"I'll try not to be jealous."

Moonlight came in through the window, making Rosie's face white and angelic. "I'm doing it for you." Tears shone in her eyes. "I'll do my best. You know I will. But Elise has to want a friend."

"I know. What I don't know is what will happen to her now. It would've been better if Mama hadn't protected her so much." Marta rubbed tears away angrily. "If anyone tried to rape me, I'd scream and claw and kick!"

"Maybe she did."

Marta doubted it. "I swear before God, Rosie, if I'm ever fortunate enough to have a daughter, I'll make sure she's strong enough to stand up for herself!"

When Rosie fell asleep, Marta lay awake staring at the beamed ceiling. What would become of Elise? How long before the Meyers' cook told someone what happened in that house? Rumors spread like mold on the damp wall of Marta's *Germania* basement bedroom. What if Herr Meyer or his son Derrick bragged to friends about the beautiful little angel they had used over the summer? Papa would not likely have the courage to confront Herr Meyer!

If only her little sister could walk to market, head up in the knowledge that she was not to blame for any of it. But that would never happen. More likely, a word from Papa, and Elise would take the shame onto herself, absorbing it, plagued by it. And Mama, filled with pity, would allow her to hide inside the house. If Elise didn't show her face, people might even begin to wonder if she had been culpable, which would only distress Elise even further. Her sister would hide away and help Mama sew fine seams and hems. As time passed, Elise would become more withdrawn, more frightened of the outside world, more dependent. Walls would give Elise the illusion of safety, just as Mama's arms had seemed to. Papa might allow it to happen just to make things easy on himself. After all, two women working day and night and neither asking for nor expecting anything would be to his benefit!

Marta pressed fists against her eyes and prayed. *Lord, You say blessed are the meek. Please bless my sister. You say blessed are those who are gentle and pure in heart. Please bless Mama. Lord, You say blessed are the peacemakers. Please bless Rosie. I ask nothing for myself because I'm a sinner. You know me better than I know myself. You knit me in my mother's womb. You know how I burn. My head pounds. My hands sweat for vengeance. Oh, God, had I strength and means, I would send Herr Meyer and his son to the depths of hell for what they did to my sister, and Papa right after them for letting it happen!*

Turning away from Rosie, Marta covered her head with the blanket and wept silently.

She got up early the next morning and thanked the Gilgans for their kind hospitality. Rosie walked with her down the hill. "Are you going to see your family before you leave?"

"No. And I'm not coming back."

Her mother had already given her permission to fly.

MARTA RECEIVED A letter from Rosie ten days later.

I saw your mother and father in church. Hermann came, too. Elise didn't. Most people think she went back to Thun. Of course, she hasn't. I asked your mother if I might come to call on Elise. She asked how much you had told me and I said everything. She seemed upset about that, but I reassured her. She said Elise isn't ready to see anyone. I'll try again next week. . . .

Mama wrote a week later.

Rosie said you told her and no one else. Rosie is a good girl who can keep a confidence. She is kind. Papa went to Thun. The Meyers had closed up the house and gone back

*to Zurich. A man asked if he had come to look at the
house. The Meyers plan to sell.*

Marta sent a brief letter in reply.

*Perhaps now that the Meyers have fled, you will help
Elise come out of exile. Rosie wants to be a friend to her,
Mama. Please encourage Elise to allow it.*

Mama wrote back.

*Elise is doing better. She helps me in the shop. Papa
agrees the best place for her is here with me. She cries
so easily.*

Marta tried to put it all from her mind, but she couldn't. She
dreamed about Elise at night. She dreamed of burning the Meyers'
house down with them inside.

"Go out for a walk." Warner brushed her aside. "If you knead
the dough any more, we'll have bricks instead of loaves!"

"I'm sorry."

"You haven't been yourself since you came back from Steffisburg. You helped your sister, *ja*? It's been a month. Are you ready
to tell me what happened?"

"No." She made a decision in that split second. "I'm done here.
I'm going to Montreux."

Warner's head jerked up. "Just because I won't let you knead
dough?"

"The dough has nothing to do with anything."

"Then why?"

"I have to get away!" She burst into tears.

The only sound in the kitchen was the burbling soup. Everyone
stared at her. "Get back to work!" Warner shouted. He pushed

Marta into the cold room off the kitchen. "Are you leaving or running away?"

She sat on the edge of the bed, head in hands. "What does it matter?" She wiped her face. She thought of Elise staying in the same place, remaining a child for the rest of her life. "I know what I want in life, and I'm going after it. I'm not going to let things happen to me. I'm going to make things happen!"

Warner sat beside her. "Why are you in such a hurry? You're only sixteen. You have time."

"You don't understand, Warner." Sometimes *she* didn't understand. One day she wanted to run as far away and as fast as she could, and then the guilt would set in and she wondered if she shouldn't go home, take care of Mama and Elise, and forget all about her dreams of making a better life for herself.

"You want to own a hotel, *ja*?" He snorted. "You think life will be good then. Work, work, and more work. That's all you'll ever do if you get what you want."

"Work, work, and more work is what I have now." If she went home, Papa would rule her life forever. "I'd rather work for myself than work to put money in someone else's pocket!"

"Pigheaded girl." When she tried to stand up, he grabbed her wrist and pulled her down again. "You still have much to learn from me about German cooking."

"You've taught me enough, Warner." She gave him a watery smile. "And I am grateful. But I'm going to Montreux."

"What will your family have to say about that?"

"Nothing." Hermann had followed his dream and joined the Army. Mama would always have Elise, and Elise would have Mama. Let Papa shoulder the responsibility for those God had given into his care.

"I see the pain in you, Marta."

She wrenched free and went back into the kitchen to work.

Warner Brennholtz came to the train station as Marta left. She hadn't expected to see him again. When she tried to thank him for coming to see her off, no words would come.

"You didn't tell your family, did you?"

She shook her head.

Stepping close, Warner took her hand and pressed several heavy coins into her palm, closing her fingers around them.

"Marta, don't cry. Enjoy this money; don't hoard it." He planted his hands firmly on her shoulders. "I'm going to speak to you like a father. You're young. Have some fun when you get to Montreux. Go dancing! Laugh! Sing!" He kissed her on both cheeks and let her go.

Marta stepped up behind the last man boarding the train.

Warner called out to her before she went inside the passenger car. "When you have that hotel, write to me." He grinned broadly. "Maybe I'll come cook for you!"

❄ ❄ ❄

Luisa von Olman invited Marta to stay until she could find work in one of the Montreux hotels or restaurants. Marta thought it would be easy. Montreux sat perched on the mountainside, Bernese-style houses, mansions, and grand hotels tucked like elaborate nests into winding cliff roads. Wealthy patrons strolled along cobbled pathways lined with linden trees and scented with lavender and lilacs, or sat on lawn chairs enjoying the view of cerulean Lake Geneva. Servants offered cake and melted chocolate for dipping.

Marta walked the steep streets for days. She found all the grand hotels and restaurants uninterested in a girl who could speak only German. Broadening her search to lesser neighborhoods, she spotted a Help Wanted sign in the window of Ludwig's Eatery. From the unkempt exterior, Marta could understand why.

The owner, Frau Gunnel, gave Marta a curt nod. "You'll have a week to prove yourself. Room and board and thirty francs a month." Marta held her tongue about the paltry pay. "Hedda!" Frau Gunnel called out. A pretty blonde setting beer steins on a tray glanced their way. Two other girls older than Marta worked with heads down, silent. "Show this new girl upstairs. Quickly!

We have a lot to do before the dinner crowd arrives." Frau Gunnel looked at Marta again and shook her head. "I hope you're as good as all your fine papers claim." She held a bowl locked in one arm as she stirred fiercely with the other.

Hedda led Marta upstairs. Glancing back, she raised her brows. "I'm surprised you came here with all your qualifications, Fräulein."

She looked at the drab stairwell walls. "Unfortunately, I don't speak French or English."

"Neither do I." Hedda opened a door and stepped aside. "This is where we sleep. It's small, but comfortable. I hope you aren't afraid of mice. We have a nest of them somewhere in the wall. You can hear them scratching at night. Take that bed over there."

Marta saw a row of plank platforms with uninviting graying feather beds rolled at the end. The room was cold. The small, narrow windows faced east, leaving the room dimly lit in the afternoon. No curtains to keep out the dawn. When Marta peered out, she could see only empty window boxes and the street below.

"I'm leaving soon," Hedda announced from the doorway. "I'm marrying Arnalt Falken. Have you heard of him?"

"I'm new to Montreux."

"His father is very rich. They live in a mansion up the road from here. Arnalt came one evening by himself and ordered beer and sausage. He says he took one look at me and fell in love."

Marta thought of Elise. Hedda had periwinkle eyes and long blonde hair, too. She hoped the girl had good sense.

Hedda nodded toward the window. "Frau Gunnel will expect you to plant flowers soon. She made me pay for them last year."

"Why should either one of us pay for them?"

She shrugged. "Frau Gunnel says we're the ones who get to enjoy them."

Marta dumped her knapsack on the bed. "If Frau Gunnel wants to dress up the outside of this place, she'll have to pay, or there'll be no flowers."

"I wouldn't argue with her, Fräulein, not if you want to keep your job. Flowers don't cost too much, and the patrons give good tips." She laughed. "Arnalt dropped a ten franc coin down my bodice the first time he came."

Marta turned away from the window. "No one is going to drop anything down my bodice."

"They will if you're friendly." The gleam in Hedda's eyes told Marta the girl valued money more than reputation.

❄ ❄ ❄

By the end of the first week, Marta saw ways to improve the eatery. When she overheard Frau Gunnel complaining about poor business, Marta shared her thoughts.

"With a few changes, your business would improve."

Frau Gunnel turned. "Changes? What changes?"

"It wouldn't cost much if you repainted the front window boxes with bright colors and filled them with flowers that would attract the eye. The menus you have now are greasy. You could reprint them and put them in sturdy folders. Vary your menu occasionally."

Plump face reddening, Frau Gunnel put her hands on her ample hips. She looked Marta up and down in contempt. "You're sixteen and you think you know so much with your fancy certificate and recommendations. You know nothing!" She jerked her head. "Go back to the kitchen!"

Marta went. She hadn't meant to insult the woman.

Frau Gunnel came in a few minutes later and went back to work on a hunk of beef, using a mallet as though attempting to kill a live animal. "I know why customers don't come. I have one pretty waitress who used to attract customers before she decided to marry one of them. And I have little Fräulein Marta as plain as bread and as friendly as *Sauerkraut!*"

No one in the kitchen looked up. Marta felt the heat rush into her face. "No one wants to eat in a dirty restaurant." Marta barely managed to dodge the flying mallet. Stripping off her apron, she

tossed it like a shroud over the embattled beef and headed for the
stairs. She threw her few things into a bag, marched downstairs and
out onto the street. People up and down the block turned when
Frau Gunnel stood in the doorway cursing her.

By the time the woman slammed the door, Marta's body felt so
hot, she was sure steam came off her. She walked uphill rather than
down. She pounded on one door after another, making inquiries.
The first few opened the door, took one look out, and ducked
back inside their houses, closing the door quickly in her face. Still
fuming, Marta realized what a sight she must be and tried to calm
down.

Now what? No job. No place to live. Her prospects were
dimmer than when she had arrived in Montreux a month ago.
She didn't want to go back to Luisa von Olman's and be a burden.
She didn't want to go home and admit defeat. Bending over, she
covered her face with her hands. "God, I know I'm impossible, but
I work hard!" She fought back tears. "What do I do now?"

Someone spoke to her. "Mademoiselle?"

She burst into frustrated tears. "I came here to learn French!"

The man switched to German as easily as someone might strip
off a glove and toss it aside. "Are you unwell, Fräulein?"

"No. I'm unemployed. I'm looking for work." She apologized
and wiped her face. The man standing in front of her looked to be
in his eighties. He wore an expensive suit and leaned heavily on a
cane.

"I've been out walking. Do you mind if I sit, Fräulein?"

"No, of course not." She moved to give him room, wondering if
he expected her to leave.

"I passed a house with a sign in the window in German, French,
and Italian." He sank gratefully onto the bench. Lifting his cane,
he pointed. "If you go up that way three or four streets, I think you
will find the house."

Thanking him, she began a search that took her the rest of the
afternoon. Just as she was about to give up, she saw the sign in
the window of a three-story house. No chipped paint here, and

the eaves had been painted red. She heard muted laughter when she approached the front door. Brushing down her skirt and pushing the straggling damp tendrils of hair back from her face, she said a quick and desperate prayer before rapping the door-knocker. Clasping her hands in front of her, she forced a smile as she waited, hoping she looked presentable and not like some worn-down, bedraggled waif who had been walking up and down the mountain all afternoon.

Someone spoke French behind her. Marta jumped as a man reached past her and opened the door. "Excuse me?"

He spoke German this time. "Just go in. They won't hear you out here. They're already serving."

Marta entered behind him. "Would you please tell the proprietor I'm here to answer the sign in the window?"

He walked quickly down the hall and disappeared into another room.

Smells inside the house made Marta's stomach growl with hunger. She hadn't eaten since early morning, and then, only a small bowl of *Müsli*. Men's laughter swelled, startling her. She heard mumbled conversation and more laughter, less loud this time.

A young and attractive dark-haired woman came into the hallway. She wore a high-necked, long-sleeved blue dress covered with a white apron that accentuated her advanced pregnancy. Cheeks flushed, she dabbed her forehead with the back of her hand as she came toward Marta. "Mademoiselle?"

"Fräulein Marta Schneider, madame." She dipped in a curtsy. "I've come to apply for a position." She scrambled for her documents.

"I'm serving dinner now." She spoke fluent German, glancing back over her shoulder as someone called out.

"I can help you now, if you'll allow. I worked in the kitchen of *Hotel Germania* in Interlaken. We can talk about the position later."

"*Merci!* Just leave your things there by the door. We have a room full of hungry lions to feed."

The dining room had a long table, its straight-backed chairs filled with men on both sides, most young and professional by the look of their clothing. The room reverberated with loud talk, laughter, the clink of wineglasses, and the call for bread being passed in a large basket. Pitchers of wine moved from hand to hand.

"Solange!" the handsome man at the head of the table called out. Solange went to him and put her arm around his shoulder, whispering in his ear. He looked at Marta and nodded.

Solange clapped her hands. The men around the table fell silent. She waved her hand toward Marta while speaking rapid French. The men gave Marta a cursory glance before returning to their conversations. Solange pointed to a large tureen at the end of the table; Marta hastened to it and tried to pick up the heavy bowl. "No, mademoiselle," Solange protested quickly. "Too heavy. Let them pass their bowls to you."

Marta filled each with thick, delicious-smelling stew, her stomach cramping with hunger. The tureen held just enough for each man to receive one full bowl. She followed Solange into the kitchen and set the empty bowl on the worktable. Solange sank onto a stool. "You did well, mademoiselle! Not a drop spilled." Lifting her apron, she dabbed beads of sweat from her forehead. "God be praised you came when you did. Those men . . ." She laughed and shook her head. "They eat like horses."

Marta's stomach growled loudly. Solange raised her brows. Murmuring in French, she crossed the room, opened a cupboard, and took out a soup bowl. "Eat now. We have a few minutes before they start shouting for more." She rubbed her back as she sat on the stool again.

"This is wonderful, Madame . . . ?"

"Fournier. Solange Fournier. My husband, Herve, was the one sitting at the head of the table."

Marta quickly finished her stew, mopping up the last bit of juice with a piece of bread. Setting the bowl in the washbasin, she took the pitcher on the stove. "Shall I refill the tureen?"

Solange nodded. "I need someone to help me clean house, change the linens, do laundry, and work in the kitchen."

Marta poured thick stew. "I need room, board, and sixty francs a month." As soon as the words came out, Marta held her breath. Perhaps she had spoken too quickly and asked too much.

"You are a girl who knows her mind and is willing to work." She planted her hands on her thighs and stood. "Done. How soon can you come?"

"All I need to do is move the knapsack I left in the foyer upstairs."

"*Magnifique!*"

"Do all of those men live here, Madame Fournier?"

"Call me Solange, *s'il vous plaît*." She smiled brightly. "And I will call you Marta." She put more bread in a basket. "Only twelve live here. The others come for dinner when they are in town on business. A friend invites them the first time and they keep coming back. Sometimes we have to turn them away. Not enough room." Laughter made the walls shake. "They are noisy, *oui*?" She laughed when a man called out loudly. "And my husband has the loudest voice of all." She tossed the last few pieces of bread into the basket. "He doesn't speak German. Do you speak any French?"

"No, but I'm eager to learn."

"*Je pense que vous allez apprendre rapidement.*" Smiling, she pushed the door open and held it so Marta could follow her with the filled tureen.

Marta wrote to Rosie.

At last, I will learn French. I have found a position in a boardinghouse full of bachelors. The house is run by a lovely couple, Herve and Solange Fournier. Madame Fournier insists I call her Solange. She speaks German, but French is her first language. She also speaks Italian and Romanian. She is a fine cook. I will need to learn French quickly if I am to be any help to her. She is enceinte. The baby will come the middle of January.

Marta sent Mama the Fourniers' address and asked how she and Elise fared.

Dearest Marta,

I am pleased you have found a better situation. Frau Gunnel is a woman to be pitied, not despised. We never know what another person suffers in this life.

Do not worry so much about Elise. She helps me in the workroom. She does all the cutting and basting now. My cousin Felda Braun came for a visit. She lost her husband, Reynard, last year, and is very lonely. I took you to Grindelwald when you were a little girl. You loved Reynard's cows. Do you remember? God never blessed Felda and Reynard with children. If anything happens to me, Elise will go to Grindelwald and live with Felda. This is her address . . .

Marta wrote back immediately.

How ill are you, Mama? Should I come home?

Mama's handwriting had changed. The perfectly formed letters now showed signs of a tremor.

Do not be afraid for me, Liebling. I am in God's hands, as are you. Remember what we talked about on the mountain before you went to Interlaken. Fly, Liebling. I fly with you. Do not forsake the gathering *of believers, Marta. It is the love of brothers and sisters that has strengthened me over the years. We are one in Christ Jesus. Let it be so for you, too. You are precious to me. I love you. Wherever you go, know my heart goes with you.*

Mama

Marta wrote to Rosie.

I'm afraid for Mama. Her last letter made me believe she is dying, but she tells me to fly. Have you seen Elise?

Each day, Marta got up before dawn and started the fire in the kitchen stove. She baked pull-apart bread drenched in butter and rolled in cinnamon and raisins. She prepared two platters of sliced fruit, then filled a large bowl with *Müsli* and a pitcher with milk. She set out carafes of coffee and hot chocolate. By the time Solange came downstairs, Marta had everything set out on the sideboard for the morning buffet. Marta poured her a cup of hot chocolate as they sat on two stools in the kitchen.

"I've had more rest in the last month than I've had in over a year. You will have to cook all the meals when the baby comes."

"I have some wonderful recipes from the *Hotel Germania*, and I know how to make the best sausage in Switzerland."

"Herve doesn't like German food. I will share my best recipes." Solange winked as she sipped hot chocolate. "More to write in that book you carry."

Marta patted her apron pocket. *"Un jour, quand j'aurai une pension à moi."*

"You are learning French *très rapidement*, though we will have to work harder on your accent." She gave a teasing grimace.

A letter arrived from Rosie.

I have gone to your home three times this week. I met your mother's cousin, Felda Braun. She is a kind woman. I didn't see Elise. Your mother made no excuses this time. She said Elise doesn't want to see anyone. Your brother attended church last Sunday. I asked about your mother and sister; he said Elise had stayed home to look after your mother. He and your father are going to Bern. Things cannot be too bad if they feel they can leave. . . .

Marta felt the tension mount inside her. She wanted desperately to go home and see Mama and Elise for herself, but winter snows had come and Solange's baby could come any hour. Marta could not leave her alone with a boardinghouse full of residents. Torn between fear and guilt, she prayed for God's mercy.

Each day that Herve came with the mail, Marta waited tensely.

"*Rien pour vous aujourd'hui*, Marta."

Each day, she heard the same words. Nothing for her today. The silence filled her with fear.

7

Awakening with a start, Marta heard Herve yelling. He pounded on her door and she called out to him. She slipped into her coat and opened the door enough to look out. "Solange?"

"Oui! Oui!" He spoke French so fast, Marta couldn't understand him. She waved him away and told him she would come down in a moment. Throwing on her clothes, she headed downstairs while still buttoning her shirtwaist. Men had come out into the hallway. She waved them back inside as she hurried down the second-floor hall to the Fourniers' large bedroom. Herve had pulled a chair over to the side of the bed and held Solange's hand. He still wore his night-clothes. Marta stood at the end of the bed, not sure what to do.

"Ah, Marta," Solange said, but her relief was short-lived as pain made her gasp. Herve stood and started rattling off French again, pacing back and forth, raking his hands through his dark hair.

Marta gathered Herve's clothes from the floor and dumped them in his lap. "Get dressed and go for the . . ." Marta searched for the French word for *midwife*. Solange had taught her. What was it? *"Sage-femme! Maintenant,* Herve. *Vite. Vite!* Don't forget your shoes."

Men talked in the corridor. Hoping they hadn't delayed Herve, Marta stepped out. "Is anyone a doctor?" They looked at one another and shook their heads. "Then unless you want to help deliver a baby, go back to your rooms." They disappeared like a thundering herd of mountain goats, doors closing quickly behind them.

Oh, God, what do I do now? Pretending calm she didn't feel, Marta came back into the bedroom. Other than one afternoon lecture at the *Haushaltungsschule Bern* on assisting at a childbirthing, Marta knew nothing at all of such matters. But she supposed she could do better than a panic-stricken husband. "Everything will be fine, Solange. The midwife will be here soon."

An hour later, the door slammed and feet pounded up the stairs. Herve spoke so rapidly, Marta couldn't understand a word he said. She did understand the look on Solange's face. "The midwife isn't coming."

"Herve says she is delivering someone else's baby. *Mon Dieu.* What are we going to do?" She groaned, another contraction coming within a few short minutes of the last one. Herve looked wild-eyed. He moaned with his wife, looking from her to Marta. When he started talking again, Marta cut him off and told him to boil a big pot of water and bring clean towels and a knife. When he just stood there, gaping, Marta repeated her words with quiet authority. "Go, Herve! Everything will be all right."

Solange began to sob and speak French as rapidly as her husband had. Marta took her hand. "German, Solange, or French more slowly."

"Keep Herve out of here. He makes me nervous. He gets upset if I so much as cut myself, and this is—" Another contraction came and stopped her from saying more. "Do you know what to do?"

Marta didn't want to lie and claim knowledge she didn't have. "God made women to have babies, Solange, and He knows what He's doing." She put her hand on Solange's damp brow. "You're going to manage this as well as you do everything else, *ma chère.*"

Herve came up with a pile of towels. He disappeared again and returned with a bowl and steaming kettle. When he came to the bed, Solange raised her head. *"Partez! Sortez!"* Stricken, Herve went, closing the door quietly behind him.

Solange relaxed against the pillows Marta had put behind her, for a few minutes at least, until the next contraction took her breath away. Marta worked through the night, dabbing Solange's forehead, holding her hand, speaking words of encouragement. Solange screamed when the baby pushed his way into the world, just as the sun peeked over the horizon. Marta tied two strings around the cord and cut it with shaking hands. Wrapping the wailing baby boy in a soft blanket, she placed him in Solange's arms.

"He's so beautiful." Solange gazed raptly into her son's face. She looked pale and drained, damp tendrils of dark hair framing her face. "Where is Herve?"

"Downstairs, I think, waiting to find out if you and the baby are well."

She laughed. "Tell him he can come back now. I won't bite him."

The door opened and a heavyset, gray-haired woman came hurrying in. Her face looked weary with exhaustion.

"Madame DuBois!" Solange smiled. "He's already come."

"So I see." The midwife removed her shawl and tossed it aside as she approached the bed. "Two babies in one night." She drew down the blanket to look at the baby. "Herve is bringing warm water and salt. We must wash you both to prevent infection." She drew blankets aside and encouraged Solange to nurse the baby. "It will bring the afterbirth." She straightened and turned to Marta. "We must strip the soiled sheets and replace them." Marta followed the woman's quick instructions.

Herve came in with another pot of hot water and a bag of salt. "You have a son, Herve." Tears of joy ran down Solange's cheeks. The midwife told him to wash his hands before he touched either babe or mother. Herve sloshed water into a basin and scrubbed past his wrists, grabbing one of the towels. When he sat on the edge of the bed, Solange gasped. Herve dropped to his knees beside the bed, murmuring endearments as he kissed Solange and beheld his son.

Feeling useless, Marta gathered up the soiled sheets. "I should

soak these right away." No one noticed when she left. When she
came downstairs, she found several men dressed for work sitting
in the empty dining room. She had had no time to set out the
usual breakfast buffet. "*Müsli* this morning, gentlemen. And no
lunch today. You'll need to find a nice restaurant. We've had a busy
night. The Fourniers have a healthy son. Everything will be back to
normal tomorrow morning."

The midwife came down to the kitchen. "Solange and the baby
are sleeping. Herve fell asleep on the settee. You did well, mademoiselle. Solange speaks very highly of you."

"Solange did all the work, Madame DuBois. All I did was
dab her forehead, hold her hand . . . and *pray*." Madame DuBois
laughed with her. "You'll need something to eat before you leave."
Marta prepared an *omelette*, fried bread, and hot chocolate.
Madame DuBois left as soon as she finished breakfast, and Marta
went upstairs to her attic room to rest for a few hours before starting preparations for dinner.

Unexpected emotion welled up inside Marta. She had never
seen anything more beautiful than the way Solange and Herve
looked at one another and at the perfect infant they had made
together. Would a man ever look at her with such love? Would
she ever have a child of her own? Perhaps her father was right: she
had no beauty to offer and she lacked Mama's gentle spirit. How
many times had Papa said no man would look at her, and in truth,
not one of the bachelors in the house had given her a second look,
other than to ask for some needed service. "*Mademoiselle, would
you mind ironing my suit?*" "*How much to do my laundry, mademoiselle?*" "*More sausages, mademoiselle.*"

Marta put her arm over her eyes and fought tears of longing
and disappointment. She must concentrate on what she could have
with hard work and perseverance, and she must not long for things
beyond reach. Solange had her Herve. Rosie would have her Arik.
Marta would have her freedom.

She could thank God she would never again live under her
father's roof. She would never again bear the bruises of a beating.

She would never again sit in silence as a man told her she was ugly, ill-tempered, and selfish.

"*Fly*," Mama said. "*Be like an eagle.*" In those words, Mama had acknowledged that Marta would not have the comfort of a loving husband or children of her own. "*An eagle flies alone.*"

As she fell asleep, Marta thought she heard a voice. "Mama?" She dreamed Mama flew above her, face radiant, arms spread like angel's wings. Elise stood below, hands raised, snow swirling around her until she disappeared.

❄ ❄ ❄

Over the next few weeks, Marta worked such long, hard hours she had no time to think about anything but what needed to be done. Herve hired another servant, Edmee, who took over the household chores. Marta prepared all the meals for the Fourniers and twelve boarders and looked after Solange during her first weeks of recuperation. Baby Jean proved demanding of his mother's time. After the first few days, Herve slept in the parlor.

Herve came into the kitchen one afternoon. "Two letters, Marta!" He tossed them onto the worktable. "Ah, *ragoût de bœuf.*" He lifted the lid from the bubbling beef stew and inhaled while Marta slid the bread from the oven and set it on the counter to cool. She picked up the two letters, one from Elise, another from Felda Braun.

Heart thumping with dread, Marta took a paring knife and sliced both open. She felt something inside Elise's envelope and carefully opened the note. Folded inside were Mama's gold earbobs.

Mama gave these to me before she died. I love you, Marta. I have asked God to forgive me. I hope you will, too.

Elise

Marta sat down heavily on the stool.

"*Est-ce qu'il y a quelque chose de mal?*" Herve stood looking at her.

What was wrong? Marta remembered the dream and felt her throat close tight with pain. Hands shaking, she put the earbobs onto the note and folded it back into the envelope. Slipping it into her apron pocket, she opened Felda Braun's letter.

Dear Marta,
It is with greatest sorrow that I write this letter. . . .

"Mademoiselle?"

Marta couldn't see through her tears. While she was here helping Solange bring a baby into the world, her mother was dying. She dropped Felda's letter and covered her face. *"Ma mère est morte."*

Herve spoke quietly. She didn't understand anything he said. He came around the worktable and put his hand on her shoulder. "I should've gone home." Marta rocked back and forth, muffling her sobs with her apron. Herve squeezed gently and left the kitchen. "I'm sorry, Mama. Oh, God, I'm so sorry." Trembling violently, she picked up Felda Braun's letter, expecting further details of her mother's passing and Elise's move to Grindelwald.

Your mother wrote to me some months ago about her illness and asked if I might consider taking Elise to live with me when her time came. I went to Steffisburg immediately to speak with her in person. I hardly recognized Anna. The doctor confirmed her own belief that she had consumption. She did not want you to know she was dying because she knew you would come home. She said if you did, your father would never let you go again. She said the minister would write to me when it was time to come for Elise.

When I went home, I began to prepare her way. I told my friends about your mother's illness and how your sister had lost her husband in a tragic accident. In this way, I could assure Elise that she could raise her baby without fear of scandal.

Marta went cold. *Her baby?* She read more quickly.

When I heard from the minister, I went immediately to Steffisburg, but Elise had already disappeared. Your father thought he would find her in Thun. Everyone was looking for her, but I grieve to tell you that we did not find her in time. Your friend Rosie found her body by a stream not far from the house.

Marta cried until she felt sick. She pulled herself together enough to set the table and serve dinner. Clearly, Herve had told the men about her mother, for they offered condolences and spoke in subdued voices. Marta did not mention Elise. Edmee stayed to help wash dishes and clean the kitchen, insisting Marta go upstairs to her attic bedroom and try to rest. Curling on her side, Marta cried as she remembered dreaming of Elise standing in the snow with her hands raised to heaven.

A few days later, Marta received a wire from her father.

Return immediately. Needed in shop.

Tears of fury filled Marta's eyes. She shook with the power of her rage. Not one word about Mama or Elise. Crumpling the message, she threw it in the stove and watched it burn.

❄ ❄ ❄

Solange sat in the kitchen with Marta, baby Jean sleeping contentedly in a basket on the worktable. *"Je comprends."* She took Marta's hand. "God brought you to us when we needed you most, and now you must go. *C'est la vie, n'est-ce pas?*"

Marta felt little guilt about leaving. Solange had healed quickly and was eager to resume her duties. Edmee had agreed to stay on full-time. She was a hard worker like Marta and would help with the baby while Solange resumed the cooking.

Solange lifted the baby from his warm nest. "Would you like to hold Jean one more time before you leave?"

"Yes. Please." Marta held him close, pretending just for a moment he belonged to her. She sang a lullaby in German as she walked around the kitchen. Then she placed Jean in his mother's arms. *"Danke."*

Tears slipped down Solange's cheeks. "Write to us, Marta. Herve and I want to know what becomes of you."

Marta nodded, unable to speak. As she came out of the kitchen into the hallway, Herve and the bachelors stood waiting. Each wished her well as she passed by. When she reached the door, Herve gave her a brotherly kiss on each cheek and handed her an envelope. "A gift from all of us."

She looked from him to the other men. Pressing her lips together so she wouldn't cry, she gave a deep, respectful curtsy and left the house. Despair filled her as she walked to the train station. She looked up at the departure times. A dutiful daughter would return to Steffisburg, work in the shop without complaining, and take care of her father in his old age. *Honor your father and mother,* God commanded, *that your days may be long in the land the Lord your God will give you.*

Marta took a coach to Lausanne, where she boarded a train to Paris.

8

1906

Bern had invigorated Marta, but Paris overwhelmed her. She found her way to the Swiss Consulate. "I'm afraid no positions are open this week, Fräulein." The clerk gave her directions to an inexpensive boardinghouse in the crowded streets of the *Rive Droite*. She paid for a week's lodgings.

Early each morning, Marta went back to the consulate and then out to spend the day exploring the city and practicing her French. She asked directions and visited palaces and museums. She walked into evening along the Seine, lost among the crowds out enjoying the city of lights. She went to the *Musée du Louvre* and wandered through the *Jardin des Tuileries*. She sat in *Notre Dame* cathedral and prayed for her sister's soul.

Prayers did not ease the grief consuming her.

Mama whispered in her dreams. *"Fly, Marta. Don't be afraid, mein kleiner Adler. . . ."* And Marta would awaken, weeping. She dreamed of Elise, too, disturbing dreams of her sister lost and trying to find her way home. Marta could hear the echo of her voice. *"Marta, where are you? Marta, help me!"* she cried out, as the swirling snow enfolded her.

After seven days, Marta gave up on finding a position in Paris and bought a coach ticket to Calais. She boarded a boat across the English Channel and spent most of the trip leaning over the side.

❄ ❄ ❄

Rain came down in sheets over Dover. Weary, Marta continued by coach to Canterbury, part of her wishing she had traveled southeast to the warmth of Italy rather than come to England. She consoled herself that learning English would bring her closer to her goal. After one night in cheap lodgings, Marta took another coach to London.

By the time she arrived, her wool coat smelled like a wet sheep, her boots and the hem of her serviceable skirt felt like they were caked with ten pounds of mud, and she had a head cold. Stomping her feet, she tried to loosen the mud from her boots before going inside the Swiss Consulate to look for lodgings and work.

"Add your name to the list and fill out this form." The harried clerk slid a paper across his desk and went back to another pile of papers.

Ten girls had already written their names on the list. Marta added hers to the bottom and filled out the form carefully. The clerk looked it over. "You have a good hand, Fräulein. Do you speak English?"

"I've come to learn."

"Do you plan to return to Switzerland?"

She didn't know. "Eventually."

"Too many of our young people are going to America. The land of opportunity, they call it."

"I miss the snow. I miss the mountains."

"*Ja.* The air is not so clean here." He continued reading her form. "Ah! You worked with Warner Brennholtz at the *Hotel Germania!*" He smiled and nodded as he pulled his wire-rimmed glasses down. "I spent a week in Interlaken three years ago. Best food I've ever eaten."

"Chef Brennholtz trained me."

"Why did you leave?"

"To learn French. I'm here to learn English. There are more opportunities for employment for those who can speak multiple languages."

"Very true. Do you speak French?"

She gave a prim nod. *"Assez de servir."* Enough to serve, but little more.

"You've accomplished much for one so young, Fräulein Schneider." He glanced over her form again. "Dressmaking, graduate of *Haushaltungsschule Bern*, trained by Frau Fischer and Warner Brennholtz, delivered a baby, and managed a boarding-house in Montreux . . ."

"I am a long way from accomplishing what I want, Herr Reinhard."

Herr Reinhard put her form on the top of the pile. "I will see what I can do."

Marta moved into the Swiss Home for Girls and waited. She had spent more than she intended seeing Paris. While other girls came and went, Marta kept to the house, trying to shake the head cold she had contracted on the journey to London and helping the housemother, Frau Alger, keep the common rooms clean and neat. She wondered if she had made a mistake in coming to England. The drizzling rain and heavy, soot-scented mists of London depressed her, and Frau Alger said good jobs were scarce.

A message came from the consulate, signed by Kurt Reinhard. The wife of the Swiss consul needed an assistant cook for a dinner party that evening. Marta washed and put on her uniform, packed quickly, and headed to the consul's mansion by taxi.

She went to the servants' entrance and found herself greeted by a harried maid. "Thank goodness!" She waved Marta inside. "Frau Schmitz is frantic. She has twenty guests arriving for dinner in less than two hours, and Chef Adalrik's wife became ill this afternoon and had to be taken to the hospital. Another maid quit this morning. We have only one upstairs maid and me."

After the cold, damp air outside, the heat of the kitchen felt momentarily wonderful. The familiar smell of good Germanic cooking reminded her of the *Germania Hotel* and Warner Brennholtz. Other things struck her as well, but she decided it was better to be in a smoky, windowless kitchen than out in the damp looking for work. She set her suitcase aside and removed her coat as the maid introduced her to the grim-faced, gray-haired chef. Adalrik Kohler barely glanced at her. "Go with Wilda. Help her set the table for twenty."

"How many courses?"

"Four. Frau Schmitz wanted six, but I can't manage more without my wife. When you finish, come back to the kitchen. Oh, and, Fräulein, this is not a permanent position. As soon as Nadine recovers, you will go."

"I came to learn English. It is more likely I can accomplish that in an English household."

"Good. Then you will not be disappointed."

With Wilda's help, Marta covered the table with white damask and set out the Royal Albert Regency Blue dishes with crystal stemware and silverware. Two silver candelabras and an arrangement of purple and white lilacs adorned the center of the table. Marta folded the white napkins into peacock tails and set them in the middle of each plate. Frau Schmitz, a dazzling blonde woman in her forties, came in dressed in a blue satin gown. Diamonds sparkled at her throat as she walked around the table, inspecting each setting. "It will do." Marta gave a quick curtsy and headed for the kitchen.

By the end of the evening, Marta's legs ached from going up and down the stairs from the basement to the second-floor dining room. When the guests left and the kitchen had been cleaned from top to bottom, Wilda took her upstairs to the fourth-floor maids' quarters.

Over the next week, Marta worked in the smoky, airless kitchen and carried breakfast trays to Frau Schmitz in her third-floor bedroom. She carried trays to the day nursery and served the nanny and the three polite, but rambunctious, Schmitz children. She carried trays laden with crumpets, cucumber sandwiches, and tea cakes to the second-floor parlor, where the lady of the house liked to have high tea using her Royal Albert Regency Blue dishes and silver tea service. She carried more trays into the dining room each evening when Herr Schmitz came home for dinner with his wife, and more trays up to the children's dining room on the third floor, where the nanny presided.

Nadine returned, and despite Frau Schmitz's complaints about money, Adalrik insisted Marta remain in her employ or he would leave. "Nadine is not fully recovered. She hasn't the stamina to go up and down the stairs twenty times a day. Marta is younger and stronger. She can manage."

After a month, Marta caught another cold, which sank into her chest. By the end of each day, her legs ached so much she could barely drag herself up the four flights to the cold room she shared with Wilda. Collapsing into bed, she dreamed of stairs winding up like Jacob's ladder to heaven. Flights of stairs angled to the right and left, until they disappeared in the clouds. Even after a night of sleep, Marta awakened feeling drained.

"Your cough is getting worse." Nadine poured hot water and brewed tea with lemon. "This will make you feel better."

Adalrik looked grim. "See a doctor before you get any worse. You don't want to end up in the hospital the way Nadine did."

Marta had no illusions. Adalrik wasn't concerned about her health, but about whether Nadine would have to return to upstairs duties. "A doctor will only tell me to rest and drink plenty of fluids."

Nadine made certain she had plenty of broth and tea with milk, but rest proved elusive and the chest cold grew worse.

"She's ringing again," Adalrik told Marta. An evening soiree had lasted far into the night, and Marta had been on duty until the last guest left and everything had been washed and put away. "She'll want her breakfast served in bed."

Marta prepared Frau Schmitz's tray. She managed to climb the first flight of stairs before a fit of coughing gripped her. She set the tray down heavily and coughed until the spasm passed. Lifting the tray, she climbed the rest of the stairs.

"This breakfast is cold." Frau Schmitz waved her hand. "Take it away and bring me another tray. And be quicker next time."

Marta made it halfway down the first flight of stairs when she began to cough again. Struggling for breath, Marta sank onto a step, the tray on her lap. Frau Schmitz came out and peered down the stairwell and disappeared back into her room. A moment later, Nadine went up the stairs. Marta managed to stand and make it downstairs to the kitchen.

Nadine came in right after her. She gave Marta a pitying look. "I'm sorry, Marta, but Frau Schmitz says you must go."

"Go?"

"She wants you out of the house. Today."

"Why?"

"She's afraid of contamination. She says she doesn't want her children getting croup."

Marta gave a bleak laugh. Oddly, she felt relieved. Another trip up those stairs and she would have come tumbling down. "I'll go as soon as I receive my pay. And would you ask Wilda to collect my things please? I don't think I can walk up those stairs again." Chest hurting, she coughed violently into her apron.

When Nadine left, Adalrik put the back of his hand against Marta's forehead. "You're burning up."

"I just need rest."

"Frau Schmitz is afraid you're consumptive."

Marta felt the shock of alarm. Was she destined to die like Mama? Nothing Dr. Zimmer had done had prevented Mama from drowning in her own blood.

"Do you know of a good doctor who speaks German?"

❉ ❉ ❉

A nurse helped Marta dress after the examination and showed her into Dr. Smythe's office. He rose when Marta entered and told her to sit. "I've seen this often before, Fräulein. Swiss girls are used to good, clean mountain air, not heavy smoke and damp fog. You should go back to Switzerland. Go home to your family and rest."

Fighting tears, Marta imagined how her father would greet her. "I'll get more rest in England." If Papa's heart had not softened over Mama's illness, he certainly would show her no kindness. She coughed into her handkerchief, thankful when she didn't see spots of red against the white. "What I need is work in a smaller house with fewer stairs and a kitchen with a door or window." The pain built in her chest until she couldn't hold back another cough. When the spasm eased, she raised her head.

"Rest is what you need, not work."

Gathering her courage, she looked him in the face. "Do I have consumption?"

"You are as pale and thin as a consumptive, but no. Frankly, Fräulein, if you don't take better care of yourself, this can kill you quicker than consumption. Do you understand me?"

Disheartened, Marta relented. "How much rest do I need?"

"A month at the least."

"A month?"

"Six weeks would be preferable."

"Six weeks?" Marta coughed until she felt light-headed.

The doctor gave her a bottle of elixir and ordered her to take a spoonful every four hours. "Rest is the best cure, Fräulein. Your body can't fight infection when exhausted."

Sick and depressed, Marta went back to the Swiss Home for Girls. Frau Alger took one look at her and assigned her a bed in a quiet corner of a street-level dorm room. Too tired to undress, Marta flopped down onto the cot, her coat still on.

Frau Alger came with a pitcher of warm water and a bowl. "That won't do."

Marta shivered as the woman helped her undress and put on her nightgown. She felt an unbearable longing for Mama. When she burst into tears, Frau Alger helped her get into bed. She took the bottle of elixir and read the directions. She went for a spoon and gave Marta her first dose of laudanum, then covered her with thick blankets and tucked them snugly around her. She put her hand on Marta's head. *"Schlaf, Kind."* Marta whispered a bleak thank-you. Already, her eyelids grew heavy.

She awakened at Frau Alger's touch. "Drink." She helped Marta sit up enough to drink a cup of thick soup, take another dose of medicine, and sink back into bed. She dreamed of climbing stairs up and up, flights turning right and left and disappearing into the clouds. She held a heavy tray balanced on her shoulder, then paused to rest. Her legs ached so terribly, she knew she would never make it to heaven. "I can't do it."

"Yes, you can." Mama stood above her dressed in white. *"Don't give up,* Liebling.*"*

She awakened to the sound of church bells and fell asleep again, dreaming Mama held her hand as they walked up the road to St. Stephen's Church. Rosie called out to her, and Marta found herself in the Alpine meadow above Steffisburg, picking spring flowers with Rosie.

Rain battered the windows, awakening her briefly. Shivering, Marta pulled the blankets up again. She wanted to dream of Mama and Rosie, but instead dreamed of being lost in the snow. She heard Elise crying out her name over and over. Marta tried to run to her, but her feet kept sinking into the snow. Crawling on her hands and knees, she looked down at the rushing water of the Zulg and saw Elise lying asleep, a baby in her arms, and a blanket of snow covering them both. "No." She moaned. "No. No." Frau Alger put cool cloths on her brow and spoke to her. Mama sat in the graveyard, embroidering another dress. She looked up with sunken eyes. *"Don't come back, Marta. Fly,* Liebling. *Fly away and live."*

Marta awakened to the sound of coach wheels rolling by. She cried, afraid if she went back to sleep, she would dream again. She heard girls come and go, and she pretended to be asleep. Frau Alger came in with a tray. "You're awake." She set the tray aside and put a hand on Marta's forehead. "Good. Your fever has broken." She helped Marta sit up.

"I'm sorry to be so much trouble." Marta felt the tears come and couldn't stop them.

Frau Alger patted her shoulder. "Hush now, Marta. You're no trouble. And you will be well soon. It's hard to be so far from home, *ja*?"

Marta covered her face, feeling the loss of Mama and Elise more acutely than ever. "I have no home."

Frau Alger sat on the bed and gathered Marta close, murmuring to her as she would a hurting child. Giving in to her grief, Marta clung to her, pretending for just a moment this kind, older woman was Mama.

❄ ❄ ❄

After a week in bed, Marta felt able to get up. The house was empty, so she fixed herself a bowl of hot porridge. Why had she come to England? She felt lost and at odds with herself. Perhaps she should have stayed in Steffisburg and helped Mama. She could have watched over Elise. Too late now to think about those things. What sort of future would she have now if she obeyed Papa and went back? Mama had known. Mama had warned her to stay away.

She gathered her courage and wrote to Rosie.

I am in England. Papa sent a wire telling me to come home. He said nothing about either Elise or Mama, and I knew he would expect me to spend the rest of my life in the shop. If I had not received a letter from Mama's cousin, Felda Braun, I would not have known Elise had died.

I fled, Rosie. I will never return to Steffisburg. The last time I saw Mama, she said I had to go. In truth, I would rather die a stranger in a foreign land than spend another day under my father's roof.

Cousin Felda said it was you who found Elise. I dream

of her every night. She cries out to me and disappears before I can reach her. I pray God forgives me for being such a poor sister. I pray God will forgive her for what she did to herself and her child. And I pray you will forgive us, too. I will be forever in your debt.

Marta

❄ ❄ ❄

After another week of convalescence, Marta grew restless and discontented. Mama had told her to fly, not perch inside the walls of the Swiss Home for Girls. Rest, the doctor had said, but rest wasn't just lying in bed tucked beneath a mound of covers. Marta leaned her forehead against the glass, feeling the walls of her prison close in around her. She imagined what Mama would say if she stood in the room right now.

"God is my strength, Marta. He is my help in times of trouble. . . . God has a plan for your life. . . . Perhaps it is God who has put this dream in your heart. . . . God is the one driving you away. . . . An eagle flies alone. . . ."

She thought of Elise, too. Mama's little barn swallow spoke to her. *"I gave in to despair, Marta. If you give up, you're giving in, too."*

Marta dressed and buttoned up her wool coat.

Frau Alger intercepted her at the front door. "Where do you think you're going?"

"Out for a walk."

Each day, determined to regain her strength, Marta went a little farther, pushed herself a little harder. At first, she could barely walk more than a block without finding a place to sit and rest. Gradually, she went two, then three. She found a small park and sat surrounded by trees and grass, spring flowers beginning to emerge, slivers of sunlight slicing through the clouds. Sometimes she rose and stood in a spear of light, closing her eyes and imagining she stood in the Alpine meadow with Mama or Rosie.

Soon, she could walk a mile before exhausting herself. When it rained one day, she sought warmth and rest in the Hare and Toad pub. Three men sat drinking from mugs of beer, giving her a cursory glance as she found her way to an empty table in a dimly lit corner. Though she felt out of place and uncomfortable, she decided to stay. At least here, she would hear English spoken.

The men talked in low voices and then, forgetting her presence, spoke more naturally. When another entered, the three greeted him and made room. He spoke to the proprietor, handed over some coins, and took a mug of ale to the table. A few minutes later, the burly proprietor came out with meals stacked up his arm— fish, judging by the smell, and cooked in some sort of dough. She listened, trying to pick up words. Some sounded familiar, no doubt derived from German.

Gathering her courage, Marta went to the counter and tried to make sense of the English words written on the menu overhead. She understood the prices well enough. The proprietor stood behind the counter, drying a beer mug. Pointing to the menu, Marta took out a few pence from her pocket and lined them up on the counter. She put her palms together and moved her hands like a fish.

"Fish and chips?"

"Fish and chips," she repeated. *"Danke."*

He brought her meal and a glass of water. He took a bottle of malt vinegar from another table and set it in front of her. "For the fish." He pointed.

Marta ate slowly, experimentally, not sure her stomach could stand deep-fried fish caked in dough. Others came in over the next hour, and the pub began to fill with men and women. Some had children. Marta felt self-conscious taking up a table by herself and left. The sun had gone down and the mist had turned to rain. It took an hour to walk back to the Swiss Home for Girls.

"Look at you, Marta!" Frau Alger shook her head. "Do you

want to catch your death this time?" She made her sit by the stove and drink hot tea. "Here. I have a letter for you."

Heart pounding, Marta tore Rosie's letter open.

My dearest friend,

I feared you would blame me for not keeping better watch over Elise. I went to see her the day after your mother's funeral. I should not have waited. Had I gone right after the services, Elise might still be alive. But I did wait and will forever be sorry for it. My mother went with me.

Your father said he didn't know where Elise had gone. He said she would not come out of her room on the day of the funeral. He didn't look in on her until the next. Your father went out to call the alarm.

I remembered how Elise loved to sit by the stream and listen to the living water. When I found her, she looked like an angel asleep beneath a white blanket of eiderdown.

I don't know how much Felda Braun told you, but I discovered why Elise hid herself away. She was heavy with child. May God have mercy on the Meyer men for what they did to your poor sister.

I found Elise curled up on her side, as though to embrace the baby inside her and keep it warm. My father told me people who freeze to death feel no pain. I pray that is true.

You asked me to forgive you. I ask now for your forgiveness. Please do not stop writing. I love you like you are my own sister. I miss you desperately.

Ever your friend,
Rosie

Marta wrote back and asked where Papa had buried Elise. She wept at the thought of Elise buried somewhere other than beside Mama, but she knew the church would not want a suicide laid to rest in consecrated soil.

Marta bundled up the next morning, walked to a coach stand, and rode down to Westminster Abbey. She sat on a pew, wondering what Mama would think of this magnificent coronation church. Massive gray columns rose like enormous tree trunks holding up a shadowed canopy above. A rainbow of color splashed across the marble mosaic floors, as sun shone through the stained-glass windows. But the light quickly faded. She listened to the living walking among the shrines to the dead, standing and whispering in the naves lined with crypts holding the bones of great poets and politicians, or gazing at some bronze effigy tomb or sarcophagus.

Oh, God, where does my sister sleep? Can You show mercy and carry her home to heaven? Or must she suffer the agonies of hell because she lost hope?

A woman touched Marta on the shoulder and spoke. Startled, Marta wiped tears away quickly. The woman spoke to her in English. Though unable to comprehend the words, Marta took comfort in the woman's gentle smile and tone. Mama might have comforted a stranger in the same way.

Marta went to Hyde Park the next day and sat on the grass, watching the boats drift by on the blue Serpentine. Even in the open air and sunshine, Marta felt grief weigh down upon her. Mama said God offered her a future and a hope. But what did that mean? Was she supposed to wait until God spoke to her from the heavens? *"Go,"* Mama had said, but Marta didn't know where to go anymore.

She only knew she couldn't continue this way, drowning in sorrow and living with regret. She had to remember what had driven her away from home in the first place. She wanted freedom to become all she could be. She wanted something to call her own. She couldn't have either of those things by sitting and feeling sorry for herself.

Before heading back to the Swiss Home for Girls, Marta went to the Swiss consul's offices.

"Fräulein Schneider!" Kurt Reinhard greeted her warmly. "It is good to see you. I heard you left the consul's house."

Surprised he remembered her at all, Marta told him what had transpired. "I would like to put my name on your list again, Herr Reinhard. But may I request an English household this time, preferably one away from the soot and smoke of London?"

"Of course. How soon will you be able to work?"

"The sooner the better."

"Then I think I have just the place for you."

MARTA RODE TO Kew Station and walked the rest of the way to
Lady Daisy Stockhard's three-story Tudor house near Kew Gardens.
She expected to meet with the mistress of housekeeping. Instead,
a stooped butler showed her into a parlor with daybeds and wingback chairs, and a large, low, round table covered with books.
Every wall boasted a gilt-framed landscape. The floor was covered
with a Persian rug. Curved, carved-legged tables with marble tops
held brass lamps, and a pianoforte stood in the far corner with a
marble bust of Queen Elizabeth. Over the fireplace hung a portrait
of an English army officer in dress uniform.

It took but a few seconds to take it all in and redirect her attention to a white-haired lady dressed elegantly in black, sitting in
a straight-backed chair, and another much younger, plump and
dressed in frothy folds of pink, sitting on a chaise, her back to the
windows and a book open on her lap.

"Thank you, Welton." The older woman took Marta's documents from him and put on tiny, wire-framed glasses as she read.

The younger woman, whom Marta took to be the lady's

daughter, said something in English and sighed. Her mother answered pleasantly, to which the daughter lifted her book and made a dismissive sounding comment. The only part of the conversation Marta was fairly certain she understood was that the young woman's name was Millicent.

Lady Stockhard removed her glasses carefully and looked up. She addressed Marta in passable German. "Don't stand in the doorway, Fräulein Schneider." She beckoned. "Come in and let me have a good look at you." Marta came a few steps into the room and stood with her hands clasped in front of her. "Mr. Reinhard tells me you don't speak English. My German is limited. Enid, my cook, will teach you English. Honore and Welton will help as well. He takes care of the gardens. I used to love gardening. It's good for the soul."

Millicent sighed in annoyance. She said something that Marta didn't understand.

Lady Stockhard answered pleasantly and then indicated that Marta should sit in a chair close to her. "I like to get to know the people who would join my staff."

Her daughter glowered and spoke again in English. Marta had no difficulty understanding her condescending tone or dismissive look.

Lady Stockhard said something to her daughter, then smiled and spoke to Marta. "I told her you have training as a dressmaker. That will please her."

Millicent snapped her book shut and rose. A rustling of skirts announced her departure.

"Do you like gardens, Fräulein?"

"Yes, ma'am." She didn't know what to make of Lady Stockhard with her inviting attitude.

"Kew Gardens is a short walk away. I used to spend hours walking there. Now I can only just manage to walk around the house. Someone must take me to Kew Gardens in a wheelchair. Welton is too old, poor dear, and Ingrid met her handsome coachman. I have Melena, but she misses Greece and her family so much, I doubt she'll stay long. Are you homesick for your family?"

Marta couldn't hide her surprise that an English lady would talk to her as though passing time with a friend. "I've been away from home nearly two years, ma'am."

"And your mother doesn't miss you?"

She felt a stab of pain. "My mother died in January, ma'am."

"Oh." She looked dismayed. "Please accept my condolences. I don't mean to pry." The lady looked down at the documents on her lap. "Marta. A good Christian name. Mr. Reinhard writes you are a good worker, but Swiss girls always are." Lady Stockhard raised her head and smiled. "I've had three in my employ over the years, and not one has disappointed me. I'm sure you won't either." She took a small silver bell from her side table and rang it.

A dark-haired, dark-eyed maid appeared. "Yes, Lady Daisy?"

"Honore, please show Marta to her quarters, and then introduce her to Enid and Melena." She leaned over and put her hand on Marta's knee. "English from now on, dear. It will be difficult at first, but you will learn more quickly that way."

Enid, the rotund and loquacious cook, spoke German, English, and French. When Marta said she had never met anyone like Lady Stockhard, who treated a servant so kindly, Enid nodded. "Oh, our lady is someone very special. She's not like so many others who look down their noses on those who serve them. Not like her daughter, who gives herself airs. Lady Daisy always hires foreign servants. She says it's an inexpensive way to visit another country. Melena is from Greece, Honore comes from France, and I'm from Scotland. Now, we have you, our little Swiss maid. Lady Daisy says if people can get along, then countries can also."

"And Welton?"

"British, of course. He served with Sir Clive in India. When Welton returned, he came to pay his respects to our lady. He had retired and needed work. Of course, Lady Daisy hired him immediately and gave him the room over the carriage house. Welton and my late husband, Ronald, became good friends. Enough talking in

German. I find it exhausting. And we have much to do." As they worked side by side, Enid pointed out objects, said the English word, and had Marta repeat it.

The next morning, the more reticent Honore taught Marta English phrases while they made beds, freshened rooms, and folded away clothing Miss Millicent had cast on chairs and floor that afternoon before going to call on a friend.

"Good morning, Miss Stockhard." Marta repeated the phrase. "Do you wish the drapes drawn, Miss Stockhard? May I bring you breakfast in bed, Miss Stockhard?"

Even the taciturn Welton became Marta's instructor. When Enid sent her out for fresh vegetables from the garden, Welton carried on with names posted at the ends of rows. "Lettuce, cucumber, string, pole, beans, gate," he told her, then shouted, "Rabbit!" He followed the last word with a string of others Marta knew better than to repeat.

Every afternoon, Lady Stockhard rang her little silver bell, sat in her wheelchair, and waited for Melena to come and take her for an outing to Kew Gardens. Marta helped Enid prepare savories and sweets for high tea. As soon as Lady Stockhard and Melena returned, Marta wheeled the tea cart into the conservatory. She set a table with a silver pot of Ceylon or India tea spiced with cinnamon, ginger, and cloves and plates of cucumber sandwiches, Scotch eggs, and currant brioches.

"What would you like, Melena?"

Lady Stockhard never ceased to surprise Marta. "She's serving tea to Melena, as though she's a guest and not a servant," she told Enid.

"She often does when Miss Millicent is out of the house. Sometimes, when her daughter goes traveling, Lady Daisy will even join us in the kitchen."

Enid, like Warner Brennholtz, shared her culinary knowledge openly. She didn't mind when Marta wrote notes in her book, even going so far as to read what she wrote and add tidbits Marta may have forgotten. Marta filled pages with recipes for crumbly scones,

Scottish shortbread, Chelsea buns, Yorkshire pudding, steak and kidney pie, and Lancashire hotpot.

"I've got a dozen others to give you," Enid told her. "Shepherd's pie, toad-in-the-hole, and oxtail soup are a few of our lady's favorites, but Miss Millicent would rather have rack of lamb and beef Wellington. When the young lady goes off on her next trip, we'll have ourselves some plain English cooking again." Enid rubbed seasonings into a hunk of meat.

"Miss Millicent must love to travel."

Enid snorted. "She has her motives." She shrugged and rolled the roast, rubbing more seasonings on the underside.

Marta received a letter from Rosie.

Elise is buried in our favorite meadow. Spring flowers are in bloom. I have not gone to church since Elise died, but I sit on our log and pray for her soul every day.

Father John came up yesterday afternoon. He told me he would rather lie beneath a blanket of flowers with a view of Thunersee and the mountains than be under six feet of dirt in the confines of stone walls inside town. When I cried, he held me.

He said the church must have rules, but God is Elise's Maker and God is just and merciful. He said the Lord promised not to lose any of His children. His words helped me, Marta. I hope they will help you, too.

Marta wished she could feel at peace, but she couldn't shake the guilt. Had she gone home, Mama might still have died, but surely Elise would have lived. How dared she go on making plans for herself when it had been her dream that made her leave them behind—vulnerable, unloved, and unprotected? Though she despised her father, perhaps he was right after all. She did think of herself first; she did think she could do better than her brother. She was ambitious and unrepentantly disobedient. Perhaps he was also right in saying she deserved nothing more than to serve in someone else's household. But before God, she swore it would never be his.

When Melena went home to Greece, Marta found herself assigned to new responsibilities.

Dear Rosie,

I have become Lady Daisy's companion. She is a most unusual lady. I have never known anyone to discuss so many interesting topics. She doesn't treat her servants like slaves, but is genuinely interested in our lives. She had me sit with her in church last Sunday.

Often, during their outings to Kew Gardens, Lady Stockhard talked about books. "Feel free to use my library, Marta. I can only read one at a time, and books shouldn't gather dust. It's lovely in spring, isn't it? Of course, the gardens are always lovely, even in winter. The holly leaves look greener and the red berries redder against the snow. You must need to rest by now. Let's sit awhile by the pond."

Waxy purple and yellow lilies rose on thick stems above the huge, green, plate-shaped leaves floating on the murky surface of the water. Mama would have loved Kew Gardens with all its varied beauty, birds flitting and fluttering from tree to tree, and rainbows in the misty spring rain.

Marta pushed the wheelchair along the walk through a wooded glen. It reminded her of the lush green of Switzerland. Flowers popped bright faces up among the green grasses. Marta felt suddenly homesick for the Alpine meadows covered with spring blossoms. Grief welled up as she thought of Elise sleeping beneath a blanket of spring green and flowers and Rosie sitting on the fallen tree, praying for her soul. Wiping away tears, she pushed Lady Daisy along in the wheelchair.

"Do you miss your mother?"

"Yes, ma'am." And Elise, though she never spoke of her.

"I know what it is to mourn. I lost my husband to fever in India twenty years ago, and there isn't a day that passes that I don't miss him. Millicent was six when I brought her home. I wonder sometimes if she remembers her father or India with all its exotic scents and sounds." She laughed sadly. "We rode together on an elephant more than once, and she loved to watch the local snake charmer."

"No one would ever forget such things, Lady Daisy."

"Not unless they wanted to forget." Lady Stockhard smoothed the blanket covering her legs. "We grieve for those we've lost, but it's the living that cause us the most pain. Poor Millicent. I don't know what will become of her."

Marta didn't know how to boost Lady Daisy's spirits.

"Don't worry about Lady Daisy," Enid told Marta that evening. "She gets like this sometimes after Miss Millicent leaves on holiday. She'll be herself in a few days."

"Why doesn't Lady Daisy travel with her daughter?"

"She did for a while, but things never worked out when our lady was along. Miss Millicent prefers going alone. She sees the world differently than our lady. And who's to say who's right. The world is what it is."

None of the staff had any fondness for Miss Millicent, especially Welton, who stayed to the garden as much as possible whenever Lady Daisy's daughter was home. The air grew colder in the house when Miss Millicent was present. When summoned, Marta went quickly to wherever Miss Millicent might be, curtsied, received her instructions, curtsied again, and departed to do what she had been told. Unlike Lady Stockhard, Miss Millicent never addressed a servant by name, asked how she felt, or discussed anything.

After six months in Lady Stockhard's employ, Marta had learned enough English to follow whatever instructions might be given.

She disliked Miss Millicent almost as much as she liked Lady Daisy. The young woman treated her mother with contempt. "One might think you prefer the company of servants to that of peers, Mother."

"I like everyone."

"Everyone is not worthy. Did you have to talk to the gardener in the front yard?"

"His name is Welton, Millicent, and he's part of the family."

"It's about time tea arrived!" she complained. "The point is, everyone in the neighborhood saw you. What will people think?"

"That I'm talking to my gardener."

"You're impossible." Miss Millicent treated her mother like a recalcitrant child. Leaning forward, she looked at the tiered dishes and groaned. "Egg and watercress sandwiches again, Mother. Cook knows I prefer spicy chicken and currant brioches. And it would be nice to have chocolate *éclairs* more often than once a month."

Marta positioned the trolley and set the silver tea service on the table, closer to Lady Stockhard than her daughter, turning the handle so her lady could easily grasp it. She felt Miss Millicent's cold glare. When Marta put the tiered dishes within easy reach as well, Lady Daisy smiled at her. "Thank you, Marta."

"The girl doesn't know how to set a table." Miss Millicent rose enough to reach across and grasp the teapot. Pouring herself a cup of tea, she returned the pot to where Marta had placed it. Then she proceeded to fill her plate with sandwich wedges, sponge drops with jam, and cream-filled strawberry meringues. "No one needs to talk to a gardener for longer than a few minutes, Mother, and you were outside for the better part of an hour. Do you have any idea what people will say about that?" She sat and put an entire sponge drop into her mouth. Her cheeks bulged as she chewed.

Lady Stockhard poured her own tea. "People always talk, Millicent." She added a bit of milk and two scoops of sugar. "If they have nothing to talk about, they'll invent something."

"They won't have to invent a thing. It doesn't even occur to you how I feel, does it? How can I show my face outside the front door when my mother is the scandal of the neighborhood?"

Fuming, Marta returned to the kitchen. "Miss Millicent wants spicy chicken sandwiches tomorrow."

"If I make spicy chicken, she'll want something else. There's no pleasing her."

"I'm surprised Miss Millicent receives so many invitations."

"She can be quite charming when she has reason to be. And I understand she can be quite pleasing to young men." Enid shrugged. "I'll be needing more carrots and another onion. Why don't you go on out to the garden? You look like you could use a breath of fresh air. But don't be long. Her Highness will be wanting the tea things removed from the parlor. She's invited guests for dinner."

Miss Millicent stayed home for two months, then left again.

"She must love to travel."

Enid gave a snort. "She's gone hunting. And I don't mean foxes."

"What, then?"

"Miss Millicent is off on another one of her husband-hunting expeditions. It's Brighton this time because she heard a friend has a brother who's eligible. She'll be home in a few weeks, disappointed. She'll be moody and disagreeable, and she'll stuff herself with scones and marmalade, cakes and spicy chicken sandwiches. Then, she'll start writing letters again, and she'll keep writing until someone invites her to come for a visit on the Continent or in Stratford-upon-Avon or in Cornwall. She meets people everywhere she goes, and she keeps their names and addresses."

Enid's prophecy proved true. Miss Millicent came home after two weeks, and she stayed in her room for another, demanding that all her meals be brought to her. Marta would find her propped up in bed, reading Jane Austen romances. After exhausting the staff with constant demands, she went off to Dover to visit a sick friend.

"I heard her tell Lady Daisy the lady must be on her deathbed," Marta told Enid. "The vicar comes to visit several times a week."

"A vicar, you say? Well, maybe Miss Millicent is beginning to see the light and lowering her standards. But if the man has a lick of sense, he'll heed the apostle Paul's advice and remain unmarried!"

Miss Millicent returned in a foul temper.

Lady Daisy ordered beef Wellington. Enid clucked her tongue as she iced a chocolate cake. "Things must not have gone well in Dover. No big surprise there. Miss Millicent will be off again soon enough, to Brighton or Cambridge."

Millicent didn't spend a week in her room this time. She lounged in the conservatory, regaling her mother with complaints. "It's a perfectly horrid place, Mother. I don't know why anyone would want to live in that cold, dreary place."

"Did you attend church with Susanna?"

"Of course, but I didn't like the vicar at all. For all his kind attention to Susanna, he was quite dull."

Back in the kitchen, Enid sighed. "More likely she tossed out her line and didn't even get a bite."

Another letter came from Rosie. She had married Arik, and she expected to be blissfully happy for the rest of her life. She wished the same to Marta, who felt a sense of loss and envy. Ashamed she could resent such happiness, Marta prayed God would bless them and spent a month's salary on white lawn, Irish lace, satin ribbons, silk embroidery thread, needles, and a hoop. While others slept, Marta sat in an alcove with a candle burning and made a dressing gown fit for a princess. It took two months to finish it.

I have never worn anything so beautiful in my life! Even my wedding dress could not compare. I have wonderful news. Arik and I expect a baby to arrive just before our first anniversary.

I can't express to you how happy I am. I pray God will bless you with happiness, too, Marta. I pray you will meet someone you can love as much as I love Arik.

Marta folded the letter away and added it to the growing bundle. Love could be a two-edged sword. What guarantee was there that it would be returned? Solange and Rosie had been blessed by the men they loved. Mama had not been so fortunate. Marta began work on a christening gown and bonnet.

A STRAINED AMBIVALENCE took hold of Marta. She continued to save money, but she stopped making grandiose plans about having her own boardinghouse. She tried to follow Mama's advice and count her blessings. She had grown deeply fond of Lady Daisy and enjoyed being her companion. She respected and had great affection for Enid. She liked Welton, and she had befriended Gabriella, the new girl from Italy. Marta set herself the task of learning Italian while teaching her English. Life was good enough in Lady Stockhard's household. Why change things?

Marta had collected the best of Enid's recipes and tucked away the book Rosie had given her. She didn't write letters to Rosie as often as she had during her first three years away from Steffisburg. Rosie's letters still arrived with regularity, filled with glowing words about Arik and going on and on about every little change in baby Henrik. And now she expected another. Rosie had always been a wonderful friend, but there was an unconscious insensitivity in the way she shared her joy. Each time Marta read one of her letters, she felt as though salt were being poured over her wounds.

She could almost empathize with Miss Millicent's increasing frustration over not finding a suitable husband.

Every Sunday when Marta went to church, she imagined Mama sitting beside her. She prayed God would have mercy on Elise's soul. Although the dreams had stopped after a year, she sometimes longed for them to return, afraid she was already forgetting Mama's and Elise's faces. The ache remained like a heavy stone inside her. Occasionally, unexpectedly, the grief would swell up and catch hold of her throat until she felt she was choking on it. She never cried in front of anyone. She waited, searching desperately for something to do to keep her mind occupied. At night, she had no defenses. In the dark, she felt free to release the pent-up pain inside her.

When she couldn't sleep, she borrowed another book from Lady Daisy's library.

Time passed most pleasantly when Miss Millicent was off on one of her hunting expeditions, far less amiably when the miss languished at home. Marta liked having Lady Daisy all to herself. She thought Miss Millicent the most foolish girl she had ever met to take her mother so for granted. Lady Daisy had entered her declining years. Someday she would be gone. Who would love Miss Millicent then?

A year passed and then another. Marta took comfort in her routine. She got up early every morning and helped Enid prepare breakfast, then did housekeeping chores with Gabriella. Every afternoon, rain or shine, she took Lady Daisy on an outing to Kew Gardens. If Miss Millicent was home, Gabriella did the running to and fro. Marta wrote once a month to Rosie, though she had less and less to tell her friend.

Often after everyone had gone to bed, Marta would sit in the library and read. One night Lady Daisy found her standing by the shelves. "What have you been reading?" She held out her hand, and Marta handed over the book she had intended to return. "*The Battle for Gaul* by Julius Caesar." She chuckled. "Rather grim reading, don't you think? Certainly not something I would ever choose." She smiled at Marta. "It was one of Clive's favorites." She handed the book back to Marta, and Marta slid it back into its place. Lady Daisy pulled a slim volume from a shelf. "I prefer Lord Tennyson's poems." She held it out to Marta. "Why don't you take this with you tomorrow when we go to the gardens?"

After Tennyson, Lady Daisy told Marta to select something. After one afternoon of listening to Charles Darwin's *The Origin of Species*, Lady Daisy brought *A Tale of Two Cities* with her. Sometimes Marta would read to her in the evening. Lady Daisy selected Sir Walter Scott's *Ivanhoe* next and followed that with Maria Edgeworth's *Castle Rackrent*. Sometimes Miss Millicent became so bored or distraught, she came along to listen.

Marta continued reading whenever she had a moment to herself, often keeping a book tucked in her apron pocket.

Rosie wrote with surprising news.

Your father married a woman from Thun the summer after your mother died. I didn't know how to tell you. She manages your father's shop, and if I dare say it, she manages your father as well. Apparently, his wife has connections. She saw that he had two men assigned to help him.

After the initial shock, Marta felt numbed by the news that she had a stepmother. How would Mama feel if she knew she had been so easily replaced? Did Papa ever grieve over her or Elise? She considered writing to him and congratulating him on his marriage, then decided against it. Though she felt no ill will toward the woman, she didn't want to extend good wishes to her father. Instead, she hoped his new wife would be as great a trial to him as he had been to Mama.

Marta continued to take Lady Daisy to Kew Gardens every day. Lady Daisy knew the name of every plant, when they bloomed, and which had medicinal value. She would lose herself in thought at times, and she'd be silent. They went often to the Palm House with its Pagoda and Syon Vistas and the steam rising from underground boilers into the ornate campanile. The steamy heat soothed Lady Daisy's aching joints and reminded her of India. Marta preferred the Woodland Glade with its deciduous canopy, flowering shrubs and hellebores, primroses and red poppies.

Every season had its delight; winter with its witch hazel and ordered beds of viburnums along the Palm House pond, and snow covering the lawn with white. February brought thousands of purple crocuses peeking up through the grass between the Temple of Bellona and Victoria Gate, and bright yellow daffodils along Broad Walk. In March the cherry trees bloomed and left a carpet of pink and white on the path. April filled the dell with red and purple rhododendrons and magnolias with their plate-size white, waxy blossoms, followed in May by azaleas covering themselves in shawls of peachy-pink and white. The scent of lilacs filled the air. Roses climbed the Pergola and giant water lilies spread out across the pond while laburnum dripped sunlight-yellow streamers in celebration of spring. The tulip and mock orange trees hinted scents of heaven, before autumn came in a burst of color, fading by late November with the advance of winter.

"It's a pity I can't be buried here," Lady Daisy said one day. Death seemed to be on everyone's mind these days, ever since the "unsinkable" *Titanic* had hit an iceberg and sunk on its maiden voyage. Over fourteen hundred lives had been lost in the frigid Atlantic waters. "Of course, I'd rather be buried in India beside Clive. India was like another world with its strange architecture and jungles. It had a scent of spices. Most ladies I met longed to return to England, but I would've been happy to stay forever. I suppose that had everything to do with Clive. I would've been happy in a bedouin tent in the middle of the Sahara."

Lady Daisy hardly said a word the next afternoon as Marta pushed her along in the Broad Walk in Kew Gardens.

"Are you feeling all right, Lady Daisy?"

"Sick at heart. Let's rest by the lily pond." She pulled a thin volume from beneath her blanket and held it out to Marta. "Lord Byron used to be Millicent's favorite poet. She doesn't read him anymore. Read 'The First Kiss of Love.'" When Marta finished, Lady Daisy sighed wearily. "Again, and with a little more feeling this time."

Marta read the poem again.

"Have you ever been in love, Marta?"

"No, ma'am."

"Why not?"

It seemed an odd question. "It's not something that can be ordered, ma'am."

"You have to be willing."

Marta felt her face heat up. She hoped silence would end such personal inquiries.

"A woman should not go through life without love." Lady Daisy's eyes grew moist. "It's why Millicent is so desperate and bitter now. She thinks all her opportunities are gone. She could still marry, if she had the courage." Lady Daisy sighed heavily. "She has a good education. She's still lovely and can be charming. She has friends. But she has always set such high expectations. Perhaps if she had had Clive's mother to help, but you see, she would have nothing to do with me. I was a pub owner's daughter, nothing more. Millicent thought the lady's heart might soften for her only grandchild. I warned her, but she went anyway. Of course, she was not received."

Lady Daisy fell silent for a long time. Marta didn't know what to say to give her comfort. Her mistress smoothed the blanket over her legs. "It's a pity really. Millicent is like her grandmother in some ways." She gave Marta a bleak smile. "She doesn't approve of me either." She lifted her shoulders. "And, in all truth, no one knows that better than I. But Clive saw something in me and wouldn't take no for an answer."

"I am sorry about Miss Millicent, ma'am." Marta couldn't deny what she had seen with her own eyes. "You are a remarkable mother."

"Less than what I should've been. It's my fault things turned out this way, but if I lived my life all over again, I wouldn't have changed a thing. I wanted him. That's how selfish I am. Besides, if I had done things differently, Millicent wouldn't even exist. I comfort myself by remembering how much Clive loved me. I tell myself he wouldn't have been happy behind a desk overseeing his father's landholdings or sitting in Parliament."

She shook her head sadly. "Millicent met a fine young man when she was sixteen. He was absolutely mad about her. I advised Millicent to marry him. She said he didn't have the proper connections and therefore would never amount to anything. He's in Parliament now, and married, of course. She saw him with his wife and children in Brighton last summer. That's why she came home so soon. One poor decision can change the entire course of your life."

Marta thought of Mama and Elise. "I know, Lady Daisy. I made a decision once that I will regret for the rest of my life, though I don't know what I could have done to change anything."

Lady Daisy looked pale and upset. "Clive was always the one to call me Milady Daisy, and Welton called me Lady Daisy when he came. I'm not a lady at all, Marta. I'm just plain Daisy. I never knew my father. I grew up in Liverpool and worked in a theater. I was Clive's mistress for a year before he took me off to Gretna Green to make an honest woman of me. Millicent knows enough about my past to think I have nothing good to teach her. I may be lower than a guttersnipe under my nice clothes, but at least I knew quality when I saw it, and I wasn't afraid to grab hold. I knew what I wanted, and what I wanted was Clive Reginald Stockhard!" She gave a broken sob.

"You are a lady. You are as much a lady as my mother was, ma'am."

Lady Daisy leaned forward and grasped Marta's wrist tightly. "What are you waiting for, Marta Schneider?"

Marta started at the question. "I don't know what you mean, ma'am."

"Of course you do." Her hand tightened and her blue eyes glistened with angry tears. "You didn't come to England to be a servant for the rest of your life, did you? You could've done that in Switzerland. A dream brought you here. I knew that the minute I saw your application. I saw in you a girl driven by something. I thought you would only stay for a year or two before you set off to get what you wanted."

Marta's heart pounded heavily. "I am content, ma'am."

"*Content.* Oh, my dear." Lady Daisy's voice softened and became pleading. "I have watched you grieve and punish yourself for nearly six years."

Marta felt the punch of those words. "I should've gone home."

"Why didn't you?"

Because Solange needed her. Because the winter snows had piled up outside the door. Because she had been afraid that if she did, she would never be able to escape.

"Don't come home again," Mama's words whispered in Marta's mind. She pulled her wrist free and covered her face.

Lady Daisy sat beside her on the park bench. "You have served me faithfully for five years. Soon it will be six. Even with the little you have told me of your mother, I doubt she wanted you to spend the rest of your life as a servant." She put her hand on Marta's knee. "I am very fond of you, my dear, and I'm going to give you some advice because I don't want you to end up like Millicent. She puts a shawl of pride around herself, and life will pass her by."

"I'm not looking for a husband, ma'am."

"Well, how could you when you spend six days a week working in the kitchen or taking me on outings and then most of the night reading? You never go anywhere other than church, and you never linger there long enough to meet any young man who might be interested."

"No one has ever been interested. Men want pretty wives."

"Charm is deceitful, and beauty never lasts. A man with sense knows that. You have strong character. You are kind. You are honest. You work hard and learn quickly. You left home to better yourself. You may not have formal schooling, but you've read the best books in my library. These are qualities a wise man will value."

"If my father could find nothing about me to love, Lady Daisy, I doubt any other man will."

"I beg your pardon, Marta, but your father is a fool. Maybe you aren't beautiful, but you are attractive. A woman's hair is her glory, my girl, and besides that asset, you have a very fine figure. I've seen men look at you. You blush, but it's true."

Marta didn't know what to say.

Lady Daisy laughed. "Millicent would be appalled to hear me speak so bluntly, but if I don't, you may go on for another five years before you come to your senses." Lady Daisy folded her hands. "If you want to marry and have children, go to an English colony where there are more men than women. In a place like Canada, a man will see the value of a good woman and not care whether the blood in her veins is blue or red. These are things I have said to my daughter, but she won't listen. She still dreams of meeting Mr. Darcy." She shook her head. "Be wise, Marta. Don't wait. Go down to Liverpool and buy passage on the first ship heading for Canada."

"And what if my ship hits an iceberg?"

"We'll pray that doesn't happen. But if it does, you climb into a life raft and start rowing."

Marta laughed. She felt exhilarated and afraid at the same time. Canada! She had never even thought of going there. She'd always thought she would return to Switzerland. "I'll leave at the end of the month."

"Good for you." Lady Daisy looked ready to cry. "I'll miss you terribly, of course, but it's for the best." She took out a handkerchief and dabbed her eyes and nose. "A pity Millicent hasn't the sense to do it."

11

1912

Four days passed in abject misery, but gradually, Marta gained her
sea legs and felt well enough to leave her bunk in steerage, ventur-
ing onto the deck of the SS *Laurentic*. Her first sight of the vast
open sea with waves catching the sunlight filled her with terror.
The ship that had appeared so enormous in Liverpool now seemed
small and vulnerable as it steamed west toward Canada.

She thought of the *Titanic*, so much bigger than this humble
vessel, and how it had gone to the bottom of the ocean. The
owners of the *Titanic* had bragged that the ship was invincible,
unsinkable. Who in his right mind would make such a boast?
It flew in the face of God, like the foolish people who built the
tower of Babel, thinking they could climb to heaven on their own
achievements.

Marta gazed over the rail, passengers lined up on both sides of
her like seagulls on a pier. The air felt cold enough to freeze her
lungs. She was afloat on a cork bobbing on the surface of a vast sea
with bottomless depths. Would this ship come near any icebergs?

She had read that what was seen on the surface was a mere fraction of the danger hidden below.

Stomach queasy, Marta closed her eyes so she wouldn't see the rise and fall of the horizon. She didn't want to go back inside to her bunk. The accommodations had turned out to be far worse than she had expected. The cacophony of voices speaking German, Hungarian, Greek, and Italian made her head ache. People fresh off farms and from small villages submitted with docile ignorance to being treated like cattle, but Marta minded greatly. If two hundred people had paid passage in steerage, then two hundred people should have a place to sit and eat and not have to find space on the floor or the windblown deck. Rather than be served, a "captain" was chosen to fetch the food for eight to ten others. And then, each passenger was required to wash his own "gear"—the tin saucepan, dipper, fork, and spoon she had found on her bunk the day she boarded the ship.

She breathed in the salt air. Despite her attempts to keep clean, her shirtwaist smelled faintly of vomit. If it rained, she might just take out a bar of soap and wash right here on the deck, clothes on!

The ship surged up and dipped down, making her stomach roll. She clenched her teeth, refusing to be sick again. Her clothes hung on her. She couldn't go forever on so little food and still have her health when she arrived in Montreal. After spending an hour waiting to use one of the washbasins so she could clean her gear and then finding it in such fetid condition, she had almost lost the cold porridge she had managed to get down that morning. She lost her temper instead. Shoving her way through a group of Croatians and Dalmatians, she marched to the gangway, intending to take her complaints to the captain himself. A master-at-arms blocked her way. She shouted at him to move aside. He shoved her back. Sneering, he told her she could write a letter to management and mail it when she arrived in Canada.

At least the boiling anger helped her forget the misery of *mal de mer*.

Now, clutching the rail, Marta prayed God would keep her

on her feet and keep what little food she'd eaten in her stomach. *Please, Lord Jesus, bring us safely across the Atlantic.*

She cast any thought of ever getting on another ship into the undulating sea. She would never see Switzerland again. Tears streaked her cheeks at the realization.

By the time the ship entered the Saint Lawrence Seaway, Marta felt rested and eager to find her way around Montreal. Handing over her papers, she spoke French to the officer. He gave her directions to the International Quarter. Shouldering her pack, she took a trolley and walked to the Swiss Consulate. The clerk added her name to the employment register and gave her directions to an immigration home for girls. Marta purchased a newspaper the next morning and began looking for employment opportunities on her own. She bought a map of Montreal and began a systematic exploration of the city. She spoke to proprietors and left applications, and she found a part-time position in a garment shop in downtown Montreal a few blocks from the Orpheum Theatre.

Expanding her exploration, she came across a large house for sale on Union Street near the railroad. When she knocked, no one answered. She peered in the dirty windows and saw an empty parlor. She wrote down the property agent's information and then walked up and down the street, knocking on doors and asking neighbors about the house. It had been a boardinghouse for women, and not the sort of women who would be welcome in any decent home. Railroad men came and went. The roof had been replaced four years ago, and the house had solid foundations as far as anyone knew. A woman had been murdered in one of the bedrooms. The house shut down shortly afterward and had stood vacant for eighteen months.

Marta went to the Records Office and learned the name of the property owner, who now lived in Tadoussac. She spent Saturday walking and thinking. Excitement welled up inside her at the thought of her goal being within reach. On Sunday, she went to church and prayed God would open the way for her to buy the house on Union Street. The next morning, she went to the property agent's office just down the street from the garment shop and made an appointment with Monsieur Sherbrooke to see the inside of the house later that afternoon. He seemed dubious of her intent and said he had little time to satisfy someone's idle curiosity. Marta assured him she had the resources to make an offer, if the house turned out to be what she wanted.

She hired a ride to Union Street and found Monsieur Sherbrooke waiting at the front door. As soon as he ushered her in, Marta thought of Mama. She had been the first one to believe in her. *"You have set your heart on a mountaintop, Marta, but I have seen you climb. You will use everything you are learning to good purpose. I know this. I have faith in you, and I have faith in God to take you wherever He wills."* She had laughed and cupped Marta's face. *"Maybe you will run a shop or manage a hotel in Interlaken."*

Monsieur Sherbrooke began talking. Marta ignored him as she walked through the large parlor, dining room, and kitchen with a sizable pantry with empty shelves. She pointed out the rat droppings to Monsieur Sherbrooke.

"Shall we go upstairs?" He walked back toward the entry hall and stairs.

Marta ignored his lead and headed down the hallway behind the stairs. "There should be a room back here."

He came quickly down the stairs. "Just a storage room, mademoiselle."

Marta opened the door to the room that would share a common wall with the parlor. She gasped at the red, green, and yellow *chinoiserie* wallpaper covering all four walls. Monsieur Sherbrooke stepped quickly around her. "The servant's quarters."

With private bath? She looked in at the pink, green, and black tiled walls and floor, claw-foot tub, and water closet. "Whoever owned this house must have treated his servants very well."

He stood in the middle of the room, pointing out the brass wall sconces and elegant gaslight hanging above.

Marta looked at the floor. "What is that stain you're standing on?"

"Water." He stepped aside. "But as you can see, there's no serious damage."

Marta shuddered inwardly.

Monsieur Sherbrooke headed for the door. "There are four bedrooms on the second floor and two more on the third."

Marta followed him, walking around inside each room, opening and closing windows. The two bedrooms on the third floor were very small, with slanted ceilings and dormer windows, and in winter they would be very cold.

Monsieur Sherbrooke ushered her downstairs. "It's a wonderful house, with a good location near the railroad and well worth the price."

Marta gave Monsieur Sherbrooke a dubious look. "It needs considerable work." She enumerated the costs she would have to bear in making repairs and getting the house ready for habitation before making her offer, considerably lower than the asking price.

"Mademoiselle!" He sighed in exasperation. "You cannot expect me to take such an offer seriously!"

"Indeed, I do, monsieur. Furthermore, you have a moral obligation to inform Monsieur Charpentier of my offer."

His eyes flickered and then narrowed as he looked her over from head to foot, reconsidering her. "Do I understand you correctly, mademoiselle, that you know the owner, Monsieur Charpentier?"

"No, monsieur, but I do know what went on inside this house and why it has stood vacant for eighteen months. The stain you were standing on in that back bedroom is not water, but blood, as you well know. Tell Monsieur Charpentier I can pay the full amount I've offered. I doubt he will receive a better bid." She handed him a slip of paper with the garment shop's address. "This is where I can be reached." She decided to press for whatever advantage she could. "If I don't hear from you by the end of the week, I have another property in mind. Unfortunately, it is not one of your listings. Good day, monsieur." She left him standing in the entry hall.

A messenger arrived at the shop on Wednesday. "Monsieur Charpentier accepts your offer."

As soon as the papers were signed and title received, Marta quit her job in the garment shop and moved into the house on

Union Street. She bought pots, pans, dishes, and flatware and left everything in boxes until she finished scouring the stove, counters, and worktable and scrubbing out cabinets and pantry. She set to work scrubbing the floors, sills, and windows. She found a wholesaler and bought material for curtains. She watched personal ads and furnished the rooms with bargain-priced beds, dressers, and armoires and the parlor with two sofas, two pairs of wing chairs, and side tables. She bought a long dining table and twelve chairs at an auction, adding lamps and a few rugs.

It took six weeks and everything she had to get the house ready. She paid for a small ad in the newspaper:

> **Room for rent. Spacious. Quiet neighborhood close to the locomotive works.**

She posted a notice on the church bulletin board and hung a Vacancy sign in the front window. She framed and hung the house rules on the foyer wall:

> **Rent due the first of the month**
> **Linens changed weekly**
> **Breakfast served at 6 a.m.**
> **Dinner served at 6 p.m.**
> **No meals on Sunday**

With the last of her money, she invited her neighbors to a Saturday afternoon high tea. As she served Ceylon tea, apple *Streusel* cake, chocolate *éclairs*, and spicy chicken sandwiches, she announced that her boardinghouse was open to renters.

The evening after the newspaper came out, Howard Basler, a railroad man, showed up at the front door. "I don't need much space." He rented an attic bedroom. A railroader's wife, Carleen Kildare, came with her two small boys to ask if Marta could accommodate a family. She showed Carleen two adjoining bedrooms on the second floor with a bathroom between. Carleen brought her husband, Nally, back that evening, and they said they would move in at the end of the month. Four bachelors, all railroad men, doubled up in the last two available rooms on the second floor. Once Marta covered the bloodstain with a rug, she slept quite comfortably in the downstairs bedroom.

Only one small third-floor bedroom remained vacant.

One of the neighbors mentioned Marta's high tea to Carleen, and the boarders teased her about when they might be served like English lords and ladies. Marta told them she'd serve them all high tea on Saturday and they could talk then about whether it would become a regular event. As she served egg and cucumber sandwiches, Welsh rabbit fingers, honey spice cake, and strawberry tarts, she told them how much she would have to raise their rent to give them this added service. After a few bites, everyone agreed.

The income exceeded Marta's expectations.

So did the work.

❄ ❄ ❄

Dear Rosie,

Warner told me the truth when he said I would work harder than I ever have in my life running my own boardinghouse. I am up before dawn and fall into bed long after everyone has retired.

Carleen Kildare offered to do the laundry if I could give her and her husband, Nally, a discount on their rent. I agreed. She works when Gilley and Ryan are napping. She also helps me prepare high tea on Saturdays. Enid's Dundee cake is always a great success, as is Herr Becker's Schokoladenkuchen. I have to hide the second cake or I would have nothing to offer at the fellowship hour after Sunday services.

*I received my second marriage proposal from
Mr. Michaelson this morning. He is one of the five
bachelors living in my house. He is forty-two and a
pleasant enough gentleman, but I am content as I am.
If he persists, I shall have to raise his rent.*

Marta took off one day a week and spent half of it at the
German Lutheran Church. She liked to sit near the back, observing
people as they entered. A tall, well-dressed man came every Sunday
and sat two aisles in front of her. He had broad shoulders and
blond hair. He never came to the fellowship hour after services.
Once, when she came outside after services, she saw him shaking
hands with Howard Basler. She saw the gentleman again a few days
later walking along Union Street.

Lady Daisy wrote to her.

*I am delighted to hear you have attained your goal of
owning a boardinghouse. I told Millicent you received
a proposal already, but she refuses to be persuaded.*

One morning after a winter storm had dumped three feet of
snow on Montreal and the autumn mud had frozen, someone
knocked on Marta's front door. Since boarders had their own keys,
she ignored the interruption and went on adding up expenses.
When the knock came again, louder this time, she left her books,
expecting to find some poor, half-frozen door-to-door salesman
outside her front door. A flurry of snowflakes drifted in when
Marta opened the door.

A tall man stood on the porch, swathed in a heavy overcoat,
scarf pulled up over the lower part of his face and his hat pulled
down. He didn't have a sample case. *"Ich heiße Niclas Waltert."*
As he touched the brim of his hat, snow slipped off the rim.
"Mir würde gesagt, Sie haben ein Zimmer zu vermieten." He spoke

High German with a northern accent and had the manner of an educated gentleman.

"Yes. I have a room for rent. I'm Marta Schneider. Please." She stepped back. "Come in." She motioned when he hesitated. "*Schnell!*" Wood and coal cost far too much, and she didn't want all the warmth going out the front door.

Removing his hat and coat, he shook them both free of snow and stomped his feet before stepping inside. She wished her boarders showed such courtesy.

Marta's heart leaped when she looked up into eyes as clear and blue as the *Thunersee* in spring. "I see you at church every Sunday." She felt her face heat up as soon as the words escaped.

He apologized in German and said he didn't speak much English.

Embarrassed, she told him she had one small attic room available and asked if he would like to see it.

He said yes, please.

Heart thumping, she thought if he saw the parlor and dining room first, and knew about the high tea served each Saturday, he might be more tempted. He didn't say anything. She took him upstairs and opened the door to the empty bedroom. The room had a narrow bed, dresser, and kerosene lamp. There wasn't room for a chair, but there was a bench under the dormer window that overlooked Union Street. When Niclas Waltert stepped in, he bumped his head on the slanted ceiling. He gave a soft laugh and drew the curtains aside to look out.

"Where do you work, Herr Waltert?" When he looked back at her, she felt a fluttering in her stomach.

"I'm an engineer at the Baldwin Locomotive Works. How much for the room?"

She told him. "I'm sorry I don't have better accommodations to offer you. I think the room is too small for you."

He looked around again and came back to the door. He took his passport from his pocket, removed several bills he had hidden there, and held them out. He had long, tapering fingers like an artist. "I will be back early this evening, if that will be convenient."

Her fingers trembled as she folded the bills into her apron pocket. "Dinner is at six, Herr Waltert." She led the way downstairs and stood in the front hallway while he took his woolen scarf from the hook and wrapped it around his neck. He shrugged into his coat and buttoned it. Everything he did seemed methodical and full of masculine grace. When he took his hat from the hook, she opened the door. He stepped over the threshold and then turned back, tapping his hat lightly against his side. "Will I meet your husband this evening?"

An odd, quivery sensation spread through her limbs. "It's *Fräulein*, Herr Waltert. I have no husband."

He gave her a polite bow. "Fräulein." Putting on his hat, he went down the front steps. As she closed the door, Marta realized she was trembling.

❄ ❄ ❄

Niclas arrived in time for dinner and sat at the far end of the table. He listened, but he didn't join in the dinner table conversation. Nally and Carleen Kildare had their hands full that night with Gilley and Ryan, and Marta worried Herr Waltert would find them annoying. But he called them by name and performed a trick with two spoons that had both children awed. "Do it again!" they yelled. When his gaze met hers, her heart flipped over.

After dinner, the men moved into the parlor to play cards. The Kildares went upstairs to get their boys ready for bed. Marta picked up the empty meat platter, all too aware of Niclas Waltert lingering in his seat. "Don't you have a servant to help you, Fräulein?"

She gave a short laugh. "I'm the only servant in this house, Herr Waltert." She set an empty vegetable dish on the platter and reached for another. "Carleen helps with the washing. Other than that, I manage to get things done."

"You're a fine cook."

"Danke." When she came back from the kitchen, she found

Niclas stacking the other dishes at the end of the table nearest the kitchen. "You don't have to do that!"

He stepped back. "I thought I should do something of use before asking a favor, Fräulein Schneider."

"What favor?" She picked up the dishes.

"I must learn English. I understand enough to do my job, but not enough to carry on a conversation with the other boarders. Would you be willing to teach me? I would pay you for your time, of course."

The thought of spending time with him pleased her greatly, though she hoped it didn't show too much. "Of course, and you needn't pay me. People helped me learn and asked nothing for it. When would you like to start?"

"This evening?"

"I'll come to the parlor when I've finished the dishes."

"I'll be waiting."

Marta stood in the kitchen doorway and watched him leave the room.

It took an hour to wash the pots, pans, and dishes and put everything away. She wondered if Niclas Waltert had given up and gone upstairs. She heard the men talking over cards as she came down the hall. When she entered the parlor, Niclas stood and set his book aside. When she came closer, she saw it was a Bible, with *Niclas Bernhard Waltert* engraved in gold on the black leather cover. "You are a religious man, Herr Waltert?"

He smiled slightly. "My father intended me for the church, but I learned early I was not suited to the life of a minister. Please." He stretched out his hand, inviting her to sit. Marta realized he would not take his seat until she was comfortably settled in hers. No man had ever treated her so respectfully.

"How are you not suited?"

"A minister's life belongs to his flock."

"Our lives belong to God whether we're in church or outside it, Herr Waltert, or so my mother taught me."

"Some are called to greater sacrifice, and some things I was unwilling to give up."

"Such as?"

"A wife, Fräulein, and children."

Her heart raced. "It is a Catholic priest who can't marry, not a Lutheran minister."

"Yes, but the family forfeits for the sake of others."

He fell silent. When she met his gaze, she was frightened by the feelings he stirred in her. *Is this what Rosie felt when she looked at Arik? or what Lady Daisy felt for her Clive?* Marta glanced away, lifted her chin, and looked back at him. "Shall we begin our lessons?"

"Anytime you wish, Fräulein."

Marta found Niclas waiting for her in the parlor every evening after dinner. While the other Canadian bachelors played cards, she taught Niclas English.

"Mr. Waltert seems quite taken with you," Carleen said one day while gathering the sheets for washing.

"He asked me to teach him English."

She laughed as she piled the sheets in her arms. "Well, that was a handy excuse."

"As soon as Herr Waltert learns enough to carry on a conversation, he'll be playing cards with the other men."

"Not if the way he looks at you tells me anything."

"He doesn't look at me in that way, Carleen."

"You're saying you don't like him?"

Embarrassed, Marta gathered the rest of the sheets and stuffed them into a basket. "I like him as well as any of my other boarders."

Carleen grinned. "You never blushed when Davy Michaelson looked at you."

❊　❊　❊

"I don't have your gift of languages, Fräulein. I'm not sure I will ever learn."

"No German, remember," Marta insisted. "English only."

"English is a difficult language."

"Anything worth learning is difficult."

"Why can't we just talk in German for a while?"

"Because you won't learn English that way."

"I want . . . learn more . . . you," Niclas said in faltering English.

Clearly frustrated, he switched to German. "I want to find out if we are suited to one another."

He could not have said anything more shocking. She opened her mouth and closed it again.

"I can see I've surprised you. Let's dispense with English for now so I can speak clearly. I want to court you."

Marta raised her hands to cover her burning cheeks. Davy Michaelson looked toward them while the others spoke in low voices. Quickly regaining her composure, Marta lowered her hands and clenched them in her lap. "Why would a man like you want to court someone like me?"

Niclas looked astonished. "Why? Because you're an extraordinary young woman. Because I admire you. Because . . ." His gaze caressed her face and drifted down over the rest of her in a way that made her body go hot all over. "I like everything I see and know about you."

Was this what love did to a person? Turned her inside out and upside down? "I'm your landlord."

His mouth tipped. "Do I have to move out to court you?"

"No." She spoke so quickly she felt the heat flood her face. "I mean . . ." She couldn't think of anything coherent to say.

"Will you attend church with me this Sunday, Marta?"

He had never used her given name before. Flustered, she let out a soft breath. "We're in church together every week."

His expression softened. "I go. You go. We don't go together. I want you to walk with me. I want you to sit beside me."

Feeling entirely too vulnerable, she looked for escape. She knew if she said no, he would never ask again. She would end up like Miss Millicent, living in regret for the rest of her life. Hadn't she come to Canada on the slim chance she might find a suitable husband? Niclas Waltert was far more than suitable.

He searched her eyes. "What troubles you?"

That he would find her unworthy, that after a while he would see she wasn't suitable at all. She hadn't even gone to high school—and he was an engineer. He was handsome. She was plain. He was cultured. She was the daughter of a tailor.

She searched her mind frantically and blurted out the first excuse that came to mind. "I don't even know how old you are."

"Thirty-seven. Not too old for you, I hope."

She stared at the pulse beating rapidly in his throat. "No. No, you aren't too old." When she raised her eyes, she saw light come into his as he smiled.

"Then you will come with me this Sunday? *Ja?*"

"Yes." She gave a prim nod. She glanced at the mantel clock. "It's getting late. I think we can dispense with our English lessons."

Niclas stood and held out his hand. As she stood, her hand in his, she knew she would go anywhere with him, even a bedouin tent in the middle of the Sahara.

1913

Dear Rosie,

I am married!

I never thought anyone would want me, and certainly never a man like Niclas Bernhard Waltert. He came to Canada a year before I did and is an engineer for the Baldwin Locomotive Works. He is tall and very handsome.

We were married on Easter Sunday in the German Lutheran Church. I made a blue skirt to wear with my Sunday-best white shirtwaist. I saw no reason to waste money on a wedding gown I would never wear again. My boarders came, even Davy Michaelson, and some of the neighbors on Union Street and members of the congregation.

I thought I was happy when I bought my boardinghouse, but I have never been as truly happy as this. It makes me afraid sometimes. We only courted for three months. I know little about Niclas's life in Germany or what brought him to Canada. But I dare not ask because there are things I have not told him. I haven't told him I turned a whorehouse into a boardinghouse. I haven't told him a woman was murdered in the bedroom we now share. Nor will he ever know I had a sister who committed suicide.

❄ ❄ ❄

1914

Niclas never said much about his work, but Marta heard the other four men talk about layoffs and difficult times at the locomotive works. Niclas got up early every morning and went into the parlor to read his Bible. He said grace before everyone ate breakfast. He set his dish on the end of the table when he finished and left for work. When it neared time for him to come home, she would stand in the parlor and watch for him. He looked weary and unhappy when he walked up the street, but always had a bright smile when he found her waiting. After dinner, he would go into the parlor with the other men. While they played cards, he read his Bible. She would pause in the doorway before she went to bed. He always gave her a few minutes to change into her nightgown and slip between the covers before he joined her.

One night, he didn't come until almost midnight. She lay awake in a fever of worry. She heard the whisper of his belt. He folded his clothes onto the chair before he came to bed. He slid his arm around her and pulled her back into the curve of his body. "I know you're not asleep."

"I see how unhappy you are." She didn't want to cry. "Are you sorry you married me, Niclas?"

"No." He rolled her onto her back. "No! You're the best thing in my life."

"Then what's wrong?"

"They're closing the locomotive works."

She felt a wave of relief. Combing her fingers through his hair, she drew his head down. "You'll find another job."

"Rumors of war keep coming, Marta. Kaiser Wilhelm keeps ratcheting up the German Imperial Navy to take naval supremacy from Britain. I'm German. That's enough to rouse hostility right now."

"Do you think there will be a war?"

"It won't take much to start one, not with an arms race spreading over the continent. And now the political maneuverings of the Russians are turning the Kingdom of Serbia into a powder keg in Europe."

As the days passed, she saw the toll the talk of war took on Niclas as he went out every day looking for work and came home with nothing but bad news.

She was afraid to tell him hers.

"You can help me with the boardinghouse."

His eyes flashed in anger. "A man is supposed to support his wife! And what is there for me to do here? You have everything working like a finely tuned Swiss watch!"

Hurt, she pushed her chair back and stood. "Well, I won't be able to do as much when the baby comes!" Niclas looked so shocked and dismayed, she burst into tears and fled into the kitchen. She pounded her fists on the worktable and turned quickly toward the sink when Niclas came through the swinging door. "Go away." He caught hold of her and turned her around. He dug his fingers into her hair. "Let go!" He kissed her. She struggled, but he didn't let go.

"*Es tut mir leid,* Marta. I'm sorry." Niclas wiped her cheeks and kissed her again, gently this time. "Don't cry." He held her close. She felt his heart beating heavily against hers. "I'm happy about the baby. Everything will be fine."

Marta thought that meant he would help her with the boardinghouse, but Niclas went out the next morning. When he didn't come back for lunch, she worried. He came in just before dinner, hung up his coat and hat, and came into the dining room. He looked like he had exciting news, but it had to wait as the others came in for the evening meal. He said grace, and plates began to pass from hand to hand. He looked down the table at her, eyes glowing.

Rather than go into the parlor after dinner, he helped clear the table and followed her into the kitchen. "They're hiring harvest hands in Manitoba."

"Harvest hands? Manitoba? What has that to do with you? You're an engineer."

"An unemployed engineer. There's no work for me here. If a job opened, I wouldn't get it. They'd be afraid I was a German spy. I must find another way to make a living."

She shut off the water and turned, but he raised his hand. "Don't say anything. Just listen to me. As long as we remain in this house, you won't see me as the head of this family."

Realization struck her. "You've already agreed to go, haven't you?" He didn't have to answer. Her body went cold. She thought she would faint and sat heavily on the stool. "What do you know about harvesting?"

"I'll learn."

"And you expect me to go with you?"

"Yes. You're my wife."

"And what about the boardinghouse?"

"Sell it."

Marta felt everything she had worked for slipping through her fingers. "I can't."

"What matters to you most, Marta? Me? Or this boarding-house?"

"That's not fair!" She closed her eyes. "You don't know how I've sacrificed."

"Do you love me at all?"

She jumped off the stool, glaring at him. "I could ask you the same question! You didn't even mention this to me before you went out and started making plans!" She stood, fiercely angry. "Why did you study engineering?"

"Because my father demanded it. Because I was a dutiful son. The truth is I never liked engineering. It was something I did because it was what I studied, but I never had any pleasure from it."

"And you think being a farmhand in Manitoba will make you happy?" Her voice sounded strident in her own ears.

"I had a garden in Germany. I liked watching things grow."

Niclas spoke so calmly and sincerely, Marta could only look back at him. Did she even know this man? She had fallen in love with a complete stranger.

"You must decide." He left her alone in the kitchen.

She sat alone in the parlor after everyone else had gone upstairs. She hoped Niclas would come out and talk to her, but he didn't. When she finally went to bed, he turned her to him. He kept her awake far into the night. When she lay languid, he stroked her hair back from her temples. "I leave day after tomorrow."

Gasping, she jerked out of his arms. Turning away from him, she wept. Niclas didn't try to draw her close again. The bed shifted as he rolled onto his back. He sighed. "You can stay here and hold on to everything you've built for yourself, Marta, or you can risk everything and come with me to Manitoba. I leave it to you."

Marta didn't speak to him the next day.

Niclas didn't touch her that night.

When he rose early the next morning and packed his bags, she stayed in bed, her face turned away from him. "Good-bye, Marta." Niclas closed the door quietly behind him. Marta sat up then. By the time she threw on her robe and went out into the hallway, he was gone. She went back to her bedroom. Falling to her knees, she sobbed.

Someone tapped on her door a while later. "Is there a problem, Marta? There's no breakfast."

"Fix it yourself!" Marta pulled the blanket over her head and stayed in bed most of the day crying. When she served dinner that evening, Nally looked perplexed.

"Where's Niclas?"

"Gone." She went back into the kitchen and didn't come out again.

❄ ❄ ❄

Dearest Rosie,

Niclas has left me and gone off to work on a wheat farm in Manitoba. He went away three weeks ago and I have not heard from him since. I begin to understand how Elise felt when she walked out into the snow. . . .

❄ ❄ ❄

Marta worked feverishly each day, spending most of her time in the kitchen. She no longer sat at the dining room table with the tenants, using the excuse of morning sickness. In truth, she was afraid she would burst into tears if anyone asked whether she had heard anything from Niclas yet. He had told everyone of his plans the evening before he left, so they knew he had gone off to Manitoba without her. They didn't need to know she didn't think he would come back.

Rev. Rudiger came to visit her. She served him tea and cake in the parlor, then sat tensely waiting for the purpose of his visit, afraid of what he would have to say to her.

"Niclas wrote to me, Marta."

Hurt welled up inside her. "Did he?" She pressed her back against the wingback chair, feeling trapped. "He doesn't write to me. Did you come here today to tell me I have to go to Manitoba? Are you going to tell me I'm a disobedient wife and I should submit to Niclas and comply with his wishes?"

His face filled with sorrow. He set his teacup and saucer aside.

Leaning forward, he clasped his hands in front of him and looked into her face. "I came because I know how difficult this separation must be on both of you. I came to tell you God loves you, and He did not give you a heart of fear."

"God loves me." She heard the sarcasm in her tone and looked away, unable to hold her pastor's gentle gaze.

"Yes, Marta. God loves you. He has a plan for you."

"My mother used to tell me the same thing. I know He has a plan for me." She glared at him. "And a plan for Niclas."

"A plan for both of you together. God would not tear apart what He has put together."

Marta couldn't speak past the lump growing in her throat. Rev. Rudiger didn't ask questions or tell her what to do. When he stood, she walked him to the door. He put on his coat and hat. Marta stepped out onto the porch. "Please forgive me, Rev. Rudiger." As the words poured from her lips, she remembered Elise lying in the snow.

Rev. Rudiger turned. Marta saw no condemnation in his gentle expression. "My wife and I are praying for you. We love you very much. If you need anything, you've only to ask."

She blinked back tears. "Pray Niclas changes his mind and comes home."

"We will all pray God has His way with each of us."

Marta dreamed of Mama that night. *"Fly, Marta."* She sat on the log in the middle of the Alpine meadow, a little cross marking the place where Elise lay. *"Fly!"*

Marta rocked back and forth, weeping. "I did fly, Mama. I did!" The wind blew, whipping through the trees. "I built my nest."

Mama disappeared and Marta found herself standing in a desert. Her feet sank into the sand. Frightened and alone, she struggled, but couldn't pull herself out. Sobbing, she thrashed, but that only made her sink faster.

"Marta."

Heart leaping at the sound of Niclas's tender voice, she looked up. He wore a seamless robe like Jesus. When he held his hands out to her, she grasped hold. The sand swirled away with the wind, and she found herself standing on solid ground. He enfolded her in his arms and kissed her. When he let go of her, she cried. He held out his hand again. "Come, Marta." A bedouin tent stood before her.

A letter arrived the next afternoon.

Dear Marta,

Robert Madson has given me forty acres to cultivate. He has also promised me seed, six workhorses, a cow, and a few chickens. A house and wagon come with the job. I will share profits with him at the end of each harvest.

If you come, I must know a few days before you are to arrive. You can reach me at this address . . .

Please come. I miss holding you in my arms.

Crying, she read the letter over and over, torn by longing, but paralyzed by fear and responsibility. It was easy for him to say *come*. He owned nothing. She couldn't just walk away and leave everything.

Could she live in the plains of Manitoba with winters forty below zero and summers of melting heat? Could she live out in the middle of nowhere, the closest neighbor a mile away and half a day's ride for supplies in some small farm town?

And how could a man who had gone to the university in Berlin be satisfied plowing fields? How could he give up building locomotives or bridges to become a sharecropper? Surely he would change his mind. And then what would happen?

She knew what Mama would tell her. *"Go, Marta!"* But Mama's life had been one of drudgery and pain, sorrow and affliction. She thought of Daisy Stockhard, sitting in her wheelchair in the middle of Kew Gardens saying she would have lived anywhere with her husband.

It all came down to one question: could she be happy without Niclas?

❄ ❄ ❄

When Marta read the newspaper, she felt her blood go cold. Archduke Franz Ferdinand of Austria had been assassinated by a Serbian national. Niclas had been correct. That gave the Austrians the excuse they'd been looking for to declare war on Serbia. Soon every country on the Continent would be pulled into the mess.

Russia, as Serbia's ally, mobilized its army against Austria and called for France, its ally, to enter the war. As a consequence, Germany declared war on Russia and France. As German troops poured into Belgium, Sir Edward Grey, Britain's foreign secretary, sent an ultimatum ordering Germany to withdraw her troops. Germany refused and Britain declared war on them, drawing Canada into the fray as well.

By the end of August, thousands of Russians had died in the Battle of Tannenberg and 125,000 had been taken prisoner. Great Britain's ally, Japan, declared war on Germany. The Germans went after the Russians at Masurian Lakes, taking another 45,000 prisoners. The Ottoman Empire entered the war to help Germany, as they continued their advance through Belgium.

Marta grieved. "The world has gone mad."

A letter arrived from Rosie.

The whole of Europe is involved in this gathering storm. It is like an argument that starts between two boys, and then others join in to help one side or the other, and soon it becomes a mob. Oh, Marta, I fear thousands will die if this goes the course my father and brothers say it will. I thank God I am enclosed in the mountains of Switzerland and our men will not be involved in the fighting. . . .

You know how much I love you. You are my dearest friend. And so I feel I have the right to ask you: Why are you waiting? What does a house matter if the man you love no longer lives there? You have written enough about dear Niclas for me to know he is not like your father. Go to him. You will never be happy otherwise.

Marta crumpled the letter in her hand and wept. It would have been better if she had never fallen in love. She ached to be with Niclas. Her life had become misery without him. But she couldn't just go. She had to think of the baby, too. Niclas's baby.

She ran her hand over her swelling belly. She remembered Solange's screams as her flesh tore. She remembered the blood. Would there be a midwife in the middle of the plains, miles from town? What if something went wrong?

Carleen came in with the mail. She shook her head, and Marta knew there was no letter from Niclas. Everyone in the house seemed to be waiting for word from him.

Dear Niclas,

Please forgive me for not seeing you off at the train station or wishing you well. You must despise me for being such a stubborn wife.

I'm afraid to come to Manitoba now. I helped deliver a baby in Montreux. I know what it entails. It is another three months before our baby will arrive, and then I will need time to heal.

I don't want to sell the boardinghouse yet. It took years to save up for it, and I will lose what I have invested in repairs and paint and furnishings. It is not simply about the money. After one season on the plains, you may change your mind about farming. What if locusts come and there is nothing left, or blight? We have a house here in Montreal. We have a way to make a living.

Promises flow easily from the lips of the rich, Niclas. Other than Boaz, I have never heard of a man so generous to his workers as Herr Madson. If you didn't get it in writing, you may find his hands full after the harvest, and your own, callused and empty.

She received his reply two weeks later.

My dearest wife,

I thank God. I have prayed constantly that your heart would soften toward me.

A man is only as good as his word. My yes is yes. God tells us not to worry. Look to the birds of the air and the lilies of the field, and see how He feeds and clothes them. God will take care of us, too. Wait until you see the beauty of this land, the waves of wheat that ripple like waves on a sea. You are never alone. God is with you, Marta, and I would be with you, too.

But I understand your fear. You are God's gift to me, my ever-practical wife. As much as I miss you, I think you are right in remaining in Montreal until after our baby comes. As soon as you are well enough and you both can travel, come to me. Let me know well in advance when you will arrive so I will be in Winnipeg to meet you.

Marta read between the lines and knew Niclas had signed a contract guaranteeing he would work the land, but had received no written promises from the landowner. She flattened the letter on her table and rubbed her aching temples. The baby kicked strongly and she leaned back, resting her hands over her abdomen.

Sighing, she closed her eyes, weary of the battle. *God, I give up. What do I do?* In that moment of stillness and quiet, she knew. Feeling a lightness inside her, she pushed her chair back, folded the letter, and stuffed it into her apron pocket. She found Carleen in the laundry room. "I'm going to Manitoba as soon as the baby is born and I can travel."

Her face fell. "So you'll be selling the house."

"No. I'm going to train you to run it."

"Me? Oh no! I couldn't be doing that!"

"Nonsense." She grabbed hold of a sheet Carleen was cranking through the wringer, shaking it out as it came through. "You're five years older than I, and you finished high school. If I can do it, of course you can." She laughed. "The most important thing is to keep the lions well fed."

13

1915

Joy filled Marta when she saw Niclas waiting for her. He looked tan and lean, his face intent as he looked from car to car. When he saw her, he smiled broadly. Laughing, she lifted their son, swaddled in a blanket Carleen had given her, so Niclas could see him through the train window.

Gone was the anger that had consumed her during the hours of her travail, when she had felt deserted by Niclas. Still, the anger had helped her press through the pain. She had cried out only once, when her body forced Bernhard into the world and he screamed in protest. Carleen washed and swaddled him in blankets and handed him over to Marta. A bubble of joy came and she laughed. She had never thought she would ever have a husband, let alone a child, and now God had given her both. A brief cloud darkened the moment as she thought of Elise and her child dying in the cold. But she pressed it away and drank in the sight of her newborn son nursing, his small hand pressed against her flesh.

Niclas ran and caught up with the passenger car, then strode alongside until it came to a full halt. Paying a porter to gather her things and collect her trunk, she headed for the door.

"Marta." Niclas waited for her at the bottom of the steps, his blue eyes moist. He steadied her with a firm hand beneath her elbow. "I thought you'd never come." Giving her a quick kiss on the cheek, he drew the blanket down so he could get a better look at his son.

"He's beautiful, isn't he?" Her voice quavered.

He raised eyes. *"Ja. Wunderschön."* He slipped his arm around her. "Come. Let's get your things loaded into the wagon. We're staying overnight at a hotel before heading out to the farm tomorrow morning."

She looked up at him. "English, Niclas, or have you forgotten already?"

He laughed. "Let me have him." She deposited the baby carefully into his waiting arms. Niclas held him close against his heart, gazing down at him in wonder. The baby awakened. "Bernhard Niclas Waltert, I am your papa. *Mein Sohn.*" Tears slipped down Niclas's bronzed cheeks as he kissed him. *"Mein Sohn."*

Marta felt an odd twisting inside her. "And if he'd been a daughter, would you have loved him as much?" Niclas raised his head, gaze questioning. She didn't repeat the question.

When they reached the hotel room, Niclas took Bernhard from the basket where Marta had settled him. "I want to see him." He laid the baby on the bed and unwrapped the blanket. Marta protested.

"He fussed half the night. I hardly slept."

"I'll hold him if he fusses."

"And will you nurse him, too?"

Niclas looked at her. "So sharp, Marta." He returned his attention to their son, who awakened and began to kick his legs and cry. Niclas lifted him. "I have not seen you in nearly a year, and this is the first day I have laid eyes on my son. Do you begrudge my being eager to hold him?"

His reprimand stung. They could have been together all this time. She could have come into Winnipeg that last week or two and had the services of a midwife. She was his wife and belonged at his side. She watched him pace the room with Bernhard in his arms. Turning away, she unpacked the diapers, baby clothing, and blankets she would need for that night, afraid she would cry. Bernhard cried instead, and Marta felt her milk let down. Pressing her arms against her breasts, she tried to stop the moisture from seeping. Bernhard cried harder.

"What's wrong with him?" Niclas sounded distressed.

She turned and held out her arms. "He's hungry."

Niclas returned the child to her arms and stood watching as she sat on the far side of the bed facing a wall. Head down, back to her husband, she opened her shirtwaist. She jerked slightly as Bernhard took hold and suckled. When Niclas came and sat down beside her, she blushed and raised the blanket over her shoulder. Niclas drew it down again. "Don't hide from me." His expression filled with wonder.

She stood and moved away as she shifted Bernhard to the other side. Niclas watched her. When Bernhard made a loud noise, he laughed. Marta laughed, too. "In one end and out the other." When she finished nursing Bernhard, she flipped out a blanket on the bed and changed his diaper.

Niclas stood over him. "He's perfect. God has given us a great gift." When he brushed the tiny, star-shaped hand with his finger, Bernhard grasped hold. "Strong, too. *Unser kleiner Bärenjunge.*"

"Yes, and our little bear cub will probably keep us awake all through the night."

Niclas scooped him up. "You won't do that to your papa, will you?" He nuzzled him and whispered in his ear.

Someone knocked on the door, turning Marta's attention away. She opened the door wide so the servant could bring in a dinner tray. Marta paid the man and closed the door behind him. Niclas put Bernhard in the middle of the double bed while they ate dinner. Bernhard cooed and kicked, making fists and swinging his arms. "He's wide-awake, isn't he?"

"Unfortunately." Marta sighed.

Niclas lifted the baby and jostled him. After a while, he put the baby in the middle of the bed and stretched out beside him, dangling a rattle over Bernhard. Marta sat in the chair, barely able to keep her eyes open. Giving up, she closed her eyes as she listened to baby coos and Niclas's soft chuckle. She awakened when Niclas lifted her. "Bernhard?"

Niclas placed her gently in the middle of the bed. "Asleep in his basket." When he began to unbutton her shirtwaist, Marta came fully awake. As he looked into her eyes, he brushed his fingers against her throat and leaned down to kiss her. She felt everything inside her open and grow warm. She removed his shirt, and she found that months of hard physical labor had thickened the muscles across his chest and down his arms. When he lifted his mouth from hers, she felt herself drowning at the look in his eyes. "I'll be gentle." And at first he was, until her response gave them both the freedom they needed.

Pulling the blankets up over them, Niclas tucked her against his body. He let out a long, deep sigh of contentment. "I was afraid you would never come. You had everything you wanted in Montreal."

"I didn't have you."

"So you missed me?"

She raised his blistered and callused hand and kissed his palm.

He nuzzled her neck. "God has answered my prayers."

"For now. We'd better both start praying the seed you planted will sprout and the weather will—"

Niclas put a finger to her lips. "Let's not worry about tomorrow." They both went still as Bernhard cried softly in his basket. Niclas gave a soft laugh. "Today's trouble is enough." Flipping the covers back, he walked naked across the room and lifted their son from the basket.

❈ ❈ ❈

Every mile that passed furthered Marta's dismay. As Niclas snapped the reins over the horses and clicked his tongue, she could only stare at the flat land before her. She didn't see a hill anywhere, but endless prairie that reminded her of the ocean crossing. She felt a little queasy.

"Are there any trees where we're going?" She removed her jacket and wished she could unbutton her shirtwaist.

Niclas glanced at her. "We have a tree in our front yard."

"One tree?"

"Right where we need it."

She wiped beads of moisture from her forehead. Dust chafed her skin beneath her clothing. She glanced over the seat at Bernhard in the basket behind her, sleeping contentedly in the wagon bouncing over the dirt road. Marta remembered the canyon of buildings in the heart of Montreal, the trolleys and a few of the new automobiles.

"There it is!" Niclas pointed, face beaming.

She saw a small house in the distance, squat and sturdy, shaded by one tree. A barn and shed stood nearby. Four horses grazed in an enclosed pasture while a thin cow stood, head drooping, inside a corral next to the barn. "That cow is sick, Niclas."

"Madson said she could give milk."

"Has she?"

"None so far." He shrugged. "I don't know much about cows."

Oh, God, help us. "You didn't know anything about growing wheat either, and you said you have planted a lot of it. I know a little about cows." She could always write and ask Arik Brechtwald's advice. He'd grown up around cows. "You said Madson gave you chickens too."

"One rooster and four hens."

"Where are they?"

"Off somewhere scratching for food, I guess."

He guessed? "Are they laying eggs?"

"I haven't had time to look." He pointed. "There's the rooster now."

The rooster strutted out from behind the barn, two hens following. She waited, but the others didn't appear. Annoyed, she imagined a very happy fox sleeping somewhere close by. The chickens scattered again as Niclas drove the wagon into the yard. As the rooster flapped away, the hens gave chase.

Niclas jumped off the wagon and came around to help her. She put her hands on his shoulders as he lifted her down. "The first thing we have to do is build a henhouse. Otherwise we'll lose them all."

He lifted the basket and handed it to her. "Why don't you go on in the house while I unload everything?"

She looked around, fighting the sick feeling in her stomach. No mountains anywhere, not as far as she could see. And Niclas hadn't lied. They had one tree, and it was too small to cast a shadow over the house. *Oh, God, oh, God . . .* "How cold does it get out here?"

"Oh, cold enough." He hefted the trunk onto his shoulder. "The creek freezes so thick you have to make a hole in the ice so the livestock can get to water. Liam Helgerson, our neighbor, showed me how to do it. He has cattle."

She looked around again and followed him inside the house. "What'll we do for firewood?"

"We don't need wood. We have prairie chips!"

"Prairie chips?"

"Dried cow dung." He put the trunk on the floor. "Helgerson has a herd. He told me to take all I need. I pick them up by the wagonload and store them in one of the stalls in the barn. The chips fuel the stove, too. It makes the meat taste peppered."

"Peppered?"

"What's in the trunk that makes it so heavy?"

"Books." She had spent hard-earned money trying to prepare for any eventuality.

"Books?"

"On farming, home medicine, animal husbandry." She followed him outside as he headed back to the wagon. She put her hands on her hips. "You didn't write anything to me about chips. Any more good news you have to tell me?"

❄ ❄ ❄

Managing a boardinghouse had been easy compared to farming. Marta carried Bernhard in a shawl tied around herself while she put in a vegetable garden and tended the chickens. Niclas worked all day in the fields, coming in only for a noon meal before going out again. His hands blistered and bled. He didn't complain, but she would see him wince when he pulled the work gloves off at night. She gave him a pan of warm water with salt to soak his hands and then wrapped them in strips of cloth. After dinner, while she nursed Bernhard, Niclas read to her from his Bible.

Liam Helgerson came over to meet Marta. He was a big man, lean and weathered after years in a saddle overseeing his land-holdings. He had turned over much of his land to sharecroppers like Niclas, but still had enough to run a small herd of fine cattle. His wife had died five years before Niclas arrived. Both lonely, they had struck up a friendship. Marta knew after a few weeks that Niclas wouldn't have a crop to harvest if not for Liam Helgerson's good advice.

"Niclas shot a pheasant this morning, Mr. Helgerson. Would you like to stay for dinner?"

His leathered face wrinkled in a broad smile. "I was hoping you'd ask, Mrs. Waltert. Niclas has told me what a fine cook you are."

He came once a week after that, usually on Sunday. Other than seeing that the animals and chickens were fed, it was the one day Niclas rested. Marta served dinner midafternoon so Liam wouldn't have to ride home in the dark. While Bernhard played on the rug, Niclas read portions of the Bible aloud as Marta sewed or knitted and Liam sat, head back, eyes half-closed, listening.

"I feel like I've been to church when I come over here. Margaret and I went a couple of times a year when we went into Winnipeg. She got some kind of cancer. It's a long, mean kind of dying. I . . ." Liam shook his head and looked out toward the fields. "Been a long time since I've felt any peace." He raked his hand back through his gray hair and put on his hat. He looked like a lonely old soul.

That night she mentioned her observations to Niclas, as he held Bernhard on his lap. "Liam seems so alone."

"He is alone except for the men who work for him."

"He and his wife never had children?"

"They had three, but they all died before they reached adulthood. They lost two in the same week to measles; the other got kicked in the head by a horse." He set Bernhard on the floor with a pile of blocks. "I'd better see to the animals."

Marta imagined the sorrow Liam must feel and shuddered at the thought of losing Bernhard. How would she bear it? If Bernhard was to become ill, how long would it take to reach a doctor? She must learn enough to doctor him herself. Her mother had shown her the medicinal herbs that grew in the Alpine meadows, but she would have to order a book on what grew here in this windswept prairie.

Leaning over, she ran her hand lovingly over Bernhard's blond head. *Please, God, keep him healthy. Make him strong like his father.*

❄ ❄ ❄

Dearest Marta,

I thank God you crossed the Atlantic when you did. You had only to worry about icebergs, but now the danger is man-made and moves at will beneath the surface. Father read to us this morning that a German U-boat sank the Lusitania off the Old Head of Kinsale, Ireland. Over eleven hundred people went down with the ship. Several hundred were American citizens, and Father believes this will bring America into the fighting.

The war grows with no end in sight. Men are dying by the thousands in trenches. Arik, Hermann, and my brothers are all on active duty. I have heard rumors that our men will blow up the roads if they must.

The entire country is on alert. I pray our leaders can keep us out of the fray. . . .

Marta prayed constantly for Rosie and Arik. She prayed for her brother, Hermann. She prayed Switzerland would stay out of the war.

❄ ❄ ❄

The hens began laying more eggs than the family could eat. Marta took only what she needed and let the hens sit on the rest. Soon she had a dozen chickens and two roosters fighting for dominance. Having watched Niclas do it the first time, Marta built a second coop and separated the males, giving half the hens to each. She beat out and ground enough grain for feed.

The cow's health improved under Marta's watchful care. One Sunday when Liam Helgerson came over for his chicken dinner, she asked if she might pasture the bovine with one of his best bulls. "You can have the calf when it's weaned or a portion of the cheese I hope to make."

"I'll take the cheese. You've got yourself an enterprising wife, Waltert."

"She had her own boardinghouse when I met her in Montreal."

"Then what are you doing out here on the plains?"

Marta gave a short laugh. "I asked him the same thing." When Niclas's face tightened, she changed the subject. "You can change your mind about the calf, Mr. Helgerson. Being Swiss doesn't mean I know how to make cheese."

He laughed. "Maybe not, but I've no doubt you'll learn."

Niclas plowed and sowed winter wheat. While he waited for the crops to grow, he hired out to clean wells. Sometimes he would be gone for several days. Marta tried to get used to the silence and loneliness of the prairie, but it wore on her nerves.

"Helgerson said there's a soft-coal mine five miles from us," Niclas announced one evening. "I can dig out whatever we can use and sell the rest in Brandon." He stored the coal in the basement. Marta covered the coal with a tarp to keep the black dust from seeping through the floorboards.

When the weather turned, Niclas moved the coops into the barn and piled bales of hay around three sides to keep them warm. Then the snows came, and Marta looked out on a frozen wasteland.

Niclas and Mr. Helgerson went out with axes to cut holes in the frozen river so the horses and cattle could drink. Niclas returned home so stiff from cold he needed her help to walk through the door. Marta spent the rest of the night tending him, afraid he would lose his ears, fingers, and toes.

"We're going home to Montreal when the thaw comes!"

"No, we can't. I signed a four-year contract."

Four years? She wept. "I hate this place! What happens when the holes you chopped fill with snow and ice? What if you end up in a blizzard and can't find your way home? What if—?"

"I'm all right." Niclas gripped Marta's head between his bandaged hands and kissed her hard. "Don't frighten our son."

Bernhard sat in his crib, crying loudly.

She put her hands over his. "And what will our son do without his father?" She stood and went to lift Bernhard from his crib.

Niclas wiggled his fingers at them. "See? I am thawing nicely." When she glared at him, he sighed. "Bring him to me." Bernhard never cried long in his father's arms.

Marta threw more prairie chips into the woodstove while Niclas played with their son. "You can't keep the cold out of this house!" She left the stove door open and rolled rags, stuffing them tightly against the space under the door. "If we have to stay three more years in this godforsaken place, then we're going to dam the creek so you won't have to risk your life cutting holes in that frozen river."

Shortly after they began the project, a neighbor to the south appeared on horseback. Niclas had gone hunting with Mr. Helgerson, leaving Marta alone to fill in the gaps between the larger boulders he had set. Seeing the rider coming, Marta waded out and untied her skirt from above her knees. She lifted Bernhard and set him on her hip as the man came closer. "So that's why the water's so low. What do you think you're doing? You can't dam this stream. The United States owns the water rights."

"No one told me."

"Consider yourself told." He swung his horse around and rode back the way he came.

Marta set Bernhard down and put her hands on her hips, watching him until he disappeared in the distance. She went back to stacking stones. When Niclas returned that afternoon, she told him. He ran his hand around the back of his neck and rubbed.

"Well, if it's the law, we'll respect it."

"If it's the law, it's unjust! The stream goes through this land, Canadian land! Our animals need water in winter. Why should you go two miles to cut a hole in the river when we can make a pond half a mile from the house?"

"I'll see what Helgerson has to say."

Mr. Helgerson came over to help dismantle the dam. "I'm sorry, Mrs. Waltert." He heaved stones onto the bank.

"Not half as sorry as Niclas is going to be by the time he finishes digging us a well!" Swinging Bernhard up in her arms, she headed back for the house.

❄ ❄ ❄

Robert Madson came after the second harvest. Marta took an immediate and intense dislike to the man with his bulging belly and fancy new automobile. "It's a pleasure to meet you, Mrs. Waltert. I see you're expecting another baby." He bent and pinched Bernhard's cheek. "You've got a grand little fellow here."

Marta served dinner and noticed how Madson didn't hesitate to take the platter of chicken first and pick the best for himself without thought of leaving an equal share for anyone else. When the men went out onto the new porch Niclas had built, she overheard Madson say prices were down this year and he hadn't made as much profit as he had hoped. When she came to the door, Niclas took one look at her and suggested he and Madson take a walk about the place to see the improvements he and Marta had made.

Furious, Marta left the dishes stacked and brought a chair outside. She let Bernhard play in the dirt while she watched the two men. They didn't walk far, but stood talking outside the barn. Niclas walked out toward the field and Madson headed back toward the house. Marta noticed the stoop of Niclas's shoulders. She stood as Madson came closer. "Leaving so soon?" She didn't try to take the chill from her voice.

"I'll have someone come and get the cow."

"You will not."

He looked surprised. "It's my cow."

"That cow is part of our contract, Mr. Madson." She had seen enough to know the man cared nothing about those who worked for him, least of all whether they had enough to eat. "We must have milk for our children." She put her hand on her swollen abdomen to press her point.

"I'll give you another cow."

"I spent months nursing that cow back to health. Our son will not go without milk while I tend another one of your sick cows." She jabbed her finger toward the field. "That cow stays right where it is."

His face flushed red. "Then I'll take the calf."

"Only if you fathered it."

His eyes darkened. "You're a hard woman, Mrs. Waltert."

She glared back at him, undaunted. He reminded her of Herr Keller. "Hard, yes, but not hard-hearted like you." Niclas would keep his word to this man, but it remained to be seen whether Madson would keep his word to Niclas. She doubted it.

His gaze shifted. He looked here and there. When he spotted

the coops Niclas had moved outside the barn, his eyes gleamed. "If I can't have the calf, I'll take the chickens."

"Of course. You can have your rooster and four hens. That's what belongs to you. And I will fetch them for you right now." She stepped off the porch and headed toward the smaller coop. Pausing, she looked back at him. "Do you want them dead and plucked, or alive and kicking?" She looked pointedly at his nice new automobile. "They tend to make a mess."

"Put them in a crate."

"Do you have one in your backseat?"

"Oh, never mind!" Slapping dust off his hat, he headed for his dusty black car. "We'll settle up at the end of the contract!"

She stood, arms akimbo. "I know the price of wheat. I asked in Brandon. Don't take me for a fool!"

"Your husband signed a contract!" He squeezed into the driver's seat and slammed the door. "Everything on this place belongs to me!"

"We are not slaves. And workers are owed their wages! God sees what you do, Mr. Madson! And God will judge between you and my husband!"

Dust billowed up behind him as he drove away.

Marta fumed the rest of the afternoon. When Niclas came in for dinner, she released her pent-up anger. "You wait and see, Niclas." She took another roasted chicken from the oven. "That man is not going to pay you anything when the contract is up." She kicked the oven door shut. "He thinks we're his serfs!" She yanked the lid off the pan and sent it clattering into the washbasin. "You added a porch to the house and dug a well, and what thanks did you get? He wanted to steal our cow and all our chickens! The man is a liar and a thief. And now you know it. You know as well as I do he'll find an excuse to weasel out of his part of the contract and you'll have nothing after four years of hard work. We should pack up and go right now."

Niclas spoke quietly. "I gave my word."

"What about *his* word?"

"My word is what matters. My yes is yes." He looked so weary. "That chicken smells good."

Marta cleaved the roasted bird in half and put it on the platter. "Next time you're in town, Niclas, buy another gun."

He looked up in alarm. "You're not planning on shooting the man, are you?"

"I'd like to shoot him!" She put the platter on the table and slumped in her chair. "Rabbits are getting into the vegetable garden, and I saw a deer yesterday. I think they know when you're out hunting and they come here for lunch. If I eat any more chicken, I'll sprout feathers. Get me a rifle, and we'll have venison and rabbit stew!"

❄ ❄ ❄

Dear Rosie,

What I feared is happening. Niclas is being cheated by Madson, and I'm going to have our second child in the dead of winter, twenty-five miles away from the nearest town and midwife.

Niclas went to town without me last time. This baby isn't sitting as well as Bernhard, and I didn't want to take any risks riding so far on a bouncing wagon. Niclas had three crates of chickens, butter, and eggs to sell, but came home with empty pockets. Mr. Ingersoll gave him credit at the general store. I told Niclas credit is fine, but cash is better.

I have never seen a man work so hard. But at the end of his contract with that thief Madson, he will have nothing to show for it but muscle and calluses.

14

1917

Niclas and Mr. Helgerson had gone out to look for some missing
cattle the day Marta went into labor. When her water broke,
she started to cry, which frightened poor Bernhard. She calmed
herself with an effort and reassured him Mama was fine, just
fine. Then she tried to remember what preparations she needed
to make.

She stoked the stove with prairie chips. She spilled blocks on
the floor to distract Bernhard. Thankfully, he grabbed them and
banged them together happily while she paced, rubbing at her
aching belly.

The contractions came fast and hard. Sweat beaded her forehead. As the pain bore down heavily, she sat and closed her eyes.
*Oh, God, oh, God, bring my husband home soon. This baby is not
going to take all day and half the night like Bernhard did.*

Bernhard didn't want to play anymore. Pushing himself up, he
toddled over to her. "Mama, Mama," he said over and over again,
holding his arms up. He wanted her to hold him.

"Not now. Mama is busy." He clutched at her, trying to climb up, but she had no lap on which to hold him. Her swollen abdomen became as hard as a rock. She groaned and Bernhard cried. When the pain eased, Marta pulled herself up and tried to lift him, but another contraction had already begun. When she set him on the floor again, Bernhard screamed.

Taking him by the hand, she pulled him along to his crib. As the pain eased slightly, she lifted him. "Go to sleep. Mama's all right. You'll have a little brother or sister soon. . . ."

Rubbing her back, she went to the window and looked out, tears streaming down her cheeks. "Papa will be home soon. Take your nap, Bernhard." Wiping tears away, she leaned heavily against the sill, counting the seconds through another contraction. It lasted longer this time.

Still no sign of Niclas.

"Oh, God." She moaned, wanting to bend her knees and lower herself to the floor. "Help me. Jesus, help me. . . ."

Marta spread a blanket over the rug. She went outside and scooped snow into a pot and put it on the stove to melt. The contractions were coming closer together and lasting longer. She cut twine and dropped it into the steaming water. Yanking a drawer open, she took out her paring knife and dropped that in as well. Trembling violently, she waited a moment before fishing the twine and knife out of the hot water. She had no more time to wait.

Thankfully, Bernhard had cried himself to sleep.

The urge came to push. She rolled a clean rag and bit down on it, muffling the groan. Lowering herself to her knees, she faced the warmth of the stove and hitched up her skirt, cutting away the flour-sack undergarment she had made.

One contraction rolled into another. She bit on the cloth to stifle her moans. Perspiration dripped from her face. Her flesh tore as the head came. Marta bore down again and the baby slipped from her body into her hands. Shaking violently, Marta sat back on her heels.

The baby didn't cry. Wrapped in its white and red womb's coat, the infant lay curled on its side, the umbilical cord still linked with Marta.

"Breathe." Marta leaned forward, gritting her teeth against the pain. She took one of the diapers she had laid out and wiped the infant's face and body. A little girl. "Breathe!"

She turned the baby over and gave the tiny bottom a gentle slap. "Oh, Jesus, give her breath. Please. Please!" She rubbed gently, praying over and over. A soft, mewling cry came, and Marta sobbed in thanksgiving. Another contraction came and her body expelled the placenta.

The door opened, filling the small cabin with a blast of cold winter air. She heard Niclas cry out her name. He closed the door quickly, stripped off his coat, and came to her. "Marta. Oh, *mein Liebling*! What can I do for you?"

"She's hardly breathing." Marta sobbed harder. "Bring the hot water in that pan. And snow! Quickly, Niclas." She mixed the scalding with the cold and tested the temperature. Then she carefully lowered her daughter into the pan, supporting the baby with one hand while washing her gently with the other. The infant's arms and legs jerked, and her tiny mouth opened and wobbled in a weak cry.

Bernhard had been large and chubby, his skin pink. He had screamed so loudly, his face turned beet red. This little girl had spindly little legs and a thatch of dark hair. Her tiny body quivered as from cold. Heart breaking, Marta dried her tenderly and swaddled her in a cloth Niclas had warmed by the fire. "I need a fresh pan of hot water and salt." She felt the blood running down her legs and remembered the midwife's warning about infection.

Niclas quickly did her bidding. "What can I do?"

"Take her. Hold her close against you, inside your shirt. Keep her warm or she'll die."

"But what about you?"

"I can take care of myself!"

Though the pain was excruciating, Marta completed all she knew she must. "I need your hand." Niclas helped her to her feet while holding the baby. She sank onto the bed. "Give her to me now." Lying on her side, she tucked the baby close.

It took several minutes of trying before the little one finally latched on to her breast.

Bernhard awakened and saw Niclas. "Papa! Papa!" He held out his arms.

Marta felt the prickle of tears. "He'll be hungry."

"I shouldn't have left you." Niclas cut a piece of the bread Marta had made that morning and gave it to their son. "I should've been here."

"We didn't know she'd come two weeks early."

"She's so small. She looks like her mother."

Marta gazed at the tiny girl lying so still and quiet, her little fist clenched against Marta's white flesh. She felt a sudden overwhelming love for this child, a bond so tight, she felt her heart ripping open. *Oh, Mama, is this what you felt when you held Elise for the first time?*

"We should name her now."

She heard what lay behind Niclas's quiet, broken words. He didn't think their daughter would live long. *Please, God, don't take her from me! She's so tiny and weak, so helpless. Give her a chance, Lord.*

Brushing her finger lightly against the silky pale cheek, Marta watched the tiny mouth work again, tugging lightly at her breast for sustenance. "Your mother's name was Ada."

"Yes, but let's not give her that name. What about Elise?" When Marta glanced up sharply, he frowned. "What's wrong?"

She had never told Niclas about her sister. "Nothing. It's just not a name I will ever give any daughter of mine." When he searched her face, she lowered her head and closed her eyes. She felt his hand rest gently on her head.

"You decide."

"Her name will be Hildemara Rose."

"It's a strong name for such a frail baby."

"Yes, but God willing, she'll grow into it."

❄ ❄ ❄

While Marta healed, Niclas went into town, taking Bernhard with him. He came back with supplies and a long-awaited letter from Rosie.

Dear Marta,

Even if you are out in the middle of nowhere, you are fortunate to be in Canada, far away from this war that never seems to end. It must be strange to have only one neighbor closer than five miles. Liam Helgerson sounds like an admirable man.

The news we receive is never good. Germany is bleeding France dry. Two hundred thousand Frenchmen died at Somme, and half a million German boys with them.

London is being bombed by Germany's new aeroplanes. Your brother remains on guard with his unit on the French border. Your father was recalled to duty along with my father and the other men in our town. Only young boys and old men are left in Steffisburg. No one has crossed our borders, thanks be to God.

Herr Madson sounds like a despicable sort of man, but I admire Niclas more and more. How many men keep their word no matter the provocation to break it? You can count on a man like that to love and cherish you in sickness and in health for as long as you both live.

Marta wrote back, but had to wait a month before Niclas took her to Brandon and she could post it.

My dear friend,

I am delivered of a baby daughter I have named Hildemara. Her middle name is Rose after you. She is very small and delicate. She barely cried when she was born, and she doesn't cry much now. Bernhard was big and robust from the beginning.

I fear for this little one. I understand now how Mama's heart broke every time she held Elise. She was small and frail, too. Bernhard put on weight right away, but this little one isn't much bigger than she was a month ago. Bernhard screams for what he wants. My little Hildemara is content to sleep warm at my breast.

Bernhard is fascinated by his little sister. We let him hold her in his lap while Niclas reads from the Bible.

Pray for your namesake, Rosie. One breath from heaven could blow her away, but God forbid I go too far in protecting her and bring her up to be weak like Elise.

❄ ❄ ❄

1918

When Niclas's time under contract came to an end, Madson returned.

Marta saw the car approaching and went out onto the porch, Hildemara riding on her hip. Niclas, covered with dust, came in from the field to welcome Madson in his tailored suit and hat. He tipped his hat to Marta. She gave a cool nod and went back inside the house, keeping watch through the window. She had no intention of inviting the man to dinner.

Madson didn't stay long. After he climbed into his car and drove away, Niclas stood with his hands shoved in his overall pockets, shoulders stooped. Rather than come to the house, he went out to the field and stood staring off into the distance. Marta knew the reason for his despair and struggled between anger and pity.

When Niclas finally came inside, she placed his dinner in front of him.

Sighing heavily, he put his elbows on the table and covered his face. "Four years of hard work, all for nothing." He wept. "I'm sorry, Marta."

She put her hand on his shoulder and pressed her lips together, saying nothing. "We all learn hard lessons in this life."

"He wants me to sign on for another four years. He said things are getting better. . . ."

The hair rose on the back of Marta's neck. She lifted her hands and stepped back. "You didn't sign anything, did you?"

"I said I'd think about it."

"Think about it? You know the man is a cheat and a liar!" Bernhard looked between them. Hildemara started to cry.

"I won't sign." Niclas lifted Hildemara from her high chair.

"It's good you didn't tell him that. He'd have put our two cows on leads and carted away all our chickens!"

Niclas sat again, bouncing Hildemara on his lap and trying to soothe her. He raised bleak eyes to Marta. "Quiet down. You're scaring her."

"She's not half as scared as I am you'll keep us here another four years!"

"I've got to figure out what we're going to do."

She put her hands on her hips. "We'll sell what belongs to us and go back to Montreal. That's what we'll do!"

He raised his head, eyes darkening. "We're not going back to Montreal. That much I do know! There's no work for me there. And I'm not living off my wife!"

"Winnipeg, then. It's another railroad hub. There'll be work for you there. I'll wire Carleen and offer her the boardinghouse for a fair price. If she can't buy it, I'll put it on the market. As soon as I get the money, I'll buy another boardinghouse."

"No, you won't! You can't run a boardinghouse with two children and another baby on the way."

"Watch me!"

He stood and thrust Hildemara into her arms. "You'll take care of our children and whatever house we find to rent. That's what you'll do! I'll get a job. I'll support my family!"

Marta turned away, afraid she'd remind him he'd done a lousy job so far. "How long before Madson wants an answer?"

Niclas let out his breath. "He said he'd be back in ten days."

"That gives us ten days to build enough crates for two hundred chickens. We'll take the cow and calf to Mr. Helgerson. He'll pay a fair price and add our calf to his herd and have one of his men take care of the cow until Madson comes back."

"I don't think Mr. Ingersoll will take two hundred chickens."

"I don't plan to sell them in Brandon. We'll load the wagon and take them to Winnipeg. We'll get a better price in city markets."

"We can't take the wagon, Marta. It doesn't belong to us. Neither do the horses."

"We're not stealing them, Niclas. We're borrowing them. Or do you expect us to walk back to Winnipeg, dragging our trunks behind us? Once we're there, we'll send word to Mr. Madson and he can send one of his other serfs to fetch them."

Marta thanked God she had gone to Brandon with Niclas the last time. Knowing the contract was coming to a close, she had told Mr. Ingersoll he needed to settle the account with her. He hadn't been happy about it, but she had cash enough to pay rent and buy what they would need to set up housekeeping in Winnipeg.

❄ ❄ ❄

Dear Rosie,

Niclas found work at the locomotive works. His old supervisor, Rob MacPherson, transferred to Winnipeg. When he saw Niclas had applied, he hired him. And just in time. Our third child, Clotilde Anna, arrived a month after Niclas went back to work. She is as robust as Bernhard, and every bit as loud in her demands. Think of it, Rosie—two miracles in the very same month! We have finally seen an end to this awful war, and we have been blessed with little Clotilde.

Hildemara Rose has none of the sibling jealousy you talk about with your children. She adores her brother and sister, so much so she will give up anything if one of the others wants it, whether it's a toy or food off her plate. They take advantage and she lets them. I will have to teach her otherwise.

Carleen and Nally Kildare bought my boardinghouse in Montreal. They couldn't afford the full price, but they managed to get a loan from the Bank of Montreal. I don't intend to touch the money unless Niclas loses his job again. God forbid that happens! I mentioned buying this house once, but he was adamant we should wait and see how things go. As far as I can see, things are going very well.

Rumors abounded as soldiers returned home from Europe. The locomotive works let some foreign workers go in order to rehire those who had served overseas. When she asked, Niclas said his job was secure as long as MacPherson was supervisor. Other than that, Niclas didn't talk about much of anything. He came home from work each day and sat in the parlor, head back, eyes closed. He roused enough to play with Bernhard and Clotilde. Hildemara always stood back, waiting her turn.

After dinner, Niclas read Bible stories to the children before Marta settled them in bed. Then he would fall silent again, sitting in his chair, gazing out the window. He always seemed worn down when he came home from work. She wondered how he could be so tired all the time when he no longer had to get up before dawn and work until dusk. Surely working at a drafting desk was preferable to the backbreaking work of plowing forty acres.

Marta waited until they were alone in bed, the lamp extinguished, before she asked. "Will you stay angry with me forever, Niclas?"

He turned to her in the darkness. "Why would I be angry?"

"Because I insisted you work for the railroad." She knew he had loved working the land. He loved seeing the wheat and barley grow. He had felt such pride in the crops he brought in. Would he become like Papa, blaming her for making him give up an impossible dream and eventually taking out his discontent on her and their children?

"I took the work available."

"But you're miserable." Her voice broke.

He drew her into his arms. "A husband tries his best to make his wife happy."

When he kissed her, she wanted to weep. She had seen little joy in him since they had moved to Winnipeg, and guilt tore at her. What if he tired of her? What if he began to see her as Papa always had: a homely, ill-tempered, selfish, and worthless girl? "How can a wife be happy when her husband is miserable?"

"You hated the wheat farm, and I hate my job." He tilted her chin and cupped her cheek. "I promise I won't take you back there, but I don't know how long I can bear to stay here."

"You'll leave me someday."

"Never."

"Do you promise?"

He rolled her onto her back. "I promise." She remembered what Rosie had said about him and drew his head down.

A long time later, she lay facing him again. She combed her fingers through his hair. "What are we going to do?"

"Wait." He took her hand and kissed it. "God will show us a way."

Niclas's hours were cut the next day.

❄ ❄ ❄

Marta knew something had happened when Niclas came in
the door. He didn't look tired this afternoon. His eyes glowed.
"MacPherson is leaving."

Her heart sank. "Is he going back to Montreal?"

"He's going to California. He has a job lined up in Sacramento."
He hung up his coat and hat. "He told me my hours are being cut
again." Bernhard and Clotilde clamored for attention.

Marta shushed them and sent them in the parlor to play.
Hildemara stood in the doorway, watching them with wide hazel
eyes. "Go with Bernhard and Clotilde, Hildemara. Go on!"

"How can they cut your hours again?" He only made seventy-
five dollars a month, barely enough to keep a roof over their heads
and good food on the table.

"It could get worse."

She knew that meant he might lose his job after all. "I'll start
looking for property. We can open another boardinghouse. We
could manage it together."

"Railroad men are leaving. The company is giving away free
tickets to California."

California? She tried to absorb the shock. "What would you do
in California?"

"MacPherson said he will do what he can to help me find a job.
If not, there's good land in California."

"You can't mean you want to go back to farming!"

"I miss the plowing and planting. I miss harvesting crops I've
sown with my own hands. I miss wide-open spaces and fresh air."

She tried to remain calm. "I remember frigid winters. I remember thunderstorms and flashes of lightning that filled us both with
fear because one strike could burn away a year's work in minutes!"

"The weather is temperate in California. There's no ice and
snow in the Central Valley."

She started to shake. "Please tell me you didn't sign another
contract."

"No, but I applied for tickets. It'll be a miracle if we get them. They're going to men who have worked for the company five years or more. But I had to try. There won't be any more in a week."

Even having been warned of what might come, Marta wasn't prepared when Niclas came home with train tickets to California. "This is the answer to my prayers," he told her, holding them up in his hand. She hadn't seen that look on his face since they left the wheat fields.

Marta remembered how much they had at the end of four years of farming. Nothing! She knew he wouldn't listen to that reasoning, and she searched for excuses to delay. "We could wait until after Christmas, at least."

He laughed. "We'll spend Christmas in California!"

Bursting into tears, she fled into the kitchen. She thought Niclas would follow, but he didn't. As she set the table, she heard him telling the children about California, the golden land of opportunity, the place where the sun was always shining. Even after she called everyone to dinner, he kept on about it. She picked at her food and tried not to glare at him and upset the children. Hildemara kept looking at her. "Eat!" she told her. Clotilde already looked like the older sister with her greater height and weight.

"When are we going, Papa?" Bernhard sounded like he'd been invited to a world's fair.

"The end of the week. We'll take only what we need." His eyes met Marta's. "We'll sell the furniture and buy what we need when we get to California."

"All of it?" she said faintly. "What about the new bedroom set we bought last year, and the couch, and—?"

"It would cost more to have them sent by freight than buying new when we get there."

She lost her appetite completely. Niclas took seconds. "They say you can pick oranges off the trees all year long."

Bernhard's eyes grew big. He'd had his first orange for Christmas last year. "As many as we want?"

"If we end up with an orange tree on our property."

"What property?" Marta said, steaming.

Niclas ruffled Bernhard's hair. "We don't have property, yet, *Sohn*. We'll have to spend time looking around first."

Marta cleared and washed the dishes while Niclas took the children into the parlor to read Bible stories.

"Off to bed." Marta shooed them up the stairs and got them ready for bed. Niclas came up and kissed them each good night. When he headed for their bedroom, she headed for the stairs.

"Where are you going?"

"I'm not tired yet." Her heart pounded fiercely.

He followed her downstairs and into the parlor. She wrapped her arms around herself and refused to look at him. She could feel him standing behind her, looking at her. She heard him sigh heavily.

"Talk to me, Marta."

"What is there to talk about? You've already made up your mind."

"What better gift can we give our children than the chance of a better life? Isn't that what you've always wanted? Isn't that why you left home as young as you did?"

"I left because I wanted to make my own choices!"

He put his hands at her waist. "You chose me."

For better or for worse, whether rich or poor . . .

Niclas drew her back against him. The feelings he stirred with a touch always defeated her. She wanted to resist, but found herself surrendering to him again. When she leaned into him, he turned her around and embraced her. When he raised his mouth from hers, she leaned her head against his chest. His heart beat hard and fast.

"Trust me."

Marta closed her eyes and said nothing.

"If you can't trust me, trust God. He opened the way."

Marta wished she could believe it.

Hildemara Rose

15

1921

The passenger car bumped and jerked, moving slowly down the track. On her knees, Hildemara looked out the window at the passing houses as the train picked up speed. She slid down onto the seat again, feeling dizzy, her stomach queasy. Mama had made her eat breakfast even though her appetite had waned with excitement over the trip south in the United States of America. Now, she felt her full stomach rolling as the wheels clicked along the track.

"You look pale, Marta." Papa frowned. "Are you feeling all right?"

"No better than I felt coming across the Atlantic." Mama leaned her head back against the seat. "Watch the children."

Bernhard and Clotilde ran up and down the aisle, until Papa told them to sit down and be quiet. Mama took one look at Hildemara and called Papa back. "You'd better take her to the washroom and quick." Hildemara barely made it inside the little cubicle at the back of the car. She cried when nothing more came up, feeling no better for it. Papa brought her back to Mama.

"She lost her breakfast. She's sweating and feels cold."

"Lie down, Hildemara." Mama stroked the hair back from her face. "Go to sleep."

One day rolled miserably into the next as they traveled. Hildemara was too sick to care when they went through customs or changed trains. Bernhard and Clotilde chattered about every little thing they saw out the window while Hildemara couldn't raise her head from the bench. Mama snapped at Papa. "You have to watch them, Niclas. I can't. I don't feel much better than Hildemara. I can't get up and chase after Bernhard and Clotilde."

"What am I supposed to do with them?"

"Keep them from annoying other passengers. And don't let them out of your sight."

"They can't go anywhere."

"They can fall between cars! They can get off the train when it stops! If you're going to the dining car to talk with those men again, take them with you. I can't run after them."

"All right, Marta. Lie down and rest. You look worse than Hildemara."

"I hate trains!"

Papa called Bernhard and Clotilde back and made them sit and look out the window. "Be good for your mama. She's not feeling well. I'll be back soon."

"Niclas!" Mama half rose from her seat before lying down again, a hand over her eyes. Antsy after a few minutes, Bernhard wanted to know how long before the train reached California. "We'll get there when we get there, and stop asking that same question over and over. I'm not so sick I can't turn you over my knee!"

Clotilde poked at Hildemara, wanting to play, but Hildemara couldn't open her eyes without feeling everything spinning around her.

"Leave your sister alone, Clotilde."

Papa came back with bread, cheese, and a bottle of water. Hildemara sipped a little water, but the smell of the cheese made her stomach turn again.

"She's not going to get better until we get off the train, Niclas."

"What's it going to be like in California?"

"Papa's already told you, Bernhard."

"Tell me again!"

"California has orchards of orange trees. You'll be able to eat as many as you want. The sun shines all year. That's why they can grow anything in California. We'll find a nice house on some land, and you and your sisters will have space around you, too. You'll be able to run and play in the orchards. No more having to stay inside a house all the time."

Mama got a pinched look around her eyes. "You said Mr. MacPherson has a job waiting for you in Sacramento."

"He said he would do what he could for me if I came." Papa ruffled Bernhard's thatch of blond hair and sat Clotilde on his lap. "We will go to Sacramento first. If there is no job, Papa knows where to find good farmland. Where would you rather be, children? In a house near the railroad with lots of dirt and smoke, or in a nice house in the sunshine in the middle of an orchard of orange trees?"

Hildemara heard her mother say something in German. Papa ignored her, listening to Bernhard and Clotilde shrieking about how many oranges they would eat when they got to California.

Papa laughed. "Farming is a job, *Sohn*. You'll have to help me."

"Be quiet!" Mama snarled. "There are other people around us." She glared at Papa. "You're filling their heads with fairy tales!"

"I'm only telling them what I was told, Marta."

"*Ja!* And Robert Madson told you wheat farming was profitable, too, didn't he?"

Papa set Clotilde beside Mama and got up. When he headed down the aisle toward the door that went to the dining car, Mama shooed Bernhard and Clotilde. "Go on with Papa. Hurry before he leaves you behind." They both ran noisily down the aisle, catching up just before Papa went through the door.

Hildemara wished she felt well enough to scamper through the cars. She wished the world would stop spinning. She felt afraid when Papa and Mama spoke in German to one another. Would the train ever stop longer than a few minutes? "Are there really orange trees in California, Mama?"

Sighing heavily, Mama put her hand on Hildemara's brow. "We'll all find out when we get there." Hildemara liked the coolness of Mama's hand. "Try to sit up for a while. You have to try to eat something. A little bread, at least. You have little chicken legs."

"I'll be sick."

"You won't know unless you try. Now, come on. Sit up."

When she did, the dizziness returned. She gagged when she tried to swallow a piece of bread.

"Hush now, Hildemara. Don't cry. At least you tried. That's something, at least." Mama tucked a blanket around her again. "I was seasick for days crossing the Atlantic. You'll get over it soon. You just have to set your mind on it."

Setting her mind on it didn't help one bit. By the time they reached Sacramento, Hildemara was too weak to stand, let alone walk off the train. Mama had to carry her while Papa collected the two trunks.

They stayed in a hotel near the train station. Hildemara ate her first meal in days in the dining room: a bowl of soup and some crackers.

It rained all night. Papa went out early the next morning and still wasn't back when Mama said it was time for bed.

Hildemara awakened. "Don't touch me!" Mama cried out. Papa spoke softly in German, but Mama answered angrily in English. "You lied to me, Niclas. That's the truth." Papa spoke quietly again. "English, Niclas, or I won't answer you." Mama dropped her voice. "Americans won't like Germans any better than Canadians did."

The sun didn't shine for days. They didn't see an orange tree until Mama took them for a walk to the capitol building. Mama spoke to a gardener and told them they could each have one orange. They thanked him politely before peeling the skins. The gardener leaned on his rake, frowning. "They're still a little green, ma'am."

"It's a good lesson for them."

Mama and Papa argued all the time. Papa wanted to look

for land to buy. Mama said no. "You don't know enough about farming to waste money on land."

"What do you want me to do? We're spending money staying in this hotel. I have to find work."

"If I buy anything, it'll be another boardinghouse."

"And then what would I do? Strip beds? Do the laundry? No! I'm the head of this family!" He spoke German again, fast, furious.

"It's in my name, Niclas. Not yours! You didn't earn that money. I did!"

A neighbor pounded on the wall, shouting for them to shut up. Mama cried.

Papa came back to the hotel the next afternoon with train tickets. At the mention of another train ride, Hildemara started to cry. "Don't worry, *Liebling*, this will only be a short ride—just eighty miles."

Mama hunkered down and gripped her by the shoulders. "Stop it! If I can stand it, so can you." Mama took her by the hand and pulled her along to the train station.

When Papa took his seat, Mama swung Hildemara up and planted her on his lap. "If she throws up, let it be all over you this time!" Mama sat on the other side of the aisle, face turned away, staring out the window.

"*Schlaf, Kleine,*" Papa said. A man in front of them turned around and stared coldly. Papa spoke English this time. "Go to sleep, little one."

"German, are you?"

Mama got up and sat next to Papa. "Swiss! We came down from Canada. He still has some trouble with English. My husband is an engineer. Unfortunately, the supervisor who promised him a position moved to Southern California."

The man looked between Mama and Papa. "Well, good luck to you folks." He turned around again.

Papa set Hildemara on the seat with Bernhard and Clotilde. "Take care of your sisters, *Sohn*." Papa took Mama's hand and kissed it. Mama stared straight forward, her face pale and set.

Hildemara roused when a man came through the car announcing Murietta.

Bernhard pushed at her, and Clotilde slipped by and ran for the door until Mama told her to stop and wait. The air felt cool against Hildemara's face when she climbed down the steps. Papa swung her onto the platform and gave her a light swat. Mama stood waiting beneath a big sign. She looked down a long, dusty street. She sighed heavily. "We left Winnipeg for this?"

"It's not raining." Papa hefted one trunk onto his shoulder and dragged the other toward an office.

Hildemara looked up at Mama's stony face. "Where's Papa going?"

"He's going to have the trunks stored until we find a place to live."

Papa came back empty-handed. "The station manager said there is only one place to stay in town."

Bernhard and Clotilde skipped ahead while Hildemara reached for Mama's hand. Mama wouldn't let her take it. She patted Hildemara's back. "Go on with your brother and sister."

"I want to stay with you."

"Go on, I said!"

Papa leaned down and tipped Hildemara's trembling chin. "No need for tears, *Liebling*. We're right behind you."

Hildemara walked ahead, but kept checking back over her shoulder. Mama looked annoyed. Papa looked relaxed and happy. Hildemara stayed close enough to hear Papa say, "It is a fine town, Marta, everything dressed up for Christmas." When Bernhard called out, Hildemara ran to join them at a big window. She gasped at the beautiful glass Christmas ornaments in boxes.

"Come on, children." Mama herded them along.

Across the street was a theater. They passed by a general store, a shoe repair and tack shop, a bakery, pool hall, and café. When they came to a two-story brown building with white-trimmed windows and a long wooden porch with four rocking chairs, Mama told them to stay with Papa, glancing at him. "You can take the children for a walk while I take care of business." Lifting her long skirt, she went up the front steps.

Papa told Bernhard to run to the first intersection and back. He did it twice before he was settled enough to walk quietly and stop asking questions. Papa took them around the corner and down to another street lined with large trees. "We're walking on Elm Street. What kind of trees do you suppose those are?"

"Elm!" Bernhard and Hildemara said at once. "I said it first!" Bernhard insisted.

Each house had a lawn. When Papa came to another street, he turned back toward Main. "Look over there at that big pink-brick building. It's a library. That should put a smile on Mama's face." He led them across Main Street and kept walking. They hadn't gone far when they came to orchards and vineyards. Exhausted, Hildemara lagged behind. When she cried out for him to wait, he came back and swung her up onto his shoulders.

Bernhard never seemed to tire. "Are those orange trees, Papa?"

"No. I don't know what they are. Why don't we ask?" He swung Hildemara down and told her to watch out for Clotilde while he talked to the farmer digging a ditch between two rows of vines. Almond trees, the man said, and wine grapes across the road.

"Thirsty," Clotilde said. Hildemara took her by the hand and led her under the shade of one of the trees. Bernhard asked if he could dig. The man handed over the shovel. The two men went on talking while Bernhard tried to scoop more sandy dirt from the ditch the man had been digging. Clotilde got up and went over to Papa, tugging at his pants. "Hungry, Papa." He patted her on the head and kept asking questions. Clotilde tugged again, harder. When Papa ignored her, she cried. Papa shook the man's hand, then asked if he could come back tomorrow and talk some more.

Face flushed, Mama got up from a rocking chair on the porch. "Where have you been?"

"We met a farmer!" Bernhard bounded up the steps. "He let me dig a ditch!"

When Papa put Clotilde down, she tugged at Mama's skirt. "Hungry, Mama."

Hildemara was too tired and parched to say anything.

"Did you give a thought to how weak Hildemara is after that awful train ride from Winnipeg? She looks ready to faint."

"You told me to take them for a walk."

Mama took Hildemara's hand and started across the street. "Around the block, not out into the countryside. It's past three! They haven't eaten since breakfast."

"Time got away from me."

Mama went into the café. They took seats by the window looking out onto Main Street. Papa asked what they wanted to eat, and Mama told the waitress everyone would have "the special." Mama folded her hands on the table. "The town is having a Christmas pageant tonight. That's something, at least."

"There's a library one street over and two blocks down."

Mama brightened, but her expression clouded over quickly enough. "Mrs. Cavanaugh would only come down twenty-five cents a night if I guaranteed a week."

"Stop worrying. God will lead me to work." When the waitress brought the plates, Papa said grace.

Hildemara didn't like the thick, greasy stew. After a few bites, she put her spoon down. Mama frowned. "You have to eat, Hildemara."

"She hasn't eaten much of anything for a long time. Maybe her stomach isn't up to it. Would you like something else, Hildemara? some soup?"

"Don't baby her!" Mama leaned forward. "You're down to skin and bones. You eat that food or you'll be sitting in the hotel room while the rest of us go to the Christmas pageant."

Head down, fighting tears, Hildemara picked up her spoon. Bernhard and Clotilde finished their dinner quickly and wanted to play. Hildemara still had half a bowl of stew left to eat. Papa took Bernhard and Clotilde outside. Mama sat watching her. "The meat, at least, Hildemara." Leaning across the table, she poked through the bowl of stew, separating bits of meat and a few vegetables. "Eat this much and drink all of the milk." Other families came in and ordered meals.

"It'll be dark before you're finished." Mama sounded annoyed. "But we're not leaving this table until you do. You won't grow stronger otherwise." Leaning back in her chair, Mama grimaced.

"Are you mad, Mama?"

Mama stared off down the street. "Not at you."

When Hildemara finally managed to swallow the last piece of carrot, Mama took some coins from her purse and gave them to the waitress. Hildemara's legs ached after the long walk with Papa, but she didn't complain. She clutched Mama's hand more tightly when they came near a crowd gathering at the center of town. Other children stood with their parents, and everyone looked at them as they walked through the crowd. Hildemara stayed as close to Mama's side as she could without stepping on her hem. Mama kept craning her neck. "There's Papa." He stood with the man who had been digging a ditch, and several others had joined them. "Where's Bernhard? Where's Clotilde?" Mama looked around.

"Over there." Papa pointed toward a group of children standing near a platform. He grinned. "Santa Claus is coming." He returned his attention to the men.

"Go on, Hildemara."

"No." She didn't want to let go of Mama's hand.

Mama leaned down. "Clotilde is almost two years younger than you and she's not afraid. Now, go on." She looked into Hildemara's eyes and her expression softened. "I'm right here. I can see you, and you can see me." She turned Hildemara around and gave her a gentle push.

Hildemara looked for her brother and sister. She could see them toward the front, near the platform. Biting her lip, Hildemara stayed near the back, afraid to make her way between the others.

A man mounted the wooden platform and gave a speech. Then four men came up in vests, one with a harmonica, and they sang. Everyone clapped so loudly, they sang another. A little girl in a short green and red satin dress, black tights, and an embroidered vest came up onto the platform. While someone played a fiddle, the girl's feet tapped, her red curls bouncing up and down.

Hildemara stared in fascination. When the song ended, the girl held out her skirt and curtsied, then ran down the steps to her proud mother.

"Santa's coming!" someone shouted, and bells jingled as a big man dressed in a red suit fringed with white appeared. He wore high black boots and carried a big sack on his back and called out "Ho! Ho! Ho!" to the excited laughter of children.

Terrified, Hildemara looked back. Mama was laughing. When Papa put his arm around her, she didn't try to pull away. Hildemara turned back to the platform and watched her brother and sister swarming onto the platform with the other children. Hildemara didn't move.

The man in red raised his head and called out in a booming voice. "It's a stampede!" Laughing with the crowd, he bent down and pulled out a small bag, handing it to the little girl in the green and red dress with the shiny black shoes. More bags appeared, clutched by excited hands.

When Bernhard came down from the platform, he had already opened his. It was filled with hard candy with flowery designs, peanuts covered in chocolate, and candy-covered almonds. Clotilde had a paper sack, too. "Can I have one?" Hildemara asked. Clotilde jerked her sack away and turned her back.

"Hildemara!" Mama called. She waved her hand. Hildemara understood. She was to go up on that platform and get a sack, too. Only she couldn't. When she looked up at the big man and all those children surrounding him, she couldn't move.

"Aren't you going?" Bernhard jutted his chin. When she shook her head, he thrust his sack into her hand and dashed up the steps.

"Back again?" Santa shook his head. "One sack per customer, sonny."

"It's for my sister." Bernhard called out and pointed at her.

Santa looked down at her. "Come on up here, little girl. I won't bite you." People laughed all around her. Someone pushed her. Hildemara dug her heels in and started to cry. Looking back over her shoulder, she saw Mama frown and close her eyes.

Bernhard returned to Hildemara's side. "Stop crying like a baby!" Bernhard growled, thrusting the sack of candy into her hand. Clotilde shrieked and ran toward Mama and Papa, holding her sack high. Head down, Hildemara followed Bernhard back to where Mama and Papa waited.

Mama stared at her. It wasn't the first time Hildemara had seen disappointment in her mother's eyes.

16

PAPA WENT OUT every day to look for work. He met another nice man who said they could live temporarily on his property near an irrigation canal. Mama and Papa argued about it, and then Mama bought canvas to make a tent. Her fingers bled before she finished it, but she kept on, jaw set tight. "I used to dream about living with you in a bedouin tent, Niclas. Now I know it for romantic nonsense!"

Papa said Mama knew how to make all kinds of things. "Her papa was a tailor."

Later that night, Hildemara awakened to shouting. Mama had spoken loudly many times since leaving Canada, but this time Papa shouted back. Hildemara scooted closer to Bernhard and they huddled in the darkness as Mama and Papa argued loudly in German.

"Enough!" Papa caught hold of Mama and gave her a hard shake. *"Enough!"* He spoke in a low, intense voice, but Hildemara didn't understand the words. Crying, Mama tried to break free. He wouldn't let her go. He said more and she started to cry, not soft, broken cries of defeat, but harsh, sobbing sounds that frightened Hildemara even more than Mama's anger had. Papa's hands fell away from her. He said something more and walked away.

Bernhard jumped to his feet and ran after him. "Papa! Don't go, Papa!"

"Go back to your mother!" Papa told him.

"No! I want you, Papa!"

Papa knelt in the sandy soil and spoke to him. "I'm coming back, *Sohn*." He straightened and looked at Mama. "God told me to bring my family here, and God will take care of us." He put his hand on Bernhard's head and looked down. "Do you believe me?"

"I believe you, Papa."

"Then help Mama believe. Do what she tells you while I'm gone." He walked off into the night.

Mama told Bernhard to get back inside the tent and go to sleep. She sat outside for a long time, her head in her hands. Then she came in and lay down between Hildemara and Clotilde. Hildemara turned to her. "I love you, Mama."

"Hush." Mama drew a shuddering breath and turned away. Her shoulders shook for a long time and Hildemara heard soft, muffled sounds in the darkness.

Shaking awake, Hildemara found Mama standing above her. "Get up. There's water in the bowl. Wash up and get dressed. We're going into town."

"Is Papa back?"

"No. And we're not waiting for him." She clapped her hands. "Come on. Hurry! We're not sleeping on the ground one more night!"

When they reached town, Mama took them into the biggest store. All kinds of merchandise had been stacked up on shelves reaching to the ceiling and on tables all around the spacious room. "You can look, but don't touch," Mama told them. Turning, she gave her list to the man behind the counter.

Bernhard headed for a train set in the front window. Clotilde stood at the line of jars filled with candy, while Hildemara wandered between the rows of tables. She spotted a blue-eyed doll in a fancy dress, ribbons in its curly blonde hair. Hildemara wanted to touch it, but held her hands clasped tightly behind her back.

"Do you like that doll?"

After a brief glance at the smiling lady in the blue dress, Hildemara looked at the doll. "She's very pretty."

"Maybe Santa Claus will bring you a nice doll just like that one for Christmas."

"Papa said we already had Christmas."

"Oh? And what did you get?"

"We came to America."

It rained again that afternoon. Mama sat inside the tent, looking out while Bernhard and Clotilde played with a ball she had purchased. Hildemara chewed her nails and watched Mama. When they became hungry, Mama gave them hunks of a loaf of bread she had bought from the bakery.

Papa came back in the afternoon. Mama got up quickly and went out to him. They talked for a long time outside. When they came back inside, Mama opened two cans of Campbell's soup for dinner.

"I'll try again tomorrow." Papa sounded tired. He didn't look happy, even when he smiled at Hildie.

It was almost dark when they heard a woman call out to them. "Hello!"

Mama mumbled something in German and Papa went outside. When he called to her, Mama rose. "Stay inside! It's sprinkling again." Bernhard and Clotilde crawled over to the tent opening and peered out into the misty dusk. Hildemara joined them.

Two women sat in a carriage. Hildemara recognized the lady in blue who had spoken to her that morning. They handed boxes down to Mama and Papa. Papa brought two inside the tent while Mama talked to the ladies. When Mama came in, her eyes were moist with tears. Hildemara leaned forward, inhaling deeply. Something smelled wonderful. When she peered out again, the lady waved to her. Hildemara waved back.

"What did they bring us, Mama?" Bernhard fell to his knees as Mama opened the first box.

"Close the flap, Hildemara," Mama said hoarsely. "You're letting the cold air in."

Papa carefully removed a large covered roasting pan. When he lifted the lid, he looked happy again. "Look how God provides. Turkey and stuffing, roasted yams."

"It's those women who provided," Mama told him tersely.

"It's God who works on the heart. Look at this feast, children."

Mama took out a jar of cranberry sauce, two tins of cookies, two loaves of fresh-baked bread, a dozen eggs, two jars of home-made jam, and several cans of milk. Sniffling, she turned away and blew her nose.

"What's in the gunnysack, Papa?"

"Well, I don't know. I guess we have to look." Papa opened it and took out the beautiful doll with blue eyes and blonde curls. "This looks exactly like you, Clotilde."

"Mine! Mine!" Clotilde clapped her hands and reached out. Hildemara's heart dropped as Papa handed the doll over to her younger sister. She bit her lip, but didn't tell Papa she knew the doll had been meant for her. She looked at Clotilde clutching it tightly against her heart and knew she'd never have it now. Hildemara sat back on her heels and blinked away tears. When she glanced up again, she saw Mama staring at her. Mama had seen her talking to the lady, and Mama had seen her admiring that doll.

"Are you going to speak up, Hildemara?"

Hildemara looked at the doll again and back at Mama.

"You'd better start learning right now you have to speak up for yourself."

"What's wrong?" Papa's eyes moved between Mama and Hildemara.

Mama was still looking at her. "Is anything wrong?"

Hildemara looked at her sister playing happily with the doll. She knew if she said it had been meant for her, Clotilde would scream and cry. Maybe if she simply waited, Clotilde would get tired of the doll after a while and then she could play with it.

"What about me, Papa?" Bernhard pressed. "Is there anything for me?"

"Well, let's see." Papa reached into the sack and pulled out a wooden airplane. Bernhard took it and started right off pretending to fly it around the tent while Papa fished in the sack. "One more." He pulled out a rag doll with a simple blue and white dotted swiss dress, brown yarn hair, and big, brown button eyes. "And this is for you, Hildemara." Papa tossed it to her.

Bernhard spoke up. "Hildie liked the other one, Mama. She saw it at the store. She was talking to that lady—"

"Well, she didn't say so, did she? So she gets what she gets."

Papa looked at Mama. "Why didn't you tell me?"

"She has to learn to speak up!"

"She's a little girl."

"She's almost five! Clotilde is only three, and she had no trouble telling you what she wanted."

"Marta." Papa spoke in soft reprimand.

Bernhard edged between them. "There's something else in the bag, Papa."

The kind ladies hadn't forgotten anyone. Papa received a pair of leather work gloves, and Mama got a beautiful white crocheted shawl.

Papa prayed and carved the turkey, and Mama filled the plates with food. When they all finished eating the feast, Bernhard went back to playing with his airplane and Clotilde with her doll.

Hildemara felt an uncomfortable twisting inside her as she watched her sister play with the blonde, blue-eyed doll. When she noticed Mama looking at her, Hildie felt her cheeks bloom hot with shame. She bowed her head.

Mama wrapped the new shawl tightly around her shoulders and went outside. Papa put his hand on Hildie's head. "I'm sorry, *Liebling*." He rose and ducked out of the tent.

Hildemara could hear her parents talking in muted voices.

Mama sounded agitated. Papa spoke German. Hildemara felt worse, knowing they were talking about her.

She sat the doll on her knees and studied it again. She thought of the lady in blue who had brought the boxes. Maybe she had made the rag doll. That made it special. Hildemara touched the glassy button eyes again and traced the stitched pink smile. "I love you no matter how you look." Hugging it close, she lay on her mat and pulled the blanket up over her shoulders.

❄ ❄ ❄

Mama got up before dawn every morning, made the fire, and fixed breakfast for Papa. Hildemara always awakened to their quiet voices. She felt easier with them talking to one another. When Mama yelled, Hildemara felt sick to her stomach.

"English, Niclas. You can't keep falling back into German. They will wonder if you backed the Kaiser."

"Mr. Musashi is teaching me to prune trees and vines. Mr. Pimentel has taught me a lot about the soil."

"And what good is all that if you haven't a place of your own; isn't that what you want to say?"

"Marta . . ."

"Not yet. I'm not willing to gamble."

Mama packed Papa cheese, bread, and two apples before he went off to work. Mama never ate until after Papa left, and most of the time, her breakfast didn't stay down long. "Are you sick, Mama?"

"It'll pass in a month or two." She dabbed at her forehead with the back of her hand. "And don't say a word about it to Papa. He'll know soon enough."

Mama usually felt better by midday, but she had no patience with Bernhard or Clotilde, and even less for Hildemara. Everyone did his best to stay out of her way. Mama had Bernhard bring water, and she had Hildemara straighten up the sleeping bags she had sewn out of old blankets. Clotilde played with the doll.

Bernhard went fishing in the irrigation canal, but never caught anything, and Hildemara peeled potatoes while Mama washed clothes in a big washtub and hung garments on a rope she strung between two trees.

When Papa came home dusty and dirty, she had warm water and soap so he could wash. Hildemara stayed close enough to hear. "I'm taking the children to school tomorrow and register them. It would be better for them if they had a permanent address."

"Yes. And when you open your purse, we'll have a permanent address."

"Find a place to sharecrop. When you prove to me you know enough to make a living at farming, I'll give you what you need."

"I could take it, Marta. What's yours became mine when we married."

She stiffened. "We're in America now, not Germany. What's mine stays mine unless I say otherwise. Don't think you can boss me around and I'll sit quietly by as your slave!"

Papa looked sad, not angry. "I'm not your father."

Mama winced. "No. You're not. But you refused to listen to me once before, and look what happened."

He wiped soap from the back of his neck. "Don't keep reminding me."

"You choose to forget."

He threw the towel down. "I choose to try again!"

She stepped forward, chin jutting. "And I choose to wait and see if this is God's will or man's whim!" She headed back for the washtub.

"You get more ill-tempered by the day!"

Mama lifted her head, her eyes filling with tears. "Maybe it has something to do with crossing a continent and coming to this end-of-the-road town. Maybe it has to do with winter and being cold and no roof over our heads and expecting another baby!" She wadded up his shirt and threw it in the dirt. "Wash your own clothes!" She walked off toward the irrigation canal and sat with her back to him.

When Papa finished washing, he went out and sat beside her. He put his arm around her shoulders and drew her close to his side.

❄ ❄ ❄

They dressed in their finest before Mama ushered them to town the next morning. "Stay out of the puddles and try to stay clean!" Bernhard ran ahead, but Clotilde and Hildemara walked behind Mama like goslings behind a mama goose. They walked past fragrant willows, down Main Street with its spread of buildings, across State Highway 99, and past one small general store, ending up at a small white building with a bell tower and red shingle roof.

Mama ran her hands through Bernhard's thick, blond, spiky hair and brushed down Hildemara's gingham dress. She lifted Clotilde to a bench. "You sit right here, all three of you, and don't move." She gave Bernhard a stern look. "If you wander off, Bernhard, I'll use Papa's belt on you when we get home." She had never used the belt on any of them, but the look in her eyes told them she meant business.

Bernhard fidgeted. He looked longingly at the teeter-totter and swings, the monkey bars and sandbox. Clotilde sat forward and swung her legs. Hildemara sat still, hands folded, praying she wouldn't be accepted, praying she would be able to stay home with Mama.

Mama came back. "Christmas vacation will be over after New Year's. Bernhard, you and Hildemara start school Monday next."

Hildemara's lip began to tremble.

Clotilde stuck her lower lip out. "I wanna go, too!"

"You'll have to wait. You have to be five to go to school."

"I'm not five, Mama."

"You'll be five before the end of January. That's close enough."

17

1922

Hildemara couldn't sleep the night before school. She pretended to be asleep when Mama got up and made Papa's breakfast. She roused Bernhard first and pulled the covers back from Hildemara's shoulders. "I know you're awake. Get up and get dressed."

When Mama gave her a bowl of *Müsli*, Hildemara couldn't eat it. Her stomach felt like something had gotten in and kept fluttering as it tried to get out. She looked up at Mama. "I'm sick. I can't go to school."

"You're not sick, and you are going."

"She is a little pale." Papa put his palm against Hildie's forehead. Hildie hoped he would say she had a fever. "She feels cool."

"She's scared, that's all. As soon as she gets there, she'll find she doesn't need to be." Mama jerked her head. "If you don't eat something, everyone in your class is going to hear your stomach growling by ten in the morning." Hildemara looked at Clotilde, still bundled in a sleeping bag.

Papa looked at Hildemara. "I can walk them to school."

"No. They need to learn to stand on their own. They'll be fine walking by themselves."

Papa ruffled Bernhard's slicked-back hair. While Mama ran a comb through it again, Papa kissed Hildemara. "You will meet lots of other little girls your age." He patted her cheek. When he went out, Mama went with him. When Mama ducked back inside the tent, she didn't look at Hildemara. She picked up the small buckets with their lunch and told them it was time to be off. She grabbed Bernhard by the shoulder before he went out. "You walk with your sister. You keep an eye on her."

They hadn't gone a quarter mile when Bernhard kicked the dust angrily. "Come on, Hildie! Stop dragging your feet!" When she didn't walk much faster, he started to run. She cried out, but he shouted back at her that she'd have to catch up or walk alone.

Hildemara ran as fast as she could, but she knew she wouldn't be able to catch him. A stitch in her side made her slow down. She cried out again, tears streaming down her cheeks.

He looked back over his shoulder. Stopping, he put his hands on his hips and waited until she caught up with him. "You'd better stop crying now or they'll all call you a crybaby." He stayed beside her the rest of the way.

Children played in the yard. Some stopped to stare when Bernhard and Hildemara came near. Bernhard pushed the gate open. When children came over, Bernhard did all the talking. Hildemara stood beside him, looking from one face to the other, her throat dry. One of the boys looked at her. "Is your sister dumb or something?"

Bernhard's face turned red. "She's not dumb."

When the bell rang, everyone lined up and filed into the building. A slender, dark-haired woman in a navy blue skirt, long-sleeved white blouse, and dark blue knitted sweater told Hildemara to share a desk with Elizabeth Kenney, the pretty girl who had worn the red and green satin dress and shiny black shoes the night of the Christmas pageant. She wore a pretty green dress today. A matching green bow tied her two long, red pigtails back. Elizabeth smiled brightly. Hildemara tried to smile back.

Bernhard made friends right away. A group of boys surrounded him on the playground. Tony Reboli stepped into the circle. "Let's play a game." He pushed Bernhard. Laughing, Bernhard pushed back. Tony put more force behind his next push. Bernhard shoved so hard Tony went down. Bernhard stepped forward and extended his hand. Tony allowed himself to be pulled up. Dusting himself off, he suggested they have a race. Tony took off, Tom Hughes, Eddie Rinckel, and Wallie Engles chasing after him. Bernhard caught up easily and passed by Tony, reaching the end of the playground first.

Sitting on a bench under a big elm, Hildemara watched her brother chum around with his new friends. He could run faster, jump higher, and play harder than any boy in school. By the end of the day, only the girls called him Bernhard. All the boys called him Bernie. By the end of the week, everyone wanted to be his best friend. Even the girls followed him around, giggling and whispering, wanting his attention. It amused Hildemara to see how embarrassed that made her older brother.

After two weeks, Hildie still hadn't made one friend. No one teased her; Bernie made certain of that. But no one paid her any attention. She became Little Sis because that's what Bernie called her and no one remembered her name. Every recess, while the others played, she sat on a bench by herself and watched. She didn't know how to join in, and the mere thought of approaching someone and asking permission made her feel sick to her stomach. Only the teacher noticed her.

Mrs. Ransom kept a chart on the wall and put up gold and silver stars, or blue and red dots. Every morning, Hildie ran to the girls' bathroom first thing to wash. It did no good. Following the Pledge of Allegiance and singing "My Country, 'Tis of Thee," which Hildemara confused with "God Save the King," Mrs. Ransom checked each child for properly combed hair, washed hands and face, clean nails, and polished shoes. Not once did Hildemara pass inspection.

Once, Mrs. Ransom went so far as to part her hair in a dozen places searching for lice. While the children twittered with laughter, Hildemara sat red-faced and sick with humiliation. "Well, at least you don't have lice. But you're not clean enough to earn even a red dot. You might earn a silver star if you bothered to polish your shoes."

When Hildemara said she needed polish for her shoes, Mama turned around and put her hands on her hips. "Polish? With all the sand and dust you walk through to get to school? We're not wasting money on polish!"

Hildemara dampened the hem of her dress to clean her shoes, but then Mrs. Ransom said her dress looked unwashed.

"Let me see your hands, Hildemara Waltert. Still chewing your nails, too. It's a disgusting habit. You'll get worms." The children around Hildie twittered. "Hold up your arms. Don't put them down until I tell you." Hildemara kept her hands in the air, her face burning with shame as Mrs. Ransom pointed. "Look at this, children. When you wash your hands, wash your arms as well. I don't want to see rivulets of dirt." She shook her head at Hildemara. "You can put your arms down now. Next time, don't just splash a little water on yourself in the girls' bathroom and call it a bath!"

"The Walterts live in a tent down by the irrigation ditch, Mrs. Ransom."

"I know where they live, Elizabeth, and it's no excuse for being filthy. If she bothered to use a little soap with the water, she might earn a silver star." Mrs. Ransom moved on to the next child. Betty Jane Marrow received a gold star every day.

Hot tears burned and Hildemara struggled to keep them back. She bit her lower lip and kept her hands clenched in her lap. She could feel Elizabeth Kenney looking at her, but wouldn't look back. A boy behind them leaned forward and yanked hard on Hildemara's hair. Elizabeth swung around. "Stop it!"

Mrs. Ransom turned and pinned Hildemara with her eyes. "Go sit on the stool in the corner."

Elizabeth gasped. "She didn't do anything!"

"All right. That's enough. Let's get to work."

When recess came, Hildemara went out to her bench. Elizabeth Kenney left her friends and approached her. "May I sit with you, Hildemara?"

Hildemara shrugged, torn between resentment and admiration. Elizabeth had a whole row of gold stars on the class chart. The only one who had more was Betty Jane Marrow. Elizabeth looked plump and pretty. No one told her she looked skinny as a rail and pale as a ghost.

"I live on Elm Street. It's not far. Just across the road and down a few blocks. You walked by my house once. I saw you through the window. My house is just a few doors down from the library. Do you know where that is? You can come to my house before school, if you like. We have hot water and . . ."

Hildemara's face flamed. "I wash every morning. I'm clean before I come to school."

"It's a long walk from where you live. I'd be covered with dust and dirt, too, if I had to walk to school every day."

"How do you know where we live? Did Bernie tell you?"

"My mother brought Christmas dinner to your family. She brought you and your sister dolls."

"Did she make the rag doll?"

"No. It was from the church rummage box." Elizabeth's friends called for her to come back. Elizabeth said she'd come in a minute. "My mother says Mrs. Ransom treats you badly because her brother got killed in the war. Your father is German, isn't he? That makes you German, too." When her friends called again, Elizabeth stood. "I guess I'd better go. Would you like to play with us, Hildemara?"

"Elizabeth!"

Hildemara looked at the other girls. They called for Elizabeth, not her. Did they think of her in the same way Mrs. Ransom did? Throat tight, Hildie shook her head. When Elizabeth walked away, Hildie watched Bernie playing marbles with his friends on the other side of the playground. Why didn't anyone care that he was

German? Everyone liked her brother. Mrs. Ransom would probably like him, too, if he were one of her students.

Mama made her and Bernie do homework every afternoon when they got home. "You have to do it now before it's too dark to see. The sooner you get it done, the sooner you can go out to play. Now, read it again."

Bernie protested.

"You'll never get anywhere in the world if you can't read better than that, Bernhard. Read it again."

After two months, Mrs. Ransom pinned a note to Hildemara's sweater. Mama unpinned it and read it. "She says you're a slow reader. You're not a slow reader. What is this note all about? She thinks you're stupid. No child of mine is stupid! Bring your book home tomorrow."

When school ended the next day, Hildemara took a reading book from the shelf.

"Where do you think you're going with that book?" Mrs. Ransom blocked the doorway.

"Mama wants me to bring it home."

"Stealing! That's what you're about!"

"No!" Blubbering, Hildemara tried to explain.

"I don't care what your mother wants, Hildemara." She snatched the book back. "Tell her to take you to the library. These books are expensive and paid for by *American* taxpayers. You don't have a right to it."

When Hildemara came inside the tent without the book, Mama wanted to know why. "Mrs. Ransom wouldn't let me have it. She said you should take me to the library."

Mama's eyes went hot, but she calmed down by the end of dinner. "We'll go to the library on Saturday." She put her fingers beneath Hildemara's chin and made her look up. "Try to make a friend. One friend can make all the difference as to whether you will be happy or miserable with the world. Rosie Gilgan is my friend and has been since the first day of school. She comes from a wealthy family who owns a hotel. I was a tailor's daughter. She lived in a large house. Our family lived upstairs from the shop. I could share my thoughts and feelings with Rosie and never fear she would tell tales or make fun of me. Rosie was always kind, a true Christian, and I knew I could trust her. You find someone like that, Hildemara Rose, and you will be a much happier girl than you are right now."

"Did you name me after your friend, Mama?"

"Yes. I did. I hope you'll grow up to have her fine qualities."

Hildemara imagined Rosie Gilgan had been fearless like Mama and popular like Elizabeth Kenney, with no worries about how others might treat her. Hildemara cried herself to sleep. She wished she could get sick like she had on the train. Maybe then Mama would let her stay home from school. Maybe then she would never have to go back and face Mrs. Ransom.

No amount of crying and begging changed Mama's mind, even on Saturday, when Mama found out she couldn't borrow books until the family had a permanent address.

❊ ❊ ❊

Papa leaned close to the lamp and translated a story from his German Bible every evening. One evening he would pick from the Old Testament, the next from the New. Bernie liked to hear about warriors like Gideon and David and Goliath or the prophet Elijah calling down fire on the altar and then killing all the priests of Baal. Clotilde didn't care what Papa read. She crawled into his lap and fell asleep within minutes.

Hildemara liked the stories of Ruth and Esther, but tonight she didn't want to get into a squabble with her brother and sister after being picked on all day by Mrs. Ransom. She had heard Mama and Papa arguing earlier, and she didn't want to add fuel to Mama's temper by complaining about anything.

"No warriors or war stories tonight, Bernhard." Papa tweaked Clotilde's nose. "And no love stories. You're going to hear Jesus' Sermon on the Mount."

Papa read for a long time. Bernie usually sat cross-legged, eager to hear. Tonight, he flopped on his cot, his hands behind his head, half-dozing. When Clotilde fell asleep, Mama tucked her into her blanket sack. Hildemara poked the needle through the sampler Mama gave her. No matter how hard she tried, she made a mess of the stitches. Mama took it and plucked at the knotted thread. She handed it back. "Do it again." Hildie hung her head, wanting to cry. Even Mama didn't approve of her efforts to do things right.

Papa kept reading.

Hildemara didn't understand most of it. What did it mean to be salt and light? Why would someone hide a lantern under a basket? Did they want to start a fire? What did adultery mean? When he started reading about enemies, Hildemara took slower, more careful stitches. *"Love your enemies,"* Jesus said. Did that mean she had to love Mrs. Ransom? Mrs. Ransom hated her. Surely that made her an enemy. *"Pray for those who persecute you,"* Jesus said. "What does *persecute* mean?"

Mama stabbed a needle through one of Papa's work shirts. "It's when someone treats you cruelly, when they spitefully use you."

Papa left the Bible open in his lap. "Jesus was treated cruelly, Hildemara. When He was nailed to the cross, He prayed for the people who put Him there. He asked God to forgive them because they didn't know what they were doing."

"Are we supposed to do that?"

Mama gave Papa an angry glance. "No one can be as perfect as Jesus."

Papa didn't look at her, but spoke to Hildemara instead. "God says if you love only those who love you, then you're no better than those who are cruel to you. If you are kind only to friends, you are no different than your enemy."

Mama tied a knot and snipped it. "That doesn't mean you let people step all over you. You have to stand up—"

"Marta." Papa's quiet voice held a note of warning that made Mama press her lips together. Papa put his hand on Hildemara's head. "It takes someone very special to love an enemy and pray for someone who is unkind."

"She's not Jesus, Niclas." Mama tossed Papa's shirt onto his bed. "And if she was, she'd end up like Him, too. Nailed to a cross!" She went outside the tent, arms crossed against the cold night air.

Papa closed the Bible. "Time for bed."

Lying on her cot, Hildemara heard Mama and Papa talking in low voices outside the tent wall.

"One of us should go and tell that—"

"It'd only make things worse, and you know it."

"She's having a hard enough time without you telling her she has to put up with people walking all over her. She has to learn to stand up for herself."

"There are different ways of standing." Papa's voice lowered even more.

Hildemara muffled her crying in her blanket. She didn't want Mama and Papa arguing about her. She prayed Mrs. Ransom would stop persecuting her. She prayed Mrs. Ransom would be nice tomorrow. She thought about what Elizabeth Kenney had told her about Mrs. Ransom's brother. Hildemara knew how sad she would be if anything bad happened to Bernie. Just thinking about Bernie dying made Hildemara feel even worse. Hildemara hadn't done anything to deserve Mrs. Ransom's hatred. Maybe Mrs. Ransom was just like those people who killed Jesus. Maybe Mrs. Ransom didn't know what she was doing, either.

All the way to school the next morning, Hildemara prayed quietly. Bernie told her to stop mumbling. "If you start whispering to yourself, people are gonna think you're crazy!"

The rest of the way to school, Hildemara thought her prayers instead of saying them aloud. When Mrs. Ransom led the children into the classroom, Hildie thought a prayer for her. *Jesus, forgive Mrs. Ransom for being so mean to me. She doesn't know what she's doing.*

The prayer didn't change anything. In fact, everything got a whole lot worse. When the hygienic inspection was over, Mrs. Ransom grabbed Hildemara by the ear and dragged her from her seat. "Come up here, Hildemara Waltert, and let the other children have a good look at you!"

Heart thumping, Hildemara tried not to cry. Mrs. Ransom let go of her ear long enough to grab her shoulders and spin her around to face the class. "Hold up your hands, Hildemara. Show these children what I have to look at every morning." Hildemara closed her eyes tightly, wishing she could become invisible. Mrs. Ransom slapped the back of her head. "Do what I tell you!" Trembling, face on fire, Hildemara held up her hands. "Look, children! Have you ever seen such disgusting fingernails? She's chewed them down to the quick."

For once, no one laughed or even twittered.

"Go to your seat, Hildemara Waltert."

When Papa finished reading the Bible that evening, Hildemara asked if he had fought in the war. He frowned. "Why do you ask such a question?"

"Mrs. Ransom's brother died in the war."

"I was in Canada when it started."

Mama interrupted before he could go on reading the Bible. "Had your papa been in Germany, he might have been killed, too, Hildemara. Hundreds of thousands died: Frenchmen, Englishmen, Canadians, Americans, *and* Germans."

Bernie asked who started it.

Papa closed the Bible. "It's too complicated to explain, *Sohn*. One angry man shot a royal and two countries went to war. Then friends of those countries took sides, and soon the whole world was fighting."

"Except Switzerland." Mama went on sewing. "They were smart enough to stay out of it."

Papa opened his Bible again. "Yes, but they made plenty of money on it."

Hildemara couldn't make sense of it. "Did anybody you know die, Papa?"

"My father. My brothers."

Mama's eyes went wide. "This is the first I've heard of them."

Papa gave her a sad smile. "I wasn't hatched, Marta. I had a mother and father and brothers and sisters. My mother died when

I was Hildemara's age. My sisters were much older and married. I don't know what happened to any of them. I've written letters." He shook his head, his eyes moist. "Only God knows what became of them."

When Hildemara got up the next morning, she asked Mama if there would be another war. "I don't know, Hildemara." She sounded angry and impatient. She finished braiding Hildemara's hair and turned her around. "Why all these questions about the war? The war is over!"

Not for some people. She didn't want to tell Mama what Mrs. Ransom did to her every day because Mama would get mad, and if Mama got mad, Mrs. Ransom would have all the more reason to be angry with Germans.

Hildemara felt sorry for Mrs. Ransom. She must be very sad to be so angry all the time. Hildemara prayed Mrs. Ransom would find another way to get over her brother's death, and not take it out on her.

Mama tipped Hildemara's chin. "Who told you Mrs. Ransom's brother was killed in the war?"

"Elizabeth Kenney."

"Well, it's no excuse. God says not to hold a grudge. Do you understand what I'm saying to you?" When Mama's eyes grew moist, she stood abruptly and turned away. "Don't forget your lunch bucket. You'd better hurry, or Bernhard will be halfway to school before you catch up."

When Hildemara looked back, she saw Mama standing outside the tent, her arms wrapped around herself, watching. Hildemara ran down the road.

A FEW DAYS later, Papa came home, his blue eyes bright with excitement. "I've found a place for us."

Mama stopped stirring the stew over the outside cookfire and straightened. "Where?"

"It's west of Murietta, about two miles outside the town limits, across the big canal. Mrs. Miller lost her husband last year. She needs someone to work the place until her daughter finishes high school. She said she might sell the place then."

"How long before the girl finishes school, Niclas?"

"Four years, I think."

"You didn't sign a contract, did you?"

"Well, I—"

"Tell me you didn't."

"Only two years. You told me to get experience! This is the best way to get it!"

Mama walked off toward the irrigation ditch. Papa followed her. When he put his hand on her shoulder, she shook him off. He talked for a long time, but Mama kept her back to him.

Bernie stood by Hildemara, watching them. "I hope Papa wins. At least we'd have a roof over our heads instead of living in a leaky tent."

❊   ❊   ❊

The one house on the property belonged to Mrs. Miller and her daughter, Charlotte, but Mrs. Miller gave Papa permission to build a temporary shelter on the property, with conditions. She didn't want a shack. Mama wanted to speak to the woman herself when she heard Papa had to pay the expenses of building the structure, but Papa ordered her not to go near "the big house."

Over the next few days, Papa built a wooden platform, half walls, and a framework over which he and Mama stretched tent canvas. The canvas sides could be rolled up on warm days, and rolled down in an attempt to keep rain and wind out. Cold air and water still managed to seep in. Papa stacked bricks and made a lean-to where Mama could cook without jeopardizing the tent-house.

Mrs. Miller and her daughter had running water inside the house, but Mama had to use a hose near the barn and carry it bucket by bucket for tent use. Mrs. Miller also had an indoor bathroom, but Papa had to dig a deep hole and build an outhouse over it. Mrs. Miller also told Papa the children were not allowed near her flower garden. "She has prize roses and shows them at the fair each year." The widow didn't want the children near the house. "She doesn't like noise."

"Mercy, Niclas, what does she expect?"

"Peace and quiet."

"Why don't you ask her where our children can play?"

Papa winked at them. "Anywhere out of sight of the house."

Bernie climbed almond trees and caught frogs in the irrigation ditch and horned toads in the vineyard. Clotilde played with her pretty china doll. Hildemara stayed close to the tent-house and Mama.

The mulberry tree provided shade, but dropped fruit on the canvas roof, staining it with red and purple splotches. Mama grumbled about living like a vagabond. It seemed the bigger Mama's belly grew, the more her temper soured. She had no patience with anyone. Even Papa couldn't soothe her temper.

Summer came early. Mama gave Hildemara the broom and told her to keep the platform swept. Too uncomfortable to stoop, she showed Hildemara how to peel and cut vegetables, how to fry meat, how to make biscuits. Summer boiled and the ground dried up in the heat.

Mama sewed the tent seams tighter, but short of keeping the sides down all day, which made the tent like an oven, she had to leave the canvas rolled high, which allowed dust and sand to blow in all day. Buzzing flies flew circles around Mama, who sat with a swatter in her hand waiting for them to land. Hot August nights had everyone sweating on their cots.

When the baby started coming, Papa had already gone out to work the harvest. Mama called out softly. "Hildemara, go tell Mrs. Miller I'm having a baby. Maybe she'll show some compassion."

Hildemara ran to the back door and pounded. "Stop that racket!" Mrs. Miller peered out through the screen without unlocking it. "If your father needs something, tell him he'll have to wait until it cools off. I'm not coming out in this heat."

"Mama's having the baby!"

"Oh. Well. Congratulations. Go find your father and tell him. He'll have to put one of the men from the work crew in charge until he can see about your mother." She closed the door.

Hildemara ran all over the ranch looking for Papa, then finally found him loading a truck at the far side of the property. When he heard Mama was having the baby, he said something to one of the Italian workers and ran back to the tent-house. Mama lay on the platform floor, sweat pouring from her beet red face. Hildemara stood in the doorway, not knowing what to do. Mama reached out to her. "Did you talk to Mrs. Miller?"

"Yes, Mama."

"What did she say, Hildemara?"

"Congratulations."

Mama laughed wildly. "What did I tell you about that woman,

Niclas?" Mama moaned. "We'll get no help from her or that lazy daughter—" She cried out in pain.

Hildemara started to cry. "Don't die, Mama." Shaking, she sobbed. "Please don't die!"

"I'm not going to die!" She clutched Papa's shirt, her fingers white. "Oh, Jesus. Oh, God of mercy . . ." After a moment, she let out a harsh breath and fell back, panting. "Go on outside, Hildemara. We don't need you."

Papa looked around. "Where's Clotilde?"

Mama gasped, a look of horror filling her face. "Oh, mercy. I don't know!"

"I'm here, Mama." Clotilde stepped around Hildemara and held out a fistful of Mrs. Miller's perfect yellow roses.

❄ ❄ ❄

Baby Rikka turned out to be Mama's easiest child, or so Papa said. He tugged Hildemara's pigtail gently. "You were so scrawny, Mama thought you'd die before the end of your first month. But you hung on like a little monkey."

"She's still scrawny." Bernie gave her a pitying look. "Tony says she's skinny as a rail."

Rikka was so plump and sweet, even Hildemara became enamored. Clotilde liked Rikka well enough the first day or two, but when the baby consumed Mama's attention, Clotilde asked if the stork could come back and take her away again. Papa laughed long and hard over that.

"She's beautiful, Niclas." Mama smiled down at Rikka as she nursed. "She has your blonde hair and blue eyes. She's going to be even prettier than Clotilde."

Hildemara took Mama's hand mirror and ran to the barn. Sitting in an empty stall, she studied her face. Did she look like a monkey? She had Mama's hazel eyes and brown hair. She had Papa's straight nose and fair skin. Somehow, even sharing those traits, she wasn't pretty at all. She burned instead of turning brown like Bernie. Her neck looked like a stalk growing up out of the flowered gingham dress.

Hildemara wished she had been born with Elizabeth Kenney's long red curls and green eyes. Maybe then Mama would be proud of her. Maybe then Mama would speak to her in that loving voice she used with Rikka; look at her with that soft, doting smile. Instead, Mama often looked at her with a frown. She would let out her breath with impatience. She would wave her hand at Hildemara and say, "Go play somewhere else, Hildemara." She would say, "Don't be hanging on to my apron strings all the time!" Mama never said, "Look how sweet Hildemara Rose is . . . look how pretty and sweet . . ."

Maybe Mama didn't like looking at her straight, mousy brown hair and hazel eyes, though Mama had the same. Sometimes, Hildemara wished Mama would hide her disappointment and make excuses for her the way she did the others. Maybe Mama regretted having wasted the name Rose on her. She wasn't poised, pretty, or popular the way she imagined Mama's friend Rosie Gilgan had been. She didn't have Papa's fine singing voice or Mama's intellect. She made a "joyful noise to the Lord," Papa said, and she had to study hard and long to get things into her head.

Whenever Hildie stayed inside the tent-house and offered to help, Mama became impatient. "If I need help, I'll ask for it. Now go on out there! Find something to do! There's a whole world outside the door. Stop hiding in here."

She wasn't hiding. "I want to help, Mama."

"It's no help having you underfoot all day! Go! Fly, Hildemara. For heaven's sake, fly!"

Hildemara didn't know what she meant. She wasn't a bird. What had she done wrong? Maybe Mama never loved her. If Mama loved plump, pink-white babies, then having a scrawny, sickly one would have been a great disappointment. Hildemara tried to gain weight, but no matter how much she ate, she still had skinny legs and bony knees and collarbones that protruded. Clotilde, on the other hand, grew plump and pink and added inches. "Clotilde's going to be taller than Hildemara in another year," Papa said one evening, and Hildie felt even worse.

Sometimes Hildie felt her mother looking at her. When she looked back, Mama would get that troubled expression again. Hildemara wanted to ask what she'd done wrong, what she could do to make Mama smile and laugh the way she did every day with baby Rikka. Sometimes when Mama did smile at her, it didn't seem to come from pride or pleasure, but sadness, as if Hildemara just couldn't help disappointing her.

Like today.

"Why are you so quiet, Hildemara?"

She looked at Mama nursing the baby. Had her mother ever held her that tenderly? "I was just thinking about school. When does it start?"

"Not until mid-September. So you can stop worrying. You've got a little more time to play and enjoy your summer."

Hildemara started praying for Mrs. Ransom. She taught kindergarten and first grade, so Hildie had only one more year to suffer before she moved up.

❋　❋　❋

At the end of the harvest, Papa collected his share of the crop money. It wasn't as much as he had hoped, but some other farmers fared worse. Some others fared better, too, Mama said. She'd been to town. She'd talked to people. Papa told her Mrs. Miller said there were extenuating circumstances. Grim-faced, Mama sent the children to bed early. Bernie and Clotilde, having played all day, went to sleep right away, but Hildemara lay awake, troubled and listening.

Papa sighed. "We'll do better next year."

"Not here, we won't. Mrs. Miller told me this morning she expects me to cook and clean for her. Just to make things even, she said. She thinks I should be thankful for the place she's given us." Mama gave a hard laugh. "She can do her own cooking and cleaning. Or hire someone else to do it."

"I'll talk to her."

"When you do, tell her to find someone else to sharecrop her place. They should know they won't get a share of anything."

"We've got no place else to go."

"We'll start asking around. Look what you've done with this place, Niclas. And think how much you learned!"

"I didn't earn any money."

"Because Mrs. Miller isn't any different than Robert Madson. You're a hard worker, Niclas. I've watched how you manage a work crew. The men respect you. You listen to people. You take advice, from men, at least. And with all your engineer training, you've been able to fix Mrs. Miller's farm equipment and get that well pump going. We'll find a place of our own."

"And how do I pay for it?"

"*We* pay for it with the money I made from the sale of the boardinghouse."

Papa didn't speak.

"Don't look at me like that. I told you why I wasn't willing to give it to you sooner. Madson took advantage of you. So has Mrs. Miller." She gave a soft laugh. "Well, I've decided if anyone is going to take advantage of my husband, it's going to be me."

Hildemara lay in the dark, watching and listening, holding her breath until Papa spoke quietly.

"I could lose everything you saved."

"Not if you listen to me. I've talked to a lot of people around town. I've spent time at the library. I've read the back newspapers. I had to be sure this is where we belong. God may talk to you, Niclas, but He hasn't said anything to me. If I had my choice, you'd be an engineer again. We'd be living in Sacramento or San Francisco. I'd own a hotel with a restaurant! But you hated working for the railroad. If you went back to it, you'd eventually hate me, too."

"Never."

"My father took his misery out on everyone around him."

"Maybe it's just a dream."

Mama's voice softened. "I've had bigger dreams than you. And

I haven't given up on them yet. Why should you?" Her voice grew firmer. "But you'd better decide what you want right now. I can start packing tonight. We can go back to Sacramento. You can work for the railroad."

Bernie stirred. "Are they fighting again?"

"Shhhh . . ." Hildemara chewed her fingernails.

"I'm not going back to work for the railroad, Marta. Not now. Not ever."

"All right. Then while you finish out the contract here, we start looking around for land with a house. By this time next year, we can start working for ourselves." When Papa didn't answer, Mama raised her voice. "Can we do any worse than we are right now, living here? How many times have the children been sick during the cold months? And in the summer, we bake like bread in an oven. No matter how much I sweep, I can't keep the place clean! And the flies! I'm lucky I didn't die of infection when Rikka came."

Papa walked away into the night.

Mama let out her breath harshly and sat in the green-willow chair Papa had made for her. Hands folded in her lap, she waited. Hildemara fell asleep and awakened to hear them talking again, more quietly this time.

"We'll do as you suggest, Marta. I pray to God you won't hate me if I lose all your money."

"*We* won't lose it. We'll stand together and fight for it. We'll do whatever we have to do to make a go of it." She gave a faint laugh. "Think of it, Niclas. With a permanent address, I'll be able to get a library card."

Papa pulled her into his arms and kissed her. He dug his fingers into her hair and held her head back as he looked down at her. "Don't let that fire go out, Marta. The world would be too cold for me to bear." Leaning down, he said something in a low, husky voice. When he stepped away, he held out his hand. Mama hesitated, turning her head slightly as though listening for Rikka. Then she slipped her hand into Papa's, and they headed out into the night.

1923

On the last day of school, Hildemara skipped down the road, heart light. She had all summer to forget how much she hated going to school. She had been devastated by Mrs. Ransom's announcement that starting next year, the second-grade class would be combined with kindergarten and first grade, and she would be teaching all of them. Hildemara had hoped that after this year, she would have a new teacher. But then she decided it just meant God didn't want her to stop praying for Mrs. Ransom quite yet.

Hildemara had learned not to complain about Mrs. Ransom. It only made Mama more angry and changed nothing. She had prayed every morning on her way to school and prayed often while in class, especially when Mrs. Ransom's eyes fell upon her like a hawk on a mouse. When she hauled Hildemara in front of the class to make an example of her poor attire or dirty shoes or chewed fingernails or scraggly hair, Hildemara prayed the words would float out the window and off into the air, never to be remembered. The room would become so silent, Mrs. Ransom's harsh words seemed to echo, and she would tire of carrying on and tell Hildemara to go back to her chair.

Now she sang thank-you prayers until Bernie said she sounded bad enough to crack the sky wide open. So what if she had one more year in Mrs. Ransom's class before she moved on to another teacher. She could be brave for another year. She wouldn't let any tears slip down her cheeks. *"Sticks and stones may break your bones,"* the children chanted, *"but words will never hurt you."* She wondered whoever came up with such a thing because it wasn't true at all. Sometimes Mrs. Ransom said things that ripped at Hildemara's heart and left her hurting for days.

Papa said to forgive, but forgiveness wasn't easy. Not when the same thing happened over and over again.

Summer passed in a haze of heat. Hildemara did chores around the house. She fed the chickens and collected the eggs, washed dishes and helped weed the garden. She took Papa's lunch out to him while Mama tried to batten down the canvas sides of the tent to keep the dust from blowing in on a napping Rikka.

As school approached, Hildemara worried and prayed continuously that Mrs. Ransom wouldn't be mean to Clotilde, who would be in kindergarten this year. Maybe Mrs. Ransom just didn't like ugly children, any more than Mama did. Hildemara prayed her younger sister's pretty blue eyes and blonde hair would soften Mrs. Ransom's heart in a way her own respectful silence and obedience never had.

She decided not to warn Clotilde about Mrs. Ransom. She didn't want her to have nightmares and start chewing her nails, too. When they bathed in the big tub together the night before school started, she told Clotilde to wash behind her ears and around her neck. Clotilde splashed soapy water in her face.

The next morning, Hildemara felt sick to her stomach, but she didn't say anything. She knew Mama would send her to school anyway, and she didn't want to answer questions. Bernie ran ahead to meet his friends. Mama had put Hildemara in charge of Clotilde, so Hildie allowed her younger sister to set the pace. "Stay on the road, Clotilde! Don't get dusty."

"You want a wagon to run over me?"

"You have to keep your shoes clean!"

"I can get dirty if I want!" Sticking her tongue out, she kicked dust all over Hildemara.

"Stop it!"

Clotilde took off running, and Hildemara ran to catch up. Laughing, Clotilde shrieked and ran faster. Hildemara tripped and fell headlong on the macadam, scraping her hands, elbows, and knees. Shocked by the pain, she pushed herself up. When she looked at her hands, she saw tiny pebbles under the bleeding skin. Now what was she going to do?

Clotilde ran back. "Ohhhh." She looked at Hildie's knees and elbows.

Still crying, Hildemara dusted herself off as best she could. "We're going to be late." She limped alongside her little sister. "When we're called to line up, we have to be in alphabetical order. There's no one after Waltert. So we're last."

When they arrived at school, Hildie went into the girls' bathroom to wash. Her hands stung like fire. She dabbed cold water on her knees, dismayed to see how the blood had already dripped down her legs and stained her socks. The blood from her scraped elbows had gotten on her dress as well. What would Mrs. Ransom have to say about that? What would Mama say?

Giving up, she went outside, worried Clotilde might be frightened on her first day of school. But Clotilde had already met a girl her own age and was playing hopscotch.

Mrs. Ransom came out. "Kindergarten, first, and second, line up here!" The other children ran to make two lines, boys and girls. Hildemara limped after them, taking last place in line behind Clotilde, who stood head high marching in place until the lines filed into the classroom.

Mrs. Ransom looked at them as they entered. "Another Waltert."

"Yes, ma'am." Hildemara flashed a bright smile that seemed to disarm Mrs. Ransom.

"And this one is pretty."

Hildemara's name had been taped on a front-row desk this year. Heart pounding with dread, Hildemara put her hand over her heart, recited the Pledge of Allegiance with the class, sang "My Country, 'Tis of Thee," and slid cautiously into her seat so she wouldn't bump her aching knees. She prayed Mrs. Ransom wouldn't say anything mean to Clotilde.

She kept glancing back as Mrs. Ransom checked each child's hands. Clotilde held her hands with limp wrists, turning them up and down so Mrs. Ransom could see. Mrs. Ransom looked dubious, but didn't say anything. Letting out her breath in relief, Hildemara turned around and faced the front of the class.

"Hildemara." Mrs. Ransom stood beside her desk. Head down, Hildemara held her hands out, palms down. "Turn them over." When she did, Mrs. Ransom gasped. "Your hands are a mess. Go wash them."

"I did."

"Don't talk back to me." Mrs. Ransom grabbed Hildemara by the hair, yanking her from her seat. Hildemara banged her scraped knee on the desk and cried out in pain.

Clotilde ran at Mrs. Ransom, screaming, "Leave my sister alone!" She grabbed the teacher's skirt and yanked. When Mrs. Ransom let go of Hildemara and turned, Clotilde kicked her hard in the shins. "You're hurting my sister!" Clotilde stomped on Mrs. Ransom's toes.

The class erupted in laughter and shouts.

Terrified at what Mrs. Ransom would do to Clotilde, Hildemara grabbed her sister by the hand and ran for the door. Mrs. Ransom cried out. Hildemara didn't stop running until they were around the side of the building.

"Why did you do that, Clotilde? Why?"

"She hurt you! She's mean! I hate her!"

"Don't say that! Papa says we aren't supposed to hate anyone." She tried to calm her sister. "Papa said people were mean to Jesus, too, and He didn't kick anyone."

Clotilde started to blubber. "I don't want to be crucified." Her blue eyes became glassy with tears. "Is Mrs. Ransom going to pound nails in our hands and feet?"

"We have to be kind to Mrs. Ransom no matter what she does. Her brother got killed in the war, Clotilde. She hates us because Papa's German. We have to pray for her."

Clotilde's chin wobbled. "Papa didn't kill anyone."

"She doesn't know that, Clotilde. She's very sad and angry. Jesus prayed for the people who hurt Him. I've been praying for Mrs. Ransom for two years. We have to keep praying for her. Mrs. Ransom is just like those people who killed Jesus. She doesn't know what she's doing." Hildemara heard a strangled sound behind her and her heart raced in fear. Glancing up, she saw Mrs. Ransom standing at the corner of the building, her hands covering her mouth, her eyes wild with pain.

Hildemara put herself in front of Clotilde. "She didn't mean to do it, Mrs. Ransom."

Mrs. Ransom uttered that awful sound again. When she reached out, Hildemara grabbed Clotilde's hand and ran.

"Hildemara!" Mrs. Ransom called after them. "Wait!"

Hildemara and Clotilde kept running.

❋   ❋   ❋

"Do we have to go back to school tomorrow?" Clotilde sat beside Hildemara. They had hidden in the first orchard after leaving town. Hildemara said they couldn't go home. They had to go back when school let out, or Bernie would be looking for them.

"I don't know what we're going to do." Hildemara wiped tears away with the back of her hand.

"Is Mama going to be mad at me?"

"Mama put me in charge of you. Remember? She'll be mad at *me*."

"I'll tell her why I kicked Mrs. Ransom."

Hildemara sniffled. "That will just make everything worse." When she pulled her legs up, her knees throbbed with pain. Sobbing, Hildie didn't know what to do or where to go.

Clotilde snuggled close to her. "Don't cry, Hildie. I'm sorry."

They waited all morning and went back to school in the early afternoon. They stood at a distance, hiding behind the trunk of an old elm tree. The children came outside for their last recess. Mr. Loyola, the principal, stood on the playground. Mrs. Ransom was nowhere in sight. Whenever he looked their way, Hildemara and Clotilde ducked back behind the tree. Finally school let out, and Bernie came outside the fence.

"We're over here, Bernie." Hildemara waved from their hiding place.

Bernie ran to them. "Boy, are you two in trouble! People have been out looking for you all day. Where have you been?"

Hildemara shrugged.

Bernie looked at Clotilde. "I heard you attacked Mrs. Ransom."

Hildemara and Clotilde looked at one another and didn't say anything. They had already agreed to a pact of silence.

"Well, come on then. We'd better go home."

The three of them hurried across the highway and walked through town, Hildemara dreading every step, wondering what Mama and Papa would say when Bernie told them what he had heard. They had just turned onto the road out of town when Mr. Loyola pulled up alongside them in his motorcar. "Climb in, children. I'll take you home."

Bernie jumped in. "This is my first time in an automobile!" Clotilde climbed in behind him just as eagerly. Hildemara didn't want to get in. She didn't want to go home either. She didn't know what to do.

Mr. Loyola leaned forward, looking past Bernie and Clotilde. "You too, Hildemara." Feeling doomed, Hildemara sat in back next to Clotilde. Bernie asked all kinds of questions about the car on the way home. Clotilde bounced excitedly, Mrs. Ransom forgotten.

Mama came out of the tent-house when Mr. Loyola pulled into Mrs. Miller's yard. She looked surprised when Bernie jumped out of the motorcar, and then Clotilde. Hildemara

climbed out last, dizzy and feeling sick to her stomach. She dared
a glance at Mama.

The principal took his hat off and held it in both hands. "May
I speak with you, Mrs. Waltert?"

Bernie had already run off for the orchard to find Papa,
undoubtedly eager to tell him about the ride and what had
happened at school. Clotilde stood beside Hildemara, looking
from Mr. Loyola to Mama and back again.

"Go on and play, you two." Clotilde didn't need a second invitation. She took off after Bernie, leaving Hildemara standing alone
and feeling exposed. Mama gave her an odd look and then forced
a pleasant smile at Mr. Loyola. "Why don't you come inside, Mr.
Loyola? You'll have to sit on a cot. We don't have any furniture.
Shall I fix some coffee?"

"No, ma'am. I won't stay too long."

Hildemara sat with her back against the wall of the pump
house. Mama and Mr. Loyola talked for a long time. When the
principal came outside, he looked around the yard. Raking his
hand back through his hair, he put on his hat, got in his car, and
drove away.

Mama didn't come outside for a long time. Hildemara pushed
herself up and crossed the yard. Mama sat on a cot, her face in her
hands. "I'm sorry, Mama."

"What are *you* sorry about?" Mama sounded angry. She
dropped her hands in her lap and raised her head. Eyes red,
face blotchy, Mama winced. "What happened to your knees,
Hildemara?"

"I fell on the road."

"Where else are you hurting?"

Hildie showed her elbows and hands.

"And that's all?"

Hildemara didn't know what her mother wanted her to say.

"We're going to have to clean those wounds or they'll get
infected." Mama grabbed the water bucket and went out to fill it.
Hildemara didn't think her day could get any worse until Mama

came back. "It's going to hurt, Hildemara, and there's nothing we can do about it." She gave her Papa's razor strop. "We have to get the pebbles and dirt out, then scrub with soap before putting on antiseptic. You bite down hard on that strop when you feel like screaming or Mrs. Miller will think I'm out here beating my children."

When it was over, Hildemara lay limp on her cot, drained of tears; hands, knees, and elbows on fire.

"We'll put on bandages when the wounds dry."

Papa came in a few minutes later, Bernie and Clotilde trailing behind him. "How is she?"

"She's a mess!" Mama's voice broke. She tipped Clotilde's head and leaned down to kiss her. "At least we have one girl who knows how to fight back!" Turning away, she went outside. Papa went outside and talked with her. When he came back, Mama wasn't with him.

Hildemara lay on her cot, watching Mama walk away. She had disappointed her again.

Clotilde peered out the tent-house door. "Where's Mama going?"

"She's taking a walk. Don't bother her. Go on outside for a while. Everything is fine. Bernhard, make certain she doesn't get near Mrs. Miller's roses." Papa lifted Hildemara carefully onto his lap. He brushed the hair back from her face and kissed her cheeks. "Mrs. Ransom won't be your teacher anymore. She went to Mr. Loyola after you and Clotilde ran away. She quit her job, *Liebling*."

"She hates me, Papa. She's always hated me."

"I don't think she hates you anymore."

Hildie's mouth wobbled and she burst out crying again. "I prayed for her, Papa. I wanted Mrs. Ransom to like me. I prayed and prayed and my prayers never changed anything."

Papa pressed her head gently against his shoulder. "Prayers changed you, Hildemara. You learned to love your enemy."

1924

Papa heard about a farm for sale on Hopper Road, two miles northwest of Murietta. When he went to town for supplies, he came back the long way to see it; he talked to Mama about it. After seeing it for herself, Mama bargained with the bank over the property, but—"They wouldn't budge on the price, so I left."

"Well, that's it, then." Papa despaired.

"We're just getting started, Niclas. That place has stood fallow for two years. No one has made an offer. If we wait, they'll come around."

While they waited, Mama told Papa to make up a list of what he would need in the way of equipment and tools to work the farm, as Mama made up her own list of needed items. She went into town three times over the next week, but never set foot in the bank. She went again the following week, and the banker came outside to talk with her.

"He wanted to negotiate." Mama laughed. "I told him I'd done my negotiating. The place isn't worth any more than we offered."

"So? What did he say?"

"We can have it."

Both Mama and Papa went back two days later to sign the papers. They came home arguing. "We could've paid the full amount in cash and not had a mortgage."

"You have to spend money to make it, Niclas. We're not going to run up debt at the hardware store and the general store and the feed store. Let the bank carry the paper for a few years, not ordinary folks who work hard to keep food on the table and a roof over their heads."

Papa went out and bought a sorrel farm horse and sturdy wagon. He had just started dismantling the tent-house when Mrs. Miller came outside and said Papa had deserted her in her time of need. She said a decent man wouldn't leave a widow and her daughter to fend for themselves, then claimed Papa had no right to take what belonged to her, and he had better leave the tent-house exactly where it was or she'd have the sheriff after him.

Mama held her temper until the last demand. Then she stepped between them. "Now that you've had your say, I'll have mine." Papa cringed as Mama went nose to nose with Mrs. Miller. When Mrs. Miller stepped back, Mama stepped forward. "Ring up the sheriff, Mrs. Miller. *Please!* I'd like to show him all the receipts for everything we've had to buy over the last two years just to keep a canvas roof over our heads. People ought to know how you and that lazy daughter of yours sit around all day doing nothing but stuffing your faces." For every step Mrs. Miller took backward, Mama advanced, hands in tight fists. When Mrs. Miller turned and ran, Mama shouted after her. "Maybe I'll post a notice in town. *Looking for work? Don't go to the Miller place!*"

Hildemara shook with fear. "Will she call the sheriff now, Papa? Will he come and take you and Mama to jail?"

Mama gave her *such* a look. "We're in the right, Hildemara Rose." She gave Papa a hard glare, too. "Scripture says a worker is due his wages. Doesn't it? It's about time the ox got his meal!" She pulled a stack of receipts out of one of the boxes. "And I have the papers to prove we haven't stolen one thing." She kicked her foot out. "Not even the dust!" She stuffed the receipts in her pocket and went back to packing.

When everything was ready to go, Papa and Mama rode on the high seat of the wagon, baby Rikki on Mama's lap. Hildemara climbed into the back with Bernie and Clotilde. They whooped like wild Indians as they drove off Mrs. Miller's place. Mama laughed. They stopped in town at the hardware store and Papa bought shovels, rakes, hoes, pruners, short and tall ladders, large and small saws, a bucket of nails, and sailcloth. He placed an order for poles, baling wire, and lumber to be delivered later. Mama went to Hardesty's, her own list to fill: a sewing machine, buckets of paint, brushes, and a bolt of yellow and green chintz.

On the way to the new place, the wagon bed piled high with all their purchases, Clotilde pressed in between Papa and Mama on the high seat, while Mama held Rikki. Hildie followed on foot with Bernie. When Papa turned in to the yard, Hildemara thanked Jesus she wouldn't have to walk any farther. She felt a rush of excitement at the sight of a barn, an open shed with an old plow, a windmill, and a house with a towering chinaberry tree in the front yard. A huge century plant grew on the opposite side of the driveway.

"All this belongs to us?"

"Us and the bank," Papa called back.

Hildie ran up the steps, but the front door had a padlock. The windows had been covered with plywood to protect them from vandals, so she couldn't see inside. She ran to the end of the porch. "An orange tree! We have an orange tree!" She didn't care that all the fruit lay rotten on the ground.

"Hildemara!" Mama called as Papa drove toward the barn. "Help unload the wagon!"

As Papa handed tools down, Mama, Bernie, and Hildemara stacked them against the wall. Clotilde sat on the ground holding baby Rikka in her lap. Papa unloaded Rikka's crib and carried it to the back door of the house, where Mama and Bernie had stacked the folded cots. A huge California bay laurel tree grew thirty feet from the back of the house, its massive arms stretching leafy branches in a hundred directions.

Mama had the keys to the padlock. Papa took them from her. Then he took Rikka and handed her off to Hildemara. "Stand with your brother, Clotilde." He removed the padlock and tucked it and the keys into his pocket. Grinning, he scooped Mama up in his arms, shouldered the door open, and carried her inside. Muscles straining, Hildemara lugged Rikka up the back steps behind Bernie and Clotilde.

Papa set Mama on her feet. He gave her a quick, firm kiss and whispered in her ear. As he headed for the back door, Mama's cheeks turned bright red.

Hildemara stood awed. The house had one front bedroom, a large rectangular living room, a kitchen, and a potbelly stove. "It's so big."

Mama looked around and sighed. "I used to own a three-story boardinghouse with a big dining room and parlor." Shaking her head, she went to work. She took Rikka from Hildemara and jerked her chin at Bernie. "Help Papa bring in the cots. Hildemara, you can start sweeping out the bedroom. Start at the far wall and sweep toward the door and then out the front so it won't blow right back in again."

As soon as Papa brought the crib inside, Mama put Rikka down for a nap. Mama opened the door of the potbelly stove, took one look inside, and ran out the back door. "Niclas! I need a hammer to take the plywood off the windows, and you have to take the chimney pipe apart! It needs to be cleaned out or we'll have the house burn down over our heads!"

Papa came in with a bucket of coal. He'd found a bin full in the barn. When Mama finished cleaning out the stove, she started a fire. She left the door open to warm the house, warning Clotilde to stay away. Then she went to work scrubbing the kitchen. "We won't get it all done today, but we'll get a good start."

It started to rain before Papa and Bernie returned from looking over the property. They went right out again after lunch. When Rikka awakened and fussed, Mama nursed her and then told Clotilde to play with her doll and keep Rikka entertained. Mama got on her knees and scraped hunks of congealed grease off the inside walls of the oven and dumped them into a bucket. "Who could cook on a stove like this? *Pigs!*"

When Mama finally finished, she built another fire in the cookstove. By then, Hildemara had finished sweeping and been put to work scrubbing the floor. "Back of the room to the front door, Hildemara. Don't start in the middle. Use both hands on that brush, and put your back into it!"

At last they could pump water into the kitchen sink and not have to tote buckets from a well. And the house was blissfully warm with two fires going. No more wind and rain coming in through canvas seams.

Papa and Bernie returned at dusk and hung their coats on hooks by the back door. Papa pumped water into a bucket and took it out to where he and Bernie washed in the cold January wind. Mama opened cans of pork and beans. "Find the plates in the trunk, Hildemara. Lay out the blue blanket and set things out. When you're done with that, put another shovel of coal in the stove."

Exhausted, Bernie sprawled in front of the potbelly stove. Edgy, Papa paced. Mama glanced over her shoulder. "How do things look?"

"Nothing has been pruned in years."

"Good thing it's winter, then. You can start now."

"Some of the trees are diseased, some dead."

"Anything that might affect the rest of the orchard?"

"I don't know." He rubbed the back of his neck. "I'll find out."

"If you have to pull out the trees, we can plant alfalfa."

"Twenty trees at the most, but alfalfa is a good idea. There's room enough to grow what we need for two horses in the strip of land alongside the road."

Bernie sat up. "Are we getting another horse, Papa?" His eyes gleamed.

"No." Mama spoke before Papa could answer. "We are not getting another horse. Not yet. We're getting a cow, and you and your sisters are going to learn how to milk her." She looked up at Papa. "You'll need to build a henhouse first thing. I'm going to buy a rooster and half a dozen hens."

"We can't do everything at once. The windmill needs repairs. I'll put up a shower house in spring. We can mount a tank on top. Good reserve, and the sun will warm the water."

"Warm showers can wait. The cow and chickens come first. Milk, eggs, and meat, Niclas. We all have to be strong enough to work. I'll start laying out a vegetable garden tomorrow."

Papa and Mama took the bedroom. Baby Rikka in her crib and Hildemara, Bernie, and Clotilde on cots slept in the living room. Hildemara lay curled up as content as a cat in front of the fire, even with rain pattering against the roof and windows.

Mama came out of the bedroom just as dawn lightened the horizon. She swung her shawl around her shoulders and went out the back door, heading for the outhouse. Papa came out a few minutes later, pulling up his suspenders. He took his coat from the hook and went outside. Hildemara heard Mama and Papa talking outside the back door. Mama came back inside alone, bringing a rush of cold winter air with her. She started the fire in the stove and pumped water into the coffeepot. She opened the potbelly stove and stoked the fire.

"I know you're awake, Hildemara. Get dressed, fold up your cot, and put it on the front porch." Mama shook Bernie awake.

"Where's Papa?"

"Working."

And they would be, too, when Papa finished building the henhouse and hutches for the rabbits Mama wanted to buy.

❄ ❄ ❄

It was a long, cold, two-mile walk to school, and it rained most of January. Bernie didn't care that his pant legs were caked with mud, but Hildie stood in line with her classmates, mortified and waiting for Miss Hinkle, the new teacher, to say something about her mud-soaked shoes and socks and the dirty hem of her coat and dress.

"I hear you have a new home, Hildemara."

"Yes, ma'am. It's on Hopper Road."

"Congratulations! That's a long way to walk in the rain. Take off your shoes and socks and put them by the heater." A few, like Elizabeth Kenney, had nice clean shoes beneath pairs of nice yellow galoshes they lined up by the door. Relieved, Hildemara saw she wasn't the only student who had shoes and socks to dry.

It was still raining when school let out. Hildemara felt damp to the skin despite the rain slicker and hat she'd kept pulled down over her head. Mama shook her head when they came in. "You look like drowned rats."

Hildemara sat silent through dinner, too tired to eat. Mama leaned over and put her hand against Hildie's forehead. "Finish what's on your plate and set up your cot. You're going to bed right after dinner." Mama scooped more potato and leek soup for Papa. "We need a table and chairs."

"We can't afford furniture."

"You're an engineer. You can figure out how to build a table and chairs and a bedframe. I already ordered a mattress from a catalog at Hardesty's General Store, and a sofa and two chairs."

Papa stared at her. "Anything else?"

"Two reading lamps."

Papa paled. "How much did all that cost?"

"The floor is clean, Niclas, but I'd rather eat at a table. Wouldn't you? It would be nice to have a comfortable place to sit and read in the evenings after a long, hard day of working in the vineyard and orchard." She cut off a piece of freshly baked bread. Slathering it with apricot jam, she held it out as though making a peace offering. "It isn't enough to just live inside a box with a woodstove."

Papa took the proffered bread offering. "Seems to me a lot of money is going out and nothing coming in."

Mama looked at him for a tense moment, mouth tight, but she didn't say another word.

For some reason, winter always made Mama pensive and quick to anger. Sometimes she would sit and stare into space. Papa would sit beside her and try to draw her into conversation, but she would shake her head and refuse to talk, other than to say January brought back memories she would rather forget.

Hildemara's birthday was in January. Sometimes Mama forgot that, too. But Papa would remind her, and she would go through the motions of celebrating. Long, cloudy days made Mama go quiet and cold like the weather.

❄ ❄ ❄

A month after they moved onto the property, Papa mounted a big brass bell next to the back door. When Clotilde reached up to pull the cord, Mama slapped her hand and told her to listen to Papa. "This is for emergencies only," Papa told them in a grim voice. "It is not a toy. You ring it only if someone is hurt or the house is on fire. When I hear it, I'll come running. But if I come and find someone rang a false alarm, they'll have a very sore bottom." He pinched Clotilde lightly on the nose and looked from Bernie to Hildemara. *Versteht ihr das?*

"*Ja*, Papa."

Hildemara lay in bed that night imagining all the terrible things that might happen. What if the potbelly stove caught on fire? What if Clotilde tried to put coal in and fell in headfirst? Hildemara smelled smoke. She saw flames coming out the windows and licking up the outside of the house. Crying out, she ran around the outside of the house. She tried to reach the bell cord, but it was too high. She jumped, but still couldn't reach it. She could hear Mama and Clotilde and Rikki screaming.

Mama shook her awake. "Hildemara!" She put her cool hand on Hildemara's forehead. "Just a dream." Pulling her shawl around her shoulders more tightly, she sat on the floor. "You were crying again. What were you dreaming this time?"

Hildemara remembered, but didn't want to say. What if speaking it aloud made it come true?

Mama stroked her hair and sighed. "What am I going to do about you, Hildemara Rose? What am I going to do?" Standing, she leaned down and brushed a light kiss against Hildie's forehead. Pulling the blanket up, she tucked it in firmly around Hildie. "Pray God gives you better dreams." She crossed the room and quietly closed the bedroom door behind her.

❄ ❄ ❄

Papa hired four men to help him prune the almond trees and make burn piles in the alleyways between the rows. Then they went to work pulling up old posts and putting in new ones on which they strung wire. They pruned the vines and tied the healthy shoots, wrapping them so they wouldn't freeze.

While Papa and Italian day laborers worked on the orchard and vineyard, Mama worked on the house. Every room got a fresh coat of yellow paint. The windows had flowered chintz curtains. The mattress, sofa, chairs, and standing lamps arrived. Her trunk became a coffee table. Papa built the bedframe. When he said he was too busy to make a table and chairs, Mama walked to town and ordered them from Hardesty's catalog.

Papa put his head in his hands when she told him. She put her hand on his shoulder. "It cost less than if you'd bought the materials and built them yourself." He got up and left the house.

Mama didn't have much to say for the next few days. Neither did Papa.

"We should build a big porch bedroom along the back," Mama said over dinner.

"We're not spending another dime. It's going to be months before this place produces anything but weeds, and we have to pay taxes."

Not even Bernie talked after that.

Hildemara could hear Mama and Papa talking in low, intense

voices behind the closed bedroom door. "Well, what did you expect? It would be easier having your own place?" Papa's voice stayed low, indistinct.

The next evening, Mama turned their world upside down. After grace, she scooped meat loaf, mashed potatoes, and carrots onto a plate and gave it to Bernie to pass to Papa. When everyone was served, she prepared her own plate. "I have a job at Herkner's Bakery. I start tomorrow morning."

Papa sputtered. Coughing, he put down his knife and fork and took a gulp of water. "A job!" He coughed again. "What are you talking about? A job!"

"We can talk about it later." Mama cut up meat loaf for Rikka.

Papa glowered at her through dinner. Mama cleared dishes and told Hildemara to keep out from underfoot. "Go and sit with Papa. He'll want to read to you." Papa always read the Bible after dinner. Tonight, he told them all to go to bed. Hildie watched and listened silently from her cot.

"Let me do them. You're going to break something."

"You're not going to work," he said in a low, hot voice.

"I'm already working. This way I'll get paid!"

He grabbed a wet dish from her hand, dried it, and shoved it in the cupboard. "We need to talk. Now!"

She wiped off her apron and tossed it on the counter, marching into the bedroom. Papa closed the door firmly behind him when he followed.

Clotilde started to cry.

"I've never seen Papa that mad." Bernie flipped over on his cot. "Shut up, Cloe." He put his pillow over his head.

Hildemara listened.

"What about Rikka? She's still nursing!"

"She'll come with me. I can nurse her as well in a bakery as I can at home. Hedda Herkner has a playpen she used for her son, Fritz."

"You didn't ask me."

"Ask you?" Mama's voice rose. "I didn't ask because I knew what you'd say. I talked to Hedda the day after Mrs. Miller told me she expected me to cook and clean for her. I told her I worked for a bakery in Steffisburg. I can make tarts and *beignets* and—"

"Make them for your family!"

"I'll be paid by the hour, and we'll have as much bread as we need."

"No, Marta. You're my wife! You didn't even consult me before you went off and—"

"Consult you? Oh, you mean the way you consulted me before you left for the wheat fields?" Mama's voice kept rising. "You never thought enough of my opinion to ask for it! You thought nothing of signing my life away, first to Madson, and then to Mrs. Miller and her good-for-nothing daughter!"

"Keep your voice down! You'll wake the children."

Mama lowered her voice. "We need another way to bring in money besides farming. We all have to make sacrifices."

"Who's going to do the washing, the cooking, the sewing, the—?"

"Don't worry. The work will get done. The children are going to learn to pitch in. Bernhard, too! Just because he's a boy doesn't mean he can go off and do as he pleases while the girls do all the work. Someday he's going to be on his own. Until he finds a wife to take care of him, he'll have to cook his own meals, wash his own shirts and underwear and pants, and sew on his own buttons!"

"My son is not doing housework! You leave Bernhard to me. Do what you want with the girls."

"Isn't that always the way?" Mama's voice had a strident edge Hildemara had never heard before. "The son always comes first. Well, so be it, as long as Bernhard learns how to be a man and not a master!" Mama came flying out of the bedroom, throwing her shawl around her shoulders. The front door closed firmly behind her.

Hildemara sat up. "Go back to sleep, Hildemara." Papa went out the front door after Mama.

Hildemara chewed her lip, listening. She didn't hear footsteps going down the stairs, but she heard voices again. Papa spoke low. He wasn't angry anymore. She crept out of her cot and went to the front window. Papa sat beside Mama on the steps.

Hildemara crept back to bed and prayed until she went to sleep.

When she awakened, Papa sat at the table, reading his Bible. He got up and poured himself another cup of coffee. Hildie shivered as she sat up. "Where's Mama?"

"She had to be at the bakery before dawn. She took Rikka. When you have your lunch hour, Mama wants you to come to the bakery. She'll have something for the three of you."

When they arrived, Mrs. Herkner called out to Mama. Hildemara saw Rikki asleep in a playpen behind the counter. Mama came out of the back of the bakery wearing a white apron with *HB* embroidered on a pocket. "Oh, heavens, Hildemara! Didn't you bother to brush your hair this morning?" Mama waved them behind the counter and into the back workroom. "Sit right there." She gave them each a thick slice of fresh bread, a wedge of cheese, and an apple, then found a brush in her purse. Planting a hand on top of Hildemara's head, she brushed hard and fast while Hildemara tried to eat her lunch. "Hold still." Hildemara's scalp burned, but when she put her hands up, Mama rapped her knuckles with the brush. "How on earth can you get so many knots in your hair?"

"I'll do better tomorrow, Mama."

"You sure will."

When Hildemara arrived home from school, Mama got out her scissors. She took a chair and set it on the porch outside. "Sit down. I'm cutting your hair short. You can't go to school looking like you did this morning."

"No, Mama. Please." What would the other students say if she showed up with short hair?

"Sit down!"

Mama started cutting, and Hildemara started crying.

"Stop blubbering, Hildemara. Hold still! I don't want to make any more of a mess of it." Hunks of dark brown hair fell on the floor. Frowning, Mama looked her over and decided to cut bangs. "I need to even this side up." After a few more snips, Mama pressed her mouth tightly and fluffed Hildemara's hair on one side and then the other. "That's the best I can do."

When Mama turned to put her scissors back in her sewing box, Hildemara felt her hair. Mama had cut it all the way up to her ears! Sobbing, Hildemara fled to the barn and hid in the back stall. She didn't come out until Mama called her to dinner.

Bernie looked horrified when Hildie came in the back. "Holy cow! What did you do to your hair?"

Mama scowled. "That's enough, Bernhard."

Clotilde giggled. Hildemara stared at her resentfully. Clotilde still had long, curling blonde hair. No one would laugh at her at school.

Papa sat at the head of the table, staring at her. "What happened to your hair, Hildemara?"

Hildemara couldn't hold the tears back. "Mama cut it."

"For mercy's sake, Marta, why?"

Mama's face reddened. "It's not that short."

Clotilde giggled again. "She looks like the little boy on the paint cans."

Mama served Hildemara after Papa. "It'll grow out in no time."

Hildemara knew it was as close to an apology as she would ever get from her mother. Not that it helped. Her hair wouldn't grow out in time for school tomorrow.

Just as she feared, the students laughed when they saw her. Tony Reboli asked if she had put her head in a lawn mower. Bernie punched him. Tony swung and missed. They started shoving each other around the playground. Miss Hinkle came outside and told them to stop at once. "What started it?"

Tony pointed. "Little Sis's hair!" He laughed. So did others.

Miss Hinkle turned to Hildie. She looked shocked for a second and then smiled. "I think it's very becoming, Hildemara." She leaned down and whispered, "My mother used to cut my hair short, too."

Hildemara took last place in the line of girls. Elizabeth stepped out of line and waited for her. "I like it, Hildie. I like it very much." Hildemara felt a wave of relief. Anything Elizabeth said she liked, everyone else liked, too.

When break came, Clotilde went off to play on the bars with her friends. Hildemara sat on the bench and watched Elizabeth playing hopscotch with several other girls. Gathering her courage, Hildie walked across the playground. Heart thumping, she clasped her hands behind her back. "May I play, too?"

Elizabeth smiled broadly. "You can be on my team."

That night, Hildemara lay awake, feeling euphoric. Mama sat at the kitchen table, the kerosene lamp burning, the stack of books on American history that she'd borrowed from the library sitting in front of her while she wrote a letter. Papa had gone to bed an hour ago. Bernie snored softly. Clotilde lay curled on her side, facing away from the lamp. Mama looked sad as she wrote.

Hildemara got up and tiptoed to the edge of light. Mama raised her head. "How was school today? You didn't say much at dinner."

Bernie and Clotilde usually dominated the table conversation. "I made a friend."

Mama straightened. "Is that so?"

"Elizabeth Kenney is the prettiest and most popular girl in class. You can ask Clotilde."

"I believe you, Hildemara." Her eyes shone.

"Elizabeth said she's always liked me. She wants me to go to church with her sometime. Would that be all right?"

"Depends on the church."

"I told her we were Lutherans. She didn't know what that was and I didn't know how to explain. Her family goes to the Methodist church on Elm Street."

"They probably think we're heathens. I think you'd better go."

"I'll tell her tomorrow." Hildemara climbed back onto her cot. Mama took up her fountain pen and began writing again, more quickly this time. "Mama?"

"Hmmmm?"

"Elizabeth said she liked my hair."

Mama's eyes glistened moist in the lamplight. "Sometimes all you need is one true friend, Hildemara Rose, just one you can depend upon to love you no matter what. You did well in finding one."

Hildemara snuggled down under her blankets, feeling for the first time as though she had Mama's approval.

❄ ❄ ❄

Dear Rosie,

After two years of hard work and living in a dusty tent, we finally have a place of our own. Mrs. Miller couldn't cheat us out of the profits because I was on hand when the crops were sold and collected Niclas's share before she could find a way to spend it on her worthless daughter.

Our place is two miles outside of Murietta, which is not too far for the children to walk to school. We have twenty acres of almond trees and twenty acres of wine grapes with an irrigation canal running along the back of the property. The house and barn are in need of repairs, but Niclas is already at work on fixing the roof. He fixed the windmill yesterday. I couldn't watch, worried the whole thing would tumble down, him with it.

Hildemara is very excited about running water inside the house. She won't have to tote water anymore. She gained some muscle from the work, which is good. She never complains. I push and she always yields, unlike Clotilde, who sticks out her chin and argues over everything. Even Rikka knows how to get her way. I hope for more fight from Hildemara. She must learn to stand up for herself, or everyone will walk all over her. Niclas thinks I am harder on her than the others, but for her sake, I must be. You know what I fear the most. . . .

❄ ❄ ❄

Hildemara learned Mama was not one to let any opportunity pass by. After six months at the Herkners' bakery, Mama knew most of the people in town. But she took time on the long walk into Murietta to get to know people along Hopper Road.

"These people are our neighbors, Hildemara. And it pays to be neighborly. You listen, too, Clotilde. Always keep your eyes and ears open to learn whatever you can. If they need help, we'll extend a helping hand. It'll come back someday if we ever get into trouble."

Clotilde stopped kicking up the dust. "What kind of trouble, Mama?"

"You never know. And never visit empty-handed. Remember that most of all." One day she would drop off a loaf of bread to Widow Cullen, the next a bag of rolls to the Aussie bachelor Abrecan Macy, or a jar of strawberry preserves to the Johnsons.

"You need to get to know people, Hildemara. You can't be hanging on to my skirts forever. You, too, Clotilde. Let the neighbors get to know you."

"They know Bernie!" Clotilde grinned.

"Well, you and your sisters aren't going to be athletes. Rikka, stay with us." Rikka was hunkered down, studying a flower. She picked it and carried it along after them. "Everyone has something to teach you."

Mama tried to make friends with everyone, especially the immigrants. Greeks, Swedes, Portuguese, and Danes, even the scowling old Abrecan took time to talk with Mama when she came by. After the first few meetings, she bartered and bargained with every one of them. She traded chickens for cheese with the Danes and Greeks. She traded shelled almonds and raisins for lamb from the Aussie. When the milk cow dried up, Mama traded vegetables for milk from the small Portuguese dairy just down the road and traded the cow to the butcher as credit for meat.

Mama liked the Johnsons best of all. Swedes from Dalarna, they had hospitable ways, always offering a cup of coffee and a sweet while passing time. Mama liked their cozy red house with white trim. Clotilde and Rikka liked the profusion of blues, reds, yellows, and pinks surrounding it. Hildemara just liked to sit by Mama and listen to the conversation between the two women. Carl Johnson and his two sons, Daniel and Edwin, tended the orchard of peach trees. Mama traded quince jelly for preserved peaches. One jar of Mama's quince jelly yielded four mason jars of Anna Johnson's peaches.

Hildemara always slowed when walking by the Johnsons' place, drinking in the rose scent. Mrs. Johnson was as fussy about dead-heading her flowers as Papa was about getting rid of every weed on their property.

"Hello, Hildemara." Mrs. Johnson stood from where she had been thinning marigolds and brushed off her skirt. "Your mama already came by this morning. I was just putting on the coffee when she went by."

"Yes, ma'am. She goes in early Tuesdays and Thursdays to make the *beignets* and *Torten*."

"They'll all be gone by noon. She brought me cardamom bread last week. Your mama is a good baker. Is she teaching you?"

"I'll never be the baker Mama is."

"Mama's teaching me to sew." Clotilde leaned over the fence and pointed. "What are those, Mrs. Johnson? They're so pretty."

"Sweet Williams." She plucked a stem of bright pink and white flowers and handed them to Cloe. "Wait just a minute and I'll bring you some seed packets. You can start a nice flower garden for your mama, *ja*? If you plant the seeds now, you will have a nice summer garden. In fall, I will give you bulbs."

Mama had Bernie turn the soil around the front porch and prepare it for planting. "Not too much manure. It'll burn the seed-lings." She and Clotilde planted lady asters, pink and white carnations, marigolds, hollyhocks, coneflower, and bachelor's buttons all around the farmhouse on Hopper Road.

Rikka liked to follow Mama around the house, holding the flowers Mama snipped. Mama would fill a mason jar with water and let Rikka arrange the flowers. Mama said it had symmetry, whatever that was. "I think Rikka could be an artist," Mama told everyone. She came home one day with a box of color crayons and let Rikka draw on old newspapers.

Bernie wanted to be a farmer like Papa. Clotilde wanted to be a dressmaker. At three, Rikka could already draw pictures that actually looked like cows and horses and houses and flowers.

Everyone assumed Hildemara would grow up to be someone's quiet, hardworking wife. No one thought she had any ambition to do more than that, especially Mama.

❊ ❊ ❊

Days passed in a blur of chores, school, study, and more chores, but every Sunday, Papa hitched up the horse and wagon and they all went into town to attend services at the Methodist church. Most of the parishioners had known each other all their lives. Some didn't like Mama because she worked for the Herkners, who had taken business from the Smiths, bakers who had been in Murietta for years.

"I wouldn't work in the Smiths' bakery if they paid me twice what Hedda and Wilhelm do. I went in there once and never went back again. The place is filthy, flies buzzing everywhere. Who'd want pastries from that place?"

Many of the men didn't like Papa either. Some called him a Hun behind his back. Those who had hired him the first year as a day laborer thought better of him, though. A quiet man, Papa didn't try to press his way in among people who viewed him with suspicion. Mama, on the other hand, lingered after services, talking to as many members of the congregation as she could.

Papa wasn't as easy with people as Mama. He didn't like answering personal questions, or mingling with people who liked to ask them. After a few months of trying to break into the tight circles, Papa gave up. "I won't stop you, but I'm not going back to church, Marta. I've got too much to do to stand around talking to people. And I can spend time with the Lord out in the orchard or vineyard." Papa flicked the reins.

"Even God took one day off a week, Niclas. Why can't you?"

"I'll rest on Sundays. But not there. I don't like the way people look at me."

"Not everyone thinks of you as a Hun, and those that do would change their minds if you'd make an effort to talk to them. You know more about the Bible than the pastor."

"You're better at making friends, Marta."

"We need to get to know people. They need to know us. If only you'd—"

"I'll stay home with you, Papa," Bernie volunteered a little too brightly.

"No, you won't. You'll go to church with your mother."

During lunch that day, Clotilde frowned. "What's a Hun, Papa?"

Mama put more pancakes on the table. "It's an insulting name for a German."

Bernie stabbed two pancakes before anyone else could get to them. "Who would want to insult Papa? He helps everybody who needs it."

"Fools and hypocrites, that's who." Mama leaned over and forked one of Bernie's pancakes onto Hildemara's plate. "Try sharing once in a while, Bernhard. You're not king of the roost. And put your napkin on your lap. I don't want people thinking my son is a complete barbarian."

Bernie did what Mama told him. "How long has the war been over, Papa?"

"It ended in 1918. You tell me."

"Six years." Hildemara answered with scarcely a thought. "I wonder whatever happened to Mrs. Ransom."

Mama gave her an impatient look. "Why would you care what happened to that woman?"

Hearing the anger in Mama's voice, Hildemara shrugged and said no more. But Mrs. Ransom stayed on her mind for the rest of the day. Hildie prayed her teacher's grief had eased by now. Every time Mrs. Ransom came to mind, she prayed again.

21

1927

After three years of working the farm, Papa made enough money from the harvest to build a long, enclosed sleeping porch on the back of the house. He put in screened windows and a partition with a closet on each side. He built bunk beds for ten-year-old Hildemara and eight-year-old Clotilde, and a fold-down platform bed for Rikki—at five, still the family baby. On the other side of the partition, Bernie had a room to himself with a real bed and a catalog dresser. Mama ordered mattresses.

Hildemara loved the new bedroom until cold weather came. Even winter screens couldn't keep the chill out. Papa hung canvas on the outside and hooked it down through December and January, which made the room dark and cold. Mama came out the back door each morning after the potbelly stove had been stoked. The girls piled out of bed, grabbed their clothes, and made a mad dash into the house, crowding around the potbelly stove to get warm. Hildemara slept on the top bunk and always ended up being last and therefore outside the ring of warmth. While Clotilde and

Rikka pushed at one another, Hildemara wormed in as close as she could, shivering until the heat penetrated her thin arms and legs.

"I'm going over to the Musashis' this afternoon," Mama announced one morning.

"Give it up, Marta. They like to stay to themselves."

"It won't hurt to try again."

The Musashi family owned sixty acres across the road, twenty in almonds, ten in grapes, and the rest in vegetables that changed by season, and not a weed anywhere. The barn, sheds, and outbuildings were sturdy and painted, as was the wooden post-and-beam house with sliding doors. Hildemara wondered where they slept seven children until Bernie said Andrew told him his father had built a dormitory for the boys and another for the girls, each with sliding doors into the living area and kitchen.

Bernie, Hildemara, and Clotilde saw the Musashi children every day at school. They had American names: Andrew Jackson, Patrick Henry, Ulysess Grant, George Washington, Betsy Ross, Dolly Madison, and Abigail Adams. Every one of them was a good student, and the boys impressed Bernie with their skill on the field. He had to work hard to be the best whenever the Musashi boys joined a game. The girls were quiet, studious, and polite, but they never had a lot to say, which made Hildemara uncomfortable. She preferred to be the one who listened rather than having to think of things to say. Hildemara preferred Elizabeth's company. Elizabeth always had things to talk about—the latest movie she saw at the theater, visiting her cousins in Merced, riding in her father's new automobile all the way to Fresno.

Papa had finally made the first inroad when Mr. Musashi's truck broke down on the way back from Murietta. Papa slowed the wagon when he saw him tinkering with the engine and looking perplexed. He had a wagon loaded with lumber and a water tank for the shower house he planned to build, but didn't see any reason not to stop and see if he could help. Papa got the truck running enough to choke its way back up Hopper and pull into the Musashis' yard, where it died again. Papa called Bernie to tend the horse and put supplies away while he went across the street to the Musashis' place to finish the repair job. It took the rest of the day, but Papa fixed it. Mr. Musashi wanted to pay him, but Papa refused.

The next time Papa pruned the trees, Mr. Musashi showed up with his boys and equipment.

Determined to break down the rest of the barriers, Mama made apple *Streusel* and crossed the street for a visit. She came home resigned. "I give up. She can't speak English and I haven't time to learn Japanese. And I think she's too afraid of me to say much of anything anyway."

Only the "town kids" had time to play during the week, and when Saturday rolled around, the Musashi children had to spend all day at Japanese school. "I learn to read and write Japanese," Betsy told Hildemara on the way to school. "I learn old country customs, courtesies, and games."

"May I go with you sometime?"

"Oh no." Betsy looked embarrassed. "So sorry. Just for Japanese."

Bernie had no better luck getting the Musashi boys to teach him Japanese fencing.

Mr. Musashi struggled to sell his vegetables in the valley. One morning, he loaded his truck with crates of broccoli, squash, beans, and onions and drove away. He didn't return that evening. Mama told Hildemara to ask Betsy if the family needed any help. "No, thank you. My father is taking the produce to the Monterey markets. He won't be back for two more days. My brothers will manage." Mr. Musashi left Andrew in charge over Patrick, Ulysses, and George. Problems cropped up like fast-growing weeds. A grass fire started down the road, threatening their orchard. Papa and Bernie ran with shovels to help put it out. When the water pump broke the next day, Andrew asked Papa for help. While Papa worked on the pump, Bernie asked if Patrick would show him how Mr. Musashi grafted the fruit trees.

"You should see them, Papa. They have three types of apples on the same tree! I'll bet we could do the same thing with the orange tree; graft in lemon and have lemonade!"

❊ ❊ ❊

On the way to school, Hildemara saw Mama coming up the road from Murietta. She never came home this early. She always worked until two. "Is something wrong, Mama?" Face like stone, Mama walked right past Hildemara and the other children without saying a word. Hildemara ran after her. "Mama? Are you all right?"

"If I wanted to talk about it, I would have answered you. Go to school, Hildemara! You'll see what's wrong with me when you walk through town!"

She was right. "Holy cow!" Bernie uttered and half whispered to Hildemara, "You think Mama did it?" The Herkners' bakery had burned to the ground.

"Why would she? Mrs. Herkner is her friend." The children stood staring at the pile of blackened boards, broken windows, and ash.

Not even the town children knew what happened other than there had been a fire the night before. Hildemara spent the day wondering. Hurrying home, she found Mama in the washhouse.

"What happened to the Herkners' bakery, Mama?"

"You saw what happened. Someone burned it down!"

"Who?"

"Go feed the chickens."

"Mama!"

"Put feed in for the horses. And if you ask me one more question, Hildemara, you'll be cleaning the stalls."

Mama was finally ready to talk when everyone sat down to dinner that evening. "Hedda said someone threw something through the front window, and the next thing they knew, the place was going up in flames. They were lucky to get down the back stairs alive. Wilhelm thinks he knows who did it, but the sheriff needs proof."

Papa didn't say any names, but he looked as though he knew as well as Mama who would want to put the Herkners out of business.

"Hedda says they've had enough. They're leaving."

"Are they all right?"

"About as all right as they can be after seeing everything they've worked for go up in flames." Mama scooped beef stew into bowls. She served Papa first, then Bernie, Hildemara, Clotilde, and finally Rikka. She served herself last and sat at the foot of the table.

Papa said grace and then glanced at Mama. "There's a blessing even in the hardest things, Marta. Last harvest put us ahead. We have enough set by that you don't have to work anymore. We have enough to make payments and pay taxes." He forked a piece of juicy beef into his mouth. "Hmmmm . . ." He smiled. "I can tell when you've had more time to cook."

"That's all a man thinks about, his stomach."

Papa chuckled, but didn't add anything to Mama's comment.

Mama dipped her spoon in the stew. "Hedda and Wilhelm are going to San Francisco. They have friends there who can help them get started again. She's worried about Fritz missing more school." Hildie knew Mrs. Ransom had given Fritz a hard time, too. Unlike Mama, Mrs. Herkner had allowed her son to stay home from school whenever he felt sick.

Papa stopped chewing and lifted his head, sensing something in the wind. Hildie went on eating, pretending she wasn't all ears as Mama went on talking casually. "He was out of school for over a month with pneumonia. He's just catching up. If they take him out now, he'll lose the whole year. I told her we'd keep him."

Papa swallowed. "Keep him?"

"Bernhard has a big bedroom."

"Mama! He's not moving in with me, is he?"

Mama ignored Bernie's protest and spoke to Papa. "You'll have to build bunk beds like in the girls' room. We have enough wood left over, haven't we? I already ordered a mattress. It'll be delivered in a few days. He can sleep on the couch until then." She took a piece of bread and buttered it lightly.

Papa glowered. "I don't remember saying yes to this idea."

"You take care of the orchard and vineyard. I take care of the children, the house, and the animals, except the horse."

Hildemara felt the storm threatening family harmony. "It would be a good deed, wouldn't it, Papa? It would help the Herkners."

Bernie's face flushed in anger. "It's my room! Shouldn't I have a say if someone lives in it?"

Hildemara gaped at him. "His home just burned down, Bernie."

"I didn't burn it down!"

"They just lost everything!"

"Fritz Herkner can't even make a base hit! Last time he played basketball, he sprained an ankle. He has less coordination than you do! He's going to be about as much help around the farm as Clotilde and Rikka!"

"That's enough, Bernhard!" Mama slammed a fist on the table, making everyone except Papa jump. "Who do you think you are? If you don't make Fritz Herkner welcome in *my* house, he'll be sleeping alone in your room and you'll be living in the barn!"

Bernie stuck out his chin. "It's Papa's house, too."

"That's enough, *Sohn*." Papa spoke quietly.

Bernie looked suitably cowed, but Hildemara's stomach sank at the look on Papa's face. She knew Mama's money had bought the farm, but Papa worked hard and brought in the crops that made it all a success. Mama talked as though he hadn't contributed anything. She could feel tears welling at the hurt look in his eyes. She looked at Mama and saw the shame she tried to hide.

"*Our* house." Mama amended, but it was too late. The damage had been done. When Papa pushed his plate away, her eyes glistened. "She wasn't just my employer, Niclas."

Papa said something in German and pain flickered across her face. Tears slipped down Hildemara's cheeks. She hated it when her parents fought. She hated to see the hurt in Papa's eyes and the stubborn tilt of Mama's chin.

"When is he coming?" Papa asked.

"Tomorrow." Mama seemed to prepare herself before saying more. "Hedda is paying us. He'll stay with us through summer."

Papa's eyes flashed. "Is everything always about money, Marta? Is that all that's important to you?"

"I didn't ask for anything! Hedda insisted! I lost my job when the bakery burned down, and she didn't think I should be paying to take care of her son. She wouldn't leave Fritz otherwise!"

Bernie stabbed a hunk of beef. "Five months." He grumbled, slumping in his seat as he poked the meat in his mouth and chewed with a sullen scowl.

Mama turned on him. "They won't lower themselves to living in a tent and then slaving for some lazy widow. You watch, Bernhard. The Herkners will have a city apartment and successful business going before the end of the summer!"

Papa shoved his chair back and left the table.

Mama paled. "Niclas . . ."

Hildemara watched Papa go out the front door. She knew how hard he worked, how hard he tried to make Mama happy. And then Mama said some thoughtless thing to crush him. Hildie's sorrow burned away in white-hot anger. She glared at Mama through her tears, wondering why she couldn't be thankful instead of resentful. Hildie knew what it was like to try to please Mama, never measuring up to expectations. For once, she didn't care. "Why do you have to be so mean to him?"

Mama slapped her across the face. Jolted back, Hildemara put a shaking hand to her burning cheek, too shocked to utter a sound. Mama had never hit her before; her face went white. When she reached out, Hildemara drew back from her and Bernie shot out of his seat. "Don't hit her again! She didn't do anything wrong!"

Mama stood, too. "Get out of this house right now, Bernhard Waltert!"

He slammed out the front door and pounded down the steps.

Clotilde stared at Mama, openmouthed. Rikka cried softly, her napkin covering her face. Blinking back tears, Hildemara hung her head. "I'm sorry, Mama."

"Don't apologize, Hildemara! Why do you always apologize, no matter what people do to you?" Her voice sounded ragged. "You clear up. You can wash the dishes and put everything away, too. You might as well get used to people walking all over you for the rest of your life!" Mama uttered a choking sound and went into her bedroom, slamming the door behind her.

Clotilde gathered the bowls. "I'll help you, Hildie."

"Mama might not like it."

"She's sorry she hit you."

"Play with Rikki, then. Give her the crayons. Anything. Just make her stop crying." Gulping down her own tears, Hildemara took over clearing the table.

Papa still hadn't returned by the time Hildemara finished clearing the table and washing, drying, and putting away the dishes. Bernie came back inside. "He's sitting outside on the porch."

Hildemara tried to lighten the heaviness in the house. "If it was daylight, he'd be currying the horse."

Papa always curried the horse when something preyed on his mind.

❊ ❊ ❊

It has been a bad time all around, Rosie. Someone burned down the Herkner Bakery and I am out of work. Niclas works hard, but it will be months yet before we see any money from this year's crop. Thus is a farmer's life. Drudgery and clinging to hope.

But that is not the worst of what's happened. After all this time, my girl speaks up to me and what do I do? I slap her across the face. I did it without even thinking. I had said something hurtful to Niclas, and he left the table, and Hildemara Rose exposed my shame.

I have never slapped any of my children in such a manner, and for me to do it to Hildemara appalled me. I wanted to cut my hand off, but the damage was already done. When I reached out to her, Bernhard told me not to hit her again, as if I would, and I sent him out of the house. Clotilde looked at me like I had grown horns. Perhaps I have. Rikka cried as though her heart had broken. Mine had.

And all Hildemara did was sit there with my hand-print on her cheek. She said nothing. I could see the hurt in her eyes. I wanted to shake her. I wanted to tell her she had every right to scream at me. She doesn't have to sit there and take it! She would have turned the other cheek if I'd raised my hand to her again.

I have not cried so much in years, Rosie. Not since Mama and Elise died. I could hear Hildemara working in the kitchen, like a good little slave.

I have failed her in every way.

22

MAMA WENT TO town the next morning, pushing Rikki in the wheelbarrow. Fritz Herkner didn't show up at school. When Hildemara came home that afternoon, she found Fritz sitting at the kitchen table with a glass of milk and a plate of cookies in front of him. He looked sallow and miserable, his brown hair a little too long and a little too much meat on his bones. Hildemara felt sorry for him, but not sorry enough to sit at the table and have Mama within arm's reach.

"I'm sorry about your home burning down, Fritz." Fritz didn't look up. His mouth worked and tears spilled down his cheeks. Mama patted his hand and gave Hildemara a jerk of the head, enough to tell her she wasn't wanted. She went to her bedroom and did her homework on the top bunk.

Mama called Bernie inside and told him to take Fritz out for a look around the place. "Show him the orchard and vineyard. Take him over to the irrigation ditch. Do you like chickens, Fritz? No? How about rabbits?" Bernie led Fritz through the porch screen door, letting it bang behind him. Clotilde went out after them.

Hildie overheard Mama talking to Papa in the kitchen later. "Hedda said he's very intelligent."

"Is he?"

"I don't know yet. She said he likes books. So I picked up a few at the library. I couldn't get him to talk about anything on the way home. He cried all the way. He's worse than Hildemara with the tears. Of course, Hedda wasn't much better. She cried harder than he did when we saw them off at the train station. We need to toughen up this boy."

"If Hedda was that upset, they'll probably come back for him in a week."

Fritz ate hardly anything the first three days, even though Mama fixed *Hasenpfeffer*, *Sauerbraten*, and *Wiener Schnitzel*. Bernie said Fritz cried himself to sleep at night. "I hope he stops pretty soon or I'm going to strangle him!"

Hildemara defended him. "How would you feel if our house burned down and Mama and Papa had to leave you behind while they went away to San Francisco?"

"Let me think." Bernie grinned. "I'd be free of chores and could do anything I wanted!"

"I know what it's like not to have a friend, Bernie. It's even worse when someone is always picking on you. He's our summer brother. We have to be nice to him."

A letter arrived from San Francisco a week after the Herkners left. Fritz cried when he opened it. He cried all through dinner. Bernie rolled his eyes and ate Fritz's share of potato dumplings.

When Hildemara leaned over to say some comforting words, Mama shook her head and looked so fierce, Hildie left Fritz alone. Papa called everyone into the living room and read the Bible. Fritz sat on the sofa, staring out the window until the sun went down.

Letters flew back and forth every few days. Every letter brought Fritz down into the doldrums again. "He needs chores to take his mind off his troubles." Mama sent Fritz out with Hildemara to feed the chickens. When the rooster came after him, Fritz ran screaming from the henhouse, leaving the door open long enough for the rooster to slip through and have three hens chasing after him. It took Hildemara an hour to catch them, and then she had to walk to school alone and explain to Miss Hinkle what happened.

"He can muck the stable," Bernie suggested to Mama. "Might get rid of some of that baby fat he's carrying around."

Mama put Fritz in charge of the rabbits instead. Fritz stopped crying. He stopped waiting at the mailbox for his mother's letters. Hildemara worried about what would happen when Mama decided to make *Hasenpfeffer* again, but it seemed Mama had already thought of that, too. "We only have one rule about the rabbits, Fritz. You can't name them."

"Not even one?"

"No. Not even one."

Luckily, they were all white. If one went missing, it wouldn't matter as much if he didn't know it personally.

Mrs. Herkner's letters still came every few days, but Fritz didn't write back more than once a week. Sometimes he went longer than that and Mama would get a letter from Hedda. "Time to write a letter to your mother, Fritz."

Hildemara envied Fritz his doting mother. She knew Mama would never miss her so much. She kept asking what Hildemara wanted to do with her life, as though she couldn't wait for Hildie to grow up and leave home.

❄ ❄ ❄

By the time school ended, Fritz had more than settled in. He'd started infecting Bernie with new ideas gleaned from the books he read. "Can we build a tree house, Papa? one like in *The Swiss Family Robinson*?"

Mama didn't think much of the idea. "Papa has enough to do. If anyone builds anything, it's going to be you boys."

Papa didn't trust them with good lumber. "They'd just waste it." He told Bernie and Fritz to draw up the plans. He'd do the measuring and marking; they could do the sawing. By the end of the first day of hard work, they came in with palms looking like raw meat and broad grins on their faces.

"We need a trapdoor to keep enemies out." *Enemies* being Hildemara, Clotilde, and Rikka, of course. "We can use a rope ladder and pull it up once we're on the platform."

Papa joined in the fun of building, adding a second smaller, higher platform as a watchtower with a ladder and trapdoor. He built a bench around the inside wall of the large platform ten feet above ground. "So you boys won't fall asleep and roll off. We can't have you breaking your necks."

Tony Reboli, Wallie Engles, and Eddie Rinckel came out to help. Hildemara sat on the back steps watching them. They looked like a bunch of monkeys climbing around in the big bay tree. She wished she could be part of the fun, too, but Bernie told her, "No girls allowed." Clotilde didn't care. She was too busy cutting out a new dress and learning how to use Mama's sewing machine. And Rikka liked to stay inside the house, sitting at the kitchen table drawing pictures and adding Crayola color. Hildemara wished Elizabeth could come over and play, but her one friend had gone to Merced to spend the summer with cousins.

"Abrecan Macy sold his place." Mama told Papa over dinner. "Another bachelor, I guess. He's from back east. Abrecan doesn't know anything about him other than he had enough to take over the place. He didn't say what the man plans to do with it."

"It's his business, isn't it?"

"His land butts up against ours. We ought to know something about him. Seems odd, doesn't it? Come all the way out here to buy a place and not have any plans for it. His name is Kimball. Abrecan couldn't remember his first name."

Mama took the new neighbor a loaf of fresh cinnamon raisin bread. "He's not very friendly. He took the bread and closed the door in my face."

"Maybe he wants to be left alone."

"I didn't like his eyes."

July turned hot, melting the macadam. The boys dared one

another to stand in the hot black tar to see how long they could bear boiling the bottoms of their feet. After a few weeks of running around barefoot, it wasn't a challenge anymore, and Fritz invented a new game of daring: standing on a red ant hill, while someone stood by with a hose. Fritz barely lasted ten seconds and had ant bites up to his ankles. Eddie, Tony, and Wallie did better, but no one did as well as Bernie, determined to win every game he ever played. Gritting his teeth against the painful bites, he stood until the ants bit their way up his thigh before jumping off the mound and yelling for Eddie to blast him with the hose. A few tenacious survivors managed to crawl into his underpants. Bernie started screaming and hopping around. Mama came running out the front door. Bernie finally grabbed the hose from Eddie and took care of business himself while Mama stood on the porch, hands on her hips, laughing. "Serves you right for being such a fool!"

Hildemara followed the boys to the irrigation ditch, where they swam. Bernie had taught Fritz to swim. She wanted to learn, too. "Just get in!" Bernie yelled at her. "Move your arms and kick your feet and stay away from us. We don't want any stupid girls around!" Hildemara slid into the water cautiously. It felt wonderfully cool in the heat of the day. When she touched the bottom, slime covered her feet and slithery weeds encircled her ankles like snakes in the slow current. She treaded carefully along the side, arms in the air. Something big and dark moved behind the bamboo stand on the other side of the ditch, startling her. When she called out and pointed, Bernie made fun of her again.

"Oooooh, Hildie see a bogeyman!" The other boys joined in. "Come on!" With his long legs, Bernie climbed easily out of the ditch. "Let's go over to the Grand Junction. The water's deeper there. This ditch is for babies!" Grand Junction was the big cement irrigation ditch that spilled water into the smaller ones running between the farms a quarter mile from theirs.

"Bernie! Wait!"

"No girls allowed!" Bernie yelled over his shoulder as he took off along the ditch, the others racing after him.

Hildemara kept wading carefully, trying to build her confidence. She saw movement behind the stalks of bamboo again, and she climbed quickly out of the water. Heart pounding, she looked across the irrigation ditch and tried to see what stood there. Nothing moved. The beads of water dried quickly on her skin. She could hear Bernie and the boys laughing and shouting at one another farther down the ditch. Their voices drifted as the distance widened. She wasn't ready to try anything deeper than this ditch, and the boys wouldn't welcome her anyway.

Still feeling uneasy, Hildemara sat on the edge of the ditch and put her feet in the water. Her skin prickled with the sensation of being watched, but nothing moved. Bernie and the others were across the road by now. She couldn't hear the boys anymore. It was so quiet.

The sun baked her shoulders and back. Her clothes dried quickly. Her legs burned in the heat. She slipped carefully back into the water, cold after the heat, and lowered herself until it lapped up around her neck. She moved her arms back and forth just under the surface. Gathering her nerve, she lifted her feet and promptly slipped beneath the surface. She stood quickly, sputtering and wiping the water from her eyes.

"Careful there. You could drown."

Heart lurching, she looked up at a man standing on the bank. He looked bigger than Papa above her, but didn't wear coveralls. He looked like Mr. Hardesty, who worked behind the counter at the Murietta General Store.

"You shouldn't swim by yourself. It's dangerous."

"I'm all right."

The man shook his head slowly. His smile taunted her, as though catching her in a lie. "You don't know how to swim."

"I'm learning."

"Those boys left you all alone. That wasn't nice."

He spoke quietly, his voice deep. Her skin crawled at the sound. He had an accent, not like Papa's or the Greeks or Swedes or anyone she knew. He didn't take his eyes from her. The water seemed to grow colder around her. Shivering, she hugged herself and took a step toward the side of the ditch.

"Careful! Snapping turtles can bite off your toes."

"Snapping turtles?" She looked down at the murky water. She couldn't see to the bottom.

"They stay on the bottom and open their mouths wide. They wiggle their tongue to attract fish. One swims close and *snap*! I knew a man who caught one and put it in his boat. It bit off four of his fingers."

Hildie's heart pounded. Bernie hadn't said anything about snapping turtles or fish. Would he swim in this canal if he knew about them? The bank seemed so far away, closer on the man's side. He hunkered, extending his hand. "Let me help you out." His dark eyes glowed so strangely, Hildemara almost forgot about the turtle hiding in the mud beneath her feet. Her stomach knotted in fear. "I won't hurt you, little girl." His voice turned silky.

Panting now, she felt the fear rising faster. His hand looked so big. He wiggled his fingers like the tongue of the turtle he'd told her about, beckoning her closer. He didn't have calluses like Papa. His hands looked strong and smooth. She leaned away from him. "Careful. You'll go under again." He reminded her of the cat when it watched a gopher hole, waiting for the perfect opportunity to pounce. "What's your name?"

Mama said never to be rude to neighbors. This must be Mr. Kimball, the man who bought Abrecan Macy's place. Mama wasn't afraid of neighbors. She talked to everybody. "Hildemara."

"Hill-de-mara." The man dragged out her name as though savoring it. "It's a pretty name for a pretty little girl."

Pretty? No one had ever called her pretty, not even Papa. She felt her face go hot. Mr. Kimball's mouth tipped. Beads of sweat dripped down the sides of his face. His gaze shifted as he looked around furtively.

The silence suddenly bothered Hildie. She didn't even hear any birds. She slid her foot cautiously along the bottom of the ditch, her breath catching every time something brushed against her ankles. When Mr. Kimball got to his feet, something inside her said, *Get away from him!*

Gasping in panic, Hildemara pushed her way through the last few feet of water to her side of the bank. Reaching up, she grasped a hunk of grass and pulled, legs wheeling.

A big splash sounded behind her.

Hildemara had just reached the top of the ditch when she felt a hand grasp her ankle and drag her back. Another hand grasped the back of her shirt. Buttons popped and her shirt came off in his hand as she thrashed. She flipped and flopped like a fish out of water, kicking her free leg and catching him hard on the nose. Uttering a grunt of pain, he let go.

Scrambling to her feet, Hildie ran. She looked back once and tumbled head over heels, sand flying in all directions. Scrambling up again, she didn't look back this time. Her thin legs pumped up and down, breath coming in frantic sobs, and she raced along the ditch and headed toward the last row of grapes next to the house. The big bay tree loomed ahead.

Mama stood in the backyard, pinning up clothes on the line. Rikka sat on the floor of the washhouse, drawing pictures in the wet sand. Hildemara ran past Mama and up the stairs, yanked the screen door open, and let it slam behind her as she dove into her bedroom. She stepped on the lower bunk and threw herself onto the top one. Her whole body started to shake. Her teeth chattered. Pressing herself into the far corner against the wall, she pulled her legs up against her chest.

23

"HILDEMARA?" MAMA STOOD in the bedroom doorway. "What's wrong with you?" Her eyes flickered. "Where's your shirt?"

The man had her shirt.

"Did you leave it at the ditch?"

Hildemara panted softly, looking past Mama, afraid he might be outside.

Mama glanced out the screen door. "Where are the boys?"

"Grand Junction."

"What happened to your leg? How did you get those scratches?"

Hildemara didn't feel anything, and she didn't want to look. Mama came into the room and stepped up on the bottom bunk. "Come on down from there."

"No."

"Hildemara . . ."

"No!"

"What happened to you?" Mama spoke firmly this time, demanding an answer.

"He . . . he . . . was in the bamboo."

"Who?"

Hildemara started to cry. "Mr. Kimball, I think. I don't know." When Mama reached for her, she screamed. "No! I'm not coming down."

"Hildemara!" Mama held her tight in her arms though she struggled.

Clotilde appeared in the doorway. "What's wrong with Hildie?"

"Go get Rikka. She's in the washhouse."

"But—"

"Now!"

Clotilde ran out the screen door. It banged, making Hildemara jerk, then banged twice more, each time more softly. Mama lifted Hildemara down and carried her into the hallway.

"Come on, girls!" Clotilde hurried inside with Rikka. "Inside the house. Go on." She locked the door behind them and told Clotilde and Rikka to play in the living room while she talked with Hildemara in the front bedroom. She sat on the edge of the bed, Hildemara on her lap. "Now tell me what happened."

Everything poured out of Hildie. She hiccuped sobs and stammered. "Are you mad at me? I don't want to go back for my shirt. Please, Mama, don't make me."

"I don't care about the shirt. You're going to stay right here inside the house." She sat Hildemara on the bed. She held Hildemara's face firmly and looked into her eyes. "You listen to me now. That man is *never* going to touch you again, Hildemara. He's *never* going to get near you. Not ever again. Do you understand me?"

"Yes, Mama." She had never seen such a look in her mother's eyes before. It frightened her all over again.

Mama let go of her and straightened. "Stay in the house." She went out of the bedroom. Hildemara heard a drawer being yanked open. Trembling, she rushed to the doorway and saw Mama standing with a butcher knife in her hand. "You girls stay inside this house."

"Mama!" Hildemara ran out of the bedroom. "Don't go. He's bigger than you."

"He won't be much longer. Lock the door!" The screen door slammed.

What if the man took the knife away and used it on Mama?

"No!" Hildemara yanked the screen door open. "Mama, come back!" Mama was running along the row of grapes. She disappeared around the end. "Papa!" Hildemara shouted. *"Papa!"*

"Ring the bell!" Clotilde stood behind her.

Hildemara grabbed the cord and pulled and pulled and pulled. The bell clanged loudly. Sobbing, Hildemara kept pulling. Cloe held Rikka by the shoulders, both pairs of blue eyes wide.

Papa came running across the yard. "What's wrong?"

Hildemara ran down the steps. "Mama went that way! She has a butcher knife! *She'll get herself killed!*"

Papa didn't wait to ask questions. He ran in the direction Hildemara pointed. "Marta!"

Bernie and Fritz, the others on their heels, came flying around the front of the house. "What's happened?" Bernie panted. "We heard the bell!"

Hildemara sank onto the back steps, covered her head, and sobbed.

"Holy cow!" Tony laughed. "Little Sis is half-naked."

Mortified, Hildemara jumped up and ran inside the house. Gulping sobs, she put her foot on the bottom bunk and dove into the top, pulling a blanket over her.

"Leave her alone!" Cloe shrieked, following after her. She climbed up onto the bunk with Hildie. Rikka climbed up, too. When Bernie came inside, Cloe yelled, *"No boys allowed!"*

It seemed forever before Hildemara heard Bernie's voice again. "I see Papa. Mama's with him. What in the heck is Papa doing with a butcher knife?"

Hildie let out her breath, but stayed under the blanket. She heard Papa's voice. "Tony, Wallie, Eddie, go on home."

"Did we do something wrong, Mr. Waltert?"

"No, but Bernhard's got work to do. Go on now. Everything is fine." He sounded as though nothing bad had happened. The boys called out their good-byes and left. Papa's voice changed. "Into the house, *Sohn*. Keep the children in the house until I get back."

"Where's he going, Mama?"

"To the sheriff."

❄ ❄ ❄

Sheriff Brunner came to the house late in the afternoon. Bernie and Fritz were sent to the tree house, Clotilde and Rikka to the porch bedroom. Hildemara had to sit at the table and tell the sheriff what had happened at the ditch. He looked at the scratches on Hildie's left leg, his face grim.

"I stopped by Kimball's house on the way out here. He wasn't there."

Mama gave a hard laugh. "That doesn't mean he won't come back."

Hildie's heart tripped. Papa sat her on his lap and held her close.

"I'll swear out a warrant for his arrest, but I can't promise anything. He has a car. He's probably miles from here by now."

That night, Hildemara awakened to the smell of smoke. A fire bell clanged in the distance. Mama and Papa stood in the yard, talking in low voices. "Maybe lightning set the place on fire." Mama sounded hopeful.

"There hasn't been any lightning." Papa spoke grimly.

"Let it burn, and him with it." Mama came back inside the house.

The sheriff returned the next morning and spoke to Mama and Papa. "Kimball's house and barn burned down last night." He didn't sound pleased. "You know anything about it?"

Papa answered simply. "No."

Mama spoke her mind as usual. "I went after him with a butcher knife, Sheriff Brunner, with the full intent of killing him. I saw him driving off in his fancy black automobile. I may wish the man dead and in hell, but I wouldn't have any reason to burn down a perfectly good house or barn. Unless he was in it. Was he?"

"No."

"Now, there's a real pity."

Sheriff Brunner stood silent and then decided, "It must have been Providence."

Bernie and Fritz didn't come down from the tree house until Mama called them in for dinner. "What'd the sheriff want?"

Mama looked between the two of them. "He asked if we knew anything about the fire last night. If he finds the arsonists, he'll arrest them. And before you ask what an arsonist is, Clotilde, it's a person, or persons, who burn down houses and barns."

Bernie and Fritz slunk down in their chairs. Papa stared hard at the two of them. "Whoever started that fire last night had better not brag about it. He'd better not breathe a single word about it, or he—or they—might grow up behind steel bars eating bread and drinking water."

Mama piled potato dumplings on both their plates. "By the way, we're having chocolate cake for dessert tonight."

❄ ❄ ❄

Dear Rosie,

One of our neighbors attempted to ravish Hildemara. If I'd been able to get my hands on him, he would be dead now. Niclas stopped me. We called the sheriff. Of course, by the time he made it out our way, Kimball had fled. If I could have torched his house with him inside, I would have watched him die and been satisfied. Instead he is loose like a mad dog and will harm some other child.

Hildemara is a frightened mouse, sitting in the corners of the house. I fight tears every time I look at her, remembering how difficult life was for Elise. Mama coddled her, and my sister became a prisoner of her own fears.

I could have taken a switch to Bernhard for leaving her

*alone at the canal, but what Kimball did is not my son's
fault and I will not lay the blame where it does not belong.*

*But what do I do now? What happened has happened
and there is no undoing it. Life goes on. Somehow, I
have to find a way to make Hildemara step out into the
sunshine again and not fear every shadow.*

❄ ❄ ❄

Hildemara didn't want to leave her room, let alone the house, but
Mama insisted she do her usual chores. "You are not going to let
that man turn you into a prisoner to your fears."

When Hildie went outside, she felt light-headed and sick to
her stomach. She kept looking around as she fed the chickens. She
felt a little better weeding. The vegetable garden was closer to the
house. Bernie came over and hunkered down next to her. "You
want to go swimming again? I won't leave you alone. I swear on
a stack of Bibles." She shook her head.

"We're going to a movie tomorrow," Mama announced at
dinner that night. Everyone but Hildemara whooped with excitement. She didn't want to walk by Kimball's property.

"Maybe we'll even have ice cream after, if you all behave."

Hildemara walked beside Mama while the others ran ahead
and then back. She came around to the other side of Mama when
they crossed the irrigation ditch with the bamboo growing on the
south side.

"No, you don't." Mama made her walk on that side of
the road. "Take a good long look when we pass his place,
Hildemara." Two blackened piles of rubble sat where the house
and barn used to be. "Abrecan Macy was a nice man. Remember
the sheep? You loved the lambs, didn't you? Abrecan Macy was
our friend. Abrecan Macy was a gentleman." Mama took her
hand and squeezed it tight. "You let your mind dwell on the
things that are right and true and lovely." She squeezed again

and let go. "You think about Abrecan Macy the next time you pass this property."

✳   ✳   ✳

Every week after that, Mama took the gang of kids to town for a matinee. The boys always raced down the aisle to grab front-row seats. Hildemara and Cloe sat a few rows behind them. Mama sat in back with Rikka on her lap, whispering to other mothers who kept watch over their children.

The boys talked through the short newsreels, laughed raucously through the slapstick comedy with pie-throwing antics or *Our Gang* mischief with Buster Brown. When the main feature came on, they howled and whooped, spending the next hour booing and hissing bad guys and cheering on the hero. They stamped their feet through chases and shouted, "Get 'em, get 'em, get 'em!" as the horse galloped across the scene. Hildemara developed her first crush, on Hollywood cowboy Tom Mix.

Papa decided they needed a dog on the farm. Everyone but Mama thought that was a good idea. "I'd rather have a gun." Mama sniffed.

Papa chuckled. "A big, mean dog is safer than Mama with a gun!" Everyone laughed.

Bernie and Fritz walked down to the Portola Dairy the next morning. Bernie came back carrying the covered tin of milk, a stray dog on his heels. Mama stood on the porch. "Where did you find that scrawny excuse for an animal?"

Fritz grinned, patting the black dog on the head. "He found us. We heard what Mr. Waltert said last night. God must have heard him, too."

"God, my foot!" She came down the steps. "Just like that, you have a big dog follow you home from the dairy. More like you petted him. Did you let him stick his nose in our milk, too?"

"He'll bark if anyone comes on the place, Mama."

Mama stood on the lawn. "He's no watchdog. Look at him, stirring up a cloud of dust with his tail."

"He's just a pup right now. He'll get bigger."

"Who told you that? Aldo Portola?"

"He's smart. We can train him. He was real hungry."

"Was?" She took the milk tin from Bernie. "Oh, for heaven's sake!"

Hildemara sat on the porch, giggling. The dog trotted over and sat in front of Mama. He stared up at her with big, limpid brown eyes, his pink tongue lolling out the side of his wide canine grin. He edged closer, stretching out his neck, tail waving faster.

"Look, Mama!" Hildemara came down the steps. "He's trying to lick your hand."

"Balderdash!" Mama's face softened. "He's trying to get more milk."

"Balderdash!" both boys shouted. "That's his name!"

Mama shook her head, mouth twitching. "I doubt we can get rid of him now that you've given him food." She headed for the steps. The dog followed on her heels. She stopped and pointed down at him. "Don't get any ideas."

Hildemara petted him. "Can he sleep in the house, Mama?"

"He can sleep in the tree with the boys, if they can get him up the ladder."

The dog didn't cooperate.

❄ ❄ ❄

All through the rest of that summer, the family accumulated animals. Papa bought a second horse. Mama bought another rooster to "improve the flock." Fritz caught a horned lizard and kept it in a box in the tree house. A tabby cat showed up and had kittens in the barn.

Papa wanted to get rid of them. "I don't want my barn turning into a cathouse."

Mama laughed so hard, tears ran down her cheeks. "You need to work more on your English, Niclas." He asked what he had said. When she explained, his face turned bright red.

Last, Mama brought home a cow. "The children are growing so fast, we might as well have milk at hand, rather than have to walk a mile to get it." Dash stood by the cow, panting and smiling. "Don't worry. You'll get your share." Mama put a big bell around the cow's neck. "Reminds me of Switzerland, where all the cows wore bells."

Summer blazed by in a haze of heat. In late August, the almond harvest began. Papa and the boys stretched out canvas under the trees, using bamboo poles to knock the stubborn almonds that wouldn't fall after shaking the branches.

Mama received a letter from the Herkners. "They're coming on Friday."

They arrived in a new black Ford Model A with sideboards. Hedda jumped out and ran straight to Fritz, hugging and kissing him until he protested.

Bernie stared at the car. "Holy cow! Will you look at this thing?" He walked around the Model A. "Can I sit in it, Mr. Herkner?"

Wilhelm laughed. "Go ahead." He pried Hedda off their son and held him at arm's length. "Look how tan and fit he looks!" Hedda grabbed and hugged him again, tears running down her cheeks.

Fritz turned beet red. "Ah, Mama. Don't call me Fritzie."

Bernie laughed. "Fritzie! Hey, Fritzie!"

Mama took the Herkners inside for coffee and angel food cake. It had taken twelve egg whites to make it. Papa had wanted a slice, but Mama said he would have to wait. "It's not polite to serve left-overs to guests." She had made Papa custard with the yolks.

The Herkners didn't stay long. Fritz looked as miserable as the first day he arrived, but at least he didn't shed a tear. Bernie needled him mercilessly. "Fritzie. Oh, Fritzie."

"See if I come back."

"Who invited you in the first place?"

"Your mother."

Cloe joined in the heckling. "Poor Mama didn't know what she was getting."

Hildemara laughed. "You've been nothing but a big pain in the neck."

"And you're nothing but a *girl*."

Mr. Herkner put the car in gear. "We'd better get out of here!"

"Whiner!" Bernie called out, running alongside the car.

"Toad-faced pollywog!" Fritz yelled back.

The black car paused briefly at the end of the driveway and then pulled out onto the road. The car picked up speed. Fritz leaned out the window and waved.

Bernie scuffed his bare toes through the dust. "Summer's over." Shoulders hunched, he headed off to do his chores.

24

Sometimes Mama would invite a dusty, tired-looking salesman into the house. She'd make a sandwich, brew some coffee, and sit awhile listening to his sad story. Hildemara listened while studying the American history books Mama brought from the library. She and Papa had to pass a citizenship test, and Mama decided the children should learn everything too.

Mama made everyone but Rikka memorize the Bill of Rights and Lincoln's Gettysburg Address. She drilled them on the Constitution and the amendments. "Rikka doesn't have to be naturalized. She's a citizen by birth." She poked Rikka's nose. "But don't think that gets you off the hook. You're going to learn all this so when you're older, you won't be like most natural-born Americans taking their freedom for granted, not even bothering to vote and then complaining about everything."

Sometimes, just to get away from Mama's demands, Hildemara climbed the chinaberry tree in the front yard and hid among the leafy branches. Almost twelve years old, she liked to be high up where she could see her world.

Mama opened a window and Hildemara heard the rapid clicking as Cloe pumped the sewing machine. She had started another sewing project, a dress for Rikki this time. Rikki sat on the front steps, holding a jar with a captured butterfly inside. She studied it intently, a drawing pad and pencil beside her. Hildemara knew her sister would open the jar when she finished her drawing and release the butterfly. She hadn't kept one more than a few hours after Papa told her some only lived a few days. Papa led the horses into the barn. Bernie went into the shower house. Across the street, the Musashi girls weeded among rows of strawberries.

Leaning back against the trunk, she listened to the hum of insects, rustling of leaves, and birdsong. Everyone seemed to have his place in life. Papa loved farming. Mama managed the house, bills, and kids. Bernie dreamed of grafting trees and improving plant production like Luther Burbank. Mama said Clotilde had the talent to be a better seamstress than her own mother. Rikki would be an artist.

Hildie felt content sitting in the tree, staying at home on the farm, being near Mama and Papa, even when Mama became annoyed that she didn't "find something to do!"

Mama opened the front door. "Come on down from there, Hildemara. Time to stop daydreaming. There's work to be done."

Lucas Kutchner, another German immigrant, came to dinner again that evening. Papa had met him in town, where he made his living as a mechanic. He worked on bicycles and cars and anything else that broke down, including pumps and clocks. "He can fix anything," Papa told Mama when introducing them for the first time. Mr. Kutchner didn't have a wife and didn't know many people in town.

Papa and he sat at the kitchen table and talked about politics and religion, railroads and cars replacing wagons, while Mama cooked dinner. Sometimes Mr. Kutchner would bring clothing that needed mending and let Clotilde sew on a button or stitch a seam back together.

Mr. Kutchner believed in the same rules Mama did and never

came empty-handed. He brought a box of chocolates the first time, which endeared him to Mama. He brought a bag of licorice on the next visit. He had an automobile like the Herkners, and he let Bernie sit behind the steering wheel and pretend to drive. Mr. Kutchner took Papa out for a ride once. Papa wiped sweat and dust off his face when he got out. Mr. Kutchner slapped the hood. "So what do you think, Niclas? Are you ready to buy one? I could get you a good deal."

"I have two good horses and two good feet. I don't need a car." Papa said it with such conviction, Mr. Kutchner didn't bring up the subject again.

Mama went to town one day and came back in the front seat of Lucas Kutchner's car, Rikka sitting on her lap. She pushed the door open and got out, setting Rikka on the ground. Hildemara stood from where she had been working in the garden. Mama looked flushed, her eyes bright. "Hildemara! Come look after your sister." Bernie stopped digging the big hole for the water reserve near the garden. He jammed the shovel in the ground and came out to take a look.

The car chugged several times, coughed once, and died.

Mr. Kutchner got out, a big grin on his face. "So what do you think of her, Marta?"

Mama's expression changed. She shrugged as she faced him. "Not much. That thing wheezes and grunts more than any sick animal I've ever tended."

Mr. Kutchner looked surprised. "She needs a little work, but I can fix her up. I'll give you a good price."

Hildie told Rikka to go in the house and get her sketchbook, then followed Bernie into the yard. "Are you buying that car, Mama?"

"A horse runs better!"

"A car runs faster and goes longer!"

Mama gave Bernie a quelling glance, but his eyes were fixed on the shiny black Tin Lizzie. "Did I ask for your opinion, Bernhard Waltert?"

"No, ma'am."

"Go on back to your digging."

Bernie let out a deep sigh of suffering and headed back. Rikka and Cloe came out the back door and sat on the step.

Mama put her hands on her hips. "I don't like the look of those tires either."

"They just need more air."

"I wouldn't buy a car without new tires."

"Tires cost money."

"So does tailoring and mending. So do roast beef dinners. Not that you're not always welcome, of course."

Mr. Kutchner scratched his head and looked befuddled. Mama smirked, but quickly covered it. She walked over to the car and ran her hand over the hood the same way she ran her hand over a sick cow. Hildie knew Mama had already made up her mind. She just had more whittling to do on the price. Mr. Kutchner saw the way she stroked the car and knew he had a buyer. "I'll have her purring like a kitten."

Mama took her hand away and looked him straight in the eye. "Get her to work like a Swiss watch and we'll talk about it. And another thing, Lucas. You and I both know that car isn't worth what you're asking for it. Maybe you should try selling this car to Niclas again. See what he says about your offer." She headed for the house. "Thank you for the ride, Lucas. Nice you just happened to see me walking home. Providential, wasn't it?"

"All right!" Mr. Kutchner called out. "Wait a minute!" He started after her. "Let's talk about it now."

Mama stopped and turned slowly, cocking her head. "Go get potatoes and carrots for dinner, Hildemara."

Hildemara took her time pulling up potatoes and carrots while keeping an eye on Mama, wondering what Papa would have to say about her conversation with Lucas Kutchner. When they shook hands, Hildemara knew what that meant. Mr. Kutchner headed back for the car, kicking the dust before he got in and started the engine. Mama waved. When he pulled out onto the road, she danced a little jig and laughed.

Lifting the basket of dirty potatoes and carrots, Hildemara met her at the back door. Cloe stood up from the step where she'd been sitting. "Papa's going to kill you."

"Not if I kill myself first."

"Did you do it?" Bernie yelled.

Bernie just couldn't keep his mouth shut. As soon as Papa took his seat, Bernie grinned. "Have you told him about the car yet?"

Papa's head came up. "What car?"

"Lucas Kutchner gave Mama a ride home in his car today. He was trying to sell it to her." He took a helping of potatoes *au gratin*. "It can go up to twenty-five miles an hour!"

"I don't think Lucas was driving anywhere near that fast when he brought me and Rikka home."

Red climbed up Papa's neck into his face. He put his knife and fork down and stared at Mama while she cut meat off her chicken thigh. Hildemara bit her lip and looked between them.

"We don't need a car, Marta. We don't have the money for one."

"You said we didn't need a washing machine. I'd still be using that bucket if I hadn't saved the two dollars myself."

"A washing machine doesn't need gas and tires!"

"Just elbow grease."

"A washing machine doesn't need a mechanic to keep it working."

"You know how to repair locomotives."

Papa's voice kept rising. "A washing machine won't run you into a tree or a ditch or turn over and crush you to death in a pile of twisted metal!"

Rikka started to cry. "Mama, don't buy that car."

Mama told Bernie to pass the carrots. "Not one dollar has passed from my hand into Lucas's."

"I'm glad to hear that." Papa sounded relieved, but not fully convinced. He kept a cautious eye on her as he ate.

Mama tucked a forkful of potatoes *au gratin* into her mouth and chewed, looking at the ceiling. Papa frowned. "I had one ride in that contraption of his and saw my life passing before my eyes."

Mama sniffed. "I grant you, Lucas isn't much of a driver. Maybe if he watched the road more and talked less . . ."

Papa froze. "What do you know about driving?"

"Nothing. Absolutely nothing." She picked up a roll and began buttering it. "Yet." She lifted the roll toward her mouth. "It doesn't look all that difficult."

"I hear it feels like you're riding the wind!" Bernie couldn't help himself.

Papa snorted. "It's more like death breathing in your face."

Mama laughed.

"What did Mr. Kutchner want for the car, Mama?"

Papa glared at Bernie. "Eat your supper! It doesn't matter what Lucas wants. We're not buying! We have two good horses and a wagon! That's all we need." Papa looked angry.

Mama lifted her hands in a light gesture. "Why don't we take a vote?"

"Aye!" Bernie called out. Cloe and Rikka raised their hands, not looking at Papa's face.

"What about you, Hildemara?"

She looked at her father. "I'll abstain."

"You would." Mama glowered at her. Sawing off another piece of meat from the chicken thigh, she lifted it toward her mouth. "Doesn't matter. Ayes win without you."

"It's only a democracy around here when you know which way the vote will go," Papa grumbled. "I hope you don't kill yourself or any of our children driving that thing."

❋ ❋ ❋

Lucas Kutchner came out to the farm after school on Friday, Mama in the passenger seat. Rikka climbed down from the front seat. Bernie and Hildemara ran into the yard to hear what Mama might say. Papa came out of the barn and stood watching, arms akimbo. Mr. Kutchner called out a hello, but Papa turned and went back into the barn. Wincing, Mr. Kutchner turned back to Mama as she walked around the car. "Well? What do you think?"

"Niclas said you were a good mechanic."

"New tires, too." He kicked one.

"So I see."

"The price is good."

"The price is fair."

"It's better than fair. This is the best deal you'll ever make in your whole life."

"I doubt that. Just one last thing, Lucas."

Mr. Kutchner looked dubious and put-upon. "What now?"

"You have to teach me to drive."

"Oh!" Mr. Kutchner laughed loudly. "Well, get behind the wheel! There's nothing to it."

Papa came back out. "Marta!" he called in sharp warning.

She slid into the driver's seat and put her hands on the wheel. "Watch out for your sister, Hildemara, and stay back. I don't want to drive over anyone."

"Marta!"

"Go curry your horses!" Mama started the car.

Cloe charged out the back door. "Is she going to do it? Is she?"

"Stay back!" Papa shouted.

The Tin Lizzie screeched in protest. Startled, Rikka covered her ears and screamed. Mr. Kutchner yelled something. The car jerked forward a couple of times and died. Papa laughed. "I hope you didn't buy it!"

Mama's face reddened. She started the car again—more screeching and grinding. Mr. Kutchner called out more instructions. "Easy now. Let your foot off the clutch and give her some gas!" The car lurched forward and bounded toward the road like a jackrabbit. "Brake!" The car skidded to a stop at the end of the drive.

Hildemara had never heard Papa swear before. "Marta! Stop! You're going to kill yourself!"

Mama stuck her arm out the window, waved, and turned right. The car lurched down the road; Papa, Bernie, Clotilde, and Rikka ran to the end of the driveway. Hildemara climbed the chinaberry tree, where she could keep watch. The car picked up speed. "She's all right, Papa! They're going over the hill right now. They're still on the road."

Papa dragged both hands through his hair. He walked in a circle, muttering in German. "Pray your mother doesn't kill herself!" He headed back for the barn.

Bernie and the girls sat on the front steps, waiting.

"Here they come!" Hildemara shouted from the top of the tree. Bernie and the girls ran to the edge of the lawn. Hildemara came down the tree fast and joined the others.

Mama whizzed by, waving her hand out the window, Mr. Kutchner shouting. "Slow down! Slow down!" And off they went in the opposite direction.

Hildemara raced up the tree again while Bernie and Cloe jumped up and down, cheering. "We have a car! We have a car!" Dash, confused, barked wildly.

Standing on tiptoes on a high branch, Hildemara craned her neck, trying to keep the car in sight, afraid any minute Mama would drive off the road and Papa's prophecy might prove true. "Here she comes again!" Hildemara made it down the tree and ran with the others to the edge of the grass.

The car raced toward them. Mr. Kutchner, face white, was yelling instructions. Slowing, Mama turned in to the driveway, a wide grin on her face. Hildemara joined Bernie and the girls running for the yard.

"Don't get in her way!" Papa shouted. "Give her room!"

Dash gave chase until Mama honked the horn. He let out a yip and ran for the barn, tail between his legs. The chickens squawked and fluttered wildly in the henhouse.

"Brake!" Mr. Kutchner yelled. *Push the brake!*" The car jerked to a stop, shook violently like an animal run hard and worn-out. Sputtering, it coughed once and died.

Mama got out with a grin broader than Bernie's. Mr. Kutchner got out on wobbly legs, wiped his perspiring face with a handkerchief, and shook his head. He swore in German.

Mama laughed. "Well, there isn't much to it, is there? Once you learn how to use the clutch, the rest is easy. Just push down hard on the gas pedal."

Mr. Kutchner leaned against the car. "And the brakes. Don't forget about the brakes."

"I'll give you a ride back to town."

Mr. Kutchner grimaced. "Give me a minute." He ran for the outhouse.

Bernie climbed into the car. "When can I learn to drive?"

Mama grabbed him by the ear and hauled him out yowling. "When you're sixteen, and not a minute before."

Hildemara felt queasy just thinking about riding in it. Papa came out of the barn, raked his hands through his hair, and went back in again.

Mr. Kutchner returned and smiled tightly. "I think I'll walk, Marta. I don't want to take you away from making dinner for your family."

"Get in, you coward. I'll have you in Murietta in a few minutes."

"That's what I'm afraid of." When Papa came out of the barn again, Mr. Kutchner called out to him with a feeble grin. "Pray for me, Niclas."

"You had to do it, didn't you?" He said something in German.

"That's no way to talk to a friend, Niclas." Mama started the car. No lurching this time. She drove smoothly to the end of the driveway, stopped, and pulled out.

Hildemara counted the minutes, praying Mama wouldn't have an accident. She heard the car coming. Mama made a wide turn into the yard, and another to the right, heading straight for the barn. Papa let out a stream of German. The horses screamed and kicked at their stalls. Papa shouted again. The car sputtered and died. A door slammed and Mama marched out of the barn, heading for the house. "You're not parking that thing in the barn, Marta!"

"Fine! You move it!"

Mama hummed while making supper. "Bernhard, tell your father dinner is ready."

Papa came in, washed, and sat, face grim. Bowing his head, he said a terse prayer, then carved the roast like a harried butcher. Mama poured milk for each, patted Papa on the shoulder, and took her seat. Papa passed the platter of mangled beef to Bernie. "I want that car out of the barn."

"It'll be out of the barn as soon as you build a shelter."

"More expense." He glared. "More work."

"The Musashi boys will be happy to help. Just tell them I'll take them for a ride. We'll have a shelter up by Saturday afternoon."

Hildemara watched the pulse throb in Papa's temple. "We'll talk more about this later."

Papa read the Twenty-third Psalm that night and then said, "Bedtime." He usually read for half an hour, at the very least.

Bernie came through the back door last, muttering. "Ring the bell. Round one starting."

Hildemara lay on the top bunk, listening to Mama and Papa fight inside the house.

"What did you pay for that piece of junk?"

"Less than you did for that second horse!"

"The car stinks!"

"And horses smell like roses!"

"Manure is useful."

"And plenty deep around here!"

Papa exploded in German.

"English!" Mama shouted back. "We're in America, remember?"

"I'm going to tell Lucas to come and get that car and—"

"Over my dead body!"

"That's what I'm trying to prevent!"

"Where's your faith, Niclas?"

"This isn't about faith!"

"God's already counted our days. Isn't that what Scripture says? I'll die when God plans for me to die and not before. You're just afraid of driving it!"

"I don't see the sense in taking needless risks. People have gotten along without cars for this long—"

"Yes, and people died younger in those days, too. I'm exhausted most of the time, walking back and forth to town. With that car, I can be home in minutes. And maybe, just maybe, I'll have time one of these days to read a book just for the pure pleasure of it!" Her voice broke. She said something in German, her voice stressed and frustrated.

Papa spoke more quietly, his voice a gentle rumble, words low and indistinct.

Hildemara let out her breath slowly, knowing the war was over and they had negotiated a truce. Cloe snored loudly on the lower bunk. Rikka lay curled on her side looking like a little angel in blue flannel pajamas. They never worried about anything.

Mama and Papa talked for a long time, their voices muffled. No more clashing swords, no more cannons firing. Only the low drone of two people talking out their differences.

❄   ❄   ❄

The car did make life easier. It opened up the world for Hildemara. Every Sunday after church, Mama took them for a ride, packing a picnic and sometimes going as far as the Merced River.

Papa never came along, but he stopped worrying. Or said he did. "Be careful." He'd brush Mama's cheek. "And bring them all back in one piece." Papa liked being alone. Sometimes he'd go out in the orchard and sit under one of the almond trees, and read his Bible all afternoon. Hildemara understood him. She liked to hide herself away in the chinaberry tree and listen to the bees hum in the blossoms.

The car came in handy when Cloe got sick. Mama loaded her in the car and took her to town. "She has mumps." Hildemara and Rikki moved out of the bedroom, but not soon enough—they both came down with it, as did Bernie a few days later. He had it far worse than anyone. His face swelled so much, he didn't look like Bernie anymore. When the pain moved down low in his body making him swell in places Mama wouldn't talk about, Bernie

screamed out in pain whenever moved or washed. He begged
Mama to do something, anything, to make it stop. "Mama . . .
Mama . . ." He cried and Hildie cried harder than he did, wishing
she could take his suffering on herself. She climbed down from her
bunk at night and prayed over him.

"Stop that!" Mama snarled, finding her there one night. "You
want him to wake up and see you hovering over him like the angel
of death? Leave your brother alone and get back to bed!"

Bernie got better, and Hildemara came down with a cold. It
got worse, changing from sniffles and a sore throat to a chest cold.
Mama moved Hildemara into Bernie's room and Bernie into the
living room. Mama made poultices, but they didn't help. She made
chicken soup, but Hildemara didn't feel up to eating anything.
"You have to try, Hildemara. You're going to waste away if you
don't eat something." It hurt to breathe.

Papa talked to Mama in the hallway. "I don't think it's a cold.
She'd be getting better by now."

Hildemara covered her head with a pillow. When Mama came
in, she sobbed. "I'm sorry, Mama." She didn't want to be the cause
of a quarrel. The cough started and she couldn't stop it. The spasm
lasted for a long time, deep, wracking, rattling.

Mama looked scared. When it finally passed, Hildemara fell
limp, gasping for breath. Mama felt her skin. "Night sweats." Her
voice had a tremor. "Niclas!" Papa came running. "Help me get
her in the car. I'm taking her to the doctor now." Mama bundled
Hildemara like a baby.

Papa carried her out to the car. "She weighs less than a sack
of flour."

"I hope it's not what I think it is."

Lying on the backseat, Hildemara bounced up and down as
Mama drove to town. "Come on, now. Help me." Mama pulled
Hildemara into a sitting position and lifted her. "Put your arms
around my neck and your legs around my waist. Try, Hildemara
Rose." She didn't have the strength.

She awakened on a table, Dr. Whiting bending over her,

something cold pressed against her chest. Exhausted, Hildemara couldn't keep her eyes open. She thought she could stop breathing and not even care. It would be so easy.

Someone took her hand and patted it. Hildemara opened her eyes to see a woman in white standing over her. She dabbed Hildemara's forehead with a cool cloth and spoke in a sweet voice. She held Hildemara's wrist. "I'm checking your pulse, sweetheart." She kept talking, quietly. She had such a pleasant voice. Hildemara felt as though she heard from a distance. "You rest now."

Hildemara felt better just listening to her. "Are you an angel?"

"I'm a nurse. My name is Mrs. King."

Hildemara closed her eyes and smiled. Finally, she knew what she wanted to be when she grew up.

25

"THE DOCTOR SAID to keep her warm and get soup into her. She's thin as a rail." Mama sounded so grim.

"I'll set up a cot in the living room near the woodstove. We'll leave the bedroom door open."

Mama aired out the back porch bedrooms, changed all the linens, and moved Cloe and Rikka back into the small bedroom. Bernie got to return to his own bedroom. Mama made milk soup with a little sugar and flour. "Drink it, Hildemara. I don't care if you don't feel like it. Don't give up!" Hildemara tried, but coughed so much, she threw up what little she ate.

Mama and Papa talked quietly in the bedroom. "I've done everything the doctor said and she's still drowning in her own body fluids."

"All we can do is pray, Marta."

"*Pray!* Don't you think I have?"

"Don't stop."

Mama gave a sobbing breath. "If she wasn't so timid and weak, she might have a chance. I might have some hope. But she hasn't the courage to *fight*!"

"She's not weak. She just doesn't confront life the way you do."

"She just lies there like a dying swan, and I want to shake her."

Bernie, Clotilde, and Rikki went to school. Papa didn't work outside all day like he usually did, but Mama went outside more. Sometimes she was gone for a long time. Papa sat in his chair, reading his Bible.

"Where's Mama?"

"Walking. Praying."

"Am I going to die, Papa?"

"God decides, Hildemara." Papa rose and lifted Hildie from the cot. He sat in his chair again, settling her comfortably in his lap, her head resting against his chest. She listened to the steady beat of his heart. "Are you afraid, *Liebling*?"

"No, Papa." She felt warm and protected with his arms around her. If only Mama loved her as much as he did.

Mrs. King came twice. Hildemara asked how she became a nurse. "I trained at Merritt Hospital in Oakland. I lived there and worked while studying." She talked about the nurses she met and patients she tended. "You're the best I've ever had, Hildie. Not one peep of complaint out of you, and I know pneumonia hurts. It's still hard to breathe, isn't it, honey?"

"I'm getting better."

Mrs. Carlson, the seventh-grade teacher, came to visit, and she brought a get-well card signed by every member of the class. "Your friends miss you, Hildemara. You come back as soon as you can."

Even her Sunday school teacher, Mrs. Jenson, and Pastor Michaelson came to visit. Mrs. Jenson said all the children were praying for her. Pastor put his hand on her head and prayed for her while Mama and Papa stood by, hands folded, heads bowed. He patted Mama's shoulder. "Don't give up hope."

"I won't give up. It's *her* I'm worried about."

Hildemara didn't know how many days passed, but one night everything had changed. A little spark flared inside her. Mama sat in Papa's chair reading a book on American history, even though she'd already passed the citizenship test and received a certificate and small American flag to prove it. "Mama, I'm not going to die."

Surprised, Mama lifted her head. She closed the book and set it aside. Leaning forward, she put her hand on Hildemara's forehead and let it rest there, cool and firm, like a blessing. "It's about time you made up your mind!"

❋ ❋ ❋

It took two months to fully recover, and Mama didn't allow her to waste a minute of it. "You may not be strong enough to do chores or run and play like the rest, but you can read. You can study." Mrs. Carlson had brought out a list of assignments and tests Hildemara had missed, and Mama sat down and worked out a plan. "You're not just going to catch up. You're going to be ahead of the class before you go back."

Mama didn't just care about getting the right answers. She wanted penmanship that looked like artwork. She wanted spelling words written twenty times. She wanted sentences built around each and then an entire essay with every word woven in. She made up math problems that had Hildemara's head spinning. "What kind of math is this, Mama?"

"Algebra. It makes you think."

Hildemara hated being sick. Clotilde got to read magazines and cut out pictures of dresses. Rikka could doze by the radio, listening to classical music. Hildemara had to sit and read world history, American history, and ancient history. When she fell asleep reading, Mama prodded her. "Sit at the kitchen table. You won't fall asleep there. Read the chapter again. Aloud this time." Mama peeled potatoes while Hildemara read. Mama bought a world map and pinned it on the wall, drilling Hildemara in geography. "With cars and aeroplanes, the world is getting smaller. You'd better know your neighbors. Where's Switzerland? No. That's Austria! Do you need glasses? Where's Germany? Show me England—England, not

Australia!" She didn't let up until Hildemara could point out every country without a second's hesitation.

When Clotilde complained about how much homework she had to do, Hildemara huffed. "I can't wait to go back to school! It'll be a vacation after having Mama for a teacher."

Mama kept Hildemara on a tight regimen, overseeing what she ate, how much she slept, and most of all, what she learned. She only balked once, and she earned Mama's ire. "I don't care if European history isn't on the list of assignments. I don't care if it isn't in your textbook. You need to learn about the world. If we don't know history, we're doomed to repeat it."

Dr. Whiting said Hildemara could return to school. Mama decided to keep her home another month. "She needs to put on five pounds or she'll catch the next bug that goes around."

Mama allowed Hildemara to go back to school in time to take tests. When the results came back, Hildemara found herself at the head of the class. Mama congratulated her. "We had to make good use of all that sick time, didn't we? Now we both know you're smart enough to do anything."

❀   ❀   ❀

A letter came from Hedda Herkner a few weeks before school let out.

"Good news? Bad news?" Papa raised his brows.

"Depends." Mama folded the letter. "It seems Fritz talked so much about his summer with us that some of his friends now want to come with him."

"He's coming back?"

"Didn't I tell you? Anyway, Hedda says the parents think it would be good for their sons to learn about life on a farm. Living in the city, those boys wouldn't have any idea. What do you think, Niclas?"

"Now you ask."

"More boys!" Clotilde groaned.

Papa sighed. "How many?"

"Counting Bernhard and Fritz, we'd have six."

"Six? Do you think you can manage that many at once?"

"I wouldn't do it alone. Hildemara can help."

Hildemara closed her eyes and breathed slowly.

Mama dropped the letter as though she had stripped off gloves and cast a challenge at anyone who dared go against her. "I can make good money running a summer camp. And it's as close to owning a hotel and restaurant as I'll ever get. The parents want these boys to learn about farm life. So we're going to teach them about farm life."

"Oh, boy," Bernie grumbled. "Sounds like fun."

Hildemara could see her mother's wheels turning. Mama voiced her thoughts aloud. "No one will work more than half a day. With six boys, Papa will have the irrigation ditches dug in no time. They can help harvest grapes and almonds. They'll learn how to take care of horses, chickens, rabbits, milk a cow . . ." She drummed her fingers on the table. Hildemara wondered what part of all that she would have to help manage. "And it might not be a bad idea to have them build something."

Papa lowered his newspaper. "Build what?"

"How about adding a bathroom to the house? Bernhard's bedroom is big enough that four or five feet wouldn't be missed."

Bernie's head shot up from his studies. "Mama!"

"You'll be sleeping in the tree house all summer with the boys, making sure they don't get into trouble."

"An indoor bathroom?" Clotilde smiled broadly, dreamy-eyed. "With a real toilet? No more using the outhouse?"

"A toilet, a claw-foot tub, and a sink, I think." Mama didn't seem disturbed by the stormy look Papa gave her. "It's about time. Everyone in Murietta has an indoor bathroom."

"God, have mercy on me," Papa said under his breath and raised the newspaper again.

"Niclas?"

"Yes, Marta?"

"Yea or nay?"

"You're the money manager."

"And a telephone, right there on the wall."

"A telephone!" Clotilde beamed.

"For emergencies only," Mama added, staring at her.

Papa shook his paper and turned a page. "Sounds like bedlam to me."

❄ ❄ ❄

June arrived in a haze of dust, blowing in Jimmy, Ralph, Gordon, Billie, and Fritz. Fritz had grown six inches in the past year, and he took relish in standing over Hildemara, who had grown barely two. Clotilde, however, could stare him in the eye. Fritz knew enough to bring only one small case with him. The other boys arrived with luggage unloaded from the back of family cars. "Rich boys," Clotilde whispered to Hildemara.

Hildemara sighed. Just watching the boyish excitement hinted at the work ahead. "This isn't going to be as easy as Mama thinks."

Mama invited the parents into the living room while Papa, Bernie, and Fritz took the new boys on a tour of the property. Hildie served tea, coffee, and angel food cake, while Mama explained the chores, projects, and recreational activities planned for the boys' "summer camp."

One mother looked dubious. "It seems like you expect them to do a lot of work."

"Yes, we do. And if you agree, I have a contract for you to sign. The boys won't be able to quibble if they know you back me up. Farming is very hard work. Your boys will learn to respect the people who provide food for the marketplace. And by the end of summer, they'll all want to be doctors and lawyers."

Smiling, the parents signed, kissed their sons good-bye for the summer, said they'd be back the end of August, and left.

No one cried.

Not on the first day.

Mama had the boys move their things into the tree house.

"Stack your clothes under the bench and put those suitcases in the shed for storage." She let them play all afternoon. Hildemara listened to them whoop and holler, and she wondered how soon that noise would turn to petulant protests and whining. When Mama rang the dinner bell, they washed and ran for the house, taking their assigned seats at the table. Mama served a feast of beef Wellington and steamed garden vegetables soaked in butter. She announced dessert would be chocolate cake.

"Wow!" Ralph whispered to Fritz. "You said she's a good cook. You were right!"

While everyone ate, Mama laid out the rules and explained the daily schedule of chores and activities. "They're posted on the back door in case you forget." Hildemara knew they would. None of the new boys bothered to listen closely. Fritz looked at Bernie and grinned with malicious delight.

The next morning, Mama awakened Hildemara before dawn. Resigned, Hildie got up without protest, put on her clothes, and went out to feed the chickens and collect enough eggs to feed their small army. Papa ate early and left "before the pandemonium starts." Mama rang the triangle at six.

The boys stirred, but no one rose. Mama went down the steps and leaned six shovels against the base of the tree and called up to the boys. "Come on down. You have chores to do." Only Bernie and Fritz did.

Mama rang the breakfast bell at eight. Bernie and Fritz came running. The new boys quickly came down the rope ladder and ran for the house. When they reached the back door, they found it latched. Jimmy tugged, then tugged again. "Hey, I think it's locked." They ran around to the front of the house and found that door locked. They stood on the porch, peering through the window at Bernie and Fritz eating a sumptuous breakfast of scrambled eggs, crisp bacon, and blueberry muffins.

"Hey!" Ralph called through the glass. "What about our breakfast?"

Mama poured hot chocolate into Fritz's mug. "Read the sign over the back door, boys." Their feet pounded down the steps.

Hildemara watched their heads bob up and down as they ran around the side of the house. She knew what they'd find. *Those who don't work, don't eat.*

Rebellion came swiftly.

"My folks paid for me to have fun! Not work!"

"I'll write to my parents and tell them she's making us work!"

"You can't do this."

Though Hildemara cringed at their begging, Mama paid no attention. "They'll learn."

Replete and smirking, Bernie and Fritz went out the back door. Hildemara went to her room to rest for the next shift of work Mama would assign. The boys argued outside the screen windows. "You guys still whining?" Bernie rubbed his stomach. "You sure missed a good breakfast!"

"We didn't come here to work!"

"Then don't. Starve. It's your choice."

"I'm going to call my mother." Gordon's voice wobbled. Tears would come soon.

"Go ahead and call her, but you'll have to walk to town to use a telephone. The one on the wall inside is for emergencies only."

"What sort of a place is this?" Ralph yelled in anger. "We're not slave labor."

Bernie laughed. "Your parents signed you over to Mama. She owns you for the whole summer. Better get used to it, boys."

"Hey!" Jimmy shoved Fritz. "You told us we'd have fun!"

"I said *I* had fun." Fritz shoved back harder. "What a baby! It's only a couple hours a day, and the rest of the time we do what we want."

Bernie couldn't resist. "As long as we don't burn down any houses or barns."

Hildemara sat up and looked out through the screen. "Bernie!"

"Okay! Okay!"

"You didn't say anything about chores, Fritz! I don't have any at home. Why do I have to do them here?"

Hildemara flopped down on her high bunk and shut her eyes,

wishing they would stop squabbling. Cloe pumped away on the sewing machine on the other side of the wall in the living room. Somehow, Rikki had such an ability to concentrate, she didn't hear the chaos outside as she lay on her bed, going through a library book on Rembrandt.

Merciless, Bernie went on mocking the city boys as he headed out toward the orchard to help Papa dig irrigation ditches. "You'd better come if you want lunch."

"I'm not a ditchdigger!" Ralph yelled after him.

"You will be!" Fritz called back.

"Hildemara!" Mama called. "There's a basket of laundry. Take it out to the washhouse and get it started." Pushing herself up, Hildemara grabbed it, propped it on her hip, and opened the screen door. Jimmy, Ralph, Gordon, and Billie wandered like lost souls looking for something to do.

Bernie and Fritz came in from the orchard just before Mama rang the lunch bell. They stepped into the back of the house and latched the screen door before the others could open it. "Read the sign, boys!" Bernie and Fritz laughed and went into the house while the others milled around outside, their defiance wilting in the Central Valley summer heat.

After lunch, Bernie and Fritz took off running for the big irrigation ditch at the back of the property. "Come on, boys!" The others didn't run as fast, but forgot their hunger long enough to enjoy themselves. Hildemara could hear them shrieking and laughing and shouting while she weeded the vegetable garden. She knew how her summer would go, and it would not be filled with play. When Mama rang the dinner bell, the boys all came running. Bernie and Fritz dove under Mama's arm and she closed the door, latching it again while Jimmy, Ralph, Gordon, and Billie gaped in misery.

"We're going to starve to death." Jimmy wiped tears away quickly.

"I gave you the rules last night, boys. I'm not in the habit of repeating myself. Tomorrow can be a fresh start. Depends on you." Mama turned her back on them and went into the house.

Fritz shook his head as he took his seat at the table. "I've never heard such whimpering and whining."

Hildemara glared at him. "Just like you last summer." She felt pity for the starving masses outside the back door.

Papa looked grim. "Those boys are going to run away."

"Let them run." Mama held out a bowl of potato dumplings to Fritz. "They'll find out soon enough they have no place to go."

Hildemara worried anyway. "What if they don't work tomorrow, Mama?" Would Mama end up handing *her* a shovel? Would she have to tend the chickens and rabbits and horses all by herself?

"Then they won't eat."

Mama went outside at six the next morning and rang the bell right under the tree house. "What do you say, boys? Are you ready to do your share of the work around here? For those who are, waffles with butter and hot maple syrup, crispy bacon, and steaming cocoa. Those who aren't can have water from the hose and air to eat."

All six boys came down the rope ladder and grabbed shovels.

An hour later, Hildemara poured cocoa and watched the new boys eat like starving wolf cubs. Mama held a platter of waffles in one hand and a fork in the other. "Anyone want a second helping?" Four hands shot into the air. "When you finish breakfast, take your shovels and report to Papa in the orchard. He'll tell you what to do next."

When Papa came in for lunch, he grinned at Mama. "Looks like you broke them." All six boys filed in, washed their hands at the kitchen sink, and took their assigned seats at the dinner table.

Mama held two platters of ham and cheese sandwiches. "Show me your hands, boys." They held them out. "Blisters! Good for you! You'll have calluses to show off before you go home. No one will ever call you sissies." She set the platters on the table. By the time Hildemara put out a bowl of grapes and apples, the platters were bare. Mama took her place at the foot of the table. "When you finish, the rest of the day is free time."

Hildemara knew she wouldn't be so lucky. She went back to the kitchen counter and made half a sandwich for herself.

26

1930

Summers meant even more work for Hildemara. She helped Mama cook, kept the house swept clean of the dust and sand always blowing in, washed clothes. In the afternoon, while Clotilde looked at movie star magazines and dreamed up new clothing designs and Rikka sat on the porch swing daydreaming and drawing, Hildemara weeded the vegetable and flower gardens. Hildemara didn't understand why Mama expected so much from her and so little from her sisters.

Clotilde repaired shirts and pants and sleeping bags. Cloe loved to sew and she was good at it. Mama bought material for shirts for Papa and Bernie and dresses for Hildemara, Clotilde, and Rikka, two new ones each year. When Cloe finished, Mama gave her money to buy fabric remnants to piece together and make whatever she wanted. Cloe could sketch garments, make patterns from butcher paper, and sew a dress that didn't look like one everyone else was wearing that year.

Rikki wandered around in a dreamy state, always seeking a

place to sit and draw whatever attracted her undivided attention. If she didn't come in for dinner, Mama sent Hildemara out looking for her. Mama never asked Rikka to do chores. "She has other things to do." Like draw birds or butterflies or the Musashi girls working in the rows of tomatoes.

Sometimes Hildemara resented it. Especially on a hot day when she could feel the dust blow against her damp skin and feel the trickle of sweat between her growing breasts. Hildemara worked on her hands and knees, pulling weeds from the flower garden around the front of the house. Rikka lay on the porch swing, hands behind her head, gazing off at the clouds. Hildemara sat back on her heels, wiping perspiration from her forehead. "Would you like to help me, Rikki?"

"Have you ever looked at the clouds, Hildie?" She pointed. "Children playing. A bird in flight. A kite."

"I don't have time to look at clouds."

Mama came out and asked Rikki if she'd like a glass of lemonade. Hildemara sat back on her heels again. "Can't Rikki take a turn weeding once in a while, Mama?"

"She knows who she is and what she wants out of life. Besides, she has such fair skin, she'd burn to a crisp pulling weeds in the garden. You do the weeding. You haven't got anything better to do. Have you?"

"No, Mama."

"Then I guess you'd better get used to doing what you're told." She went back into the house.

Rikka came to the porch railing and sat against a post. She had a sketchbook in her hand and started drawing. "You could say no, Hildemara."

"It has to get done, Rikki."

"What do you want to be when you grow up, Hildie?"

Hildemara yanked another weed and threw it into the bucket. "A nurse."

"What?"

"Never mind. What's the use of dreaming?"

She picked up the weed bucket and moved to a row of carrots. "There will never be enough money for me to go to training."

"You could ask."

And have Mama say no? "The money Papa and Mama make off the farm and Summer Bedlam has to go to mortgage payments and taxes and farm equipment and vet bills for the horse."

"They're doing well, aren't they? Papa just extended the shelter he built off the barn."

"That's so winter rains won't rust his tractor."

Rikki wandered along the row of vegetables. "Mama buys sewing supplies for Clotilde."

Hildemara bent over and pulled another weed.

Rikki put her arms out like a bird, dipping one way and then the other. "Mama buys me art supplies."

Hildemara threw weeds into the bucket. "I know."

Rikki turned. "Because we ask."

Hildemara sighed. "Tuition to a nursing school and textbooks cost more than sewing and art supplies, Rikki."

"If you don't ask, you'll never get anything."

"Maybe God has another plan."

"Oh, I already know what it is."

"What?"

"Go on being a martyr."

Stung, Hildemara sat back on her heels, her mouth opening and closing as Rikki skipped up the back steps and went into the house.

❄ ❄ ❄

Mama continued pressing her about the future, though Hildemara didn't see that she had one. "You're about to enter high school. You need to start making plans."

"Plans for what?"

"College. A career."

"Bernie's going to college. I heard you talking to Papa about how much that will cost."

"He might get a scholarship."

Might didn't mean *would*. "I hope he does." She wondered how one went about getting a scholarship and whether she might qualify.

"Well?" Mama looked annoyed. "Aren't you going to say anything?"

"What do you want me to say, Mama?"

"What you have on your mind."

Hildemara chewed the inside of her lip, but lost her nerve. "Nothing."

Shaking her head, Mama took her purse and headed out the back door. "I have shopping to do in town. Do you need anything, Clotilde?" Red thread. "Rikka?" A box of pencils. She gave Hildemara an annoyed look. "I don't have to ask you. You never want a thing, do you?"

Nothing as inexpensive as red thread and a box of pencils, she wanted to say, but then Mama might ask the question of what she did want, and she'd have to hear why she couldn't have it.

Hildemara went to the library the next day and checked out a biography of Florence Nightingale. She read on the long walk home, taking her time, knowing she'd have chores to fill the rest of her afternoon and evening. She came in through the back screen door and shoved the book under her mattress before going in to help Mama with dinner. She set the table and made the salad, then later, cleared the table and heated water to wash the dishes. Cloe got out her folder of glossy pictures from movie magazines and studied dress designs, while Rikki sketched Papa reading in his chair. Mama set her box of writing materials on the table.

Letters, letter, letters. Mama was always writing to someone. Sometimes Hildemara wondered if her mother loved all those people in other parts of the world more than she loved her own family.

Papa went to bed early. Mama followed him. "Don't stay up late, girls."

When Cloe and Rikka finished their game, Hildemara took the book out from under her mattress. "I'll come to bed in a few minutes."

✺ ✺ ✺

Mama stood at the work counter rolling out a piecrust when Hildemara came in the front door. The biography she had hidden lay on the kitchen table. Heat rushed into Hildemara's cheeks when Mama glanced over her shoulder. "I saw your mattress sticking up and felt a book. I expected to find Jane Austen. *Pride and Prejudice* or *Sense and Sensibility*. That's what I thought you'd be reading."

"It's a biography, Mama. Florence Nightingale was a nurse."

"I know what it is! I know who she was."

Hildemara picked up the book and headed for the back door.

"Put that book back on the table, Hildemara."

"It belongs to the library, Mama. I have to return it."

"It's not due until the end of the week, unless you've already finished it." Mama laid the crust over a pie dish. "Have you?" She pressed it down and poured in a bowl of pitted cherries.

"Yes, Mama." Hildie stood watching Mama roll out the top crust. It took only seconds for her to lay it over the cherries, cut away the extra crust, pinch around the edges, and poke holes in the top. Mama opened the oven, slid the pie in, and banged the door shut.

"I don't think I'll ever be able to make a pie as good or as fast as you, Mama."

"Probably not." Flipping the towel over her shoulder, Mama stood, hands on her hips. "But then that's not what you want to do, is it?"

Hildemara hung her head.

"Is it?" Mama raised her voice.

"No, Mama."

"How many times have you read that book?" Mama jutted her chin toward the offending biography. "Two times, three?"

Hildemara thought it best not to answer. She felt exposed enough without having her heart laid bare.

"It's not Florence Nightingale that fascinates you, is it? It's *nursing*. I'll bet you've been dreaming about it since Mrs. King came here with all her stories. Let me tell you something, Hildemara Rose. She filled your head with a lot of romantic nonsense. I'll tell you what nursing really is. A nurse isn't any better than a servant. I've spent most of my life scrubbing floors, cleaning kitchens, and washing clothes. I'd like to see you do something more with that brain of yours than spend the rest of your life emptying bedpans and changing sheets! If you want to know my opinion, I don't see nursing as coming up in the world from where I started out!"

Hildemara felt hurt and angry at the same time. "There's more to nursing than bedpans and sheets, Mama. It's an honorable profession. I would be helping people."

"That's what you do best, isn't it? *Help* people. *Serve* people. You're already good at being a servant. God knows, you've been mine for the last six years. No matter how hard I've pushed, you never once complained." She sounded angry about it.

"You and Papa work so hard. Why would I complain about doing my share?"

"Your share! You've done more than your share."

"You needed help, Mama."

"I don't need your help."

She blinked back tears, knowing that crying would annoy Mama even more. "I never please you, no matter what I do. I don't know why I try so hard."

"I don't either! What do you want? A badge for being a martyr?"

"No, but a little approval from you would be nice."

Mama's eyes flickered. Sighing, she pushed her hands into her apron pockets. "Life isn't about pleasing other people, Hildemara. It's about deciding who you are and what you want out of life and then going after it."

How could she make Mama understand? "For me, it's about doing what God wants, Mama. It's about loving one another. It's about serving."

Mama blinked. "That's the first straightforward thing you've ever said to me, Hildemara Rose." Her mouth curved in a sad smile. "A pity we can't agree."

"I'm sorry, Mama."

Her eyes flashed. "There you go again, apologizing. You'd better learn right now not to say you're sorry for being who you are."

She picked up a dishrag, wiped the counter, and tossed it into the sink. "If you want to go to nurses' training, you had better find work and start saving your money because I'm not paying for it."

Somehow the rejection didn't hurt as much as Hildemara had expected it would. "I didn't ask."

"No, you didn't. But then, you wouldn't, would you? You wouldn't believe you had any right to expect anything." She slid the book across the table. "Take it!"

Hildie picked up the book and looked at it for a long moment. When she looked up, she saw Mama staring at her strangely.

"One thing good has come out of this conversation, Hildemara Rose. At least I know now you won't be clinging to my apron strings or living under my roof for the rest of your life. You won't end up running away or sitting out in the cold until you freeze. You're on the edge of the nest right now, my girl. You'll fly out of here soon." She smiled, eyes gleaming. "And that pleases me. That pleases me very, very much!"

Hildemara climbed onto her bunk, hugged the book against her chest, and cried. Whatever she had thought before, Hildemara saw now Mama couldn't wait to get rid of her.

❄ ❄ ❄

Hildemara lost her pal Elizabeth to Bernie the first day of high school. She'd always suspected Elizabeth had a secret crush on Bernie, but Bernie had never shown interest in Elizabeth. He'd been too caught up in playing sports and making mischief with his friends to care much about girls. On the first day of freshman year, Hildie sat on the grass with Elizabeth, talking about the second session of Summer Bedlam, as Papa called it, and her dreams of going to nursing school. Bernie stood over them with an odd look on his face.

"Hey, Bernie." Hildemara shielded the sun from her eyes. "What're you doing in the freshmen area?"

"Why don't you introduce me to your friend, Hildie?"

She thought he must be kidding, but played along. "Elizabeth Kenney, this is my older brother, Bernhard Niclas Waltert. Bernie, this is Elizabeth. Now, what do you want? We're talking and you're interrupting."

Bernie hunkered down, eyes fixed on Elizabeth. "You sure changed over the summer."

Elizabeth's cheeks turned dark pink. She ducked her head and looked up at him through her lashes. "In a good way, I hope."

He grinned. "Oh yeah."

Annoyed, Hildemara glared at him. "Don't you have somewhere else to go, Bernie? I can see Eddie and Wallie over there, playing basketball."

He sat and leaned on his elbow. "Don't you have studying to do, Hildie? or someplace else to go?" He didn't look at her as he talked, and Elizabeth didn't look away from him either. Bernie might as well have said, "Get lost!"

"We were talking, Bernie."

His mouth tipped, his gaze never leaving Elizabeth's face. "Do you mind if I join you?"

"No." Elizabeth sounded breathless. "Of course not."

Hildemara rolled her eyes. She looked between her brother and best friend and knew everything had changed in a split second. When she got up, neither noticed. When she walked away, neither called her back. When school let out, she saw Bernie walking beside Elizabeth, her book bag slung over his shoulder. When she called out to them, neither heard her.

Bernie had the entire school following on his heels. Why did he have to set his sights on Elizabeth? "Thanks," she muttered under her breath. "Thanks for taking my one and only friend."

She met Cloe and Rikki on the other side of the highway, near the grade school. "You two go on ahead. I have something to do." Mama said she'd have to earn her own money for nursing school,

and what better time to start than now? As soon as her sisters
headed off for home, Hildemara rubbed her perspiring palms
against her skirt and went into Pitt's Drug Store. It took her a few
minutes of browsing around before she could gather the courage
to ask Mrs. Pitt if she might hire someone to work behind the
counter, serving root beer floats and milk shakes.

Mrs. Pitt was drying a glass. "Did you have someone in mind?"

Hildie gulped. "Me."

Mrs. Pitt laughed. "You can start tomorrow. I've got plenty of
other things I'd rather do around here than serve teenagers root
beer floats and milk shakes." She called out loudly. "You hear that,
Howard? Hildemara Waltert is coming to work for us tomorrow."
She winked at Hildemara. "I'll show you what's what. It's pretty
simple. Having you work here might draw some more teenagers."

Hildemara didn't want to tell her not to get her hopes up.

On the long walk home, Hildie felt flushed with success. She
relished her secret as she raced through her chores.

Hildie set the table and sat down to dinner, eager to make her
announcement, but everyone else had plenty to say. Bernie said
he was late because he'd walked Elizabeth Kenney home and her
mother invited him in for cookies and milk. Clotilde asked Mama
if she could have a dollar to buy some fabric. Rikka stared off into
space, undoubtedly thinking about some new drawing she wanted
to do, until Mama told her to get busy and eat.

Dinner was almost over before there was enough lull in the
conversation for Hildie to make her announcement. "I have a job."

Papa's head came up. "A job?"

"I start work tomorrow after school at the soda fountain inside
Pitt's Drug Store."

Mama smiled slightly. "Is that so?"

Papa wiped his mouth with a napkin. "I don't like the idea. You
have your studies, and what about Mama? She needs your help
around the house."

"I do not." Mama tossed her napkin on the table. "And if I did,
I have two other daughters who can pitch in."

Clotilde squinted a look at Hildemara. "Thanks." Rikka went on eating, her mind still off in the wild blue yonder.

Papa frowned at Mama. "Did you know about this?"

She stood up and started clearing dishes. "It had to happen sooner or later, didn't it? Children don't live off their parents forever. Or shouldn't."

"How come I'm going to have to work and Bernie doesn't?" Clotilde griped.

Bernie put his fork down. "We can trade anytime you want. I'll feed the chickens and set the table. You can help Papa with the plowing and planting and harvesting."

"I work! I made that shirt you're wearing!"

Papa slammed his fist on the table. "Enough!" Mama's mouth twitched into a smile that smoothed out when Papa looked down the table at her. "Did you know Hildemara was looking for a job?"

"I told her she'd better."

"Why?"

"Ask her. She can speak for herself." She gave Hildie a cool look, brows raised in challenge. "Can't you?" It didn't sound like a question.

Papa stared at Hildemara. "Well?"

She took a deep breath, hoping to slow her racing heart, and laid out her plans for the future. When she finished, everyone sat staring at her.

Papa broke the silence. "Oh. Well. Why didn't you say so?"

"Since you're not working yet, you can help clear the table, Hildemara." Mama didn't say anything else until she handed her the last dish to dry. "When do you plan to study? You'll have to keep your grades up."

"Between classes. During lunch break. I'll only work until six."

"You'll have to warm up your dinner when you get home."

"I'll manage." She had hoped Mama might say she'd miss having her around the house. She should have known better.

"It might be good to start a savings account at the bank, just so you don't squander your earnings."

"I planned to do that with my first paycheck."

"Good." Mama left Hildemara to finish the cleanup and went outside to sit on the porch swing.

❄ ❄ ❄

Papa said the Depression wouldn't last forever, but hard times brought more traveling salesmen to the door. Farmers fared better than most. They knew how to grow their own food. Even with the price of almonds and raisins down, Papa and Mama didn't worry about putting food on the table. Papa had enough money for the mortgage and taxes. "If we run short, I can find work," Mama told him. "Mr. Smith offered me a job at his bakery."

"You aren't going to work for him, are you?"

"He swears he had nothing to do with the Herkners' bakery burning down."

"And you believe him."

"You're the one who always tells me not to judge people, Niclas."

"There's judging, and there's discerning."

Mama sighed. "I said no, but if we need money, I know where to get work."

"Start baking more here. Take your *beignets* and *Torten* to Hardesty. He'd sell them for you."

Mama chuckled. "If you want *beignets* and *Torten* or anything else, Niclas, just say so."

"*So.*" He pulled her down on his lap and whispered in her ear.

❄ ❄ ❄

When others went to the movies, Hildemara worked. She met more students while working behind the soda fountain counter than she had during eight and a half years of school in Murietta. When the movies let out, the kids came across the street for sodas and sat in booths talking. Some of the adults left her five-cent tips.

She liked working. She liked the bustle and buzz of teenagers in and out of the drug store. She liked earning money, knowing every day she worked brought her closer to her goal. She took orders, made milk shakes and floats, washed glasses, cleaned counters, all the while dreaming of the day she would wear a white uniform and cap and walk the corridors of a hospital, bringing comfort to the sick. Maybe someday, she'd go to China and serve in a mission hospital, or tend sick babies in the Belgian Congo, or help a handsome, dedicated doctor stop an epidemic in India.

Mrs. King came in with a list from Dr. Whiting. While she waited for Mr. Pitt to fill the drug order, she sat at the counter and ordered a Coca-Cola. Hildemara told her she hoped to attend the nurses' training program at Merritt Hospital in Oakland. "That's wonderful, Hildemara! When you're closer to graduation, I'll write a letter of recommendation for you."

The first year of high school passed in a blur of study and work. When Summer Bedlam rolled around again, Hildie asked Mama if she could do without her. Of course Mama said yes. Hildemara took on a second job at the Fulsomes' chicken farm, plucking birds for market. Paid by the bird, Hildie learned to work fast.

She hoarded every dime and nickel, knowing exactly how much she had to save in order to pay for tuition and uniform fees. She would also need the tools of her trade: a pocket watch with a second hand to count heartbeats and a fountain pen to write vitals on patient charts. Mama and Papa had already made plans to send Bernie to college when he graduated at the end of the next school year. Every extra dollar would go toward getting him through school.

Hildie had seen Papa hand Bernie a dollar more than once so her brother could take Elizabeth to a movie on Friday night. "He's young. He needs to have a little fun."

Mama saw, too, and protested. "And what about the girls? They're young. They want to have fun. Are you going to hand them a dollar every time they ask?"

Hildemara covered her ears with the heels of her hands. She hated to hear her parents argue over money. She swore she would never ask them for a dime. She would earn her own way.

27

1932

Bernie graduated with honors. From the first day of school in
Murietta to the last, Hildemara's brother had been the shining star.

Elizabeth sat with the family through the ceremony. When
Hildie heard her sniffling, she handed her a handkerchief.
Elizabeth wouldn't be seeing much of Bernie that summer. Mama
wanted him on hand to organize the Summer Bedlam work crew,
and Papa needed him for harvesting.

Once a week, they let him loose and he went into town to see
Elizabeth. He typically came home depressed. "I wish I didn't have
to go so far away to school."

Mama snorted. "If you were any closer, you'd never get any
studying done. You'd be too busy chasing after Elizabeth's skirts."

Clotilde snickered. "He doesn't have to chase her."

Bernie's face turned red. "Shut up, Cloe." He left the table.

Elizabeth came into the soda fountain almost every day through
summer, bemoaning how much she missed Bernie. Hildemara let
her talk.

When school started again, she came with Hildemara and sat at the counter, doing her homework. "You watch, Hildie. Your brother is going to meet some pretty college girl and forget all about me. It's two whole years until we graduate!"

"He writes more to you than he does to Mama and Papa."

"He only wrote twice last week."

"Well, that's twice more than he's written home, and he's been gone a month."

When Bernie came home for Christmas break, he spent more time in Murietta at the Kenneys' than he did at home. At least until Mama put her foot down. "Since we're paying your way through college, you can help around here."

"Mama! I haven't seen Elizabeth since summer, and not much then. She might lose interest if I don't—"

"The roof needs repair, and we need a new garbage hole dug and the old one covered. If you have time after those things are done, then you can go court Miss Kenney, though I think she's in the palm of your hand already."

Papa wasn't so adamant about making Bernie spend more time at home. "He's in love, Marta. Slack the reins a little."

"He'll have plenty of time for galloping after Elizabeth after he finishes college. And he'll have something to offer then."

❉ ❉ ❉

Summer Bedlam had proven so successful, Mama had been holding it every year. The summer after Bernie's first year of college was the fifth session. Bernie had outgrown snipe hunts, swimming in a ditch where the water only came up to his navel, and managing a work crew of "city softies." He worked alongside Papa through the long, hot days of irrigation and harvest, then went off with his friends on the bicycle Mama had given him the first year for "keeping the boys in line."

Hildemara didn't receive a reward for the work she did helping

Mama cook, clean, and wash clothes. She also took care of any first aid needs, but she didn't mind that.

Boys kept coming, younger brothers and friends of friends. Papa never lost patience with the new boys.

Hildemara wished Mama had patience for her, but it seemed to wear thinner by the year. She'd snap orders and expect Hildie to know what she wanted before she wanted it. Hildemara tried to please her, but never knew whether she did or not. Mama never said one way or the other. For a woman who spoke her mind about everything else, Mama never seemed to say what she thought about her eldest daughter. Then again, maybe it was better she didn't.

Hildemara kept building her savings account through sophomore and junior years. No sooner had Clotilde entered high school than Mama started talking about sending her to design school. Hildemara had to listen to them talk about it over dinner. Clotilde set her sights on the Otis Art Institute, and Mama didn't seem to think it out of reach to help her with expenses. If that wasn't enough salt in her wounds, Hildemara had to listen to Mama prodding Rikka to spend more time drawing and painting so she could put together a portfolio for submission to the administrators at the California School of Fine Arts.

Mama never told Cloe or Rikki to find a job and pay their own way.

❊ ❊ ❊

1934

When Hildie's senior class Slack Day rolled around, she took extra hours at Pitt's instead of playing hooky with the rest of her friends. Clotilde came in for a soda after school, spending a portion of the allowance Mama now gave her. "Mama's going into Modesto to do some shopping. You should come and pick out something to wear for graduation. They have some nice dress stores there."

"Mama didn't offer to buy me a graduation dress, and I'm not spending a penny of my savings on one."

"What are you going to wear?"

"The dress I wear to church."

"That old thing? Hildie, you can't! Everyone else will be wearing something new, something special."

"Well, I won't be, and I don't care." She had no intention of wasting hard-earned money on a new dress. "It doesn't matter, Cloe. No one is going to remember what I wore five minutes after I receive my diploma."

"Well, whose fault is that? All you do is bury your nose in a book or work here." She waved her hand dismissively.

Annoyed, Hildemara looked across the counter at her sister. "You want to know something, Cloe? I've worked every hour and every day I can and I barely have enough saved for one year of nurses' training. *One year*, Cloe. And it takes *three years* to become a registered nurse." She felt the prick of tears coming and lowered her chin, scrubbing at the counter until she had control of her emotions. "Bernie and you and Rikki will have it all handed to you on a silver platter."

"You should talk to Mama. She'll help you."

"Mama's the one who told me I had to earn my own way. She thinks nursing is a form of servitude." Hildemara shook her head. "I can't ask her for anything, Cloe. Bernie still has two more years of college. You'll go to the Otis Art Institute and Rikki will be in San Francisco a few years after that. Papa and Mama only have so much. I can't ask Mama for anything."

"What is it Mama says? Nothing ventured, nothing gained?"

"I'll venture to Oakland and pray God gives me the rest of what I need." She didn't want to ask Mama when she knew the answer would be no.

"You're more stubborn than she is." Cloe finished her Coke and left Pitt's.

The night before graduation, Hildemara came home dog-tired and depressed. Maybe she could skip the ceremony and go in for her diploma later. She could say she was sick. It might be nice to sleep all day, if Mama would let her.

As she came in the back door, she saw a blue organza dress hanging on the foot of her bunk bed. Cloe came through the back door from the kitchen. "It's for your graduation. What do you think of it?"

Hildemara dropped her book bag and pressed her knuckles against her quivering lips.

Cloe pushed her into the bedroom. "Come on. Try it on. I can't wait to see how it looks."

"Where did you get it?"

"Where do you think? I made it!" She bustled around Hildie, tugging her sweater off. "I've never worked so hard on anything." Hildemara barely had her school dress off before Cloe pulled the new one over her head, tugging it down. She pinched one side and then the other. "Just needs a few tucks and it'll be a perfect fit. We've been working on it for days!"

"We?"

"Mama bought the fabric and I designed the dress. We've both been putting it together. There won't be another like it." She stepped back, admiring her work. "It's fabulous!" She frowned. "What's the matter? Why are you crying?"

Hildemara sat on Rikki's bed, grabbed her discarded dress, and tried to stop the tears.

"You like it, don't you?" Cloe sounded worried.

Hildemara nodded.

"I knew you would." Cloe sounded her confident self again. "And I knew you wanted a new dress for graduation, but you'd rather die than ask." She laughed, pleased. "You said people won't remember you five minutes after graduation, but they'll remember this dress. And someday, you'll be able to say you were Clotilde Waltert's first model."

Hildie laughed and hugged her.

When she tried to thank Mama later, Mama waved her off.

"Bernhard had a new suit for his graduation. You needed a dress. I don't want people saying I don't take proper care of my children."

Hildemara didn't say any more about it. When she put the dress on the next day, Papa smiled and gave a nod of approval. "You look beautiful."

Hildie turned. "The dress is beautiful."

Papa put his hands on her shoulders. "*You* are beautiful. When you cross that platform and get your diploma, you'll make me and Mama proud. Your mother never had the opportunities you've had, Hildemara. Her father took her out of school when she was twelve. It's why she's so dead-set on all her children getting as much schooling as they can." He tipped her chin. "Don't tell her I told you she never went to high school. It's a sore spot with her."

"Mama has the equivalent of a college degree, Papa. She speaks four languages and runs a school every summer. I haven't gotten an answer from Merritt yet. I may be working at Pitt's and living at home for the rest of my life." That certainly wouldn't please her mother.

"You'll have an answer soon enough, and I've no doubt it will be the one you're waiting for." A car horn honked twice. He patted her cheek. "Better go. Mama's waiting to drive you into town."

She hugged him. "She's coming back for Cloe and Rikki as soon as she drops me off. Are you walking to town or riding back with Mama later?"

He grimaced. "I'm riding. God, have mercy. I don't want to miss my daughter's graduation."

Mama didn't say a word on the drive to town. When Hildemara tried again to thank her for the dress, Mama's mouth tightened and she shook her head, staring at the road ahead.

As Hildemara crossed the platform that evening in her new organza dress and received her diploma, she paused long enough to look out into the sea of faces. She spotted Mama, Papa, Clotilde, and Rikka sitting in the second row. Papa, Cloe, and Rikki clapped and cheered. Mama sat with her hands folded in her lap, head down, so Hildie couldn't see her face.

❄ ❄ ❄

Dear Rosie,

Hildemara Rose graduated from high school today.
When she received her diploma, I feared I'd embarrass
her with my tears. I am so proud of her! Hildemara Rose
is the first girl from my side of our family to finish school.
God willing, and the crops are good, she will go on. I
wanted her to go to university, but her heart is set on nurses'
training. She still has a servant's heart. She dreams
of being the next Florence Nightingale. If the Samuel
Merritt Hospital School of Nursing refuses her, I swear
I will go down and pry open the doors with my bare hands.

❄ ❄ ❄

"There's a letter for you on the table." Mama nodded toward the envelope propped up against a mason jar full of roses.

Heart tripping, Hildie read the return address: *Samuel Merritt Hospital School of Nursing.*

Mama looked over her glasses as she mended a pair of Papa's overalls. "You won't know what it says unless you open it."

Hands shaking, Hildemara grabbed a knife from the drawer and carefully slit open the envelope. Her excitement died as she read. Mama dropped her mending on her lap. "What's the matter? They don't want you?"

"I meet all the qualifications except one: I'm not eighteen." She wouldn't turn eighteen until January. She would have to wait until the next class started the following fall.

"You don't have to be eighteen to go here." Mama took another envelope out of her apron pocket and held it out. It had already been opened.

Hildemara read the embossed printing in the left corner. "The University of California in Berkeley? Mama, I can't go there."

"Why not?"

Hildemara wanted to weep in frustration. "Because I'm still saving up for nursing school!" She tossed the letter on the kitchen table. "Besides that, a university isn't for someone like me." Fighting tears, she headed for the back door.

Mama threw her mending on the floor and stood. "Don't you ever say anything like that again! I swear I'll slap you silly if you do!" She grabbed the letter from the table and held it up under Hildemara's nose. "You have the brain! You have the grades! Why shouldn't you go to college?"

Hildemara cried out in frustration. "Tuition, plus books, plus room and board in a dorm . . . I've barely saved enough to pay the uniform fee and one year of tuition at Merritt. And that's where I want to go! After six months' training, I'll be paid by the hospital. I'll have to save every penny so I can pay for my second and third year!"

Mama flapped the envelope. "This is the University of California in Berkeley, Hildemara!" Her voice rose in frustration. "A *university*!"

Clearly, Mama wasn't listening. "It's one year, Mama, and I'll have nothing at the end of it."

"Nothing? What do you mean, *nothing*? You'll have one year at one of the best universities in the country!" She flapped the envelope again. "That's worth more than—" She stopped and turned away.

Hildemara pressed her lips together so she wouldn't cry. "More than three years of nurses' training, Mama? That's it, isn't it?"

Mama made fists and pounded them on the kitchen table so hard it bounced. Shoulders drooping, she swore twice in German.

For once, Hildemara didn't cower. She spoke her mind. "You let Cloe and Rikki dream their dreams, but I haven't the right, have I, Mama? No matter how hard I try, I'm never going to come up to your expectations. And I don't care anymore. I want to be a nurse, Mama." Something erupted inside her and Hildie screamed. *"A nurse!"*

Mama rubbed her face and let out her breath. "I know, but you'll have to wait, won't you? And while you're waiting, why waste your time at Pitt's when you could go to Berkeley? Even one semester—"

"The money I've saved is for nursing school."

"Then I'll send you! I'll pay for the year!"

"I can tell how much you like that idea. Keep your money! Spend it on Cloe and Rikka. Otis Art Institute and the California School of Fine Arts will probably cost as much as the university. And you promised them."

Mama glared at her, eyes overbright. "It never occurred to you I'd help you, did it?"

"You're not offering help, Mama! You're sending me where *you* want to go!" As soon as the words flew out her mouth, she knew the truth of them. She could see it in Mama's face.

Mama sat and put her face in her hands. "Maybe I am." She let out a deep sigh and put her arms on the table as though bracing herself.

Hildemara started to say she was sorry and caught herself. She felt a sudden wave of pity for her mother and pulled out a chair. "What would you have studied, Mama?"

"*Any*thing. *Every*thing." She waved her hand as though chasing a fly away. "It's water under a bridge." She skewered Hildemara with her gaze. "What do you plan to do for the next year?"

"Work. Save."

Mama's shoulders sagged. "I've been harder on you than the others because I felt I had to be. Well, you've finally stood up to me. I'll give you that much." She stood and turned her back on Hildemara. Grabbing up her sewing, she sat and went back to mending Papa's pants.

❄ ❄ ❄

Hildemara found a better job at Wheeler's Truck Stop on the highway. She worked longer hours and made good tips. When she came home, she often found Mama sitting at the table writing letters. Sometimes she'd be adding notes to her old brown leather journal. "How was your day?" she'd ask without looking up.

"Fine."

They didn't seem to have anything to say to one another.

When the time finally came for Hildemara to leave, she packed the few things she would need and bought her train ticket to Oakland. Mama made beef Wellington for dinner. Hildemara thanked her for making such a feast the day before she left. Mama shrugged. "We did the same for Bernhard."

Cloe jumped up as soon as dinner ended. "Stay put, Hildie!" She dashed into the front bedroom and came back with a pile of wrapped presents. She put them down in front of Hildie.

"What is all this?"

"What do you think, dopey? Your going-away presents!" Clotilde grinned and clapped her hands as she sat. "Open mine first! It's the biggest one."

"Another creation by Clotilde?" Hildemara gasped when she pulled out a navy blue dress with white cuffs and bright red buttons. A red belt, red pumps, and a red purse were in the bottom of the box.

"You'll look like a million dollars!"

Papa gave her a small, black leather-bound Bible with a red ribbon. "If you read it every morning and evening, it'll be just like we're sitting together in the living room, *ja?* The same way we have since you were a baby."

Hildemara came around the table and kissed his cheek.

Bernie gave her five dollars. "Should've been for your graduation, but better late than never." He said he'd earned good money selling his grafted lemon and lime and orange trees to a Sacramento nursery. "I plan on spending a small fortune on an engagement ring for Elizabeth."

"Don't steal your sister's thunder." Mama nodded at the last two presents. "You have two more to open, Hildemara Rose."

Rikki had framed a drawing of Mama knitting while Papa read his Bible. Hildemara's eyes welled with tears. "Someday I'll make an oil painting of that for you, Hildie. If you'd like."

"I'd like, but don't ask me to give this one back."

The last present was a small box, simply wrapped in brown butcher paper with a red ribbon tied in a bow. "Is this from you, Mama?"

"Must be, since you've opened one from everyone else." Mama folded her hands tightly in front of her.

Hildemara couldn't speak when she opened it.

"It's a pocket watch with a second hand, like one they use in a race," Mama told the others.

Hildie looked at Mama through tears, unable to utter a word. She wanted to throw her arms around her mother. She wanted to kiss her.

Mama stood abruptly. "Clotilde, clear away the boxes and paper. Rikka, you can help clear up tonight."

When Hildie got up the next morning, Papa told her he'd be driving her to the train station in the wagon. "I have to go in for supplies anyway."

"Where's Mama?" She wanted to talk to her before leaving.

"Sleeping in."

"That's a first." The closed bedroom door looked like a fortress wall.

Papa stood on the station platform, waiting with Hildie until the train whistle blew and the conductor called for all to board. He held her shoulders firmly and kissed her cheek. "One from me." He kissed the other. "One from Mama." Picking up her suitcase, he handed it to her, his blue eyes moist. "God will be with you. Don't forget to talk to Him."

"I won't, Papa." Tears streamed down her cheeks. "But I didn't get to say thank you to Mama. I couldn't say it last night."

"You didn't have to say anything, Hildemara." His voice caught. He waved and headed off, calling back over his shoulder. "Go on now. Make us proud!" He strode across the station platform.

Hildemara climbed aboard the train and found a seat. Her heart leaped as the train lurched forward and began to move smoothly along the tracks. She caught a glimpse of Papa sitting on the high wagon seat. He wiped his eyes and untied the reins. When the train whistle blew, Hildemara raised her hand and waved. Papa never looked back.

28

1935

Farrelly Home for Nurses stood on the grounds of Samuel Merritt Hospital. Hildie stood gazing up at the grand four-story, U-shaped brick building that would be her home for the next three years. Excitement pulsed through her as she asked directions to the dean of nursing's office.

Mrs. Kaufman stood a head taller and considerably broader than Hildemara. Her dark hair was cropped short. She wore a dark suit and white blouse and no jewelry. She greeted Hildemara with a firm handshake and handed over a pile of clothing. "This is your uniform, Miss Waltert. Laundry services are available. Do you have your laundry bag clearly marked with your name? You don't want anything lost. Remember to remove all jewelry, and no perfume." She explained that bracelets and rings carried bacteria, and perfume became cloying for patients in the already anesthetic-rich environment of a hospital.

"I'm glad you have short hair. Some girls complain bitterly about having to cut it, but short hair is more hygienic and easier to keep up without all the fuss and bother. Be sure to keep it above your collar. Do you have a pocket watch and fountain pen?"

"Yes, ma'am."

"Keep both tucked in your apron pocket at all times. You'll need them." She picked up her phone. "Tell Miss Boutacoff her probie has arrived." She hung up. "*Probie* stands for probational student nurse. Each new student has a big sister to welcome her and answer any questions she may have."

Hildemara heard the squeal of rubber soles on linoleum outside the door and saw a flicker of irritation on Mrs. Kaufman's face. A tall, slender young woman stepped into the office. Curling black hair framed an impish face dominated by dark eyes and winged brows. "Miss Jasia Boutacoff, this is your little sister, Miss Hildemara Waltert. Please try to teach her good habits, Miss Boutacoff. You're dismissed." Mrs. Kaufman began to sort through a stack of papers on her desk.

Jasia led Hildemara down the hallway. "I'm to give you the grand tour. Orient you to your new surroundings." Her dark eyes sparkled. "Come on." She waved Hildie along. "Rule number one." She leaned in and whispered loudly. "Don't get on Kaufman's bad side. I was supposed to write you a welcome letter, but I've never been much for correspondence." She made a clicking sound with her tongue as she winked.

Hildie had to take two steps to every one Jasia did.

"I remember my first day," Jasia reminisced. "I was scared to death. The General had me quaking in my boots."

"The General?"

"Kaufman. That's what we call her. Behind her back, of course. Anyway, I didn't meet my big sister until the second week. She forgot all about me. Oh, well. I had to learn all the ropes the hard way. By making mistakes. Plenty of them. I didn't endear myself to the General. I'm counting the days until I have my certification and I can depart the nether regions of Farrelly Hall. If I'm lucky, I'll be hired as a private duty nurse by some lonely, wealthy old man with one foot in the grave and another on a banana peel." She laughed. "You should see your face, Waltert. I'm kidding!"

Jasia took the stairs two at a time. Hildie raced after her. "We'll start at the top and work our way down. Call me Boots, by the way, but never in front of the General. She'll skin you alive. We're supposed to call one another Miss So-and-so. All very prim and proper. Come on! Keep up! This is going to be a whirlwind tour!" She laughed again. "You're puffing like a steam engine."

Boots took Hildemara from a large auditorium to a reception room to the library, kitchenette, two classrooms, and a dietetic laboratory. Hildie ran to keep up, wondering if everything would go like this. The second floor held a nurses' dormitory; the third, an open-air sleeping porch with cot beds and another auditorium.

"People are coming and going at all hours up here, but you'll get used to it. It'll be a while before you'll move up here anyway, if you make it through probation. The first six months, everyone on staff will try their best to wash you out, and anyone lacking in stamina and dedication goes! You look a little thin. You'd better get some meat on those bones. Oh, and I forgot to tell you: you can use the radio and piano. Do you play? No? Drat! We need someone around here to start up a glee club."

Boots pointed this way and that as they rushed along.

"There's a sewing machine in there. The shelves contain a fiction library. Two hundred books, but you're not going to have any time to read even one of them. A magazine in the bathroom, maybe. What a slowpoke. Come on! Let's move, Waltert!" She laughed easily, not winded at all. "You're going to have to learn to fly if you want to be a good nurse." She went down the stairs quickly, head high, not even holding the rail. In awe, Hildemara followed at a safer pace.

Boots waited at the bottom. She whispered, "As you already know, the General is on the first floor, guarding the gates to the outside world." She pointed. "She has a helper, Mrs. Bishop." She pointed to another office door. "Bishop's a peach. If you're late, she'll sneak you in. But be careful. We don't want to get her fired.

Come on. Down we go into Probie Alley, or the Dungeon as I call it."

The corridor bustled with new students finding their bearings.

"You'll be down here in the gloom for six months, with a room-mate, hopefully more fun than mine." She shuddered dramatically. "Do whoever she is a big favor and keep everything put away. There's barely space to change your mind in these cells, let alone your clothes." Her shoes squeaked to a halt. "Here's where I dump you. This humble abode is your new home! Enjoy!" She waved her hand airily.

Hildie peered in at a room with two narrow beds and two tiny dressers.

"Oh, before I forget, the most important room in the build-ing—the communal bathroom—is just down the hall on the right, and on the left farther down is the itsy-bitsy kitchenette you'll have to share with twenty classmates. Of course, there'll be fewer by the end of the month."

With that encouragement, Boots glanced at her pocket watch and squealed. "Holy Godfrey! I've gotta run! Duty in fifteen minutes! Cute doctor." She raised her eyebrows up and down. "See ya!" She ran for the stairs. Her shoes squealed again. "Let me know if you have any questions or problems!" Her voice echoed in the corridor. Girls stuck their heads out doors to see who was making all the noise, but Boots had already bounded up the stairs.

Laughing under her breath, Hildemara entered her new home. It wasn't any smaller than the room she had shared with Cloe and Rikka. And here she'd have only one roommate.

Smiling, she unpacked her blue dress with the white cuffs, red shoes, purse, and belt and put them in the bottom dresser drawer. She put two other dresses in the second drawer, along with her extra underwear. Unfolding the clothes Mrs. Kaufman had handed over, she admired the blue- and white-striped dress with puff sleeves. A pair of stiff-starched removable cuffs and a collar lay between the folds. A full white apron, long white silk stockings, and thick-soled white oxford shoes finished the ensemble. Hildie ran her hands over the garments, heart swelling with pride. No nursing cap, not yet. She would have to earn that. But even so, she couldn't wait to wear the uniform tomorrow for her first morning orientation class.

Keely Sullivan, a redheaded, freckle-faced girl from Nevada, came in an hour later and unpacked her things. Over the next few hours, Hildie met Tillie Rapp, Charmain Fortier, Agatha Martin, and Carol Waller. They all crowded into the room to share how and why they had decided to become nursing students. Tillie, like Hildemara, had dreamed of becoming the next Florence Nightingale, while Agatha wanted to marry a rich doctor. "You can have doctors," Charmain said, leaning against the doorframe, arms crossed. "My father's a doctor. Give me a farmer any day. Farmers stay home!"

"Farmers are boring!"

"Excuse me?" Hildemara pretended offense. "My brother's a farmer. Six feet two; blond; blue-eyed; football, basketball, and baseball star of our high school. He's a senior in college now."

Charmain's eyes shone. "When do I get to meet him?"

"Maybe I'll take you to his wedding. He's marrying my best friend."

Everyone laughed. They talked through dinner in the cafeteria and went on talking long after dark, too excited to go to bed. "Lights out, ladies!" Bishop called from the end of the hall. "It's going to be an early morning!"

Sometime after midnight, the last girl crept out of Hildemara and Keely's room. Hildemara put her hands behind her head and smiled in the dark. For the first time in her life, she felt completely, utterly at home.

❄ ❄ ❄

Everything moved fast the first few months. Up at five in the morning, Hildie lined up for a shower and time at the mirror or sink. She had to be at the hospital by six thirty, ready for uniform inspection at seven. After that, she helped deliver breakfast trays to patients and had lessons in how to properly make a bed: sheets folded in square corners and tucked tight enough to bounce a quarter.

Hildemara and the others followed the General like ducklings down the hospital corridors, pausing as she introduced "our new probies" to patients and then demonstrated various skills they needed to learn over the next few weeks: taking and charting temperatures and pulse rates, changing bandages, doing bed baths and massages. Hildemara got her first sight of a naked man and felt her face go hot. Mrs. Kaufman leaned close as Hildie filed out the door with the other student nurses. "You'll get over being embarrassed about anything soon enough, Miss Waltert."

By the end of the week, Hildemara received her ward assignment and reported to the registered nurse who would continue her training and then wrote a daily progress report for Mrs. Kaufman. Just when she felt she had built some kind of rapport with one registered nurse, Hildie found herself reassigned to another.

After lunch in the cafeteria, Hildemara attended class lectures conducted by the General or various doctors: ethics, anatomy, and bacteriology to start, adding nursing history, materia medica, and dietetics later. She felt the hot breath of the General on her neck frequently and feared being culled.

"It's not called Hell Month for nothing." Boots lifted her mug of hot chocolate in salute. "Congratulations on making it through." Though they addressed one another properly during duty hours and in class, Boots was Boots anywhere else. She made up nicknames for everyone. Tillie became Dimples; Charmain was Betty Boop; Keely became Red. Agatha with her impressive bosom became Pidge. She dubbed Hildie Flo for Florence Nightingale.

The days didn't get easier, but Hildemara fell into the routine: up before dawn, shower, dress, breakfast, songs and prayers in the rec room chapel, uniform inspection, four hours of ward duty, half an hour lunch break in the cafeteria—sometimes all of it standing in line, which meant going hungry—four more hours on duty, thorough shower and shampoo to disinfect herself before dinner, classes until nine, study until eleven, fall into bed in time for Bishop's "Lights out, ladies!"

She prayed constantly. *God, help me through this. God, don't let me blush and embarrass this young man while giving him a sponge bath. God, help me pass this test. God, don't let me be culled! I'd rather kill myself than go home with my tail tucked between my legs and my dreams in tatters! Please, please, please, Lord, help!*

"Miss Sullivan!" The General's voice boomed from the hallway. "Where do you think you're going at this hour of the night?"

A muffled response. Hildemara had barely looked up from her book while Keely got herself dolled up for a date with some young doctor in training.

"Probies do not date, Miss Sullivan! Get your mind off men and onto nursing." More muffled words from Keely. "I don't care if you have a date with the apostle Paul! If you leave this residence without permission, take your possessions with you because you won't be allowed back in. Do you hear me?"

Everybody in Probie Alley heard the General.

Keely came back into the room, slammed the door, and sank onto the bed in tears. "I'm so sick of her snoopervising. I had a date with Atwood tonight."

"Atwood?"

"He's that cute intern on the obstetrics ward we've all been swooning over. Well, everyone but you, I guess. He's going to think I stood him up!"

"Explain to him tomorrow." Too tired to care, Hildemara put her book on her dresser, rolled over, and fell asleep dreaming of sutures, knives, instruments, and a frustrated doctor standing over an unconscious patient and shouting at her, "He's not even shaved and prepped!"

Every waking moment, she worked and reviewed details on how to do throat irrigations, barium enemas, Murphy drips, and concise and acceptable case reports. Boots called her a workhorse. "You look pale, Flo. What did I tell you about getting some meat

on your bones? Ease up a little or you're going to end up sick."
She slung an arm around Hildie's shoulders as they walked to
the hospital.

❄ ❄ ❄

"Miss Waltert," the General breathed into her ear. Hildemara's
head snapped up and heat flooded her face, but no one laughed.
Everyone sat in some state of exhaustion, trying to keep her eyes
open and listen to Dr. Herod Bria's history of medicine. His mono-
tone voice droned on and on. Hildie glanced surreptitiously at
her pocket watch and groaned inwardly. Quarter past nine. Old
Bria should have finished his torturous, meandering lecture fifteen
minutes ago, and he was still going strong, referring to a pile of
notes still to go through.

A soft yelp sounded behind her as the General pinched Keely.
The sound made Dr. Bria look at the clock on the wall instead of
his mound of notes. "That's all for this evening, ladies. My apolo-
gies for going over time. Thank you for your attention."

Everyone made a rush for the door, crowding through. Boots, a
night owl, was waiting in Hildemara's room to see how her day had
gone. Hildie sighed and nudged her over so she could sprawl on
her bed. "And to think, I used to love nursing history."

Keely grabbed her toothbrush and toothpaste. "That old geezer
loves to hear himself talk!" She disappeared out the door.

Boots gave Hildie a catlike smile and purred. "Perhaps our
beloved Dr. Bria needs a lesson in punctuality."

The next evening, while Hildemara struggled to stay awake and
attentive, Dr. Bria lectured until an alarm went off so loudly all the
students jumped in their seats. The tinny-sounding bell continued
to jingle as the General stormed across the room, yanked the sheet
cover off John Bones, the dangling human skeleton, and tried to
pry the clock from its pelvis. Bones clacked and clattered as the
skeleton danced.

Mouths twitched, muscles ached with control, but no one

laughed when the General held up the clock and snarled, "Who did this?" They all looked around and shook their heads. The General marched up one aisle and down the other, studying each face for signs of guilt.

"I beg your pardon, Dr. Bria. Such rudeness . . ."

"It's all right, Mrs. Kaufman. It *is* nine o'clock."

Mrs. Kaufman dismissed the class and stood at the door, surveying each girl as she slipped by. Hildie hurried downstairs and ran along Probie Alley, her rubber-soled shoes squealing to a stop at her door.

Boots was lounging on her bed. "Ah. Class let out on time tonight." She laughed.

"*You* did it."

She gave Hildie a look of wounded surprise. "Would I do such a thing?"

Hildemara closed the door quickly before giggling. "I don't know anyone else around here that would play a prank like that."

Keely ducked in and closed the door quickly. "*Shhhh.* The General is standing at the foot of the stairs."

Boots sighed. "Oh, boy. My goose is cooked."

They were surprised to hear a deep belly laugh. It faded quickly, as though someone was heading upstairs at a run.

"Well, what do you know?" Boots drawled. "And here I thought the General's face would crack if she ever smiled."

❄ ❄ ❄

"It's fine to have compassion, Miss Waltert, but you must keep a professional detachment." Mrs. Standish stood outside the closed door of a patient's room. "You won't last otherwise." She squeezed Hildie's arm and walked away.

Even Boots warned her not to become too attached. "Some will die, Flo, and if you let yourself become too close, you'll break your heart over and over. You can't be a good nurse that way, honey."

Hildemara tried to keep a distance, but she knew her patients had other needs beside physical, especially those who had been in the hospital for longer than a week and had no visitors. She felt Mr. Franklin's hot glare as she changed his soiled sheets. "Fine way to treat an old man. Load him up with castor oil and then fence him in."

"It was that or leave your plumbing stopped up."

Surprisingly, he laughed. "Well, from where I sit, you got the raw end of this deal."

Boots worked a ward with her. "Check on Mr. Howard in 2B, Flo. He's a cotton picker, always at his dressings." From there, Boots sent her to check vitals on Mr. Littlefield. "Cheer him up. He's got his feet braced against getting well." When Hildie came on duty the next morning, Boots told her she had to report to a private room patient. "He's been here a week. Another face might cheer him up."

"What's his story?"

"He's a doctor, and he doesn't like hospital rules."

Hildie's mouth fell open when she found her patient standing buck naked at the window, grunting and swearing as he tried to pry it open. "Can I help you, Dr. Turner?"

"How does a man get some air in here?"

"The nurse opens the window as soon as the patient gets back in bed." She stepped by him and managed to pull the window up a few inches. "How's that?"

After checking his vitals and writing on his chart, she went out for his lunch tray.

"Meat loaf!" He groaned loudly. "What I wouldn't do for a steak and potatoes!"

When she returned for his tray, she found peanut shells all over the floor and a half-filled bag in his side table. She swept them up while he napped.

The next morning, she gave him a bed bath and changed the sheets. He clung to the railing. "Are you trying to topple me right out on my head?"

"I'm thinking about it."

He laughed over his shoulder. "I'll be more cooperative tomorrow."

And he was. He sat in his flimsy hospital gown, his ankle on his knee, while Hildie hurriedly stripped his bed.

"What is going on, Miss Waltert?" The General stood in the doorway. Dr. Turner's foot slapped down on the floor. "Is this how you make a bed? By having a poor, sick patient sit in a breeze?"

"It's the way he wanted it, ma'am."

"Well, he doesn't have a say. We don't want you to get pneumonia, Dr. Turner, now, do we? Get back in bed!" She glowered at Hildie as she marched out the door. "I'll be back in a few minutes to inspect."

Hildemara rolled Dr. Turner from one side to another as she pulled the sheets taut and tucked them in firmly. By the time Mrs. Kaufman returned, Dr. Turner lay on his back, hands folded on his chest like a corpse in a coffin, and an all-too-lively twinkle in his eyes, which he closed when the General came close.

"Very good, Miss Waltert. Good day, Dr. Turner." As she swished out the door, Hildie breathed again.

"Check the hall," Dr. Turner whispered. "Tell me when she's gone."

Peering out, Hildie watched the General stride down the hallway, pause briefly at the nurses' station, and head for the stairs. "She's gone." She heard a mighty thrashing sound and turned. "What are you doing?"

Dr. Turner kicked until all the bed linens she had carefully tucked in came free. "Ahhh. Much, much better." He grinned at her.

She wanted to smother him with his pillow or beat him over the head with the sack of peanuts someone had smuggled in. "They should have a special ward for doctors! One with manacles!" She heard his laughter as she went down the hall.

"Doc is gone. You can have Miss Fullbright now. She's down the hall on the left." Another private room patient who didn't seem sick at all. Hildemara carried in her meal trays and drew water in a tub. Miss Fullbright took her time and bathed unaided each morning while Hildie made the bed with fresh linens. The woman read incessantly while a radio played classical music on her side table. The only medicine dispensed was one aspirin a day, a child's dose.

On the fifth day, Hildie found her dressed and packing her suitcase. "I'm so glad your tests all turned out well, Miss Fullbright."

"Tests?" She laughed. "Oh, that." She folded a silk dressing gown into her suitcase. "Just routine stuff, no real complaint. I'm as healthy as a workhorse." She chuckled. "Don't look so surprised. I'm a nurse, too. A head nurse, in fact. Not in this hospital, of course. I'd have no privacy whatsoever." She handed Hildie three novels. "You can put these in the nurses' library. I'm done with them." She smiled. "It's simple, Miss Waltert. I work hard all year, overseeing a staff of nursing students just like you. I need to get away and have a little vacation now and then. So every few years, I call my friend and sign in here for a week, have a routine checkup and a good rest with room service while I'm about it."

Room service? Hildie thought of Mama's comment about nurses being nothing more than servants.

"None of my friends know where I am, and I get to read for pleasure." She closed her case and snapped the locks.

"Don't forget your radio."

"It belongs to my friend. She'll pick it up later." Miss Fullbright slid her suitcase off the bed and held it easily at her side. "You were very efficient, Miss Waltert. Henny will be pleased with my report."

"Henny?"

"Heneka and I go way back." She leaned closer and whispered. "I think you and the other probies call her the General." Laughing, she walked out the door.

29

1936

The six-month probation period proved grueling and heartbreaking. Keely Sullivan got washed out when Mrs. Kaufman caught her sneaking out for another date. Charmain Fortier discovered she couldn't stand the sight of blood. Tillie Rapp decided to go home and marry her boyfriend. By the time the capping ceremony rolled around, only fifteen remained out of the twenty-two who had come with such high hopes. Mrs. Kaufman informed Hildemara that she would head the procession as the Lady with the Lamp, Florence Nightingale, the mother of nursing.

"I knew you'd do it, Flo!" Boots secured the plain white cap on Hildie's head and helped her with the coveted scarlet-lined navy blue cape with the red SMH insignia on the mandarin collar. "I'm proud of you!" She kissed her cheek. "Keep that lantern high."

The other nursing students had friends and family among the audience. "Where are your folks?" Boots looked around. "I want to meet that handsome brother of yours."

"They couldn't make it."

Everyone had a handy excuse. Mama said it would cost too much money to bring the whole family up by train. Papa had too much work to do to leave the farm. Mama had to make plans for Summer Bedlam again. The girls couldn't be bothered, and Bernie and Elizabeth were making wedding plans. This ceremony wasn't like a graduation, was it? It was just the end of probation, right? Nothing that mattered. Not to them, anyway.

Cloe wrote.

The folks want to know when you're coming home. We miss you. We haven't seen you since Christmas.

Hildemara wrote back.

No one missed me enough to come to my capping ceremony. . . .

Papa wrote a short note.

Your words sting, Hildemara. Do you really judge us so harshly? Mama works hard. I can't leave the ranch. Come home when you can. We miss you.

Love, Papa

Driven by guilt, Hildemara finally went home for a weekend. The last person she expected to meet her at the bus station in Murietta was Mama. She snapped a book closed and stood up when Hildie came down the steps. "Well, well, so here's the grand Lady with the Lamp."

Was Mama being snide or condescending? "It was an honor, Mama, for being top in my class." Hildie carried her suitcase to the car without looking back. Flinging the suitcase into the backseat, she climbed into the front, clenching her teeth and swearing to herself she wouldn't say another word. Hurt and anger boiled up inside her, threatening to spill over and spoil the short time she had to visit.

Mama got in and started the car, saying nothing on the drive home. She turned in the driveway. Hildie broke the silence. "I see you have a new tractor." Mama parked the car, the only sign she had heard Hildie a tightening of the muscles in her jaw. Hildie stepped out, grabbed her suitcase, and slammed the door. As she headed for the back door, she noticed other things she never had before. The house needed painting. The tear in the screen door had lengthened, letting flies in. The roof covering over the sleeping porch had been patched.

Cloe swung the door wide and came charging out. "Wait until you see our room!" The bunk bed had been replaced by two single beds covered with colorful quilts, a built-in, four-drawer dresser between them. On it stood a shiny brass kerosene lamp. Hildie had become so accustomed to electric lights that she'd forgotten the porch had never been wired. "What do you think? Isn't it grand?"

After living in the pristine environment of Farrelly Hall and the polished corridors of the hospital, Hildemara noticed the unpainted, unfinished walls, the grimy woodwork, the sandy floor. She searched for something to say. "Who made the quilts?"

"I did. Mama bought the fabric, of course."

"Of course." It struck Hildie then. There was no room for her. "Where do I sleep?"

"On the living room sofa." Mama walked past her. She paused at the back door to the kitchen. "Life doesn't stand still, you know. Now that you have your own life, there's no reason we can't spread out a little and enjoy the extra space ourselves, is there? There's no law against your sisters being as comfortable as you are in that grand brick building you wrote about." The door slammed behind her.

Hildemara wished she had stayed in Oakland. Mama had managed to make her feel small and mean-spirited. "It's lovely, Cloe." She fought tears. "You did a beautiful job on those quilts." Unlike the old one Hildemara had used, these covered the entire bed. Cloe and Rikki wouldn't have to scrunch up to keep their feet warm. "Where's Papa?"

"Helping the Musashi boys. Their pump broke down again."

Gathering her courage, Hildie went into the living room and sat on the lumpy old sofa. Everything looked the same, but she saw it through the eyes of her bacteriology class. Everywhere she looked, Hildie saw places where colonies could flourish: a food stain on the sofa; scuffed woodwork; sandy grit tracked in from field and barn, undoubtedly rich with manure; linoleum peeling off in one corner of the kitchen; stacks of newspapers; the splattered, sun-bleached kitchen curtains; the cat sleeping in the middle of the kitchen table, where everyone ate.

If there was one thing Hildie had learned in the past few months, it was what people didn't know could hurt them.

Papa came in through the front door. "I saw Mama drive in." Hildie ran to him, hugging him tight. "Hildemara Rose." His voice rasped with emotion. "All grown-up." He smelled of horse manure, engine grease, dust, and healthy perspiration. Hildie cried at the pleasure of seeing his smiling face. "I've got to get back to work, but I wanted to welcome you home."

"I'll go with you." Hildie followed him across the street, waving hello to the Musashi girls working in the field. While Papa worked on the pump, she told him about her classes, patients, doctors, the girls.

He laughed over Boots's prank with John Bones. "You sound happy, Hildemara."

"Happier than I've ever been, Papa. I'm where God wants me."

"I'll be done here in a while. Why don't you go see about helping your mother?"

Mama brushed off her offer. "Just let me do it myself. I can get things done a lot faster."

Cloe had to study. Rikki had gone off somewhere to draw another picture. Bernie was in town with Elizabeth. Hildie sat on the sofa and read one of the old movie magazines Cloe collected. Several pages had been torn out. Hildie tossed it aside and looked at another. Same thing. Gathering up the old magazines, she took them out to the burn pile in the pit Bernie had dug last year. Cats wandered everywhere. Did they still live on mice in the barn? Or did Mama feed them excess milk from the cow she'd added to the menagerie?

Hildie went back inside to escape the heat. She missed the cool sea air that blew in across San Francisco Bay. She felt uncomfortable sitting in the living room while Mama worked in the kitchen, back rigid, hands flying about her tasks. Hildie didn't know what to say. Silence and inactivity grated on her nerves. "I can set the table, can't I?"

"Please!"

Hildie opened the cabinet and took out the dinner plates. "This plate should be thrown away."

"Why? What's wrong with it?"

"It has a crack."

"So what?"

"Cracks are breeding grounds for germs, Mama."

"Put it back in the cabinet if it's not good enough for you."

Angry, Hildie took the plate out the back door and threw it into the garbage hole.

When she came back inside, Mama glared at her. "Are you happy now, Hildemara?"

"At least no one will get sick."

"We've been eating off that plate for ten years and no one's been sick yet!"

Bernie came home and hugged Hildemara. "Not staying for dinner, Mama. I'm taking Elizabeth to the movie." He leaned in toward Hildie. "Want to come with us?"

She was sorely tempted. "I'm only here for a couple days, Bernie. I'd like to spend it with the whole family. Tell Elizabeth I said hi. Maybe next time."

Everyone talked through dinner, except Mama. Cloe talked enough for two people and Rikki wanted to know about nurses' training. Hildie told them about the capping ceremony and her new uniform. She didn't say anything about being Lady with the Lamp or top of her class. She hoped Mama would say something, but she didn't.

She lay awake most of the night, staring at the ceiling. When she finally dozed off, Mama came into the kitchen and lit a lamp, keeping the wick low as she moved around on tiptoes, filling the coffeepot, making rolls, beating eggs. Papa came in, pulling up his suspenders. They whispered in German. Hildemara kept her eyes closed, pretending to be asleep. As soon as they both finished breakfast, they went out to do chores. Nice that Mama let Cloe and Rikka sleep in. Hildie had never enjoyed that privilege.

Throwing on her clothes, Hildie started a fire in the woodstove and filled a big pot with water. She ate a roll and drank coffee while she waited for the water to boil. Filling a pail with hot water, she took a bar of soap and a rag, got down on her hands and knees, and started scrubbing the linoleum.

"What do you think you're doing?" Mama stood behind her, a milk bucket in her hand.

"Helping, I hope." Hildie wrung brownish water from the rag. She'd have to scrub for a week to get this floor clean. She cringed at the thought of how many germs had been tracked in on Papa's work boots.

Mama sloshed milk as she slammed the bucket on the table. "We spent two days cleaning this house for your visit! I'm sorry it's not good enough for you!"

Hildie didn't know whether to apologize or thank her and decided neither would do any good.

"Is this what you learn in nurses' training? How to scrub floors?"

Scalded by Mama's scorn, Hildie sat back on her heels. "And bedpans, Mama. Don't forget about that."

"Get off your hands and knees!"

Hildie got up, grabbed the pail of filthy water, and went out the back door. She slammed the screen door behind her and threw the water over Mama's flower bed. Tossing the bucket aside, she went for a walk, a long walk down to Grand Junction, where she sat and watched the mesmerizing flow of water. How was it possible to love Mama and hate her at the same time?

When she went back, the house was empty. She found Papa in the barn sharpening a hoe. The scream of metal against stone matched Hildie's feelings. When he saw her, he stopped. "You didn't go to the movie with Mama and the girls."

"I wasn't invited."

He shook his head and set the hoe aside. "They wanted you to go."

"How would I know that, Papa?"

He frowned. "I'm sorry no one came to your capping ceremony, Hildemara. We'll come to your graduation."

Old Dash rose and barked as Mama's car turned in to the drive. Bernie sat behind the wheel, Cloe and Rikki shrieking with laughter as they pulled in. Everyone piled out. Even Mama had a smile on her face until she saw Hildie sitting on a bale of hay in the barn. "Where on earth did you go?"

"To Grand Junction."

"You missed a good show." She headed for the house.

"I would've come if I'd been asked!"

"You would've been asked if you'd stayed at home."

Papa let out his breath and shook his head.

Hildemara headed for the house. She had tidied up Cloe and Rikka's bedroom earlier. When Hildie came in the back door, she lifted the hem of one of the quilts. "I made the bed with square corners. This is how we do it at the hospital. Everything stays tucked in this way. Looks nice and neat, doesn't it?"

Rikki threw herself onto her bed and lounged with her arms behind her head. "Mama thinks you're too high and mighty for us now."

"Is that what she said?"

"She said you wouldn't put a cracked plate on the table. She said you threw away one of her prettiest plates just because you didn't think it was good enough for you to eat off of it."

"I wouldn't want anyone in the family eating off a cracked plate. Cracks are breeding grounds for germs."

"What are germs, anyway?" Rikki shrugged.

"They're living organisms so small you can't see them, but they're big enough to make you very, very sick. I've seen patients suffering with diarrhea, vomiting, fever, and chills. . . ."

"Be quiet!" Cloe hissed. "You've hurt Mama's feelings enough."

"And it never occurred to anyone that my feelings might be hurt when no one bothered to come to my capping ceremony?"

"It's not like a graduation!"

"It was important to me."

"You've done nothing but pick since you got home."

"What are you talking about, Cloe?"

"Last night at dinner, you picked on Mama's canning!"

There had been mold growing on the top of the quince jelly. When Hildie didn't touch it, Mama wanted to know why it wasn't her favorite anymore. Hildie told her. Mama had scraped it off and plunked it down on the table. "There. How's that, Miss Nightingale?"

Hildie wanted to explain. "You've never seen people sick with food poisoning."

Cloe glared. "As if Mama's cooking would make anyone sick!"

Mama appeared in the doorway. "What are you two arguing about?"

"Nothing," Hildie and Cloe said in unison.

"Well, keep *nothing* to yourselves!" She glared at Hildemara and went out the back door with a basket of laundry. Hildemara knew she had heard everything.

Hildie hardly spoke the rest of the time at home. She went to church with the family and sat with Elizabeth and Bernie. She walked home with Papa.

"You seem to have a lot on your mind, Hildemara."

"Too much to talk about."

"I know how that is."

Mama drove Hildemara to the bus station. Hildie felt edgy with guilt. "I'm sorry, Mama. I didn't mean to insult your cooking or your housekeeping or—"

"I'm sorry; I'm sorry; I'm sorry." Mama put her foot down harder on the gas pedal.

Hildemara almost said she was sorry again, but bit her lip. "Old habits are hard to break."

Mama let up on the gas. "The world is dirty, Hildemara Rose. It's never going to be as clean and neat as you want it to be. You'll have to find a way to live with that."

Hildie sat up straight, blinking back tears, staring out the window as the vineyards and orchards flew by. She sat within two feet of her mother and felt a million miles between them.

Mama parked behind the bus station. She kept her hands on the steering wheel, the car idling roughly. "Will you be home for Easter?"

"Would you like me to come home?"

"What do you think?"

Hildie thought Mama would like it a whole lot better if she stayed in Oakland.

30

Now that probation had ended, Hildemara had moved upstairs to the higher realms of student quarters. Her new accommodations consisted of two rooms sleeping four each and divided by a bathroom with one toilet, one basin, and one bathtub. "Paradise!" She hardly had time to get to know her new roommates. Another washed out after a month, packing and disappearing quietly after a night shift.

Weeks passed in a flurry of eight-hour duty shifts, doctors' lectures, classes, and examinations. When Hildie came down with a sore throat, Mrs. Kaufman checked her into the hospital for a tonsillectomy. It gave Hildie the excuse she needed not to go home for Easter.

Once back on her feet, she was assigned to work with Mrs. Jones on the general ward. "She's a warhorse," Boots told her. "Old as Methuselah. Served in the Great War and probably knows more about medicine than half the doctors in this hospital, but I'm warning you: Jones will expect you to be busy all the time. When you finish your duties, look for something to do to help out or she'll skin, skewer, roast, and eat you alive for breakfast. Or lunch. Whichever comes sooner!"

Hildie found backs to rub, pillows to fluff, bedpans to scrub, cupboards to clean, linen cabinets to straighten.

A new patient arrived and pressed his buzzer within minutes. Hildie went running. He waved his hand frantically. "A bowl." She held it for him while he coughed violently and gagged, spitting into it. He collapsed back. "I'm so tired of this cough." He wheezed, his face white. Hildie made a notation on Mr. Douglas's chart.

Another patient buzzed and Hildemara helped him with a bedpan. As she carried it to the utility room, Jones appeared. "Let me see that." Shocked, Hildemara handed over the bedpan, wondering why anyone would want to look at such an oozing mess. If that wasn't surprising enough, Jones lifted it and took a whiff. "Smells like typhoid to me." She looked grim. "We're sending a sample of this to the lab."

"Don't we have to have a doctor's order?"

"He's away right now, isn't he? I'll fill out the lab slip. We'll get it down before he can make a fuss." She took the sample to the lab herself.

The doctor stormed onto the ward and asked who she thought she was to fill out lab slips and give orders. She wasn't a doctor, was she? Jones waited for his tirade to wind down before handing him the lab report. His face reddened. Without an apology, he handed them back. "He'll have to be quarantined."

"It's already taken care of, Doctor."

He stormed off the ward.

Boots laughed when Hildie told her about it. "She's gone horn-to-horn with more than one doctor. She can't abide fools, no matter how well educated. If she sees a hint of blood or pus, she's on it. And thank God she is. Have you ever seen a doctor hang around to look in a bedpan? Ha! That'll be the day!"

Mr. Douglas buzzed again the next morning just as Hildie came on duty. Hunched over, wracked with pain, he coughed. Exhausted, he could barely spit into the bowl she held for him.

She rubbed his back and said comforting words. Jones stood in the doorway. As he flopped back in bed, gasping, she drew the curtain around the bed. She didn't have to ask this time. Hildemara held out the bowl. Jones barely glanced at it. "How long have you had this cough, Mr. Douglas?"

"Couple of months, I guess. Can't remember . . ." He panted.

"Too long. I can tell you that much," his roommate grumbled. "Keeps me awake all night coughing."

"Sorry about that." Mr. Douglas started to cough again.

"Can't you do something for him?" his roommate called out.

Jones edged Hildemara back from the bed and took her place. She put her hand against his back. When he finished coughing, she let him spit into the bowl again. "Try to rest. We're going to move you to a private room."

Hildemara wiped Mr. Douglas's forehead while Jones read the chart hanging on the end of the bed. She put it back, eyes bright with anger. She hid her emotions quickly and patted Mr. Douglas's foot. Motioning Hildemara away, she closed the door behind them as they left. "If that's bronchitis, I'll eat my nursing cap!"

"What do you think he has?"

"Full-blown tuberculosis."

The next morning, another doctor appeared, livid and ready for her blood. "I hear you quarantined my patient."

"I'm protecting my patients and nurses from contagion."

"Can you read a chart, Mrs. Jones?" He thrust it in her face. "Can you read *bron-chi-tis*?"

"If Mr. Douglas has bronchitis, no one will be happier than I. But until I see his test results, I'm taking precautions."

"You've overstepped your authority, and I intend to have you fired!"

His white jacket flapped as he headed down the hall. Jones turned calmly to Hildie and the two other nurses hovering at the station. "All contagion safety measures stand until such time as Mr. Douglas is removed from our ward or I'm proven wrong. Is that clear, ladies?"

"Yes, ma'am."

Jones went about her business without so much as a wrinkle on her brow.

Mr. Douglas disappeared from the ward a few days later.

❄ ❄ ❄

Tension mounted and tempers flared among the roommates. "You have a dresser, Patrice. Use it!"

"My tennis racket won't fit."

"When do you have time to play tennis? Would you answer me that?"

"Would you all shut up! I'm trying to study."

"Wait until you work in pedie. That Miss Brown is a frustrated old maid. She never gives time off. I'll be lucky if I ever have a date."

Hildemara gave up and began studying in the library and sleeping in the upstairs sleeping porch. Nurses came and went. She often met Boots in the cafeteria. "When you graduate, you can move off grounds. We could find a little place to share, something close to the hospital."

Boots took Hildemara to the pediatric ward her first day. "Nice and quiet, isn't it?" She grinned. Only the soft step of their rubber-soled shoes sounded in the corridor. A cart squeaked; a door opened; another cart of breakfast trays; the metallic clink of knife, fork, and spoon; quiet voices—all the usual sounds of a working hospital. The doors to pediatrics lay just ahead.

Boots snickered as she planted her hands and shoved them open. "Hang on to your cap, Flo! You're about to find out why this section has heavier insulation and soundproofing!"

Hildemara stopped, assaulted by the sound of howling infants. Shrill and loud, low and plaintive, tempestuous whimpers and wails struck her heart. One pitiful voice among the rest cried, "Mommy, I want my mommy!" Like a wave the word moved down the hall from room to room.

Hildemara didn't know whether to cover her face or her ears. "I don't know if I can do this, Boots."

Boots grimaced. "I know it's hard, Flo, but you haven't been on the terminal ward yet. I cried, too. You'll get used to it. Dry your tears, honey. Put a smile back on your face and get busy. They need you. I'll see you later in the cafeteria."

Miss Brown gathered the nurses and introduced Hildemara, then led them from one patient to the next on rounds. Miss Brown explained every diagnosis, treatment, and home background before talking to each patient. Hildemara's heart broke at so many young patients—some in the tonsil ward, others in the surgical group. She reviewed an appendectomy, a hernia repair, plastic surgery for cleft palates. One child had a feeding problem, another pneumonia, another flu, and on to the long-term cases of post-polio, dystrophy, malnutrition, to the preemie room for babies in need of the most careful and specialized care. All through viewing the misery, Miss Brown smiled. She talked to each of her patients, knowing each one's history. She patted a bottom here and stroked a forehead there. She took extended hands, squeezed a toe, picked up another little one for a gentle rocking and back rub before putting the child back in bed.

"She's like another mother," one of the nurses whispered to Hildemara.

A mother with nursing skills beyond the ordinary.

Later in the afternoon, Hildemara went to check on a little boy who had been badly burned. She found Miss Brown sitting by his bed, holding his hand and reading him a book. "I thought you were off duty, Miss Brown."

"I only live a block away. Nurse Cooper said Brian asked for me."

Hildemara wondered if she would ever be as good a nurse as Miss Brown.

"Don't be so hard on yourself, Flo." Boots sipped coffee in the cafeteria later that afternoon. "You're doing well. Better than most, in fact."

"I dream about my patients."

"Well, you'd better stop that. You won't be much use to them if you don't get a good night's sleep." She put her cup down. "You'll learn to do all you can and let go of them when you walk off the ward. If you don't, your nursing days are numbered."

Awakened one night, Hildemara found her face wet with tears, her heart still pounding. She had been dreaming of Brian and how his father had held him down on a floor heater.

She tried to run and stop him, but her feet had been chained. She had tried to claw free, sobbing. Wiping her face, she sat up, trembling.

The sleeping porch did little to block out the sounds of the hospital. An ambulance siren came closer. Delivery trucks came and went. A nurse tiptoed across the sleeping porch and sank onto her cot. Two others whispered.

Hildemara knew she had to stop getting so involved with her patients. How could she be a good nurse if she allowed her heart to become attached to every patient she served? She rubbed her face, exhausted, heartsick. Papa came to mind. Closing her eyes, she could see him sitting in his chair, his Bible open, his face relaxed. Papa would tell her to trust in the Lord. Papa would tell her to pray.

Curled on her side, Hildemara prayed for Papa. Then she prayed for each of her patients. Names came to her mind, one after another, a dozen, two dozen, as though God was reminding her. At the end of each individual prayer, she let them go with a simple thought. "Brian belongs to You, Lord, not me. I give him into Your mighty, healing hands. Your will, not mine, be done. . . ."

Her body relaxed. She felt at peace. Tomorrow, she wouldn't wait until after midnight to pray. She would pray her way from one patient's bed to the next. She would imagine Jesus walking beside her from room to room. She would do what she could as a nurse and leave the rest to God's tender mercy.

❋ ❋ ❋

From pediatrics, Hildemara went on duty in geriatrics. From one extreme to another, she thought, depressed at the sight of the long wards, bed after bed, filled with cantankerous old men to the east and restless old ladies to the west. No matter how hard the nursing staff worked, the place often reeked of bowel movements and urine.

Hildie found herself talking to the Lord all day. *Lord, what can I say to give comfort to Mary today? What can I do to brighten Lester's mood?*

Some patients stared vacantly while Hildie checked their vitals or changed their diapers and bed linens. Others complained or stood at windows, staring out as though trying to find some escape. Some mumbled to themselves. Those still ambulatory roamed the hallway, pausing to talk to anyone who would listen. Hildemara tried to take time, but often had to rush to some patient in more dire need. She always had so much work to do and so little time. And so many had needs.

Before breakfast trays arrived, Hildemara helped awaken and refresh patients by washing faces, scrubbing dentures, smoothing sheets and blankets she would change later. Sometimes patients didn't want to cooperate. If she couldn't cajole them, she left in hope they might allow her to help them later.

The head nurse took her aside. "You can't give in, Miss Waltert. Mr. Mathers has to be moved every two hours or he'll develop bedsores. I know he complains. I know he curses like a drunken sailor. But you cannot let that stop you from doing what's best for him. Now, go back in there and be firm!"

She had to be like Mama.

Old Ben Tucker, a diabetic who had had his right leg amputated, became her favorite.

He often had his bed raised and table in position before she came in. He'd grin. "I've been waiting for you, darling. Feed me or shoot me."

"You slept well, I take it."

"The nurse woke me up last night and gave me a sleeping pill."

For all his good spirits, he looked ashen. How many hours since his last pain pill? "How do you feel?"

"With my hands." He reached out.

She pushed them down. "Behave. I need to take your pulse."

"Go ahead, but bring it back. I need it."

When she came on duty one morning and found he'd died quietly in his sleep, she stood by his bed, crying. The head nurse came in and put her arm around her. "Your first death?" Hildie nodded. The head nurse sighed and released her. "Dry your tears, Miss Waltert. Close his eyes. That's right. Fold his hands. Now cover him with the sheet. Go back to the nurses' station and call the hospital morgue."

Work healed a wounded heart. Hildie had hours to go on the shift, and others to see, to cheer, to encourage.

Nursing wasn't what she had expected, but she loved it all the same. She loved being part of a team that helped people get back on their feet and back to the business of living. She loved easing those who faced death. She loved feeling needed and useful. She loved serving others. She felt she had found her place in the world. She had purpose. She had value.

Despite the hard work, the anguish of seeing so much pain, the grief of losing a patient, Hildemara knew she was exactly where God wanted her.

31

WHEN SUMMER ROLLED around, Hildemara used a portion of her hard-earned savings to attend Bernie's college graduation. Elizabeth came with Mama and Papa, Cloe and Rikki. When she asked Hildemara to be her maid of honor, Hildemara laughed joyously and said of course, then worried how she'd afford a fancy dress. Elizabeth whispered, "My mother wants me to have a big ceremony, but I want something simple." Bernie could not have picked a better girl. When the wedding day arrived, Hildemara wore the navy blue dress with white cuffs and red buttons Cloe had made for her. She wore it again to Cloe's graduation and got a pinch from her sister after the ceremony.

"I'm going to have to make you a new dress."

"Please." Hildie grinned. "I suppose you'll be dreaming up designs for wedding dresses one of these days, too."

"Ha!" Cloe thought marriage a boring waste of time and talent. "I have a career to build. Mama's taking me down to the Otis Art Institute in a few weeks. I can't wait!"

Clotilde had looked confident and happy as she strode across

the stage to receive her diploma. Laughing, she'd tossed her mortar-
board in the air. Her hair had darkened to wheat, and she kept
it cut short in a bob that suited her heart-shaped face. Both of
Hildie's sisters had a confidence she had lacked until recently.

"Nursing seems to suit you, Hildie. You look happy."

"I've found where I belong."

"Met any guys?"

Hildie laughed. "Half of my patients are guys."

"I don't mean patients."

"I know what you mean, Cloe, but I'm not looking for romance."

❄ ❄ ❄

Boots graduated and hired on full-time at Merritt. Hildemara still
met her in the cafeteria every chance they got. "I'll give it a year
or two here, and then I'll look into hospitals in Hawaii or Los
Angeles. Might be nice to be somewhere warm and sunny all the
time." The Bay Area fog got to her.

Hildemara completed her second year of nurses' training. When
she started the last year, she received a blue SMH patch to sew
onto the corner of her cap. Six months later, she removed the patch
and pinned a tiny gold replica of the school in its place.

Every hour she wasn't on duty, she studied for her upcom-
ing examinations. The final would cover all three years of training. She gathered with the other students from her dwindling
class, which had dropped to thirteen, and joined in quizzing one
another on medical and surgical procedures, diseases, pediatrics,
obstetrics, bacteriology, materia medica, psychiatry, measure-
ments, and dosages.

Toward the end of her third year, the academic load lightened
and began to focus more on job prevalence, requirements, salaries,
professional organizations, and available college courses. Hildie
thought of Mama's push to go to UCB. Maybe she would end up
taking classes there, after all.

"You must keep up with new methods and ideologies, ladies,"

the General lectured. "Every year brings changes in medicine and nursing. Those who don't keep up fall behind and eventually find themselves out of a job."

Hildemara talked to Boots about it. "How many nurses can afford college or have the energy to attend classes after a full day's work?"

"It's a fact of life, Flo. Remember Miss Brown? She's been demoted to ward nurse. No college degree." She shrugged. "It's a pity, but that's the way it is. If you want a supervisory position like Mrs. Kaufman, you're going to have to go to college."

"I just want to be a nurse."

"You're a good one already." Boots brightened. "Say. We have to get you a nice outfit before your graduation. It's only a few weeks off."

"I don't have much money." She'd always admired the way Boots dressed off duty. She always had something stylish and classy.

"Meet me Saturday morning. I'll take you to my favorite store."

"Boots, I don't think—"

"Don't argue. You are not wearing that navy blue dress again!"

They rode a city bus downtown. Boots walked along, whistling, an impish look on her face. Hildemara had to hurry to keep up. "Here we are!" Boots stopped in front of a Presbyterian church.

"A church?"

Boots took her by the arm and led her around the side. A door stood open with a sign on the steps: *Rummage Sale*.

"You wouldn't believe some of the things I've found here. Come on!" Boots picked through the piles of used clothing with an eye to fashion that would have impressed Cloe. She put three outfits together in a matter of minutes. "One for your days off, one for afternoon teas, and one for a night on the town!" She even found a hat that would work with all three ensembles, and two pairs of shoes.

Hildemara paid for the items. "I can't believe I just bought an entire wardrobe for under six dollars! I'm going to write to my mother. Maybe it'll impress her."

"A smart girl learns where to shop," Boots told her on the walk back to the bus stop. "But don't you dare tell any of the other girls where I go." She laughed. "They all think I shop at Capwell's or the Emporium!"

As it turned out, Hildemara needed all three outfits for the week of graduation. On Monday, the nursing school treated the graduates to an afternoon tea with the top brass of the hospital. The night before graduation, the hospital VIPs and alumni took the graduating class to the Fairmont Hotel for dinner. Her classmates gaped when Hildie came into the lobby to wait for their ride.

"Holy cow!"

"Get a load of Flo!"

Hildemara blushed as they gathered around her.

"Where have you been shopping?"

She shrugged, quelling the urge to laugh. "Here and there."

The morning of graduation, Hildie went for mail call, praying Papa and Mama had written. No word. She grew more nervous as the day passed. She had written home, inviting the family to come. She'd only heard back from Cloe and Bernie and Elizabeth; all three planned to come in Bernie's new car.

That afternoon, Hildie and her classmates cleared the dining hall of tables and lined up chairs, borrowed potted ferns and palms, and set up a makeshift stage for graduation.

"Hey!" one of the girls called, rushing in to help finish setting up. "You'll never guess who's speaking tonight."

"Who?"

"Doc Bria!"

"Quick!" Hildie said in mock horror. "Someone bring in John Bones and install the alarm clock!" The girls laughed.

"Can't you just hear him already," another said, and she put her hand over her heart. "'Ah, ladies, it will be my great pleasure to pour forth in my most meticulous rhetoric all the prosaic platitudes of my professional pomposity in preposterous proportions of propitious postulations.'"

They roared with laughter.

Mrs. Kaufman appeared in the doorway. "Ladies, please, keep the noise down. Others are studying."

When it came time to dress for the ceremony, Hildie put on her white silk stockings and shoes, her new white uniform and cap with gold pin. Pulling the cape around her shoulders, she secured the mandarin collar. Nervous, she stood in the polished corridor outside the dining hall now lit with candelabras on either side of the stage. As she led her class into the room, she spotted Boots first, then across the aisle stood Bernie and Elizabeth and Cloe. She blinked in surprise when she saw Papa and then Mama, Rikki standing on the other side of them.

Mrs. Kaufman, eyes glistening with tears, handed out plaques of Florence Nightingale's pledge, which Hildemara recited with her classmates. She received her certificate and another gold pin.

The lights came on and cheers filled the room. Rikki pressed through the crowd to reach Hildie. "You look so beautiful in white! You have to sit for me. You look exactly how I imagine Florence Nightingale. All you need is a lamp."

Bernie had his arm around Elizabeth. "You look like you belong here, Sis."

And then Mama stood in front of her, Papa right behind her. He smiled broadly, his hands on Mama's shoulders. Had he pushed her forward? "We're proud of you, Hildemara. You did it."

Mama just looked at her. She didn't say a word. Hildie saw her swallow hard as if words wanted to come, but couldn't. When she raised her hand, Hildie grasped it. She couldn't speak either, and it took all the self-control she could muster not to cry.

"She's a grand girl!" Boots appeared and spun Hildie into another hug. "Best in the class." Hildie made quick introductions.

"Are you coming home for a while?" Mama asked.

Surprised she had asked, Hildie shook her head. "No. I've been hired to join the Merritt staff. I'm back on duty day after tomorrow."

"So soon?" Papa looked disappointed. "Mama and I thought you'd be home for a few weeks, at least."

"I won't be able to come home for a while, Papa. I'm fortunate to have a job so soon. I made twelve dollars a month this year, and I still need to pay Cloe for making the two uniforms."

"One to wear, one to wash." Cloe smiled, shaking her head.

"And I'll have rent. Boots found a little house a few blocks from the hospital. We're sharing expenses."

Mama didn't say anything, not one word, until after refreshments and the conversation died down. People began to go out on the town. "It's getting late." Mama looked up at Papa. "We need to start back."

Hildie fought back the tears. "I'm glad you came."

"We wouldn't have missed it." Papa hugged her hard. "Keep saying your prayers and reading your Bible." He patted her back and let her go.

"I will, Papa." She wrapped her arms around Mama and hugged her. "Thank you for coming. It meant the world to me." She felt Mama's hand on her back, and then she withdrew from Hildie's embrace.

"You did it, Hildemara Rose." Her smile seemed a little sad. "I hope the life you've chosen for yourself makes you happy."

Hildie leaned forward and kissed Mama's cheek. "I guess I'm about to find out, aren't I?"

❉ ❉ ❉

Dear Rosie,

Hildemara Rose is now a full-fledged nurse. She was the top student in her class and had the honor of leading the procession. And she did look like Florence Nightingale in her white uniform and navy blue cape. My girl stood so tall with her head high! I could imagine her standing on a battlefield with her lamp held high, giving the wounded hope.

She is not a timid child anymore. My girl knows her place in the world. I am so proud of her, Rosie. The evening would have been perfect if not for the speaker, some long-winded doctor who didn't want to leave the podium. I had a dreadful headache and it was difficult to concentrate on what he had to say. And then the press of people made the pain worse.

I wanted to tell Hildemara how proud she made me, but I couldn't get the words out. Niclas spoke for both of us. I asked if she was coming home, hoping I would have time and opportunity to talk with her, but she has already been hired by Merritt Hospital and will be on official duty long before you receive this letter. Not only that. She and her friend Jasia Boutacoff have found a house to rent. She is a woman now, with a life of her own.

❄ ❄ ❄

Hildemara moved in with Boots a week after joining the Merritt nursing staff. The house wasn't far from the hospital, so she walked every day she worked. The house felt like a palace after the small dorm bedroom, and quiet after the sleeping porch she'd shared with dozens of nurses coming in and going out. The house had a few drawbacks: a big yard to care for and a large fruit-producing lemon tree. Mr. Holmes, their next-door neighbor, said the previous tenant had driven nails in the trunk in hope of killing the tree. "Must have given it a boost of something!" Hildie sacked up lemons every week and dropped them off at the hospital kitchen.

"We've got to do something about the yard." Hildie worried. "We're going to be the neighborhood slobs."

"Who cares? It's the landlord's problem, not ours. He said he'd come by and do it when he has time."

The landlord only came on the day rent was due, and by then Hildie and Boots had learned the roof leaked and the kitchen sink had a habit of stopping up. Mr. Dawson said he'd send someone to fix it.

"When hell freezes over, he'll fix it." Boots called on a friend to do it, then sent a bill to the landlord. When he didn't pay, she deducted it from the next month's rent. When Mr. Dawson complained, Boots stood toe-to-toe with him in front of the house.

Neighbors came out to listen. Boots called Mr. Holmes to witness that Mr. Dawson had agreed to her deducting a portion of the rent for repairs. When she came inside the house, she slapped her hands together as though dusting the man off. Hildie laughed. "You remind me of Mama!"

Finally, embarrassed by the state of the front yard, Hildie asked Mr. Holmes if she could borrow his lawn mower and hedge clippers. She remembered how Papa had disdained people who "let their land go" and didn't want to be the dump of the block.

"Sorry." Mr. Holmes shook his head. "I don't loan tools, Miss Waltert. Learned the hard way people don't return them."

"I'd buy a lawn mower and clippers if I could, but I don't have the money."

"What do you do for a living?"

"We're both nurses at Merritt."

He peered over the fence at the yard, rubbed his chin, and shook his head. "Sure is a mess. Tell you what. I've got an old mower under the house. I'll sharpen the blades and grease her up a bit and you can have her. I'll give you my wife's old clippers. It's clear that place you're living in needs work. How much rent is Dawson charging you girls?" When Hildie told him, he whistled. "No wonder you don't have anything left over. He sure saw you coming, didn't he?"

Mr. Holmes brought the lawn mower and clippers over the next Saturday. "All sharp and ready to go."

After an hour, Hildie sat on the front steps to rest. Mr. Holmes peered over the fence and asked how the lawn mower was working. "It's working fine, Mr. Holmes, but I should've asked if you had a sickle." Hildie wiped sweat from her brow.

He laughed. "Looks better than it did."

"Thanks for the mower and clippers, Mr. Holmes. I'll keep you supplied with lemons."

"Call me George. And as for lemons, I already take what I want off the branches hanging over my fence."

32

1939

Germany Invades Poland

Hildemara read the headline over morning coffee and a plate of scrambled eggs. Boots shuffled in, wearing her slippers and robe, still bleary-eyed from her date the night before.

"Oh, my head." Boots groaned, sliding cautiously onto a chair across the table. "I don't even know what time I got in last night."

"After two in the morning."

"No wonder I feel like a truck ran over me."

Hildie folded the paper back to read the second-page continuation. "Have you seen this?"

Boots rubbed her temples. "Heard it on the radio last night."

Papa had worried about this kind of thing happening. German relatives had written glowing letters about the meteoric rise of Adolf Hitler and the National Socialist German Workers' Party. Papa said a man with such messianic charisma might prove to be a devil in disguise. Mama thought the Great War would end all wars in Europe. Papa said man's nature never changes.

Boots made a dismissive gesture. "I hope America stays out of it." Apparently she had other things on her mind besides what was happening in Europe. "I saw a new guy in the cafeteria yesterday." She raked her fingers through her curly black hair. "Good-looking, tall, great body, nice eyes, a smile to make a girl's knees wobble."

Hildie looked up from the paper. "Did you make a date with him?"

"Nope. He's an orderly. I only go after doctors, lawyers, and Indian chiefs. You might like him, though."

Hildie just looked at her. They'd had this discussion before. Boots accused her of becoming a social outcast. Hildie said she had enough of a social life with the nurses and her patients at work.

"Flo, you're going to become like Miss Brown."

"And what's wrong with Miss Brown?"

Boots stood, shaking her head. "Gotta get ready." She opened the bedroom door and turned back to Hildie. "I'm going out after work. Don't wait up for me."

Hildie laughed. "I never do." She had the house to herself more than she had expected, especially when it came to yard work and doing dishes. She didn't mind the quiet. When she had a day off, she slept in, caught up on laundry, housekeeping, and yard work. She kept up correspondence with Cloe, who had moved to Los Angeles, or wrote to Mama and Papa. Mama wrote back once a month, giving a chronology of what had happened on the farm. When Hildie had Sunday off, she went to church.

Hildie was sitting in the cafeteria the next evening, finishing her supper and thinking about Boots and her comment about Miss Brown, when she felt someone looking at her. She glanced up and saw a young man standing in line, waiting for the cook to hand him his dinner. He fit Boots's description of the "new guy" she'd seen. When he smiled at her, Hildie looked down quickly. Flustered, she picked up her tray, dumped the contents, and left the cafeteria.

The next day when she came on the ward, she saw him helping lift one of her patients from bed to gurney for transporting him to surgery. He had an athletic build like Bernie. Football player? When he smiled at her again, she felt herself blush. Embarrassed, she looked away quickly and busied herself with paperwork at the nurses' station. She kept her eyes down as he went by with her patient.

As she stood in line for lunch, someone came up behind her. "I saw you on the medical ward this morning."

She glanced at him and returned her attention to the cafeteria menu. Picking up her order, she headed for a table in the far corner of the room, where she could be alone. As much as she laughed over Boots's disdain for orderlies, she knew there was an unspoken rule about nurses fraternizing with them. What was it the General had said? *"Laborers work with hands. Professionals work with hands, head, and heart."*

"Mind if I sit with you?" When Hildie just stared, open-mouthed, he set his tray down and took the seat opposite hers. "Is there an unspoken rule around here that a nurse can't say more than three words to an orderly?"

Did he read minds? "No."

"One word. Hardly an improvement."

His smile did odd things to her insides. "I don't usually strike up conversations with people I don't know. I only saw you yesterday for the first time."

"That's better." He grinned, which made her heart do flips and flutters. "I'm a junior at UC Berkeley with eyes on medical school. I thought it might be a good idea to work in a hospital and get a different view on my future career."

"Good for you."

"I'm working in the psych ward for the next month."

"I hear it can be a real riot in there."

He laughed. "Good one." He was even more handsome and appealing when he laughed.

"I wasn't joking."

"Oh." He looked at her, really looked this time, and she could feel the heat coming up again, along with tingles and other feelings she had never had before that made her feel vulnerable. "Miss Waltert." He held out his hand, a big strong hand like Bernie's only without the calluses. "I'm Cale Arundel, but my friends call me Trip." When his fingers closed around hers, heat surged through her. She pulled her hand away.

"Do you like movies, Miss Waltert?"

"Who doesn't?"

"How about Friday night?"

She glanced up sharply. "Are you asking me for a date?"

"You look surprised. Yes, I'm asking you for a date."

She looked around, disturbed by his attention. She had never been asked out by a boy, let alone a man. Why would someone like Cale Arundel be interested in her? "I'm on duty."

"When are you off duty?"

"I'd have to check the schedule."

He crossed his forearms on the table and leaned forward, gazing at her with faint amusement. "Is it because I'm a lowly orderly that you hesitate?"

"I don't know you."

"I don't know you either, but I'd like the opportunity to get to know you. Hence, the invitation."

She looked at her watch. "I need to get back. Excuse me." She grabbed her tray, dumped the contents in the garbage can near the door, and left the tray on top. Her heartbeat didn't slow until she returned to the medical ward.

"What happened to you?" one of the nurses asked.

"Nothing. Why? Am I late?"

"No. You just look a little flushed and excited about something."

Cale Arundel came on her ward later that afternoon. The moment she spotted him, she grabbed a clipboard and ducked into the linen closet to check off the list of sheets, pillowcases, towels, and washcloths. One of the nurses peered in. "Someone's waiting for you at the nurses' station."

Cale walked toward her. "I came for an aspirin."

"An aspirin?" Nurses sat, heads together, whispering and

grinning at her. She glared at Cale. "You came all the way here from the psych ward to find an aspirin?"

"I didn't think you'd loan me a straitjacket."

She didn't smile. She looked pointedly at the other nurses and then back at him. Maybe he'd get the hint and stop providing grist for the gossip mill. He noticed, too, but shrugged it off. "People talk. So what?"

So what? It was her reputation at stake. Embarrassed, angry, she headed down the hallway. He followed. When she stopped out of sight of the other nurses, he stepped in front of her. "You look ready to shoot me, Miss Waltert."

"Why are you here?"

"Why do you think?"

"I have no idea!"

"I checked your schedule. You're off on Friday. I'd like to take you to dinner and a movie."

No one had ever asked her out, and the thought of this handsome young man, orderly or not, being interested in her seemed beyond comprehension. "I have no intention of being the brunt of someone's idea of a joke."

"Why would I joke about it?"

"No!"

"How do you know I'm not husband material unless you get to know me first?"

She blanched. "What did you say?"

"Boots said you wouldn't go out with anyone unless he was husband material."

"I'll kill her." Hildemara felt her face go hot. "And I'm supposed to believe you're looking for a wife?"

"I never gave it much thought until two days ago, at 12:15 to be exact, when you walked into the cafeteria."

Did he really think she'd believe such hogwash? "I'll put out the word, Mr. Arundel. You'll have women lined up and on their knees begging."

He leaned so close that she could smell his aftershave. "Keep it to yourself. I'm not interested in anyone else. Dinner and a movie. I promise I won't lay a finger on you, if that's what worries you." He raised his hand in solemn vow. "I swear I'm a gentleman."

"If you aren't, I have a big brother who'll beat the living tar out of you."

He laughed. "I take that as a yes. Friday. Six o'clock sharp." He shoved the swinging doors open and walked through. "See you then."

"Wait a minute!"

A patient buzzer went off. She pushed the doors open, but Cale had already gone into the stairwell. Frustrated, she hurried back down the hall. She'd only make matters worse by tracking him down in the hospital.

Boots! She'd tell her roommate to give him a message.

"Nothing doing." Boots shook her head. "You want to break a date, you do it yourself."

She watched for him in the cafeteria, hoping for a chance to tell him she'd changed her mind. She didn't see him for the next three days. She comforted herself with the fact that he didn't have her address. He couldn't come and pick her up if he didn't know where she lived.

"He's cute. And you haven't had a date since I've known you." Boots was scrambling eggs in the small kitchen. "Go out. Have fun." She clicked her tongue and winked. "Try not to behave."

Hildemara didn't see Cale at all that week. On Friday, she fretted about what to do. Maybe he wouldn't show up. But then that would be even more humiliating!

"Will you settle down, Flo? You're jumpy as a grasshopper."

"What was I thinking? I don't even know the guy."

"That's why you go out with him. So you can get to know him. Let me know if he's a good kisser."

"You're not funny, Boots!"

She laughed. "It's so much fun teasing you."

Hildie sat on the beige sofa she and Boots had bought second-hand and plucked at the skirt of her navy blue dress. She got up again. "This is crazy." She saw a black Model T Ford pull up and park in front of the house. "Oh no, he's here. I can't do this, Boots."

"No getting out of it now." Boots bounced over, knelt on the couch, and peered out through the curtains. "Holy cow! Red roses! This guy is serious. And a car! And I thought he was an orderly."

Hildie slapped her hands away from the curtain. "Will you stop? He'll see you! He is an orderly. He's a student at UC Berkeley majoring in medicine." She felt a twinge of something uncomfortable watching Boots watch him. "Why don't *you* go out with him?"

Boots laughed. "He's at the door, Hildie. Open up. Let him in."

They went to Lupe's on East Fourteenth Street. Over the next hour, Hildie found out Cale Arundel preferred the nickname Trip; he grew up in Colorado Springs; his father drove a city bus; his mother played piano for the Presbyterian church next door; he liked skiing, fishing, and hiking; and he'd spent three years at the University of Colorado in Denver. "I transferred to Berkeley because it's one of the top universities in the country."

Exactly what Mama had said. "Why transfer so late?"

"Didn't have the grades to get in freshman year, and even if I had, I would've had to pay out-of-state tuition. Transferring senior year isn't the smartest decision I've ever made. I lost some credits coming here, but I wanted UCB on my diploma, and I hope to do my internship in San Francisco."

"Why are you called Trip?"

He laughed. "I can thank my father for that. He said I tripped over my feet until I grew into them." He held up his hands. "Enough about me. I want to know about you."

Hildie didn't know what to say to make her life sound the least bit interesting. Thankfully, the waitress brought their spaghetti. Trip put his hand out to take hers. "Mind if we pray?" She put her hand in his as he said grace. He squeezed her hand lightly before letting it go. "Last thing I'll say about myself—God matters. I go to church every Sunday. I hear you're a praying girl. Now, it's your turn to talk." He stabbed his fork into his spaghetti.

Stomach fluttering, Hildie twirled spaghetti on a fork, wishing she had ordered something easier to eat. "My parents are farmers in Murietta, almonds and raisins. I have an older brother and two younger sisters. Bernie went to college in Sacramento. He's married to my best friend, Elizabeth. My younger sister, Cloe, is going to the Otis Art Institute in Los Angeles. She intends to design costumes for the movies. Rikka, the youngest, is a talented artist, still in high school. When I graduated from high school, I came up to train at Samuel Merritt Nursing School. When the administrator asked if I'd stay, I said yes. End of story."

Trip gave her a lopsided smile. "I doubt that." He set his fork down and studied her.

She picked up her napkin. "Do I have spaghetti sauce on my chin?"

"No, but you have a nice chin." He picked up his fork again. "Sorry. I like looking at you."

No one had ever said that to her before.

Trip took her to *Drums Along the Mohawk* with Henry Fonda and Claudette Colbert. He kept his word and didn't touch her, not even once. When the movie ended, he drove her straight back to the house, walked her to the door, said he'd had a great time, and wished her a good night.

She took the hint and retreated into the house, leaving the porch light on until he got into his car. She watched through the curtains as Trip Arundel drove away. *Well, that's that.* She plunked down on the sofa and stared at the wall.

She had had the best time of her life, but thought she must have bored Trip to death. He couldn't get away fast enough. Changing into flannel pajamas, she tried to read. Distracted, she went to bed and lay awake until Boots came home at three in the morning. "You don't have to tiptoe."

"You're still awake?" Boots's voice slurred slightly. "Have a good time?"

"Sounds like you did."

Boots stood in the doorway. "A little tipsy, tha's all. He took me dancing and then to some party. So? How did you like Trip? Nice guy, isn't he."

"Yes. He's nice." It seemed a harmless enough thing to say to her inebriated friend. In truth, she had liked him entirely too much. She had felt the loss of him when he said good night. "I don't expect to hear from him again."

"Too bad." Boots waved her hand. "I'm going to hit the hay before I end up on the floor. Nigh' night."

Trip called the next day. "How about an ice cream at Eddy's?"

And the evening after that. "It's a nice evening for a walk around Lake Merritt."

When he didn't call on Monday, Hildemara felt the hint of heartbreak coming on. How could she have allowed herself to fall for someone so fast?

When he called the next day and asked her to dinner and another movie, she declined.

"Sunday, then. Church?"

"I don't know my schedule yet. I may put in for extra shifts."

Trip didn't press.

Boots came home early. "Why are you crying? Did that guy do something . . . ?"

"No. He didn't do anything. Nothing's wrong."

Boots sat on the sofa. "He hasn't asked you out again. Is that it?"

"He did ask me out."

Boots shook her head. "So what's the problem?"

"I'm not going out with him again."

"Why not? You like him. He likes you. Put two and two together and—"

"And I end up with a broken heart. Trip could have any girl he wants, Boots. He's gorgeous. He's going to UCB. He's going to be a doctor. That should make even you sit up and take notice."

Boots gave Hildie a hard push. "Next time he asks, say yes."

Next time he asked, Hildie thought up another lame excuse to say no. "I have to study for the state board exam." She wanted to keep a distance rather than let herself hope.

The day after she received the good news that she'd passed and
now qualified as a registered nurse, Trip showed up on the medical
ward with a bouquet of daisies he'd probably bought from the
hospital gift shop. "Congratulations!"

She took the bouquet and set it on the nurses' station counter.
"How did you know?"

"Boots told me. You aren't on shift tonight and you don't have
to study. Let me take you out so we can celebrate." He said it
loudly enough for three nurses to overhear, even if they hadn't been
eavesdropping. Hildemara blushed and stepped away from the
others, moving farther down the hall.

"I don't think that's a good idea."

He frowned. "Did I do something to offend you?"

"No."

"Why do you keep saying no, Hildemara?"

"Mr. Arundel!" Jones beckoned him down the hall. They spoke
in low voices. Without looking at her, Trip strode down the hall
and disappeared through the swinging doors. Feeling a lump
growing in her throat, Hildie went to check on her patients. When
she came back to the nurses' station, Jones looked up at her. "You're
fighting a losing battle, Hildemara."

Trip showed up in the cafeteria a few days later. Hildemara
grabbed her tray and retreated to a table behind a potted palm.
Trip gave his order, waited for it, and crossed the room. He set his
tray on the table, but didn't sit. "Boots said you probably wouldn't
trust me unless I had references. So . . ." He reached into his
pocket, took out three envelopes, and slid them across the table.
"Just so you'll know I'm not the wolf waiting to devour Little Red
Riding Hood." He took his tray and left.

Annoyed, she tore open the envelopes. One letter came from
Trip's pastor claiming Trip was a morally upright young man
who attended church every Sunday. Another came from the head
nurse of the psych ward, far more serious in tone, commending
Mr. Arundel for hard work, intelligence, and compassion. The
third was in the form of a petition: *All the undersigned concur that*

Miss Hildemara Waltert, more commonly known as Flo, should go out with Mr. Cale Arundel, commonly known as Trip, of Colorado Springs, a most honorable young man. Signatures followed, with Jasia Boutacoff at the top and twenty-two other nurses' names below hers, including Miss Brown and Miss Jones!

Cheeks flaming, she folded the letters and stuffed them into her uniform pocket. She tried to eat her lunch, but felt the amused glances of several whose names were on the list. Trip sat alone across the room. He ate quickly, dumped his garbage, and came back to her table. Sliding a chair out, he turned it around and straddled it. Folding his arms on the back, he looked at her. "We had a great time, didn't we? Or was I deluding myself? I have been working on the psych ward, after all."

"Trip . . ."

"You know, it would be easier to marry you first and then ask you out."

"Don't make fun of me, please."

"I saw you before you ever saw me, Hildie. You were praying with one of your patients. I thought you were the prettiest girl I'd ever seen. I asked around about you. I liked what people had to say."

"You asked about me?"

He grimaced in apology. "Boots has a reputation. I wanted to know if her roommate plays the field like she does. I wanted to know a little more about you before I made a move." He smiled slightly. "I think you feel something for me or you wouldn't be running so scared. I'd like to spend more time with you, get to know you better, have you get to know me." He rose and turned the chair around. "Your decision." He pushed the chair under the table. "You tell me no again, and I'll take it as no." He gave her a rueful smile, his gaze caressing her face. "I'm praying you say yes." He walked away.

When she got off work, he was waiting outside the medical ward. She took the stairs instead of the elevator. He kept up with her. "So?"

"Yes."

He flashed a smile at her. "Good."

She stopped on the landing. Maybe he wasn't the Casanova she had first thought, but that didn't mean that this relationship would come to anything. He might take her out a few more times and realize she was the most boring girl he'd ever met and wonder why he'd bothered in the first place.

He was right: she was scared. She was already halfway to being in love with him. She needed to say something, but couldn't think of anything that wouldn't expose her feelings.

Trip stepped closer. He took her hand and wove his fingers through hers. "Don't worry so much, Hildemara Waltert. We'll take it one step at a time and see where this takes us."

And so they did for the next six months, until Mama called and said she needed Hildemara to come home right away. "Your father has cancer."

33

1940

Cancer meant Papa was dying. Hildie had seen patients wasting away, in pain, dying slowly, relatives coming and going, broken and grieving. Cancer meant there was no hope. Cancer meant a lingering, excruciating death. When had he been diagnosed? What had been done for him? What, if anything, could be done? How long had Mama waited before calling for help? Hildemara couldn't imagine her asking unless there was no hope at all.

She felt sick and afraid, wondering if she would be up to taking care of her father. How would she bear it? It was hard enough watching a stranger suffer.

And Trip. It meant leaving him, and she loved him so much she ached with it. She hadn't told him yet. Maybe God had kept her silent for a reason. She had no idea how long she might be gone, and then, when it was all over, what would happen to Mama? A week ago, she and Trip had had a conversation that gave her reason to hope he loved her as much as she loved him. "We can talk about the future when I graduate from UC."

"How long will that be?"

"Another year, maybe less, if I can squeeze in a few courses over the summer."

Hildie wanted to tell him two people working together toward a common goal could get there a lot faster than one man on his own. She lost her courage.

Now it didn't matter. Her father took precedence.

With newspaper headlines and radio reports blaring about the Nazis invading Denmark, Norway, France, Belgium, Luxembourg, and the Netherlands and nurses talking about possible military service, Hildie put in for emergency leave. She packed everything in two suitcases and called Trip to break their Friday night date.

"I had something special planned."

"I'm sorry, Trip." She clutched the telephone, trying not to start crying again.

"What's wrong, Hildie?"

"My father has cancer. I'm going home to take care of him."

"Home to Murietta? I'm coming over."

"No, Trip. Please don't. I can't allow myself to think about anything but Papa right now. And I—"

"I love you, Hildie."

She wanted to say she loved him, too, but that didn't mean she didn't have to leave. She felt torn between her love for Papa and her love for Trip.

"Stay put. I'll be there in thirty minutes."

Panic set in when he hung up. She called the bus station for schedules, called Mama with the time she would arrive in Murietta, raked her fingers through her hair, and wondered if she should call a cab and go before Trip arrived. With no one in the house, she felt vulnerable. She knew she would make a complete fool of herself over him.

When the knock came, she almost didn't answer the door.

Trip knocked again, harder. "Hildie!"

She unlocked the door and opened it. Trip stepped inside and pulled her into his arms. Crying, she clung to him, knowing it would be a long time before she saw him again, if ever. He nudged the door shut with his foot. She shook with sobs and his arms tightened. She could feel his heart beating fast and hard.

Pulling her arms down, she pushed back. Trip didn't try to hold on. "I only have a few minutes before I have to leave for the bus station."

"Let me drive you to Murietta. I'd like to meet your parents."

"No."

He looked pained. "Why do I get the feeling you're closing the door on me again?" When she didn't say anything, he stepped closer. "What's going on, Hildie?"

"I don't know what I'm going to find when I get there, Trip. I don't know how long I'm going to be away. Months? A year? I have no way of knowing." If she was gone too long, he might find someone else. She wouldn't want to come back. And what would Mama say if she showed up with a young man? She hadn't mentioned Trip in any letters, holding tight to her feelings, not sharing them with anyone, except Boots, who couldn't help but see. What would Trip think if Mama spoke her mind as she always did? *Well, this is the first I've heard you have a young man in your life."* What then?

Covering her face, Hildie burst into more tears. Embarrassed to have Trip see her so out of control, she turned away. She didn't dare tell him how she felt. It would only make everything worse. When Trip touched her shoulder, she moved away. Wiping her face, she gulped. "It's better if I go home alone. I'll have time to think, time to get control of my emotions. I need to make some kind of plan for how to care for him."

Trip came up behind her and ran his hands down her arms. He spoke gently, reasonably. "What are your mother and father going to think of me if you arrive on a bus?"

She bit her lip. "They won't think anything."

"I know what I'd think. My daughter is keeping company with an insensitive man who doesn't care anything about her family.

Not much of a recommendation there." He turned her around. "Hildie?"

"They don't know about you."

He went still, his eyes flickering with confusion, then hurt. "You never told them about us?" When she didn't answer, he let out his breath as though punched. He took his hands from her waist. "Well, I guess that makes it clear where I stand."

"You don't understand."

He stepped back and held up his hands in surrender. "It's okay. You don't need to explain. I get it."

"Trip. Please."

"Please what? You can't love someone if you can't trust him, Hildie, and you've never let yourself trust me." Eyes moist, he turned away. "I guess I should've seen this coming. I'm just dense." He picked up her two suitcases. "Is this it?" He didn't meet her eyes. "Anything else you want to take home with you?"

Was he giving her one last chance?

"You're right, Hildie. I don't understand." He went out the door. She had no choice but to follow, lock the door behind her, and get in his car.

Neither spoke on the drive to the bus station. He pulled up in front. When he started to open his door, she put her hand on his arm. "Don't get out of the car. Please. I can make it on my own." She tried to smile. She tried to tell him the last six months had been the happiest of her life. She tried to tell him she loved him and would never forget him as long as she lived. Instead, she gulped and said, "Don't hate me, Trip."

"I don't hate you."

So much for happily ever after. "Good-bye, Trip." Trembling all over, she reached for the door handle.

Swearing softly, Trip reached for her. "Just one thing before you go." He dug his fingers into her hair. "I've wanted to do this for weeks." He kissed her. He wasn't tentative or careful or even gentle. He drank her in and filled her up with sensations. When he drew back, they both sat breathing hard, stunned. He ran his thumb over her lips, tears filling his eyes. "Something to remember me by." He let go, leaned across, and shoved the door open. "I'm sorry about your father, Hildie."

Standing on the sidewalk with her two suitcases, Hildie watched Trip drive away. He didn't look back. Not once.

She boarded the bus, found a seat in the last row by herself, and cried all the way to Murietta.

❄ ❄ ❄

Mama stood waiting outside the bus station. She frowned when Hildie came down the steps, collected her luggage, and met her. They didn't embrace. Mama shook her head. "You look awful. Are you going to be all right? I don't want you going to pieces the minute you walk in the door and see your father. That will just make it worse for him. You understand me?"

Cover up. Pretend everything is all right. "I got it out of my system on the way home."

"I hope so."

Hildie had no intention of telling her mother she had just lost the love of her life. "How long have you known about the cancer?" She put her suitcases in the backseat and sat in front.

"It came on suddenly." Mama started the car.

"No symptoms at all?"

"I'm not a nurse, Hildemara. He looked a little yellow to me, and I told him so, but your father said he didn't have time for a doctor. Not then, anyway." She ground the gears.

Yellow? Oh, God. "Is it in his liver?"

"Yes."

Hildemara shut her eyes for a moment and then looked out the window, hoping Mama wouldn't guess what she already knew. It wouldn't be long.

Mama drove more slowly than usual. "I'm glad you're home, Hildemara."

"So am I, Mama. So am I."

❄ ❄ ❄

Papa sat in the living room, his Bible open on his lap. Hildie set her suitcases down and went to him, trying not to show the shock at his changed physical appearance. "Hello, Papa."

He rose with difficulty. "Hildemara! Mama said she had a surprise for me."

When he opened his arms, Hildie walked into them. She held him firmly, but gently, willing herself not to cry. "I'm home, Papa." She ran her hands over his back, guessing at how much weight he had lost since Christmas. She could feel his vertebrae, his ribs.

Papa took her by the arms and stepped back. "There was a time when you couldn't put your arms all the way around me." He had always stood straight and tall with broad shoulders and thick biceps. Now he was bent from weariness and pain. He edged back toward his chair, reaching back with a tremulous hand. She wanted to step forward and help him, but the look on his face prevented her. He had his pride, and she had already damaged it with her quick tactile examination.

"He doesn't have much appetite." Mama stood in the middle of the room. "But I'll get supper on the stove. I'm sure you're hungry after your long trip, Hildemara."

Hildie bent and picked up her suitcases so Papa wouldn't see her tears. "I hope I'm not sleeping on the sofa."

"Bernie's room is empty, now that he and Elizabeth are settled in the new cottage. You can sleep in there. Bernie's out in the orchard. Elizabeth loves farming as much as your brother. She grows flats of flowers for the nursery."

"Wish she'd grow us some grandchildren," Papa said with a laugh.

Hildie felt a wave of sadness. She had learned more than she wanted to know about some things while in the hospital. For Bernie to father a child, after the case of mumps he'd had as a boy, would take a miracle. She remembered him screaming in pain as the disease attacked his testicles. She hadn't understood then what she knew now. She wondered if Dr. Whiting would ever tell them. Probably not, unless they asked. "Will they be eating with us?"

"No. She cooks for the two of them."

Hildie set her suitcases in Bernie's old room and looked out through the screen. The cottage her brother had built for his bride was white with yellow shutters. A flower box held purple pansies and white alyssum. A lattice shed had been built beyond the wash-house past the bay tree. Elizabeth stood inside it, working among flats of flowers.

"Rikka will be home from school soon," Mama called out over the radio Papa always wanted turned on in the living room. Another radio music program had been interrupted with the increasingly dismal news in Europe. Germans were bombing Paris. In Italy, Mussolini declared war on Britain and France. As sick as he was, Papa still wanted to know what went on in the world.

Rikki had commencement exercises soon, Hildie remembered. Papa had already insisted he would attend the ceremony, even if he had to use a cane.

Hildie came back into the living room. "You want any help, Mama?"

"No. You just sit with Papa and visit."

Hildie sat at the end of the sofa closest to Papa's chair. He reminded her of the old gentlemen on the geriatric ward. Cancer aged a man. Her heart broke watching him lean back carefully, a hand resting lightly over his swollen abdomen. "Your baby sister is doing well in high school. Top grades in art."

"No surprise there, Papa."

Mama cut peeled potatoes into pieces over a pot. "She wanted to quit and get married a while back."

"Married! To Paul?" Or was it Johnny? She couldn't remember. Her baby sister went through boys faster than babies went through diapers.

Mama snorted. "She's had two boyfriends since Paul. The new

one is Melvin Walker. He's an improvement over the others—five years older, has a good, steady job."

Papa smiled. "She'll know when the right one comes along, and I have a feeling it isn't this one."

Hildie thought of Trip. He'd been the right one. It just hadn't been the right time.

Mama added water to the pot. "This one won't be brushed off. He knows what he wants, and he's sticking close until she sees his worth."

Papa chuckled. "Sounds like what I had to do." His eyes twinkled as he looked at Hildie. "There's nothing wrong with a little romance. How about you, Hildemara? Have you met anyone special?"

"Would she be here if she had?" Mama set the pot on the stove.

"I've had a few dates." Hildie wondered what they would say if she told them she had met and fallen in love with a man, that she had dreamed of marrying him and having his children. Better to have them think she had no luck with love than know she had given him up to take care of Papa. Papa would send her back, and she needed to be here. Now that she saw Papa, she knew how much.

Papa held out his hand. When she took it, she felt the bones through his rough skin. "I was surprised when Mama said you wanted to come home." She realized with some surprise that Papa didn't know Mama had called and asked her to come. Hildie felt guilty for not knowing how sick he was before this. If she had come home sometime during the last few months, she might have seen signs and given warning. Instead, she had been so caught up in her own life, in Trip, in love that she hadn't bothered.

"Well, it's about time, isn't it, Niclas?" Mama grabbed a towel. "I could use a little help around here." She tossed the towel on the counter and put her hands on her hips.

Hildie took the cue. "I've missed you both. I've wanted to come home for quite a while. I hope you won't mind having me around for a month or two."

"I know what's going on." Papa's voice had an edge of anger in it. "How could you do this, Marta? Hildemara's got a life of her own."

"Working. That's her life. She's a nurse, and a good one. She led the class procession as the Lady with the Lamp. She had to be the top student to do that. She knows what's what, and we need a nurse. Why not one who loves you?"

"Oh, Marta." Papa sounded so weary and defeated. He couldn't fight back anymore.

Mama's arms dropped to her sides. "It's what she's always wanted to do, Niclas. You said it was what God called her to do. Maybe it was for such a time as this. Tell him, Hildemara."

Hildie heard the pleading in Mama's voice and saw the telltale brightness in her hazel eyes. Papa looked crushed in spirit. "I didn't want to become a burden, Marta."

"You're not a burden, Papa, and I'd have been hurt if Mama hadn't called and someone else tended you. Life is short enough as it is for all of us. Time is the most precious thing we have, isn't it?" She took his hand between hers. "There's no place I'd rather be than right here." On the bus ride to Murietta, she had buried and mourned all the might-have-beens.

He looked into her eyes and went very still, comprehending. "We don't have much time, do we?"

"No, Papa. We don't."

Turning away, Mama gripped the sink. Her shoulders sagged and shook, but she didn't make a noise.

❄ ❄ ❄

Hildemara lay awake inside the screened porch bedroom, listening to the crickets and a hoot owl in the bay tree near the tree house. She prayed for her father. She prayed for Trip. She prayed God would give her the strength she would need, knowing each day would become more difficult.

When she finally slept, she dreamed of long, polished corridors.

Someone stood in the open doorway at the end, surrounded by light. She ran toward him and felt his arms go around her. She heard his whisper against her hair, inside her heart, not in words but in rest.

She awakened when a rooster crowed. The back door opened and closed, then the screen door. Sitting up, Hildie watched Mama cross the yard to feed the chickens.

Hildie went into the bathroom built by the Summer Bedlam boys and showered, brushed her teeth and hair, dressed, and went into the kitchen. She poured coffee and sat at the kitchen table reading her Bible. Covering her face, she prayed for Mama and Papa and the days ahead. Then she thought about Papa standing beneath the white almond blossom canopy in spring, singing a German hymn. She thought of him sharpening tools in the barn, digging irrigation ditches, sitting in his wagon loaded with vegetables from Mama's garden.

Today, Lord, she prayed. *Give me strength for the day. This is a day You have made and I will rejoice in it. I will. God, give me strength.*

When Hildie heard Papa groan, she went to him, prepared to play the role God had given her.

❊　❊　❊

Dear Rosie,

I do not know if you will receive this letter with all that is happening in Europe, but I must write. Niclas has cancer. He is dying. I can do nothing for him but sit and try to make him more comfortable.

I had no choice but to ask Hildemara to give up her life and come home. He needs a nurse. He worsens by the day and I can't bear to see him in such pain. She is a great comfort to us both.

Niclas still insists on listening to the radio, and all the news is depressing and frightening. As you know better than I, Hitler has gone mad with power. He will not stop until he has the whole of Europe in his hands. My old friend, Chef Warner Brennholtz, returned to Berlin several years ago. No word from him for two Christmases. And now London is being bombed. I fear for Lady Daisy. I pray the mountains will protect you and yours.

All these terrible things that are happening only deepen my worries over Niclas. I must be strong for him! Bernhard and I must continue the work around the ranch or Niclas worries everything will fall apart. I tell him that will not happen, not while I have strength in my body. But he has always been able to read my thoughts. He understands me too well. He sees too much.

A world at war mirrors the state of my heart, Rosie. I am at war with God. My soul cries out to Him, but He does not hear. Where is God's mercy? Where is His justice? Niclas does not deserve such suffering. . . .

34

EACH EVENING AFTER Papa had gone to bed, Hildie sat at the kitchen table with Mama. She read her Bible while Mama wrote letters. She had been writing to Rosie Brechtwald for as long as Hildie could remember. All Hildie knew was Mama and Rosie had been schoolmates. Mama had written to others over the years, and she received responses, usually around Christmastime, from Felda Braun, Warner Brennholtz, and Solange and Herve Fournier, all in Switzerland. Mama used to cut off the stamps and give them to Bernie. Her brother asked once why Mama wrote to people she'd never see again. "I see them here." She pointed to her head. "And here." She touched her heart.

"And God willing, we'll see them again when the last trumpet blows," Papa added.

Hildie and Mama didn't say much to one another. Before Hildie went to bed, she put her hand on Mama's shoulder and said good night. Sometimes Mama answered.

Hildie got up early one morning after she'd been home for about a week and sat waiting for Mama at the breakfast table before the sun came up. "I'm going into town and see Dr. Whiting, Mama."

"Why? He'll be out the end of the week."

"Papa needs pain medication."

Mama poured herself a cup of coffee and sat at the table. "He won't take it, Hildemara. He said he doesn't want to spend his last months on earth too drugged to think clearly."

"He may change his mind."

Mama bowed her head. "You know your father."

"I need to be ready, in case."

"You can take the car."

Hildie chuckled. "I would if I knew how to drive. I'll walk."

"Why didn't you ever learn? A nurse makes good money, doesn't she? Clotilde bought a car the first week she lived in Burbank and got that apprenticeship making costumes. Even Rikka knows how to drive."

"I lived a block from the hospital, and if I wanted to go any-where else, there was always a city bus going the same direction. One of these days, I'll learn."

"I could teach you."

"Now isn't the time." Hildie clasped her cup in both hands, staring at her coffee as she spoke. "We'll have to work together, Mama, and make him as comfortable as possible."

Mama set her cup down forcefully. "I don't want him comfort-able. I want him to live."

"I'm a nurse. Not God."

"Did I say you were? Did I ask any more of you than what you've been trained to do?"

Hildie pushed her chair back, picked up her cup and saucer, and set them on the counter. "I'll wash them later." She headed for the back door.

"Where are you going?"

"To see Dr. Whiting."

"It's not even light yet."

"It'll be light enough by the time I get there."

"For heaven's sake, sit down and I'll fix you breakfast."

"I'll eat at the café."

"You can be such a fool, Hildemara!"

Shaking, Hildie stopped and looked at her from the doorway. "Be angry, Mama. Be raging mad! But aim it at the cancer!" She closed the door as she went out.

Hugging her coat around her, Hildie walked to town. She took her time, drinking in the fresh morning air, the smell of damp sand and vineyards, the sound of water churning at Grand Junction, the scent of eucalyptus. She stopped by the site of the house her brother and Fritz had burned down. Someone had bought the property and built a new house and barn.

The café lights were on. She recognized the waitress. "You're Dorothy Pietrowski, aren't you? You graduated with my brother, Bernie Waltert."

"Oh yeah." The plump, dark-haired girl grinned. "I remember him: big, good-looking, blond guy with blue eyes. All the girls were crazy in love with him. Elizabeth Kenney has all the luck." Her smile flattened. "I don't remember you."

"Few people do." Hildie smiled, extended her hand, and introduced herself.

Dorothy seemed in no hurry to take her order. "Your father's sick, isn't he?"

"How did you know?"

"People talk. My dad has a lot of respect for him even if he is a—" She blushed crimson. "Sorry."

"A Hun?" Hildie laughed it off. "We're all naturalized Americans and proud of it. We even have little celebratory flags and documents to prove it."

"People can be so stupid." Clearly, Dorothy didn't include herself. She shrugged again. "What can I get you this morning, Hildemara?"

"The farmer's special." Eggs, bacon, sausage, hash browns, toast, orange juice, and plenty of hot coffee.

Dorothy laughed as she stuck her pencil behind her ear. "It'll be right up."

Hildie remembered Mama and Papa talking about the war to end all wars. She remembered the year the Herkners' bakery burned to the ground. It hadn't just been about business. People didn't come home from fighting a war and get over it in a day or even a year. To some, it didn't matter how long a family had been in the country or how long since they'd passed their citizens' test. All that mattered was where they came from. And Papa came from Germany.

Dorothy came back with several plates and set them down in front of Hildie. "It's a wonder how you can be so thin." She came back to replenish Hildie's coffee. They talked each time she did. Finally, Dorothy slipped into the booth and told her how Murietta never changed. Maybe that was good; maybe it was bad. Hildie told her about nurse's training, her job at Samuel Merritt, and the people she had met. The only one she didn't talk about was Trip Arundel. The bell jangled.

"This is when it gets busy." Dorothy slipped out of the booth. "It's been good talking with you." She picked up the coffeepot. "I hope you'll come in again."

"I enjoyed it, too, but I think this is the last time I'll be out of the house for a while."

❋ ❋ ❋

Dr. Whiting had tears in his eyes as he sat behind his desk. "He's a proud man, Hildemara. And a stubborn one, too. Of course, I'll give you whatever you need. The cancer is going faster than I expected, but maybe that's a good thing, if you understand what I mean."

Hildemara nodded. "It won't be long, Dr. Whiting."

"I imagine you've seen enough dying in the hospital to recognize the signs." He tented his hands and sat silent, thinking. Hildemara didn't press. The doctor got up and went out. He came back a few minutes later and put a small box on the desk between them. "Morphine. Enough dosages to last a week under normal circumstances. I'll order more. Your father is going to refuse it at first, Hildemara. When he does, you ask him how he'd manage to watch someone he loves die slowly and in excruciating pain. Once he has the first injection, he'll argue less the next time. He may even come to ask you. It's one of the most addictive substances we know, but that doesn't matter under these circumstances."

Blinking back tears, Hildemara rose. "Thanks, Doctor." She took the vials. "What dosage do you prescribe?"

"I'm leaving that up to you." Dr. Whiting cleared his throat. "You give Niclas as much as you think he needs. I promise when it's all over, I won't question your judgment."

It took a few seconds to realize what he meant. She thought her legs would go out from under her. "I can't do that."

"You say that now."

"I won't!"

Dr. Whiting stood and came around the desk to embrace her. He patted her back as she cried. When she managed to regain composure, he opened the door and walked her through the waiting room. "I'll come out at the end of the week."

Hildemara walked home, feeling like she had a hundred-pound weight in her purse rather than a small white box containing vials of morphine.

❋ ❋ ❋

Mama sat with Papa in the afternoons. Hildemara knew they needed time to be alone and went to visit with Elizabeth. The cottage Papa and Bernie had built had a concrete foundation and indoor plumbing. The kitchen had a big white stove with counters built on both sides for work space. It had a refrigerator instead of an icebox, a bathroom with sink, toilet, and tub with a shower overhead. The living room wasn't big, but cozy with a love seat and chair, a coffee table, side table, two lamps, and a radio, which Elizabeth had playing. Except for having only one bedroom, it was similar in size to the house Hildie had shared with Boots.

"It's perfect for us, now." Elizabeth looked around, still glowing like a new bride. "But we'll need more room when we have children."

Hildemara looked away. "You have a green thumb. All those flowers in the flower boxes and the flats."

Elizabeth laughed. "Who would have guessed I'd be good at something as worthwhile as growing things?" She grew serious. "I can hardly wait to be growing a child." She blushed, lowering her eyes. "We're trying. We were hoping to have good news before Papa . . ." When she looked up, her eyes were glassy with tears. "A baby would cheer him up, don't you think?"

Hildemara looked down into her coffee.

Elizabeth leaned over and put her hand on Hildie's arm. "I'm so glad you're home, Hildie. I've missed you." She squeezed and let go. "I know this is an awful thing to admit, but I was scared to death your mother might expect me to help take care of Papa. I don't know the first thing about nursing, and frankly, Mama can be a little intimidating at times."

Hildie smiled at her. "A little? At times? She still intimidates me on a daily basis!"

"Your mother is amazing, Hildie. She knows as much about running this place as your father. She gave Bernie a list of what has to be done, when and how, who to contact when the almonds and raisins are ready for market. She had it all written in her journal."

Hildemara knew Papa had no worries about the farm. He had said the other day he had full confidence that Bernie could run things for Mama, if Mama allowed. Now she couldn't help but wonder if Mama was already making preparations for Papa's passing, but she didn't dare ask.

❄ ❄ ❄

Boots wrote.

I saw Trip the other day. He asked about you and your father. He asked if you planned to come back to Merritt.

I told him I didn't know, and you probably didn't either. You should write to him, Flo. The poor guy looks like a lost soul.

Hildie gathered her courage and wrote to Trip. She kept the letter short and focused on Papa and Mama, Bernie and Elizabeth, what it felt like to be home after four years away, how little her hometown had changed. One page. A week later, her letter came back marked *No forwarding address.*

❄ ❄ ❄

Papa lost his embarrassment as the weeks passed, and Hildemara took over washing him and changing sheets. She gave a pattern to Mama for a hospital gown. "It'll make things easier for him and for me." Mama got to work right away. The flannel kept him warmer. So did the soft socks Mama knitted.

Papa took her hand one morning and patted it weakly. "God made you a nurse just in time, didn't He? He knew I'd need you."

She kissed his hand and pressed her cheek against it. "I love you, Papa. I wish you didn't have to go through this."

"I know where I'm going. I'm not afraid. Mama is going to need you, Hildemara Rose."

"I'll stay, Papa."

"For a while. Not forever."

❄ ❄ ❄

"Morphine puts you to sleep. I don't want to spend the little time I have left in the arms of Morpheus." But when the pain grew unbearable, Papa finally relented and allowed Hildie to give him an injection.

She called Cloe. She came home two days later and dumped her suitcases in the screened bedroom they had shared as girls. After an hour sitting by Papa's bed, she came and found Hildie. "He's asking for you."

Hildie prepared the morphine injection.

Mama came and went from the bedroom. She had stopped sleeping with him. "Every time I roll over or move, I'm hurting him."

When Papa cried in pain, Mama would become agitated. She'd pace, ashen, biting her thumb until it bled. "Can't you give him something?"

"I have, Mama."

"Well, it wasn't enough. You should give him more."

"Marta . . ." Papa's voice, barely above a whisper now, always caught Mama's attention. Glaring at Hildemara, she went back into the bedroom. Papa talked with her softly, in German. Hildie leaned against the sink counter, hands covering her face, trying not to sob.

"You never loved me, Niclas." Mama spoke in a ragged, grief-soaked voice. "You married me for my money."

Papa spoke louder this time. "Do you suppose there was money enough in the world to make me marry such an ill-tempered woman?"

Hildie went to the doorway, wanting to cry out to both of them not to waste time arguing, not now, not when it was so close to the end.

"You make jokes at a time like this." Mama started to rise and Papa caught her wrist. She could easily have broken free, but she didn't.

"Marta," he rasped. "Don't pull away. I haven't the strength to hold on to you anymore." When she sagged into the chair and began to weep, Papa turned toward her. "I wouldn't leave you if God wasn't calling me away." He stroked her head, his hand trembling with weakness. When she looked up, he touched her cheek. "I've warmed myself by your fire." He said more to her, softly, in German. She took his hand and held it open against her cheek. Hildemara stepped back and turned away.

How could Mama not know Papa loved her? Hildemara had seen him show it in a thousand ways. She had never heard either

Mama or Papa say aloud in front of witnesses, *"I love you,"* but she had never doubted for one moment they did.

Mama came out of the bedroom and motioned Hildemara to go in. Hildie went.

Looking at her wristwatch, she held his hand and prayed until the time came to give him another injection. When she came out, Mama sat at the kitchen table, her head buried in her arms. Hildie didn't know who needed her more, Papa or Mama. She knew how to tend Papa, how to comfort him. But Mama had always been a mystery.

That night, Papa lapsed into a coma. Hildemara stayed in the room, turning him gently every two hours. Mama protested. "What are you doing? Just leave him alone! For heaven's sake, Hildemara, give him peace."

Hildemara wanted to rise up and scream back at Mama. Instead, she went on with her work and spoke as quietly and calmly as possible. "He needs to be turned every two hours, Mama, or he'll develop pressure sores."

Mama helped after that. They worked in shifts. Mama's face looked as white and cold as marble.

The smell of death filled the room. Hildie checked Papa's pulse repeatedly, his breathing. She prayed softly under her breath as she ministered to him. *God, have mercy. God, let it end soon. God, take Papa home. Jesus, Jesus, I can't do this. God, give me strength. Please . . . please, Lord.*

Hildie changed the bed linens and changed his gown. She wondered if people felt pain in a coma. She didn't know whether to give him an injection or not. When she called Dr. Whiting and asked, he said he didn't know.

"It's my turn, Mama."

"No." She spoke firmly. "You've done enough. Go rest. I'll stay a little while longer."

"I'll wake you if—"

Mama shook her head. "Don't argue with me now, Hildemara Rose." She took Papa's hand between hers and whispered raggedly, "Not now."

❄ ❄ ❄

Hildie entered the room and knew before she touched his fore-head that Papa had gone home. His face looked so serene, all the muscles relaxed. He looked white now instead of gray, the skin taut against cheek and jawbone, eyes closed and sunken. She felt relief and then ashamed that she did. "He's gone, Mama."

"I know."

"When?"

Mama didn't answer. She just sat holding Papa's hand in both of hers, staring down at him.

Hildemara put her hand on Papa's brow and found it cold. She felt the rush of anguish rise up, catching her by the throat, but fought it down.

Papa had gone hours ago, and she couldn't help wondering how much of Mama had gone with him.

❄ ❄ ❄

Hildemara wrote to Boots the night after Papa had been taken away to the mortuary. Mama had gone to bed and stayed there all day. Cloe fed the chickens, milked the cow, and saw to the rabbits. When Bernie told Hildie she didn't have to do the chores, she screamed at him that she had to do something or run mad, then fell sobbing into his arms. "Papa's gone. He's gone. I thought he'd live forever."

Mama had already taken care of all the arrangements, of course. No open casket. Papa didn't want it. A simple memorial service at the church for whoever wanted to come. The entire town showed up, along with the last person Hildie ever expected to see.

Trip stood outside the church after the memorial service. Hildie's heart leaped and lodged in her throat. He looked so tall and handsome in a black suit, hat in his hands. He held it by the brim, turning it slowly. People clustered around Mama. Hildemara stayed close by her side, Bernie and Elizabeth on the other, Cloe and Rikka right behind. So many had come: Dr. Whiting and Mrs. King, teachers, school principals, store owners, farmers, the Musashi family. The Herkners came all the way from San Francisco, bringing Fritz with them. Everyone had a story to tell about Papa, memories they wanted to offer.

"Niclas helped plant my orchard . . ."

". . . loved God . . ."

". . . helped us out when we came here from Oklahoma . . ."

". . . knew how to manage a crew of harvesters and let them go at the end of a season with a smile on their faces . . ."

"Always knew I could trust him . . ."

Mama frowned at Hildemara. "Stop squeezing my arm so tight."

Hildie apologized and let her go. She couldn't see Trip among the mourners and wondered if he had already left.

Mama nudged her. "Mr. Endicott is talking to you."

Heat surged into Hildie's cheeks and she thanked him for his kind words. She spotted Trip again on the outer edge of the gathering. "Excuse me, Mama. There's someone I need to speak to, and then I'll be right back." She slipped away, letting Cloe take her place.

She wove her way through the throng of people, accepting condolences, trying to keep moving toward Trip. When she finally reached him, she couldn't speak. She opened her mouth and closed it like a fish drowning in the air.

His eyes glistened with tears. "I'm sorry about your father, Hildemara. I would like to have met him."

His words reminded her of her sin of omission. She had never once mentioned Trip to Papa. "Thank you for coming." How had he known about the memorial service? Boots had taken a job in Los Angeles last month.

He seemed to read her mind. "Boots called and told me."

Hildie glanced back at Mama, afraid Trip might see more in her face than she wanted him to know. She loved him so much, she wanted to cry out at the pain of seeing him again.

"You look tired, Hildie."

"I am." *Bone tired. Soul tired.* "So is Mama."

"Can I meet her?" When Hildie hesitated, his mouth tipped. "Don't worry. I won't say anything about us."

Us.

The crowd thinned enough for them to make their way easily to where Mama stood with Bernie, Elizabeth, Cloe, and Rikka. "Mama, I'd like you to meet a friend from Merritt." She introduced Trip as Cale Arundel. Trip extended his hand and spoke gently to Mama, holding hers in both of his. Mama thanked him for coming so far and looked at Hildemara, as though for further explanation in why he would.

"Come on, Mama." Bernie took her hand and drew it through his arm while giving Hildemara a pointed glance. "We should go home."

Trip touched Hildemara lightly on the arm. "Walk with me to my car?"

"I'll be right there, Bernie."

As Trip guided her, his hand slid down her arm and clasped her hand. She slipped free. When they stopped by his car, she raised her head. "It was very kind of you to come so far, Trip."

"I could drive you home. It would give us a few minutes to talk."

"I can't." Her voice broke.

"Are you coming back?"

"I don't know." Tears slipped down her cheeks and she impatiently brushed them away.

After the difficult months of watching Papa die, her emotions were in a state of confusion. She couldn't go back to Oakland and pick up her life where she had left off. It seemed almost immoral to do such a thing when so many were dying, when Papa had only just been laid in his grave. She couldn't leave Mama alone. Rikka would be off with Melvin. Cloe would be back in Hollywood, neck-deep in costume design and dating her producer. Bernie and Elizabeth couldn't do all the work, could they? Someone had to stay and take care of Mama. But that wasn't all that churned in her mind. The war! Everyone talked about the war. Men died in wars. Better not to love Trip any more than she already did. No one knew what tomorrow might bring.

"No. I don't think I will. Not now. Mama needs me." She couldn't look at him, knowing everything she felt would be written across her face. She saw Mama staring at her from the front seat. "I have to go, Trip." She stepped back. "Say hello to everyone. Tell them I miss them."

When she slid into the car, Mama didn't look at her. She sat, back straight, eyes staring forward in the front passenger seat. Bernie started the car. "Where's Rikka?"

Cloe was staring at Hildie. "She's riding home with Melvin."

Bernie glanced back from the driver's seat. "Is Cale following us to the house?"

"No." Before anyone could ask if she had invited him, she went on quickly. "He has a long drive home to Oakland." She looked out the window, hoping no one would see her tears or mention him again.

"Seemed like a nice guy, what little I could tell from the one minute he was with us."

"He's better-looking than most of the actors I've met," Cloe added, not smiling, still staring, a faint frown on her face.

"All the women in the hospital were in love with him."

"And he came all the way to Murietta—"

"Shut up, Bernie." It was Cloe who said it.

Mama didn't utter a sound.

When all the visitors left, Mama went to bed. When Hildie looked in on her later, Mama lay on her back, wide-awake, staring at the ceiling. "Do you want me to sit with you awhile, Mama?"

"No."

Hildie fell asleep on the couch. She awakened with the moonlight streaming through the window. She thought she heard someone screaming outside. She rose quickly and looked in on Mama. She wasn't in her bed. Throwing on her coat, she flew out the back door. The screaming came from the orchard. Bernie stood in the yard. "Is it Mama?"

"Yes." He caught her by the arm. "Leave her alone. She has to get it out someway." She could see the sheen of tears on his face. "She's held it in too long. Let her scream. Let her pound on the earth."

Hildemara could hear her. "She's cursing God."

"For tonight, and then she'll be holding on to Him when she's finished. Go on back to the house. She'll come in when she's ready."

"What're you going to do?"

"Papa told me to watch over her."

35

1941

Papa hadn't been in his grave a week before Mama went back to work. She got up at dawn and made the coffee, then went out to milk the cow, feed the chickens, and collect eggs. Cloe went back to Hollywood. Rikka went back to school. Bernie saw to the business of the farm. Elizabeth tended the flats of seedlings in the lattice nursery and kept the vegetable garden weeded and bug-free.

People continued to come to visit, and everyone brought something: casseroles; cakes; German potato salad; small jars of homemade jams and jellies; pickled watermelon rinds; large jars of apricots, peaches, and cherries. Over the years, Mama had taken gifts to families in need, and now she reaped what she had sowed in kindness.

Edgy with nothing to do, Hildemara set to work on the house. She scrubbed the kitchen floor, took everything out of the cabinets and scrubbed the shelves, scoured the stove and sink. She scraped peeling paint and decided it was time to freshen things up a little. She used some of her savings to buy a cheerful yellow paint, the same color Mama had originally chosen and which had faded over the years. Elizabeth had made pretty curtains for the cottage. Why shouldn't Mama have some? Hildemara bought fabric and enlisted Elizabeth's help in redoing the living room, kitchen, and bedroom curtains. She added lacy sheers so Mama could open the windows and not have dust blow in or sunlight fade the sofa after she and Elizabeth recovered it with a chintz slipcover. She made pretty decorative pillows of blue and yellow with lacy edges. Mama had never had any before.

Mama still cooked. Hildemara sent away for a Quaker lace tablecloth. She put a fresh bouquet of flowers on the table every few days.

If Mama noticed any of the changes, she never said. Hildemara didn't know whether it lightened Mama's grief or not.

She took out the ragbag and started work on an area rug. The mix of colors would brighten the living room. When she wrote to Cloe and told her what she planned, Cloe sent a box of fabric pieces. The work filled Hildemara's long, quiet evenings. She had to work or she couldn't sleep. She grieved over Papa, worried about Mama.

And she couldn't get Trip out of her head.

Even when she fell exhausted into bed, she had trouble sleeping. She'd lie awake, wondering what he was doing, if he had met someone. Of course, he would. She couldn't go back. She couldn't leave Mama by herself.

Mama put her book down one evening and shook her head. "That rug will take months to finish, Hildemara. Why did you start it?"

"Because it'll brighten the living room. Look at all the colors, Mama. If we went to the movies, we'd see some of these fabrics in costumes. Rikka is going to paint a picture of the Alps for you. We'll hang it right there on the wall. It'll add—"

"This is my house, Hildemara. Not yours."

Hildie gasped as she stabbed her finger with the needle. Wincing, she sucked at the wound. "I know, Mama. I'm only trying to fix things up a bit, make it more—"

"I like the yellow walls. I like the new curtains. But enough is enough."

"You don't want the rug?" Hildemara couldn't stop the hurt from rising inside her. "What am I supposed to do with all this—?"

"Just leave it in the box."

"The rug is—"

"Big enough for under the sink."

Hildemara's eyes flooded. "What are you trying to say, Mama?" She knew, but she wanted to hear it aloud. She wanted it out in the open.

"I don't need a servant, Hildemara. And I certainly don't need a nurse!"

Her words cut deeply. "You don't need me. Isn't that what you're trying to say?"

Emotion rippled across Mama's face, like a storm over water, and then her face hardened. "All right, Hildemara Rose. If that's what it takes, I will say it. I don't need you. I don't want you here. The sooner you leave, the better for both of us!"

Leave? And go where? Hildemara's face crumpled. "You were the one who asked me to come home!"

"To take care of Papa! And you did, and he's gone now. I can take care of myself!"

"I only want to help."

"No. You want to play the martyr."

"That's not true!"

"Then what else could it be? Why stay two months, and do all the things you've always hated?"

"I didn't want you to be alone!" She burst into tears.

"Last time I looked, Bernie and Elizabeth lived a few hundred feet from my back door." Mama gripped the arms of her chair. "You trained to be a nurse. You told me that's what you wanted to do with your life! So why are you still here? Why haven't you gone back to nursing? You had your own life before I asked for your help. Your help isn't needed anymore. Why are you still here?" She rose, face twisting. *"Go live your life and let me get on with mine!"*

She went into the bedroom she had shared with Papa and slammed the door.

Dumping the rug into the remnant box, Hildemara ran out the back door and into Bernie's old bedroom. Covering her head, she sobbed. *Go back? Go back to what?* She'd ended things with Trip. If there had ever been a chance for happiness, it had ended that day he came to the memorial service. If she went back to Merritt, she might see him again. Some other girl would have certainly said yes. How could she bear to see him again? And now Mama showed her true feelings. Mama couldn't wait to be rid of her.

What had she expected?

Packing her suitcases, she took a shower and went over to talk to Bernie and Elizabeth. "I need a ride in the morning."

"Where you going?"

"Back to Oakland."

She couldn't sleep that night. She went into the kitchen and fixed the coffee.

Mama came out. "You're up early."

"I'm leaving this morning."

"You want something to eat before you go?"

If Hildie had hoped Mama would change her mind, she had her answer. "No, thank you."

Mama poured herself a cup of coffee. "I'll get dressed and drive you to the bus station."

"Bernie's taking me."

"Oh." She sat and let out a long breath. "Well, suit yourself."

When it was time to leave, Hildemara stood in the back door-way. "Good-bye, Mama."

"Write."

As Bernie turned out on the road going by the front of the house, she saw Mama standing on the porch. She lifted her hand. Hildie felt little comfort in the small gesture.

"Sorry, Hildie." Bernie drove like Mama—fast, confident, head up with eyes straight ahead. "Are you going to be okay?" He gave her a quick glance.

"Right as rain." Miss Jones had said she would hold her job. As to the rest, she would have to wait and see how much suffering she could bear before she ran.

❄ ❄ ❄

With Boots gone, Hildie had no place to live. Mrs. Kaufman gave her a place at Farrelly Hall. "You can stay as long as you need, Hildemara." The sleeping porch was hardly a place to call home, but Hildie felt comfortable there. She would have to ask around and see if anyone needed a roommate.

Jones put her right to work. "We've been shorthanded, and it'll get worse if we go to war. We can't ignore Hitler forever, and the Army will need nurses."

Hildie dove into work. She felt useful again. Mama may not need her, but plenty of others did. And she loved her work; she loved her patients; she took extra shifts and worked six days a week.

Boots called from Los Angeles. "What are you doing in Farrelly Hall? I thought you'd be married to Trip by now."

"I haven't seen Trip."

"Are you hiding out on ward duty?"

"It's been a long time, Boots. I doubt he remembers me."

"You're such an idiot."

Standing at the nurses' station a couple mornings later, Hildemara heard a thump as someone hit the double doors and swung them open. Her heart jumped when she saw Trip striding down the corridor. He looked mad. She hadn't even caught a glimpse of him since returning to Merritt two weeks before. She had avoided the cafeteria for fear of running into him. "Hello, Trip. How are you?"

He caught her by the wrist and kept walking. "Excuse us, ladies." He half dragged her down the hall, opened a linen closet, and pulled her inside.

"Trip, I . . ."

He kicked the door shut behind him, hugged her to him, and

then kissed her. Her nursing cap came askew, dangling by a bobby
pin. When he lifted his head, she tried to say something, and he
kissed her again, deeper this time. He held her so close she didn't
have to wonder what he was feeling. Her toes curled in her white
oxfords. They bumped against a shelf. He drew back. "Sorry."

Breathless, he looked down at her. He was about to kiss her
again when someone tapped on the door. "Careful of the linen
in there!" Jones's rubber soles squeaked down the hall.

"Marry me."

"Okay."

His breath came out sharply. "Okay?"

"Yes." She stepped forward and dug her hands into his hair.
"Yes. Please." She pulled his head down. "Don't stop."

He caught her wrists and pulled her hands down. "I hoped to
get this welcome in Murietta." His mouth tipped in a lopsided
grin. "You gave me the impression you weren't coming back at
all." His eyes darkened. "Boots called."

"I'll have to thank her."

"Mama doesn't need you anymore?" He taunted her gently,
putting her cap back on her head, trying to make repairs. Her heart
hammered.

"Mama kicked me out."

"God bless Mama." He cupped her cheek tenderly, then ran
his thumb lightly over her swollen lips. "I'm going to write her a
thank-you letter." He kissed her again, as though he couldn't help
himself.

No tap this time, but a firm rap of hard knuckles. "That's
enough, Mr. Arundel. We have work to do around here."

Trip opened the door. "Yes, ma'am."

"Get that cheeky grin off your face and get off my ward." She
looked Hildemara over. "Fix your hair. What? No ring?" She called
after Trip. "You do have honorable intentions, don't you?"

"Yes, ma'am!" Laughing, he hit the door again and disappeared.

Hildie laughed, too, exultant.

❄ ❄ ❄

Trip wanted to buy a diamond solitaire, but Hildie talked him out of it. "I can't wear it to work. Fancy rings carry bacteria, and a solitaire would catch on linens when I change beds." He picked a platinum wedding band lined with tiny diamonds instead. They would have a small church wedding in Oakland right after school let out in June.

Trip took another part-time job washing windows to save money for a house. Hildemara took extra shifts. They hardly saw one another, except when they went to church together every Sunday.

As the weeks passed, Hildie began to feel lethargic. She had chills during the day and bundled into a sweater. She had night sweats. Trip put his hand against her forehead one evening. "You're hot."

"I'm probably getting a cold or something."

Trip took her back to the apartment she shared with a pulmonary ward nurse. He insisted she stop working so hard and take at least two days off a week. She cut back on her hours, but still didn't seem to feel rested. When Trip took her bowling, Hildie could hardly lift the ball and roll it down the alley. Twice, she dumped it and watched it roll slow motion down the gutter. "Sorry. I'm just too tired tonight."

"Taking care of your father took a lot out of you, Hildie." Trip wove his fingers with hers. "You've lost more weight since you got back."

She knew and had been trying to eat more. Her chest ached. She couldn't seem to get a full breath. Depressed, she took a few days off. Trip came by and opened cans of chicken soup. "No more extra shifts, Hildie. Promise me. You look exhausted."

"Stop worrying, Trip."

Jones scowled when she came on ward after a few days' rest. "Go downstairs right now and see the staff physician." She picked up the telephone. "Go on, Hildemara. I'm calling him right now and telling him you're on the way."

The doctor put his stethoscope against her chest. He reviewed her symptoms. She found it difficult to fill her lungs with air. It hurt to breathe. He thumped her chest and listened again, looking grim. "Pleural effusion." Fluid on the lungs.

"Pneumonia?"

He wouldn't answer, and Hildemara felt cold shock race through her body. When he checked her into the hospital and ordered X-rays, she didn't protest. She couldn't get Mr. Douglas off her mind, and there had been two other patients she had tended since then who had been transferred out of the medical ward into quarantine.

Trip came in before she could leave orders that she didn't want visitors. She hadn't stopped crying since being checked into the hospital. When she saw him, she put out her hand. "Stay away from me."

"What?"

"Get out of here, Trip."

"What's wrong with you?"

She held a sheet up over her mouth. "I think I have tuberculosis."

He went white. Both of them knew a student nurse had died the year before. Two other bronchitis patients turned out to have active TB.

Trip kept coming. She grabbed the cord and pressed the button over and over. A nurse came running.

"Get him out of here. Now!"

"Hildie!"

Sobbing, pulling the sheet over her head, she turned away.

The nurse escorted Trip from the room, then came back. "Shouldn't you wait until the test results come back before—?"

"And risk exposing someone? You should wear a mask! And keep people out of here!"

She didn't have to ask the doctor what the X-rays showed. She could see it plainly on his face.

"We need to send fluid to the lab before we can be sure."

Small comfort. He aspirated fluid from her infected lung and sent it to the lab, where it would be injected into a rat. The doctor ordered her to the contagion unit.

Trip came immediately. She refused to see him. He wrote a note and gave it to a nurse.

We've kissed a hundred times, Hildie. I've already been exposed! Let me come in and see you. Let me sit with you. Let me hold your hand. . . .

Crying, she insisted on plastic gloves and a mask before she wrote back to him.

I didn't know I had TB! You cannot come in. Don't ask me again. This is hard enough as it is. I love you. Go away!

She didn't want to take any chances on infecting him or anyone else.

Hildie spent the next few weeks on the isolation ward, waiting for test results. Trip kept coming back. "You're the most stubborn, willful woman I've ever met," he called through the door.

The tests came back positive.

36

"WE DON'T KNOW enough yet about tuberculosis." The doctor
looked apologetic. Several nurses had died over the last few years.
Clearly he didn't want to give false hope.

Hildemara knew she had little chance of survival with a history
of pneumonia.

"I've ordered bed rest."

She gave a bleak laugh. As if she hadn't been in bed resting for
weeks!

"Merritt doesn't have a contagion ward dedicated to TB, so you
will be transferred to a sanatorium. There are several from which
to choose, but you'll need to make your decision right away or the
hospital administration will have to decide for you."

Though Hildie had contracted tuberculosis while working, it
still remained unsettled whether Merritt Hospital administration
would pay for her care. Not wanting to accumulate debt, she chose
the least expensive facility, Arroyo del Valle, a county sanatorium
in the Livermore hills. They offered financial aid. If she survived,
she would need it. She found herself wondering who would have

to pay the bills if she died. Citizens, of course. Taxes. She felt ashamed.

Trip protested. "There's a better hospital right here in the Bay Area." He stood in the hallway, speaking to her through the barely open door.

She didn't want to tell him her reasons. Why waste money if she wasn't going to live anyway? "I'll do better out in the country with space and fresh air around me."

"I'm going to call Rev. Mathias. He can perform the wedding right here in the hospital. Jones would come."

"No!"

"Why not?"

"You know why not. There's no cure, Trip."

"I'm praying for you. I've got the whole church praying for you. My folks are praying. Their church is praying. Your mother, Bernie, Elizabeth . . ."

"Stop it, Trip!" Every breath hurt. Her heart ached even more. She panted for a moment until she had breath to speak. "What if it's not God's will?"

He pushed the door open and came in. "You're giving up. Don't you dare give up!"

A nurse appeared almost immediately. "You can't be in here!"

"I'll go for now, Hildie, but I won't go far." When the nurse took him by the arm, he jerked free. "Give me a minute!" He set the nurse aside and walked over to the bed, grabbing Hildemara by the wrists as she held the bedcovers over her mouth. "I love you, Hildie. Nothing is ever going to change that. In sickness and in health. I swear to you before God and this witness." He jerked his head back toward the nurse calling down the hall for security. "As long as we both shall live." He caressed her wrists before he let go of her. Two men appeared in the corridor. He raised his hands. "I'm going."

"To the showers first," one informed him.

Hildemara wondered if TB would be as painful a death as cancer, or if she'd die of a broken heart first.

❄ ❄ ❄

Hildemara's first letter at Arroyo came from Mama. Only one line.

I'll come down as soon as the grape harvest is over. You get better.

Just like Mama to give an order.

Several other nurses had been sent to Arroyo. Everyone got along. Hildie supposed it came from having so much in common with one another. They talked about nursing, families, friends, doctors, cases they had worked. They played games, read books, spent time outside in the sunshine, and slept. To anyone else, it probably would have sounded like a vacation.

The fluid extractions felt like slow torture. She suffered from night sweats and high fevers. After weeks of rest, she still felt weak. Frustration and grief increased her depression as time passed and she felt no improvement.

Trip came to visit. She gave up trying to make him stay away.

Her roommate, Ilea, also a nurse, shared her mother's delicious homemade fried chicken, potato salad, and chocolate chip cookies with Hildie and anyone else who came to visit. Her fiancé came often. Several patients had husbands; a few had children. One with kids died a week after Hildie came to the hospital. Not all the boyfriends and husbands proved as faithful as Trip. Some never came.

Mama wrote again.

I'll come down as soon as the almonds have been sold.

Hildie wrote back.

Don't feel you need to come. It is a long drive, and I'm not much company.

A week later, Mama showed up without warning.

❈ ❈ ❈

Hildemara glanced up in surprise and saw Mama standing a few feet away. "Mama?"

She had that look on her face that meant trouble. "You're my daughter. Did you think I wouldn't come?"

Hildie coughed into a handkerchief. Mama sat slowly, watching her, expressionless. When the spasm finally stopped, Hildemara leaned back, feeling drained. "Sorry." She saw the flash of something in Mama's eyes. "Sorry I said sorry." She offered a weak smile.

Mama had brought gifts. Cloe sent a beautiful lace-trimmed nightgown and bathrobe stylish and expensive enough for a Hollywood movie star. She had tucked a note in the folds.

This was meant for your wedding night. I don't think Trip will mind if you wear it now.

Cloe had about as much hope as Hildemara.

Rikka had sent pictures: Cloe at the sewing machine, Mama in the driver's seat of her Model T, Bernie grafting a tree, Elizabeth in the vegetable garden, Papa standing beneath the blooming almond trees, arms outspread, looking up. She had even drawn one of Hildie sitting in the branches of the chinaberry tree, leaning back against the trunk, wearing a *Mona Lisa* smile. The last was a caricature self-portrait of a girl in an artist's smock drawing a naked man who looked remarkably like Melvin. Hildie laughed and then coughed again, longer this time.

Mama had crocheted a pink lap blanket. Hildemara smoothed it over her legs. "It's beautiful. Thank you for coming all this way to see me."

"You didn't think I would, did you?"

She shrugged. "I didn't expect it."

Mama looked off toward the rolling hills and oak trees. "It's nice and peaceful here."

"Yes." *A good place to die.* Sometimes she prayed God would take her. Trip could move on with his life. She wouldn't feel like she lived in the bottom of a well. Papa said once that death was opening a door into heaven.

They talked about the ranch. Bernie and Elizabeth still hoped for a baby. Hildemara didn't want to take that hope away and tell Mama it wasn't likely to happen.

Mama talked about Papa and how he loved Hildie. They talked about Cloe and the movie stars she had met. Cloe liked to drop names like Errol Flynn, Olivia de Havilland, Bette Davis, Tyrone Power, Alice Faye. She had finally snagged her dream job and made costumes for the movies. She met many stars at pre- and post-production parties.

Other patients came outside, greeted Hildemara, met Mama, talked awhile, and moved off to rest in the sunshine. "You've made some nice friends, Hildemara."

"We try to hold one another up."

"And Trip?"

"He comes once a week, when he's not in class or on duty. He still needs a few hours before he can graduate from Cal. Some of his units didn't transfer from Colorado. As soon as he finishes school, he's taking on more hours at the hospital. He can't afford medical school yet."

Mama relaxed in her chair, mouth softening. She smoothed the wrinkles from her cotton flower-print dress and folded her hands. "Good. All you have to do now is get well."

"That's not up to me."

Her eyes flared. "Yes. It is."

Hildemara didn't try to argue. She knew more about tuberculosis than Mama could ever guess. Why tell her what it did to a person's lungs? It was enough that Hildie didn't have hope. Why strip Mama of hers?

Troubled, Mama pushed herself up. "Well, as much as I hate to say it, I'd better get going. It's a long drive back to Murietta." Hildemara drew the lap blanket aside and started to stand. "No,

Hildemara Rose. You sit right there and enjoy the sunshine." Stepping back, Mama looped her knitted sweater over her arm and picked up her worn white purse. "Before I go, I've got something to say to you." She leaned down and grasped Hildemara's chin. "Find the guts to fight, and hang on tight to life!"

Hildemara jerked her chin away and glared at her through tears. "I'm doing my best."

Mama straightened, her expression disdainful, mocking. "Really? Not from what I can see. You've been sitting here for the past two hours feeling sorry for yourself."

"I never said—"

"You didn't have to say anything. I can see it written all over your face. You've given up!" She shook her head. "I never thought any of my children would turn out to be cowards, but here you are giving in. Just like—" She pressed her lips together. "Why waste my breath?"

Hurt, furious, Hildemara pushed herself out of the chair. "Thanks so much for your compassion, Mama. Now, get out of here." Heart pounding, she watched her mother walk away. Mama looked back once, a smirk on her face.

Blood coursed through Hildie's veins for the first time in weeks. She sat again, shaking, fists in her lap. Bundling up the pink lap robe, she threw it in the dirt.

The doctor checked her that afternoon. "You have some color back, Miss Waltert. I think you're turning a corner."

❋ ❋ ❋

Dear Rosie,

I went to Arroyo del Valle to see Hildemara Rose. She had Mama's pallor and the deep shadows under her eyes. I could see no life in them when I first arrived. It terrified me. She didn't seem to care whether she lives or dies.

I wanted to shake her. Instead, I called her a coward. Though it broke my heart, I mocked and belittled her. Thank God she got good and mad. Her eyes spit fire at me and I wanted to laugh with joy. Better she hate me for a while than give up on life and be put in an early grave. She was trying to get up when I walked away. She barely had strength enough for that, but at least there was color in her cheeks. I hope that fire burns brighter each day.

❄ ❄ ❄

Though her condition improved, Hildemara had to fight the constant tug of depression at how many months passed. Several patients died. Hildemara focused on the number who improved or celebrated remission. Trip wrote daily, but letters were a poor substitute for kisses or an embrace.

As soon as you're out of that prison, we're getting married.

She started having dreams that made her awaken in a sweat, but not the kind brought on by TB. She didn't argue with him anymore.

At night, while others slept, she knelt on the end of her bed and looked out the window at the moon and stars and talked to God. Or Papa. She spent hours reading the small, black leather-bound Bible Papa had given her when she started nursing school, writing down Scriptures that promised her a future and hope. When the binding began to give way, she asked for adhesive tape.

It took a while, but she got over being angry with Mama. Mama was just Mama. She had to give up hoping she'd have a relationship with her like Cloe or Rikka. Both her sisters had always had the lion's share of love. But then, they were lionesses like Mama. Nothing would stop them from going after what they wanted.

Hildie wondered if Mama would ever give her credit for making it on her own.

Jones came to see her. "The secret of longevity, my girl, is getting a chronic illness early in life. I survived the Spanish flu. It made me aware of how fragile our lives are. When you get out of here—and you will—you're going to take better care of yourself. When you get out of here, you come on back to Merritt. I want you back on my ward."

Boots wrote often. She had met someone—a patient, this time.

I gave him a back rub one night. One thing led to another. Let's just say if we'd been caught, I would have lost my job. He says he loves me, Flo. He says he wants to get married. Just thinking about saying "until death" makes me break out in a sweat.

A few weeks later, she wrote again and said she had broken up with him.

I've probably made the biggest mistake of my life, but it's too late now. Some people just aren't ready to settle down. I think I'm one of them.

Boots took a job in Honolulu.

Surf and sand and plenty of tanned bodies. Oh, my. I think I'm in heaven.

A few weeks later, another letter arrived.

What was I thinking when I took this job? I've seen the entire island twice over. A pity I'm not an Army nurse.

There are plenty of cute soldiers around. But I can't stand it. I feel like I'm living on the head of a pin in the middle of the Pacific. Hey. Why would I feel that way? I am! I'm sending résumés to the mainland. Who would've guessed I'd become claustrophobic in paradise?

❄ ❄ ❄

Six months had passed by the time Hildemara received permission to leave. She packed her bags.

"December 1, 1941, is a day of celebration from here forward." Trip carried her suitcase out to the car. He settled her comfortably in the front seat. When he started to tuck the lap robe around her, she protested. "I'm well. Remember?" He grinned and gave her a firm kiss, the first in eight months.

When he slipped behind the driver's seat, he leaned over and put his arm around her. "Let's try that again." He took her hand and placed it, palm flat, against his chest. She could feel his heart hammering as fast as her own. Eyes black, he caressed her face. "We'd better start making wedding plans now. No more excuses."

"I can't think of a single one."

Six days later, the Japanese bombed Pearl Harbor.

37

Hildemara married Trip on December 21, 1941. Bernie and
Elizabeth came up with Mama. Melvin drove Rikka. They left
shortly after the ceremony to take the ferry to San Francisco.
Cloe sent her regrets. She had a job with a production company
working on another swashbuckler. Tyrone Power, this time.
"We're sewing night and day to get the costumes ready for the
shoot. . . ." Bad weather and lack of money kept Trip's parents
in Colorado.

Many of Hildie and Trip's local church friends attended and
gave gifts. The deaconesses put on a wedding reception in the
social hall. Everyone talked about the war, and some of the men in
the congregation had already signed up for military service. Mama
gave the newlyweds a crocheted tablecloth with fifty dollars tucked
into the folds. They used it to buy train tickets to Denver.

Trip's mother and father made Hildemara feel more like a long-
lost daughter than an in-law. When asked what she wanted to call
them, she rejected Otis and Marg and opted for what Trip called
them—Dad and Mom.

"Look out!" Trip laughed. "Dad's looking for ways to entertain you."

When he hooked a sleigh to the back of his car, Hildie climbed aboard and sailed down East Moreno to Prospect Lake. In a few short weeks, she learned the rudiments of ice-skating and cross-country skiing.

They had little time alone in the small one-bedroom house. Trip's bedroom was much like Hildie's had been, a converted back porch. At least he had snow shutters instead of screen windows. They had no trouble keeping warm.

"We're going to have to go back to California soon, so you can start medical school."

Hildie combed her fingers through Trip's thick brown hair. His parents had gone off to visit friends, leaving them alone for the day. They had spent all morning in bed, not having to worry about making a sound.

Trip took her hand and kissed it. "I joined up, Hildie."

Her heart froze. "What did you say?"

"I went to the recruiter's office on Monday and signed the papers."

She yanked her hand free and sat up. "Oh, Trip. Tell me you didn't! We've only been married three weeks!" Everything had worked together to keep them apart for so long: Papa's illness, then hers, and now he signed up to go off and fight a war? How could he?

"It's cold." Trip pulled her down again, swinging his leg across hers to hold her there. "Every able-bodied man is joining up. How can I not do my part?"

"So you join up without even saying a word about it? I'm your wife!"

"Hildie . . ."

"Let me up!"

He did. She pulled her robe on and went into the house, standing near the potbelly stove. She'd have to crawl inside to thaw the chill inside her. Trip came in, closing the door behind him. He stood behind her, running his hands up and down her arms. "I should have told you. I'm sorry I didn't. I was afraid I'd let you talk me out of it."

She shook his hands off and faced him, tears streaming down her cheeks. "Is this the way our marriage is going to be? You make life-changing decisions and tell me later?" Something else struck her. "Your parents knew, didn't they? That's why they left us alone today." She closed her eyes. "That's why Mom went to bed early last night and Dad looked so grim."

"Our country needs soldiers. The recruiter thinks I'll end up a medic with my premed background and the time I spent working in a hospital. I can be of service."

He clutched her face, his own agonized. "I can't stay here safe and happy, making love to you every chance I get, while others risk their lives for our freedom. This is a fight for America's survival, Hildie, not a little skirmish in a foreign country somewhere we've never heard of."

She felt her body shaking in reaction. She had read the newspapers, too. If the Japanese invaded California and Germany overran Europe, the whole world would be at war. "You're right. I'll enlist, too. Jones said a year ago the Army would need nurses."

He let go of her, his face flaming. "Over my dead body! You're not enlisting in the Army!"

She laughed in disbelief. "It's all right for you, but not for me. I have more training than you do, Trip. Don't expect me to sit home and wait when my husband could be among the wounded!"

"I want you safe from harm!"

"And I wanted the same for you, but you did as you pleased. And now I agree. Our country needs us."

"No . . ." He put his head in his hands and turned away.

Hildie put her hand on his back. "If it means our freedom, shouldn't we all be part of it?"

He turned to her, face pale. "Don't do anything yet. Promise me. We'll pray about it."

"Did you?"

"Yes!" He cupped her face. "I've been praying since December 7 about what to do."

"And never included me."

Trip winced. "I won't do it again. Listen to me, please. One of us joining right now is enough. Give it a little time and we'll pray and see what God wants for you."

Everything moved faster than either expected.

Trip received his orders, and Hildie followed him to Camp Barkeley, Texas, and then to Fort Riley, Kansas, and then on to Fort Lewis, Washington. She lived in boardinghouses while he lived in the barracks. When he had a day's leave, they stayed in her room, hungry for one another. Tens of thousands of Navy men and Marines headed for the South Pacific to fight the Japanese while the Army geared up to invade Europe. Trip received orders for Officer Candidate School.

"You can't come this time, Hildie. I won't be able to see you, and I don't want you living among strangers. I want you to go home."

Which home? Where? She didn't know whether to go back to work at Merritt, where she would be surrounded by friends, or to Colorado Springs and live with Mom and Dad, or home to Murietta and Mama, if Mama would allow. No place would feel like home without Trip. She would stay in Tacoma until she could figure out what to do.

Trip dressed in his uniform while she sat on the end of the bed in the dressing gown Cloe had made. He leaned down and kissed her. "Maybe God will answer my prayers by then." He brushed his fingers against her cheek and went out the door.

She didn't have to ask what he meant, though he had never spoken his prayer aloud. He wanted her pregnant. He didn't just want a child; he wanted her ineligible to join the military.

She flung a hand over her eyes and prayed God's protection on her husband. If the slight morning nausea the last few days was any indication, God might have already answered Trip's prayer. They might have something to celebrate rather than spending every moment worrying about what the future could hold. The future could hold a child! Then again, she might just be feeling sick at the thought of what could happen to Trip.

Hildemara waited another month before making an appointment. The doctor confirmed she was pregnant. Proud to be carrying Trip's child, she sat with her hand resting on her abdomen during the long bus ride back to the apartment.

She would go home to Murietta. She didn't want to add to Trip's worries, and her husband wouldn't want her living alone with a baby on the way. *God has settled it, Trip. You're going to be a daddy. I'm going home to Mama. . . .* Mama's first grandchild! Perhaps Mama would even be happy enough to crow about it.

Rikka had gone home to see Melvin before he headed off to Marine Corps boot camp and then gone back to San Francisco. She had quit full-time classes at the California School of Fine Arts, preferring to pick and choose what she studied. She had found a job as a waitress in a fancy restaurant and loved everything about living in San Francisco. She claimed she loved Melvin, but she had no intention of becoming a farmer's wife in Murietta. It remained to be seen whether romance or a lust for life would win out. With Rikka's eyes fixed on city life, Hildemara assumed there would be plenty of room for her and a new baby.

Only a fool assumes.

1942

Hildie left her trunk and suitcase at the train station and walked home. Thinking to surprise Mama, she knocked at the front door. She didn't know the woman who opened it.

She stood gaping. "Who are you?"

"I'd be asking you the same question."

"I'm Hildemara Arundel."

"I don't know no Arundels."

"Waltert. My mother is Marta Waltert."

"Oh." Her face cleared and she pushed the screen door open. "Come in, please. Your mama don't live here no more. She lives out back in the cottage." She put her hand under Hildie's arm. "Here. You set yourself down. You look a little peaked."

"Who are you?"

"Donna Martin." She patted Hildie's shoulder, poured her a glass of lemonade, and said she'd go get her mother.

A moment later, Mama raced in the back door. "What are you doing here, Hildemara?"

"Trip's gone to OCS. He said I couldn't go with him. I wanted to come home!" She burst into tears.

"Come on." Mama hauled her up, apologized to Donna Martin for the intrusion, and pushed Hildie out the back door, down the steps, and along the path to the cottage. She opened the side door into the kitchen. "It's too bad you didn't think to write first, instead of just showing up on the front doorstep."

"I thought I'd be welcome." Hildemara wiped her face. "I should've known better." She looked around. "You're living here? Where are Bernie and Elizabeth?"

Mama poured another glass of lemonade and plunked it in front of Hildie on the small kitchen table. "You look like you haven't slept in a week."

"Mama!"

Mama sat and folded her hands on the table. "Hitch and Donna Martin are sharecropping the place. They've got four children. I don't need much room, so I gave them the big house. They'll be more comfortable there, room to spread instead of living in a tent-house like we did."

"And Bernie and Elizabeth?"

"The government came and took the Musashis away. Bernie and Elizabeth moved over to their place."

"Took them away? Where?"

"To an assembly center in Pomona. We've heard rumors they're going to be sent to some internment camp in Wyoming, of all places. We sent blankets and coats a week back. Hope they get them. The government seems to think every Jap is a spy these days. I'm surprised a bus hasn't come after me and the rest of the Jerries and Wops around here, sending us all to some godforsaken camp in Death Valley." She raised her hands and shook her head. "People go crazy when a war starts. They let fear run wild. Anyway, Hitch and Donna are good, hardworking people. Papa spoke highly of Hitch. They came out when Oklahoma turned to dust, and they've had a hard time ever since they arrived in California. I know how that feels. Hitch knows farming and ranching, so I hired him to run the place. That's how Papa and I started when we came to California. Sharecroppers. Do you remember those days living by the irrigation ditch and in that tent-house Papa built? I'll treat the Martins better than we were treated, I can promise you that."

"So you're living here."

"Yes. It suits me. The Martins will have the place looking as neat and tended as Papa did when he was well."

Hildie bristled. "Bernie did a good job."

"Yes. Bernie did a good job; I'm not saying he didn't. He'll do a good job across the street, too."

"I could help."

"Not here, you can't. What, now that you've come home you think I'll put the Martins out so you can move in and play farmer? No. The cottage has only one bedroom, Hildemara, and I'm not sharing it. I don't need you down here on the farm."

Hildemara's mouth trembled. "Did you ever think I might need you?"

Mama put her hands over Hildie's and held them tightly. "No, you don't. You've been standing on your own two feet for a while now." She took her hands away. "Go on back to Merritt, back to work, back to your friends! Time will pass faster that way."

So much for being welcomed home. "I can't go back to work."

"Why not?"

"I'm pregnant."

Mama sat back in her chair. "Oh. Well, that changes things." She smiled, her eyes glowing softly. "You and Elizabeth will have a lot to talk about. Go on over. They'll be glad to see you. And there's plenty of room at the Musashis'. He built a dormitory for the girls, remember?"

Mama went with her. "Look what the cat dragged in!"

How like Mama to say it that way.

Bernie strode across the yard, grabbed Hildie, and flung her around, her feet swinging. She laughed for the first time in weeks. "Put me down, Bernie!"

"Careful, Bernhard. Your sister's expecting a baby."

Bernie set Hildie down. "Holy cow! How far along?"

"Three months." She watched Mama head back across the street. Hildie could almost imagine her brushing off her hands, having settled things so quickly.

"Elizabeth's six months along. She's still sick as a dog every morning. I thought she wrote to you. Letter probably got lost with all your moving hither and yon, following that man of yours." He put his arm around her and steered her toward the Musashis' house. "She's going to be over the moon when she sees you. She's been lonely."

Bernie stopped, looking grim. "I'd better warn you now, in case you might want to change your mind about staying here. We've had rocks thrown through the windows. Old Man Hutchinson called me a Jap lover yesterday. I can understand, I guess. His son was killed at Pearl Harbor, but try telling him the Musashis had nothing to do with it. People see Jap spies behind every bush, and a few German ones, too. Do you understand what I'm saying, Hildie?"

"Yes." Fear made fools of some people.

Elizabeth turned from the kitchen sink as Bernie and Hildie came in the door. Hildemara gave her a long, considering look. *Miracles do happen,* she told herself. Hildie hoped this pregnancy was one of them.

"Hildie." Elizabeth spoke softly. "I'm so glad you're home." They embraced.

When Hildie searched Elizabeth's eyes, her friend blushed and looked away. Hildie wanted to weep.

Bernie took Hildie back to the train station in Mama's Model T to collect her luggage. He had to muscle the trunk into the backseat. "You have more stuff than the last time you came home!"

"Mrs. Henderson, my landlady, had a sale before I left Tacoma. She's putting the house up for sale and moving in with her daughter. I helped her bring boxes down from her attic and price everything. You wouldn't believe how much stuff she'd accumulated over the years. She had things left behind by boarders, and her husband had a store. He sold all kinds of things, including china. Her attic was packed! She gave me twelve different place settings from his store displays: Royal Doulton, Wedgwood, Spode, and Villeroy and Boch. She gave me some linen tablecloths, too. We can use everything if you and Elizabeth would like."

"We'll store your trunk in the barn. Keep all those nice things for when you and Trip set up housekeeping. Elizabeth packed all of the Musashis' dishes and kitchenwares. We're using our own."

Bernie seemed to have less security than she did. "What are you going to do when the Musashis come back?"

"We'll cross that bridge when we come to it."

With the Martins living in the big house and sharecropping the farm, it seemed Bernie had been done out of a home and a job. "Whose idea was it to move over to the Musashis'?"

"Mama and I both had a brainstorm at the same time. It hit me the day I saw the Musashis walking to town with one suitcase apiece. Didn't seem right."

"Thanks for taking me in, Bernie."

Bernie gave her a droll look. "You think I'd leave my pregnant sister without a roof over her head?"

"Mama would."

He gave her an irritated glance. "What a thing to say."

She felt ashamed and defensive. "I didn't know anything about the Martins. Last I heard, you were running the place."

"Things change." He gave a mirthless laugh. "I cried when I saw the Musashis leave. Mama got mad as all get-out. She said it wasn't right. She wrote letters and called anyone who'd listen. She drove all the way to Sacramento to talk to someone in government. They wanted to know where *she* came from. We decided to keep the Musashi farm running. If the taxes don't get paid, they'll lose the place. Me and Mama and Elizabeth decided this was the best way to handle things right now. The Martins are good people, Hildie. They'll take care of the place like it's their own, and Mama's comfortable in the cottage."

While Bernie carried her trunk into the barn, Hildemara took her suitcase inside the house. Elizabeth had set the table. She glanced over her shoulder at Hildie and turned back to the stove.

"Something smells wonderful."

"Stew." Elizabeth's voice sounded choked.

Elizabeth hardly said anything through dinner. Bernie talked about the work that needed doing. Hildie talked about moving from place to place, following Trip. "No place at the inn for OCS." She shrugged, trying not to think about how many months it might be before she saw Trip again.

"I tried to enlist." Bernie tossed his napkin on the table. "I'm strong as a horse, but they wouldn't take me. I had two strikes against me before I walked in the door. I'm an only son and a farmer. Then again, maybe there's another reason they don't want me. Bernhard Waltert isn't exactly an American name, is it?" He got up. "I've got work to do."

Hildie looked from the closing door to Elizabeth with her hangdog expression. "Are things really that bad?"

"Someone called him a coward the last time he went to town."

Hildie stacked Bernie's dish on top of hers and began to clear the table. "Idiots!"

"I can do the dishes, Hildie."

"I want to do my part while I'm living here. You cooked. I'll do the dishes."

Elizabeth sat with her head down. "You know, don't you?"

Hildie stood at the sink and closed her eyes. She wanted to pretend she didn't understand. Drying her hands, she came back and sat at the table. Elizabeth couldn't look her in the face. "Who's the father?"

Elizabeth's shoulders jerked as though she'd been struck. "I love him, you know."

Hildie's heart sank. She wanted to grab Elizabeth and shake her. "Who?"

Elizabeth looked up, eyes wide, mouth trembling. "Bernie. I love Bernie!" Her voice broke. She covered her face.

"Does he know?"

"How did you?"

Hildie lied. "The look on your face when I came in the door, the way you couldn't look me in the eyes. Does Bernie know?"

Elizabeth shook her head. "He knows something's wrong." She wiped tears away. "He doesn't understand why I cry all the time. The doctor told him it had to do with hormones." She looked up, afraid. "Are you going to tell him?"

"I'm not going to be the one to tell my brother something that will rip the heart right out of him. It's your secret, Elizabeth, not mine." Still, she had to know. "You didn't say who the father is."

"Eddie Rinckel."

Bernie's best friend? "Oh, Elizabeth." Hildie stood up and moved away from her. "How could you?" She felt sick. She wanted to slap Elizabeth, scream at her.

"Do you hate me?"

Hildie closed her eyes. "Yes. I think I do." Trembling, she went back to the sink to do the dishes. Elizabeth got up quietly and went into the bedroom she shared with Bernie.

Later, lying in bed, listening to the night sounds, Hildemara cried.

Suddenly Bernie threw open her door. "Fire! Come on. I need help!"

Hildie grabbed her robe and ran. Elizabeth worked beside Bernie. The Martins, all six of them, and Mama in her nightgown, came with shovels. It took an hour, but they managed to beat out and smother the blaze that had started in the alfalfa field.

Mama tossed her long braid back over her shoulder and wiped soot on the front of her nightgown. "We need another dog." Dash had died while Hildemara was in nursing school.

Bernie gave a cynical laugh. "Make that two, Mama."

39

TRIP CALLED LATE one evening. Hildemara rejoiced at the sound of his voice. "I got your letter. I've only got a few minutes to talk. So listen. I want you safe. Go back to Colorado and live with my parents. They'd love to have you."

She shouldn't have told him about the fire or *Jap lover* painted in red on the barn wall. "I'm not turning my back on my friends. The Musashis are as American as you and I. They've been our neighbors for years. Mr. Musashi taught Papa how to prune the almond trees and vines. Papa fixed his well and his truck. I went to school with the Musashi girls. Bernie played football and basketball and—"

"Hildie . . ."

"Don't worry about me. I can take care of myself."

Bernie laughed while sitting at the kitchen table with Elizabeth. "She's beginning to sound like Mama."

"Rocks through windows? A field on fire?" Trip sounded angry. "Sounds like you're in a war zone."

"Maybe we are, but it's a different war than you'll be fighting."

Tears sprang to her eyes. She tried to calm down. "Things will settle down. People have known us around here for years, Trip. Papa was well loved, even if he was German." She couldn't help the edge in her tone. "We're sitting tight and keeping this place going. You take care of yourself." She wiped tears away at the thought of what Trip would soon face. Fear had become a constant companion, robbing her of sleep, stealing her appetite. Other sorrows came to bear, as well. Elizabeth, for one. Hildemara struggled with disappointment and the sense of betrayal, for Bernie's sake.

"I've got to go."

Hildie heard voices in the background and knew a line had probably formed at the base telephone. "Trip!" Her voice broke. She didn't want their last conversation to be an argument. "I love you."

"I love you, too. Take care of our baby."

She heard something in his voice. "You received orders, didn't you?"

"We're shipping out."

"When?"

"Soon. If anything happens to me—"

"Don't say it! Don't you dare!"

"I love you, Hildie. Stay safe." He hung up.

Hildie's hand shook as she put the receiver back on its cradle. It struck like a blow to the heart that she might never hear Trip's voice again.

❄ ❄ ❄

Bernie looked at Hildemara over his cup of coffee before dawn the next morning. "You look awful. Do you have morning sickness, too?"

"I just can't sleep for worrying."

"Elizabeth doesn't feel well enough to get up." He stole a brief glance toward the bedroom door and looked straight at Hildie. "You two have words or something?"

"No. Why would we?"

He put his cup down carefully. "I know about the baby."

"Oh, Bernie." She put her hand over her mouth, wanting to sob at the look on his face.

"It's my fault, you know." He grimaced. "I found out after I married her I couldn't give her children." He looked at her again. "We'd been trying. Doc told me mumps can make a man . . . well, you know, not worth anything."

"Don't say that."

"I'm a coward, Hildie. I didn't have guts enough to tell Elizabeth the truth. I was afraid I'd lose her. I probably will anyway."

She'd never seen her brother so despondent. "She says she loves you." She put her hand over his. "I believe her."

"It was Eddie." His eyes filled. "He told me himself."

Hildemara went hot. "Bragging?"

"No. Far from it. I knew something had been tearing him up inside. We went out for a couple of drinks before he left for basic training. He signed into the Marines. He had last-minute jitters. Wondered if he was brave enough. He got so drunk, he could hardly walk. When I dropped him off, he kept saying how sorry he was, how he wished I'd kill him, and then the Japs wouldn't have to bother. When I asked him what in the blazes he was talking about, he told me."

"He should've kept his big mouth shut!"

Bernie gave her a sad smile. "He's been in love with Elizabeth since before we came to town. I'm the one who stole her from him, not the other way around."

"That's no excuse. Not for either one of them."

Glaring at her, he rubbed his head, agitated. "Don't judge her. Some people were giving her a hard time in town, saying I was a coward for not joining up, calling us Jap lovers and Mama a dirty Nazi. Eddie stepped in and told them to shut up and back off. He gave her a ride home. Only they didn't come back right away. She was scared to death of what I might do when I found out. And he knew I'd head into town and have more than words with a few of those . . ." Bernie rubbed his face. "Anyway, they stopped at Grand Junction. He just wanted to calm her down before bringing her home. They started talking about old times, good times. She was still crying, shaken up. He held her, comforted her. That's how it started, I guess. It just didn't end there."

Bernie's face twisted, anguished. "I couldn't hate him. Not even when he told me. What right have I got to throw stones at anyone?" His eyes filled. "He's dead, you know. Got blown to bits on some piece of crap island in the South Pacific. He used to tell me he wanted to go to the beach. 'Let's go over to Santa Cruz,' he'd say. Well, he died on a beach."

Hildie put her face in her hands and sobbed. All she could think about was Trip on his way to Europe. She'd told herself over and over he was a medic. Thank God, he wasn't a Marine. They wouldn't put him in the front lines. He would follow, picking up the pieces.

Bernie gripped her shoulder. "Go gentle on my wife. She's eating herself up with guilt. And I love her; I love her so much. As far as I'm concerned, that baby she's carrying is mine."

Hildie raised her head. "Maybe you should tell her."

"Tell her what?"

"Everything."

He shook his head. "She might leave me."

She leaned over and cupped his face. "You haven't left her."

He pulled away and stood. "Two wrongs don't make things right, Sis."

"What good is love without trust?"

"What are you two talking about?" Elizabeth stood in the bedroom doorway, still in her nightgown, arms hugged around herself. She looked sick and frightened, pale and strained. She looked at Hildie and then Bernie, bereft. "Did you . . . ?"

"Did she tell me the baby isn't mine? No, sugar. She didn't. I already knew."

Elizabeth made a choking sound and stepped back, hands covering her face.

Bernie pulled a chair back. "Come and sit down with me. We need to talk."

Hildie couldn't bear the pain she saw in both their faces, the guilt and shame, the heartbreak. She got up. "I love you both." She went outside.

Sitting in Mrs. Musashi's chair out front, she watched the sunrise while Bernie and Elizabeth talked inside the house. No screaming, no shouting like Mama and Papa. The silence worried her and she stood, looking through the window. Elizabeth sat on Bernie's lap, her arms wrapped around his shoulders. He held her firmly, stroking her back as both wept.

Relief filled Hildie. She envied the fact that they could be together through this war and not have to be separated. She didn't like feeling that way. She went out for a long walk through the Musashis' English walnut orchard, thanking God Bernie and Elizabeth would be all right. She prayed for Trip's safety. She ran her hands over her abdomen, praying their baby would be born healthy and strong. She prayed the next battle would turn the tide of the war and it would end soon.

Thinking of Trip filled her with so many emotions: worry, fear, hope, hunger, an aching loneliness to have him back beside her. *God, please bring him home to me. Bring him home in one piece.*

❄ ❄ ❄

As summer moved toward fall, townsfolk had another reason to resent Bernie and Mama and anyone else in their situation. Rationing kept people in want, but farmers had plenty. Mama's forty acres of almonds and raisins and her half-acre vegetable garden, along with chickens and rabbits, produced enough to feed both families and have plenty to sell. Bernie kept up the walnut orchard, vineyard, and two acres of produce, making runs to Merced to sell tomatoes, squash, onions, and carrots. The Musashis had two cows, both healthy; a hundred chickens; a dozen rabbits; and four goats. Bernie added a dog. He called him Killer as a joke, though passersby believed it and kept their distance. Never lacking in food, Mama said they should give away whatever they could spare to neighbors and friends in town, keeping only enough for mortgage payments and taxes on the two places.

Hildemara blossomed with her pregnancy. So did Elizabeth. They laughed as they waddled around the place. Weeding became more difficult as the months passed. Bernie and Elizabeth's son came in September. They named him Edward Niclas Waltert.

Mama checked the mailbox every day. Hildemara went across to get their mail. Mama would sift through the envelopes and sigh heavily.

When Hildemara's labor started, Bernie went for Mama. Rather than drive to town for Dr. Whiting, Mama came across the street to help deliver the baby. Hildemara was too far along to argue. She had already told Elizabeth what to do to get ready.

Mama leaned over Hildie, wiping sweat from her forehead. "You scream if you want to."

Hildie knew Mama expected her to be worse than Elizabeth, who had screamed and sobbed and begged for the pain to stop. Hildie had been in hospital delivery rooms. She knew what to expect. She had no intention of making it worse for all those around her. She didn't look at Mama or listen to anything she said. She concentrated on the course of her labor, enduring the pain in silence and bearing down when her body told her it was time.

"You have a son, Hildemara Rose." Mama washed and swaddled him and placed him in her arms. "What are you going to call him?"

Exhausted, Hildie smiled into his perfect face. "Trip likes the name Charles."

She wrote to Trip the next day.

Our son arrived on December 15. Charles Cale Arundel has very healthy lungs! Mama says she can hear him across the street. He and Eddie are going to make quite a pair. . . .

She wrote every day, sometimes in a way to sound like Charles was writing the letter.

Daddy, come home soon. I can't wait to meet you. You have to teach me how to play basketball and baseball. . . .

Giving birth took more of her strength than she expected. Or maybe it was the night feedings that seemed to sap her of strength. Elizabeth had been up and around a few days after giving birth, but Hildemara felt so tired all the time. She feared relapsing with tuberculosis.

Mama came over every day. "Get some sleep. Let me hold my grandson."

❄ ❄ ❄

Dear Rosie,

Hildemara Rose has given me a second grandson. She has named him Charles Cale Arundel. She did well. No screaming or carrying on. The only time she shed a tear was when she held her newborn son in her arms. Then she cried a river of joyful tears.

I remember giving birth to Hildemara on the floor of the cabin in that frozen Manitoba wheatland. I cried! I think I cursed Niclas when he came home and found me. Poor man. I have never been easy on anyone, especially those I love most.

My girl did better than I, but I'm worried. Hildemara has not bounced back to good health the way Elizabeth did. She looks so pale and worn down. Nursing every two hours is exhausting, and I fear my girl may get sick again. I offer to help, but she gives me a look that sends me home. So I bring dinner sometimes, just to give these two girls rest.

Hildemara Rose and I get along, but there is a wall between us. I know I built it. I doubt she's forgiven me for my harsh words at the sanatorium, and I will not apologize for them. I may have to prod her again. I'll do whatever I must to keep her spirits up. Oh, but it hurts me so to do it. I wonder if she will ever understand me.

❄ ❄ ❄

After spending almost a month in bed, Hildie began to regain her strength. Mama made a sling for her so she could carry Charlie around while doing chores. He rode happily, cradled safely against Hildie's chest. When he grew too big to ride in the sling, Mama designed a backpack. When he began to crawl, Hildie and Elizabeth took turns watching their "little explorers."

Bernie laughed as the two boys crawled around the house. "They need sunshine, but I think we're going to have to cage them."

The Allies pressed on. Battles raged in Germany and in the South Pacific. Hildie wondered if the war would ever end and Trip come home.

40

1944

The war finally began to turn in the Allies' favor, and every day brought new hope as they listened to the radio.

Bernie started making plans. "We're not staying in Murietta. When the war ends, the Musashis will come back. Everything will be ready for them, and we'll look for our own place. I made good money off those trees I grafted. Lemon-orange-lime trees." He laughed. "I'd like to start my own nursery, do some more grafting. Experiment a little and see what else I can come up with. I could do landscaping. Might be nice to live closer to Sacramento or San Jose or in sunny Southern California near all those movie stars Cloe writes about. They'd have money to spend."

Hildemara didn't know what to do. She had written to Trip every day and hadn't received a letter in weeks. Every time a car came up the road, her heart lodged in her throat for fear it would stop and an Army officer would come to the door. Eddie Rinckel wasn't the only hometown boy killed overseas. Tony Reboli had died on D-day. So had two of Mama's Summer Bedlam boys, and Fritz had lost his leg when he stepped on a land mine on Guadalcanal.

Hildie knew Trip had survived D-day. By the time he reached Paris, he had become a captain. His letters, few and far between, were filled with words of love, what he remembered about their time together, how much he missed her. He didn't write about the future.

The newspapers reported tens of thousands dying on battlefields in Europe, and previously unknown islands in the South Pacific. The prejudice got worse at home. Hildemara continued to go to church with Mama. She left Charlie at home with Bernie and Elizabeth, who had stopped going. Only a few people spoke to Hildemara, and only because they knew Trip served in the Army. Hardly anyone spoke to Mama. Old friends who had known them for years kept their distance, staring and whispering. Mama sat eyes straight ahead, listening to the sermon, Papa's Bible open in her lap.

Hildemara was the one who got mad. After all the nice things Mama had done for people over the years, they turned on her now? "I thought they were our friends!"

"They were. They will be again, when the war is over. Assuming we win, of course. If we don't, we're all going to be in the same sinking boat."

"Fair-weather friends, Mama. They're not real friends."

"They're afraid. Fear makes people mean. Fear makes people act stupid."

"Don't make excuses for them!" Hildemara stared out the window, arms crossed over her chest, hurt and fuming.

Mama shrugged while driving. "When it's all over, we won't hold it against them."

Hildemara turned in exasperation. "*You* won't. I'm not going to have anything to do with those . . . those hypocrites!"

Mama's face flamed. "Where do you get off judging, Hildemara Rose?" She turned sharply in to the drive. Hildemara bumped against the door. "Keep on as you are and you're going to be just as mean-spirited and stupid as they are!" Mama slammed on the brake so hard Hildie had to grab the dash to keep from cracking her head on it.

"Mama! Are you trying to kill us?"

"Just shake a little sense into your head." She shoved her door open and got out. "What do you suppose your father would say to you right now? *Turn the other cheek!* That's what he'd say."

Hildie jumped out and slammed her door. "I never thought I'd hear that come out of your mouth!"

Mama slammed her door harder. "Well, it did." She stomped off toward the cottage.

Hildemara regretted adding fuel to the fire. "Why don't we go to Atwater next Sunday?" she called after Mama. "No one knows us in Atwater! No one will be gossiping about us there!"

Mama swung around and planted her feet. "Don't be so stupid, Hildemara. I still have a Swiss accent."

Smarting under her criticism, Hildie shouted back. "Swiss, Mama! Not German! The Swiss are neutral!"

"Neutral!" She snorted in disgust. "A lot you know. Where do you think Germany gets it munitions? How do you think goods pass from Germany to Italy? If that isn't bad enough, people around here don't know the difference between a Swiss, German, or Swedish accent!"

Hildie's shoulders slumped. "I'm not going back to church."

"Well, fine! *You* run if you want. *You* hide! But I'm going back and I'm going to keep going back! And one of these days, I'll be buried in their churchyard. You make sure of that! You hear me, Hildemara Rose?"

"I hear you, Mama! They'll probably spit on your grave!"

"Let them spit. It'll make the flowers grow!" She slammed the cottage door behind her.

Bernie stood in the yard across the street. "What was that all about? I could hear you and Mama shouting all the way over here."

"She's impossible!"

Bernie laughed as she stormed by. "I never thought I'd see the day that you'd shout back at Mama."

"It didn't get me anywhere, did it?"

1945

Franklin Roosevelt continued as president, starting his fourth term, with Harry Truman as the new vice president. London was bombarded by V-1 rocket bombs. Mama wrote letters to a friend in Kew Gardens. Rumors were confirmed about Nazi concentration camps exterminating Jews. German officers failed in an assassination attempt on Hitler and were hanged. American soldiers pushed toward Berlin.

Finally, Germany surrendered, though the war raged on against Japan. Thousands died as American troops fought to take back one Pacific island after another.

Trip wrote from Berlin.

I'm coming home.

He didn't know when he would arrive, but he would be sent to his city of enlistment, which meant if she wanted to be at the train station to meet him, she needed to return to Colorado. Hildie's joy turned to panic when she saw the letter had taken twelve days to reach her.

Bernie took her to the train station to buy tickets. She prayed she would be able to ride in a Pullman so she and two-year-old Charlie could rest on the three-day trip to Colorado.

By the time they arrived, Hildie had lost weight from motion sickness and was exhausted. The train pulled into Denver midafternoon, and she had to transfer to the Eagle streamliner to Colorado Springs. Carrying Charles on her hip and struggling with her suitcase, she made it just in time. Every muscle in her body ached. She shifted Charles in her arms.

Mom and Dad Arundel stood on the train platform waiting for her in Colorado Springs. Hildemara cried in relief when she saw them. Mom gave her a quick hug and took Charlie. "Oh, he's beautiful! Just like his daddy at this age." She kissed Charlie's plump cheeks while Dad hugged Hildie.

"Any word?" Hildie had dreamed of seeing Trip with them.

"Not yet, but he'll be home any day now." Dad picked up the suitcase. "Only one?"

"Bernie will ship everything as soon as we know where we're going to live."

She felt dead on her feet; she stumbled. Dad caught her beneath the elbow and looked her over with concern. "You're going straight to bed when we get to the house. You look like you haven't slept in three days."

"Charlie didn't sleep much on the train."

Dad smiled. "Well, you've got reinforcements now, so you can rest up before Trip gets here."

Hildie fell asleep the moment her head touched Trip's pillow in the porch bedroom. She awakened to someone stroking her face. When she opened her eyes, she saw Trip leaning over her, smiling. She thought she was dreaming until he spoke.

"Hey, sleepyhead."

She reached up and touched his face. Sobbing, she threw her arms around him. He held on to her. Gripping her hair, he drew her head back and kissed her. She tasted salt and realized they were both crying.

Embarrassed, he whispered against her hair. "I've missed you so much, Hildie." She heard the tears in his voice.

She pressed closer, nestling into the curve of his neck, inhaling his scent. "You're home. Thank God, you're home." She could feel the tremor in his hands. If not for his parents in the other room or for Charlie, who was crying again, she might have been bolder. She drew back, smiling, drinking in the sight of her husband. He looked tired. His face hadn't changed, but his eyes looked older, battle-worn. "What do you think of your son?"

"He's perfect. He's sitting on the kitchen rug playing with some of Mom's wooden spoons. Or he was. I tried to pick him up, but he didn't think much of the idea."

"He doesn't know you yet. He will." She kept touching him, running her hands over him, her heart squeezing tight at the signs of fatigue, sorrow, joy, all mixed together. His eyes darkened.

"Better stop." He took her hands and kissed them. "I want you so much I hurt, Hildie." He rested his forehead against hers. "I know what I'd like to do with you right now, but I don't want to shock the life out of my parents."

Mom prepared a wonderful lunch. They all sat around the table, giving thanks to God for Trip's safe return. Trip fed Charlie. "They say food is the quickest way to a man's heart." Trip made airplane sounds and told Charlie to open the hangar. Everyone laughed. Hildie couldn't take her eyes off Trip.

Dad got up. "Why don't we take this little fellow on a stroll, Mom?"

Mom stacked dishes and put them in the sink. "The fresh air would do him good. Leave the dishes, Hildie. You and Trip have a lot of catching up to do."

They went out with the stroller they'd bought before Hildie arrived and settled Charlie into it. The sun was warm as Trip and his dad carried the stroller down the front steps, Mom following.

"We're going down and around Prospect Lake," Dad called out. "Charlie might like to watch the kids playing."

"The Harts haven't seen him yet," Mom called. "We'll probably stop there while we're out."

"Don't you two worry if we're gone for a couple of hours." Dad winked at Trip. "We'll take care of Charlie. You take care of your wife."

Hildie watched them walk up East Moreno Avenue. Trip took her hand and drew her back inside the house, closing the door behind them. Leaning against it, he grinned. "A couple of hours, Dad said."

She blushed. "I adore your parents."

They made the most of the rest of the afternoon.

❆　❆　❆

Hildie had six perfect days with Trip before he had to report to base. His parents went with her to the train station. Mom took Charlie so Hildie could walk alongside the moving car, her hand pressed against the glass, his on the other side. "I'll see you in a few days, Trip."

His eyes filled with tears. He mouthed, *I love you.* He looked over her head to his parents and then turned away.

No one spoke on the way back to the house. Hildemara had a premonition, but didn't want to speak it. Mom reached for Charlie as soon as they entered the house. "Why don't you let me take him for a while?" She looked ready to cry. She took Charlie into the bedroom instead of setting him on the rug to play. Hildie's heart began to pound.

"Sit down, honey." Dad put his hand on her shoulder.

"What's wrong?"

"Trip couldn't tell you."

She started to shake inside as the fear came up and spread. She had read the papers. She hadn't wanted to believe it. "Tell me what?" She could barely get the words out. The war in Europe had ended. Trip had done his part.

"Trip received his orders. He's being sent to the South Pacific."

❄ ❄ ❄

Grief-stricken and angry, Hildemara returned to Murietta. Mom and Dad had wanted her to stay with them in Colorado Springs, but she said Bernie and Elizabeth could use her help holding on to the Musashi place. Dad's eyes had flickered at the Japanese name, but he hadn't argued.

Settled again, Hildie couldn't bear to read the newspapers or listen to the radio. At night, Bernie turned it on and she couldn't get away from it. Casualties mounted as ships were sunk by kamikaze pilots. Each island recaptured cost tens of thousands of lives. And still, Japan with its ancient code of honor refused to surrender. An invasion would come, and estimates ran up to a hundred thousand American soldiers dead to defeat the Japanese on their own soil. How many had already been killed at Normandy or in northern Africa, Italy, and Germany? Millions! Europe had been laid waste by war.

Trip wrote.

Rough seas. Been sick for days. Not much good to anyone.

And how long before his ship reached the shores of Japan and he would be in another beach invasion, the red cross on his white helmet a perfect target for enemy fire?

Mama told her worrying did no good, but Hildie couldn't seem to stop. She worried over Trip's ship being hit by a kamikaze. She worried about his ship sinking, leaving him lost at sea, adrift, then drowning or being eaten by sharks. She worried his ship would succeed in reaching Japan or some godforsaken island and he'd step on a land mine and be blasted to bits like poor Eddie Rinckel and a dozen others she knew from school days.

"You're going to make yourself sick again, Hildemara Rose." Mama sat at the Musashis' table, a glass of lemonade in front of her. "You can't change anything. Your husband will come back or he won't. Worrying isn't going to help him. You've got to stop moping around like a lost soul, hiding in the house. Elizabeth could use a little more help around here, in case you hadn't noticed."

"Leave me alone, Mama. What do you know about loving someone the way I love Trip?" She regretted the words as soon as they sprang from her mouth.

"Oh. Love. Is that what this is? Love?" Mama sneered. "Looks more like self-pity from where I'm sitting. And a good excuse not to carry your share of the load. Who do you think you are, some duchess? Leaving all the work to Bernie and Elizabeth because your husband made it back from Europe and got sent to the Pacific? You think you're alone in your misery? Trip would be proud of you, wouldn't he? Seeing you sitting on your backside at the breakfast table sniveling and letting Elizabeth keep watch over two babies. No. Make that three. Wouldn't he just love that?"

"Stop it!"

Mama got up and shattered the glass of lemonade in the sink. "No. You stop it! *Mein Gott!* This is war! The people who give up and give in don't survive! You know what Papa said about worry. It's sin, Hildemara! It shows your lack of faith in God! You know what Papa told me before he died? He said every time I felt myself starting to worry, he wanted me to pray. *Pray!* That's what I do! Sometimes screaming! I hang on to faith with both fists and pray. It's harder some days than others, but by heavens, I do it!"

"I'm not you."

"No. You're not." Mama let out her breath. "I didn't expect you to turn out like me. I just didn't want you to be like . . ."

Caught by the changed tone of her voice, Hildemara looked up. "Like who?"

"Never mind." She shook her head, her eyes moist. "Sometimes all you can do is pray." She looked down at Hildemara. "And hope for the best." She went to the door. "Tell Elizabeth I'm sorry about the glass. I'll get her another." She slammed the door behind herself.

Hildemara picked the glass shards out of the sink and threw them away. Putting on her apron, she went out to help Elizabeth weed the garden. She could hear Eddie and Charlie playing in the pen Bernie had set up. Elizabeth glanced up and shaded her eyes. "I saw Mama going in to talk with you. Are you okay?"

"I'll survive." She leaned down and ran her hand over Charlie's head. Whatever happened, she knew for his sake she had to do more than survive.

❇ ❇ ❇

On August 6, 1945, America dropped the atomic bomb on Hiroshima. Hildie sat with Bernie and Elizabeth listening to the radio. They had heard rumors something big was coming, but had never imagined such destruction possible. "They'll surrender now." Bernie felt sure of it.

The Japanese didn't.

Another bomb fell three days later on Nagasaki after leaflets had been dropped to warn of its coming. Bernie cheered when the Japanese surrendered, as did Hildemara and Elizabeth, dancing around the kitchen while Eddie and Charlie watched with wide eyes, confused at all the ruckus.

Two days later, the Western Defense Command revoked the exclusion orders against Japanese Americans. The Musashis would be coming home soon, but Bernie didn't seem at all worried about it. He and Elizabeth started making plans to move farther north, closer to Sacramento.

Hildemara received a letter from Trip. His ship would come into San Francisco. He didn't know what day.

Stay in Murietta. I'll come to you. . . .

Would he want to go back to Colorado or stay in California? Would he want to start medical school right away? If so, she would have to find a job and help pay his way. But then what would she do about Charles? So many decisions needed to be made. She wouldn't know anything until Trip came home.

When the phone rang, she ran to catch it.

"Do you know there are no taxis in Murietta?"

"Trip!"

"At least, none that I can find. How's a civilian supposed to get a ride around here?"

"Where are you?" She sobbed with joy.

"Murietta train station."

"We'll be right there!" She ran outside. *"Bernie!"* For the first time in her life, she wished she had taken Mama's advice and learned to drive.

On the way to town, Hildemara screamed, "Can't you go any faster?"

Bernie chuckled. "If I go any faster, we'll end up in a ditch." His eyes gleamed with amusement. "I'm surprised you didn't want to bring Charlie with you."

"Oh no!" she shrieked. She'd left him alone on the rug! "We've got to go back!"

"Forgot him, huh?" Bernie laughed without restraint. "Just left him with the door wide open. He's probably toddled off some- place. Probably eating sand by now or playing in manure. He could fall into a canal, you know, or get run over. Great mama you turned out to be."

"Bernie!"

He gave her a shove. "He's fine, you idiot. Relax! Elizabeth took him out to the garden. He and Eddie are probably yanking on the playpen bars trying to escape. Did you know you forgot to hang up the telephone? You just left poor Trip hanging on a line."

"What am I going to tell Trip? What's he going to think of me?"

Bernie laughed. "I doubt he'll be thinking about anything but getting his hands on his wife again."

Trip didn't give her a chance to breathe, let alone explain why she didn't have Charlie with her. She laughed and cried she was so happy to see him. He looked lean and fit, and handsome in his uniform, though she couldn't wait to see him out of it. "You said *civilian*."

"I am, but you have all my civvies in the trunk."

"Oh. I forgot."

Bernie grinned. "She seems to be forgetting a lot of things lately."

Mama came over to welcome Trip home. She had gone to town and bought a leg of lamb and wanted to help put on a celebratory dinner. Hildie ran out to the barn and brought back a tablecloth and china place settings. Bernie and Trip took their sons outside to play while Mama, Hildie, and Elizabeth set the table.

Mama admired the plates. "Lady Daisy had plates just like these." She ran her finger around the edge of a Royal Doulton plate before setting it on the table.

The Martins came over. The house filled up to bursting. Everyone laughed and talked and passed plates of lamb, mashed potatoes, carrots, and peas around the table. Mama had even thought of apple mint jelly. Trip chopped carrots for Charles, who chucked them on the floor, rousing more laughter. "We're going to have to work on your table manners."

They talked of more serious matters. Trip asked what Bernie planned to do when the Musashis came home.

"Start packing."

Everyone grew quiet. Hitch and Donna exchanged a glance. Mama spoke up. "Hitch, you and Donna needn't worry. We have a contract."

"We never signed anything, Marta. And Bernie's your son. . . ."

"I gave my word."

Hitch looked embarrassed. "Bernie and Elizabeth and the baby will need a place to live. What're they going to do?"

Mama smiled. "Ask them."

Bernie took Elizabeth's hand. "We've been talking about moving up to Sacramento and opening a nursery. I've got some money saved—not much, but enough to get started." He gave Mama an apologetic smile. "It's what I've always wanted to do."

Mama stared back. "Did I ever say you couldn't?" She turned to Trip. "What about you two? Where will you go?"

Trip looked grim. "We can go back to Colorado Springs for a while, until I figure out what I'm going to do with the rest of my life."

Hildie was surprised. "What about medical school?"

"Normandy killed that plan for me. I've seen all the blood I ever want to see. No more." He shook his head. "I don't think I could ever work in a hospital again either."

Mama picked up a bowl of mashed potatoes and handed them to Donna. "It'll all work out." She looked at Hildemara. "Don't worry about it."

42

Friday afternoon, Hildemara heard a heavy vehicle coming up
the road. She straightened where she had been working in a row of
zucchini and brushed herself off. An Army bus pulled up and idled
in front of the farm. Hildie swung Charlie up and sat him on her
hip as she hurried toward the yard.

Mr. Musashi got off the bus, Mrs. Musashi behind him. George
and the girls, all taller, stepped down, looking shy and uncertain.
Bernie came out of the barn. Elizabeth opened the screen door and
came outside. As the bus pulled away, Mama crossed the street.

The Musashis just stood there, tight together, silent, looking from
house to barn to orchard and fields. They looked strange in their
government-issued clothing. Hildie felt tears fill her eyes. No one
seemed to know what to do, what to say. Bernie approached them.
"Everything is pretty much the way you left it, Mr. Musashi."

They just looked at him, saying nothing. Hildemara couldn't
read anything in their faces. They had never seemed more foreign
or more vulnerable.

Bernie looked back at Elizabeth. Hildie handed Charlie to

Trip and went to Betsy. She was a beautiful young woman now, a head taller than she had been the last time Hildie saw her. "Let's bring your parents inside the house, Betsy. You all must be tired. We can make tea. Elizabeth has been baking cookies all morning."

"You live here now, too?" Betsy looked at her coldly.

Mama stepped in and spoke to Mr. and Mrs. Musashi. "Only until you all got back." She spoke firmly. "Bernhard moved into your place right after the government relocated you. He worked both sides of the road until I hired the Martins to sharecrop my place. Otherwise, my son would have worked himself to death keeping both places running. My son has done a good job for you, Mr. Musashi. Tell him, Bernhard!"

Bernie blushed crimson. "Mama . . ."

"Can't you see? They don't understand! They think you stole their place." She turned to Betsy. "Explain to your parents right now. The mortgage and taxes are paid up, and there's enough left from last year's crops to carry your family through to next year. We've been waiting for you. It's still your place."

Betsy started to cry. She bowed deeply, her hands fluttering over her mouth. Her father looked at her and spoke grimly. She shook her head and spoke in Japanese. He looked at Bernhard and Mama. He looked at Elizabeth and Hildemara and Trip. He didn't say anything. Mrs. Musashi spoke quietly in Japanese. Betsy answered. Tears streamed down Mrs. Musashi's face. Mr. Musashi bowed at the waist, and so did his wife and children.

Mama looked mortified. "What about your brothers, Betsy?" No one else had the courage to ask. "When will they be home?"

Betsy smiled, dark eyes shining, but it was Mr. Musashi who answered. "They both good soldiers, many honors from fighting Germans." He caught himself. "So sorry, Mrs. Waltert. So sorry. I not think clearly."

"No need to apologize, Mr. Musashi. I'm Swiss, not German, and Niclas believed Hitler would cause more trouble than the kaiser. He would've been proud of your sons."

❄ ❄ ❄

Hildie and Trip moved back to Oakland. They stayed in a hotel until they found a small rental house on Quigley Street. Charlie still struggled with having to share Hildie with Trip. He'd become used to sleeping with Hildemara and having her all to himself. Now that he didn't, he threw tantrums when put in his own room. Torn between husband and son, Hildie tried to please both. Still, when Charlie cried, she jumped to comfort him. Nights proved long with numerous interruptions. Trip became frustrated. "He knows exactly when to ruin things, doesn't he?"

By the end of his first month home, Trip had had enough. When Charlie wailed, he caught hold of Hildie and held her down in bed. "Let him cry."

"He needs me."

"The heck he does. You're making it worse. He has to learn he can't have you any time he wants."

"He doesn't understand!"

"He understands all right. All he has to do is cry to have his way."

"That's not fair. He's just a baby."

"He's *our* son, Hildie. He's not just yours anymore. I'm his father. Listen to me."

Charlie's cries turned to screams of rage. Hildie started to cry. She wanted to cover her ears or scream along with him.

"Don't give in." Trip held her close, his arm across her chest, his leg trapping hers.

"Let me go, Trip."

With a sigh, he did and turned his back on her.

Hildie sat on the edge of the bed, head in her hands, heart in her throat. Charlie's screams changed. He cried and then stopped, as though listening for her footsteps in the hall. He cried again. "Mama . . . Mama . . ."

He whimpered. Then silence fell in the house. She curled on her side. Trip didn't touch her for the rest of the night. She felt the wall between them, like a physical force.

❋ ❋ ❋

Charlie wasn't the only one having difficulties adjusting.

Trip had constant nightmares. He moaned, thrashed, cried out. When Hildie touched his shoulder, wanting to soothe him, he jerked awake. He always came out of it with a jolt, shaking. He wouldn't talk about what he dreamed. Sometimes he got up and went into the living room and sat with a light on, staring at nothing.

She came out and sat with him. "What do you dream about?" Maybe talking about it would break the grip the nightmares had on him.

"The war."

"Can you tell me . . . ?"

"No!" He looked bleak and despairing.

Once, she came out and found him crying, his hands raked into his hair, holding his head. She sat down beside him and put her hand on his back. He stood abruptly and moved away from her. "Go back to bed, Hildemara."

"I love you."

"I know. I love you, too. But it doesn't help."

"If you can't talk to me about what happened, you have to talk to someone."

"I'll get over it in time."

❋ ❋ ❋

The nightmares persisted. Trip entered the police academy and that seemed to make everything worse, though he felt called to it. A siren's call that would destroy him? Sometimes he drank in order to sleep.

Finally Hildie could stand the worry no more. It affected her sleep and appetite. She went to Rev. Mathias.

Sobbing, she told him everything, even how sometimes when they made love, Trip seemed to be trying to drive demons away.

"He scares me sometimes. I don't know what to do to help him. He won't let me in." When asked, Hildemara could name all the places to which she had posted letters. Rev. Mathias thought about it for a moment, his mouth a grim line.

"We must have been following in each other's footsteps. Normandy. Paris. Germany. Berlin. I can guess what he saw, Hildemara. I saw it, too. I was a chaplain."

When Rev. Mathias came to dinner, Trip looked at her with fury in his eyes, but didn't say anything embarrassing about a wife interfering. Hildemara took Charlie and went out for a long walk so the men could talk. When she came back, both of them had red-rimmed eyes. After they saw Rev. Mathias out, Trip kissed her the way he used to kiss her. Hildie didn't ask what they had talked about. She didn't want to know any more details than she already did.

That night her husband slept through the night without crying out or thrashing. She awakened once and found him so still, she feared he had died. She turned on the light and found his face at peace. He looked young again, as he had before he'd gone away to war. In the morning, he looked rested, but she knew the war had altered him in ways that would never be undone.

He and Rev. Mathias started meeting once a week for coffee just to talk. Even so, there were times when Hildie would see a look come into Trip's eyes, and she'd know he was reliving the horrors again. Some wounds broke open and had to be stitched closed with patience and prayer. She mourned the loss of the young man he had been—carefree, easygoing Trip so quick to laughter. That man had disappeared on the beaches at Normandy, and in his place another returned hardened by war, cynical about the world, and with a fierce desire to protect her and Charlie from harm.

Trip excelled at the police academy. His college degree and science background made him a prime candidate for forensics. He agreed to a transfer to the new Santa Rita jail, where he would work in a laboratory, studying and sorting evidence.

Rather than be separated by the long commute, Hildie looked for a rental near the prison. They moved into a bigger house with a bigger yard not far from his job. Paxtown, a small farming community nestled in the East Bay Hills, sat two miles away with a grocery store, department store, and theater, among other comforting amenities, including a church.

The cyclone fences with concertina wire at the top and guards at the prison gate disconcerted Hildemara. Trip had seen them before. "This time they keep the bad guys in." His cryptic comment gave Hildie her first insight into what he had seen, what had haunted his nights for so long. They never talked about those years he served.

The neighborhood women came over with cookies and casseroles and invitations to bring Charlie over to play with their sons and daughters.

Many of their husbands had served in the war, too. They talked about problems the way Mama and Papa had talked about crops, with camaraderie and hope for the future. Hildie and Trip attended block parties, barbecues, and card parties. Hildie invited women over for coffee klatches and teas. People often talked of "those dirty Japs," and Hildemara talked about the Musashi family and Andrew and Patrick serving in Europe. Some of the women stopped inviting her to their homes.

"I wonder what they'd say if they knew my father came from Germany and my mother is Swiss." If not for Mama's correspondence with Rosie Brechtwald, they wouldn't have known how the Swiss threatened to blow the main tunnel into the country if one German stood in the light at the end of it. But that didn't stop them from making money off the war selling munitions to the Germans and transporting goods between the Third Reich and Mussolini. Rosie said it was the only way they could remain free. Mama grieved over freedom being purchased with blood money.

"Don't tell them," Trip ordered her. "It's none of their business."

Trip kept his police revolver loaded and high enough to be out of Charlie's reach, but close enough to get to it fast. Hildie wondered if working homicides was good for him, but he seemed to relish the work of putting criminals in prison.

After looking at available land in the area, Trip became increasingly discouraged and despondent. "I'll be retirement age before we can afford to buy property of our own!"

"We could save enough if I worked at the veterans hospital outside Livermore."

Trip's eyes darkened. "What about Charlie?"

"I could work a night shift now and then. See how it goes." She didn't tell him she suspected she was pregnant again.

43

1947

Hildie gave birth to their daughter, Carolyn, in the spring. Carolyn wasn't as easy a baby as Charlie. She had colic and cried almost constantly. Hildemara almost felt relieved when she was able to go back to work after two months off.

At first, Trip protested. "Quit, Hildie." He ran his hand over Carolyn's downy head. "Think of the baby."

"I'll sleep late on weekends. We still need to save a lot more before we can buy land."

"You're exhausted."

"LaVonne said she'd babysit Charlie and Carolyn a couple of days a week. I can change to day shifts. That will make it easier."

"And when will we be together? Dinnertime?"

"I'm only working part-time, Trip."

"And what about your health?"

"I'm fine, Trip. Really. I couldn't be better."

And it was true.

When she said it.

❊ ❊ ❊

1948

Charlie, four years older, doted on his baby sister and liked to play with her. As Carolyn grew, she started climbing out of her crib at night and crawling into bed with Hildie and Trip. Hildie would have to get up and carry her back to her crib. "When is that child going to sleep through the night?"

Trip chuckled. "Maybe we should tie her in."

They locked their bedroom door instead. Sometimes Hildie got up in the morning and found Carolyn curled up with her blanket outside the door.

❊ ❊ ❊

1950

"You look pale, Hildie. You've got to get more rest."

"I'm trying." Still she couldn't seem to catch up on sleep, even staying in bed on weekends.

Trip got a promotion. Now a lieutenant, he drew a higher salary. "Quit work. Stay home. We don't need you getting sick again."

She knew that better than he did. She might not make it out of the hospital this time. Heeding Trip's appeal, Hildie resigned. She tried to get more sleep, but it seemed elusive in the face of rising fears.

As a nurse, she knew the signs, even if she'd tried to ignore them over the past months. She started losing weight again. It took a force of will to do even the easier household chores. She awakened with night sweats and fever. When the cough started, she gave up and told Trip she had to go back to Arroyo.

❊ ❊ ❊

1951

Hildie had been at Arroyo two months and knew she wasn't getting any better. Lying in bed at the sanatorium, she saw all of Trip's dreams going down as her bills mounted. He had to hire a baby-sitter to watch Charlie and Carolyn until he got home from work each afternoon. He had to get Charlie off to school each day, cook and do the laundry, keep up the house, keep up the yard. Any time left over, he spent with her, leaving the children behind with LaVonne Haversal.

"If I'm going to die, Trip, I want to die at home."

His face twisted in agony. "Don't talk like that."

The doctor had warned them both that depression would be her greatest enemy.

"I pray, Trip. I do. I keep crying out to God to give me answers." And only one answer came again and again. It seemed a cruel joke.

Trip prayed and came up with the same solution Hildemara dreaded speaking aloud.

"She won't come."

"She's your mother. Do you think she'd do nothing to help you?"

"I told her I'd never ask for her help."

"It's the only way to bring you home, Hildie. Or are you going to let your pride stand in the way?"

"She's never helped me before. Why would she do it now, and under these circumstances?"

"We won't know unless we ask." He took her hands. "I think she'll surprise you."

Trip called Mama while Hildemara choked on her pride and wondered why God had brought her down so low. Trip thought she feared Mama might say no. Hildie feared Mama would say yes.

The moment Trip told Mama she was sick and asked for help, Hildemara knew whatever respect she had earned from her mother would be gone. Mama would think her a coward again, too weak to stand on her own feet, incapable of being a good wife and mother.

If Mama came, Hildemara would have to lie in bed and watch her mother take over her responsibilities. And Mama would do it all better than Hildemara ever had because Mama always managed everything perfectly. Even without Papa, the ranch ran like a well-oiled machine. Mama would be the one to give Charlie wings. She'd probably teach Carolyn to read before she turned four.

Sick and helpless, Hildemara would have to watch the life she loved be taken over by her mother. Even the one thing at which she excelled, the one area of her life where she had proven her worth, would be stripped away from her.

Mama would become the nurse.

Marta

44

Marta stood in the almond orchard beneath the white blossom canopy, the heady scent of spring in the air. Overhead, bees hummed, gathering nectar and spreading pollen, promising a good crop this year. Petals drifted like snowfall around her, covering the sandy soil, reminding her of Switzerland. It wouldn't be long before new-growth-green leaves deepened into darker shades and almonds began to form in tiny nubs.

Niclas used to stand in the orchard just as she did now, looking up through the white-clothed branches to blue sky. He had always been thankful to God for the land, the orchard, the vineyard, crediting the Almighty for providing for his family. He'd never taken anything for granted, not even her.

How she missed him! Marta had thought the years would dull the pain of losing him; and in part, they had, just not in a way she wanted. She couldn't remember every detail of his face, the exact color of his blue eyes. She couldn't remember the feel of his hands upon her, the abandon when they came together as man and wife. She couldn't remember the sound of his voice.

466 || HER MOTHER'S HOPE

She *could* remember clearly those last weeks when Niclas had suffered so much and tried so hard not to show it because he knew she watched in helpless agony, anger boiling against God. As cancer ate away the hard muscle of his body and left him skin and bones, his faith had grown stronger and more unwavering. "God will not abandon you, Marta." She believed it because she believed Niclas.

Though he hadn't feared death, he hadn't wanted to leave her. When she realized his worry, she had told him she had done very well on her own and she didn't need anyone to take care of her. His eyes had lit with laughter. "Oh, Marta, Marta . . ." When she had wept, he took her hand weakly in his. "You and I are not finished," he whispered, his last words to her before he fell into a coma. She sat beside him until he stopped breathing.

Niclas had been so vigorous; she expected they would grow old together. The children had grown up and gone out on their own. She thought she and Niclas would have many happy years together, alone at last, with limitless time to talk, time together without inter-ruption. Losing him was hard enough without the awful cruelty of how he died. She had told God in no uncertain terms what she thought of that. A good, God-fearing and God-loving man like Niclas shouldn't suffer like that. She had come out here and stood in this orchard night after night crying out to God in anger, hurling her questions at Him in fury, pounding the ground in her grief.

She hadn't stopped with her complaints over losing Niclas, but had moved on to other pent-up grievances: her father's abuse, her mother's life of illness, her sister's suicide. She dredged up every resentment and hurt.

And God had let her purge herself. In His mercy, He didn't strike her down. Instead, she would feel the whisper of air, the silence, and would feel Him close, leaning in, His presence comforting.

Marta held to Niclas's promise. How she loved that man still. And they would be together again, not because of anything she or Niclas had done in this life to make it so, but because Jesus held them both in the palm of His mighty hand. They were both in Christ and always would be, though she had to endure this physical separation for however long God decided. The Lord had already set the day of her death, and she sensed it would be a long time in coming.

After those first painful weeks following Niclas's death, when she'd finally drained herself dry, she began to see God all around her. Her eyes opened to the beauty of this place, the tenderness of her family and friends who still offered aid and comfort, Hitch and Donna Martin, who shouldered the work. She took long drives to think and talked easily to the Lord while she did. She apologized for her unruly behavior and repented of it. While she had ranted, God had bestowed grace upon her. He had watched over, protected, and cared for her when she was at her worst.

She laughed now, knowing how surprised and pleased Niclas would be if he could see the change in her. She didn't just pray over meals; she prayed all the time. When she opened her eyes in the morning, she asked God to take hold of her day and lead her through it. When she closed them at night, she thanked Him. And in between, she constantly sought His guidance.

Even so, loneliness sometimes snuck up on her as it had today, catching her by the throat, making her heart flutter with an odd sense of panic. She had never been one to cling or depend solely on her husband, but he had become integral to her existence. Niclas now stood in heaven, and she remained captive on this earth. Jesus was with her, but she couldn't see Him; she couldn't touch Him. Never one for hugs and kisses from anyone but Niclas, she missed human touch.

Why this restlessness inside her? Was she floundering or simply at a crossroads?

She missed so many things, like watching her children or the Summer Bedlam boys hunting for doodlebugs and horned toads or crossing the barnyard on stilts.

She missed the sound of their laughter and shrieks when they played tag or had one of their moonlight snipe hunts. Only the humming of bees filled the silence now. The air, cool and refreshing, stood still.

Marta admonished herself. She had no patience for self-pity in others. She despised it in herself. She had started her journey alone, hadn't she?

"Look at the birds, Liebling. *An eagle flies alone,"* Mama had told her so many years ago. All right. Life wasn't fair. So what? Life was difficult. It didn't mean she had to become a grumbling old woman dragging her feet all day. She would mount up with wings as an eagle. She would run and not grow weary; she would walk and not faint. She would fly alone and trust God to keep her spirit airborne. Consider it all joy.

She had plenty of blessings to count. Her children had grown strong and flown off to build their own nests and families. Bernhard and Elizabeth's nursery in Sacramento was doing well. Movie companies pursued Clotilde for her expertise in costume design. Rikka, dreamy and lovely as ever, still had Melvin dangling. How long before that poor young man realized Rikka loved art more than any man?

Only Hildemara still troubled her. Marta had no peace about Hildemara. Her eldest daughter hadn't looked well the last time Marta saw her. And how many months ago had that been? Of course, everything could have changed for the better by now. Of the four, Hildemara shared the least about her life. She kept a distance. Or did Marta just imagine that?

She missed Hildemara terribly, but if her daughter wanted to keep a distance, so be it. Marta wouldn't poke her nose in where it wasn't wanted. At least Hildemara knew how to take care of herself, especially if she'd learned keeping up a house wasn't as important as taking care of her health.

Shaking her head, Marta chuckled, remembering how Hildemara had come home from nursing school and spent her vacation scouring and scrubbing everything in sight—floors, walls, counters, shelves. She'd been obsessed with ridding the farmhouse of germs, as if that were possible. Marta had been insulted at the time, annoyed past enduring.

Her mind often went back to the day Hildemara had left home.

Marta had pushed her hard that day. She'd hurt her girl and made her good and angry. Hildemara had never done anything easily, and stirring her anger had served Marta well in motivating the girl. If she got Hildemara mad enough, her daughter forgot her fear. But now she wondered if the anger lingered, even after the blessings became apparent. She hoped that wasn't true.

Hadn't anger had its way with her as well? Would she have left Steffisburg if she hadn't been raging mad at her father? Or had it been pride?

Her girl had been a godsend during Niclas's illness. Hildemara had proven her great worth during those last difficult months. She'd been knowledgeable, efficient, overflowing with compassion. She hadn't allowed her emotions to rule. She had been like the balm of Gilead in the house. Once or twice, she had stood up to Marta as she guarded her patient. It couldn't have been easy on Hildemara to watch her papa die. Marta was proud of her.

It had been in the weeks that followed Niclas's death that Marta had recognized the growing threat to both her and her daughter. Hildemara had remained to keep her company, to serve, and Marta had drawn comfort from it. She had become used to Hildemara doing for her. God had opened her eyes to it, and she'd been furious. Marta, who had sworn never to become a servant, was making her daughter into one. Her conscience rubbed her raw. Mama had set her free. Would she now cage Hildemara? What did an able-bodied woman need with a nurse? Mortified, she saw how Hildemara cooked and cleaned and fetched and carried. Only the constant activity and search for new things to do revealed the inner turmoil inside her girl. And it had come to Marta like a blow.

Hildemara doesn't belong here! Cut her loose!

The more Marta considered the truth of it, the angrier she'd become—at herself, more than Hildemara. It shamed her now to remember how long it had taken to do what was right. She had pushed Hildemara right out the door. It broke her heart, but a good mother teaches her children to fly.

Some, like her sister, Elise, never even spread their wings.

Others, like Hildemara, had to be shoved to the edge before they'd take wing. Marta regretted pressing her daughter so hard, but if she hadn't, where would they be now? She, sitting like the queen of Sheba in her rocker, reading for the pure pleasure of it while Hildemara worked her fingers to the bone on that wretched rag rug? God forbid!

If only she'd been able to send Hildemara off in Mama's gentle way, with words of blessing rather than a lie: *"I don't want you here."*

Marta had often been amazed at the differences between herself and her eldest daughter. Marta had set her mind long ago against ever being anyone's servant. Hildemara made a career of it. Serving others seemed to come naturally to her. Marta had dreaded being pulled home again by Mama's illness and Elise's dependency. Hildemara had come willingly, pouring her heart into caring for her papa—and mama, as it turned out.

Marta's father had clipped her mother's wings and caged her. He'd worked Mama until her health gave out. Had he the opportunity, he would have done the same to Marta. Mama knew it as well as Marta. Marta had fretted constantly, her conscience plaguing her. How could she leave Mama, ill as she was, and go after her dream? How dare she take her freedom at the cost to others she loved so dearly! Mama had understood the guilt that imprisoned Marta and lifted it.

"You have my blessing, Marta. I give it to you wholeheartedly and without reservation."

So many years had passed and Marta held fast to those words. *"You have my love."*

Words had power. Papa's crushed. Mama's lifted and sent her out free to find her way in the world. Perhaps, had Mama known how far from home Marta would go, she might've had second thoughts. Perhaps that had been an added reason for holding Elise so close, inadvertently clipping her wings and making her unable to fly.

Marta had so often been tempted to hold Hildemara as close. Sickly from birth, a tiny, homely baby prone to sickness, Hildemara

Rose had torn at Marta's heartstrings. She had wanted to protect and shower love on her girl. What a tragic waste if she'd given in and done it! No, Marta told herself firmly, she would've crippled her. She had done the right thing in stifling those yearnings.

Bernhard, Clotilde, and Rikka had all been born with an independent spirit. Hildemara Rose came into the world dependent. If it were left up to her, Hildemara might still be here, working for Mama, forgetting she had a life of her own to live. Marta hadn't been willing to wait and watch the years pass, or to see an old pattern be reborn. Mama had done the right thing by her, but the wrong thing for Elise. Marta couldn't allow herself to make the same mistake with Hildemara Rose.

Why was the girl so much on her mind lately? Why couldn't she find any peace about her?

It was time to stop second-guessing whether she had done things right or not. She had done her best by all her children. She had other decisions to make. She had her own life to consider.

As much as she had come to love the orchard and vineyard, this ranch had been Niclas's dream, not hers. She felt restless here. What of her plans set aside so long ago? Was she past the age where she could go back and pursue them? Or had they been too big? She'd wanted to own a hotel. She couldn't care less about that now, but what about getting an education? She sniffed, imagining what people would say if a woman her age showed up for a college lecture. Then again, why should she care what anyone thought about it? Had she ever cared what others said?

Would she be allowed in without a high school diploma? They would undoubtedly want to test her. Let them. She knew more than any eighteen-year-old she had met in a dozen years. Hadn't she read and reread her children's textbooks while they slept?

Maybe she was just being an old fool. Did having a high school diploma matter anymore? She should just get over not having one and be done with it. She could keep going down the shelves in the library, reading one book after another, until she lost her eyesight or dropped dead.

Self-pity again. *Lord, don't let me get into that disgusting habit.
And while we're about it, God, I don't know what to do. But it seems an
unholy waste of time to stay here and go on as I am. I pay the Martins
a fair wage and have more than enough to get by, but I feel . . . What?
What do I feel? I don't even know anymore, what I want, why I'm still
breathing air. Everything used to be so fixed in my mind.*

Hildemara.

Her mind's eye saw her daughter again. What about her? There
was unfinished business between them, but Marta didn't know
what to do about it. She wasn't even sure what it was, and she had
no intention of apologizing for being hard on her when that hard-
ness had been necessary.

*What about Hildemara, Lord? What're You trying to tell me? Just
spell it out!*

"Mrs. Waltert!" Hitch Martin came striding toward her. Niclas
had been right about the Okie being a hard, dependable worker.
Hitch kept up the place the way Niclas would have wanted, and
Marta didn't mind paying him wages above the going rate. "Donna
and me was going to town for supplies and wondered if you'd be
needing anything."

Polite, always respectful, considerate, too, he and Donna never
failed to ask, even knowing the answer would always be the same.
"Not a thing, Hitch." Marta liked having ready excuses to get in
her car and take a drive.

Hitch stood arms akimbo, admiring the trees. "Looks to be a
good crop coming, don't it?" The hives they had set out were busy.

"It does, indeed." Barring a strong wind or late driving rain to
ruin it. The bees were certainly doing their work.

"Someday I hope to have a place of my own like this." He
gave her a quick, shy glance. "In case I haven't said it lately, Mrs.
Waltert, I surely do appreciate you hiring me and letting us use the
big house." Hitch looked more fit than when she'd hired him—
plenty of good food, a decent roof over his head, and fewer worries
about how he was going to take care of his four children brought
change.

"It's as much to my benefit as yours." Maybe more so. She had hours to herself these days to do what she pleased, which made her grateful. She remembered what it had been like to live in a drafty tent with four children and only a barn for respites of privacy with her husband. She remembered spending three years slaving through blistering summers and arctic winters for a man who cheated them of their fair share of profits. She swore she'd never treat anyone who worked for her that way. The Martins were good people and she intended to see they did well.

Hitch seemed in no hurry to leave. "Listen to them bees."

"We'll have plenty of honey to sell." She would smoke the hives and steal the honey soon. Donna spun the rich sweetness from the combs and filled and labeled the jars for market.

"Nothing tastier than honey from almond blossoms, ma'am. Oh, by the way, I heared your phone ringing on the way out."

Probably one of her friends from church needed something cooked for someone sick or bereaved. "They'll call back."

Marta and Hitch talked farm business on the walk back to the wide drive. The windmill needed repairs. They'd have to start digging the irrigation ditches soon, get a head start. Now that they had a bathroom with a shower in the house, the small building with a water tank on top could be converted to something more useful. The barn would need repainting in another year. She could hire extra help if he wanted it for that project. "I don't want to see you up on an extension ladder, Hitch." He laughed and said he'd send one of his sons up to do the high work.

Hitch told her the tractor was acting up again, but he felt sure he could fix it, if he had a few parts. Marta gave him the go-ahead to buy whatever he needed. She always had a list of chores, but he'd begun anticipating her requests and getting the work done before she needed to ask. He was a good man, a good farmer.

After the Martins drove off in their old truck, Marta wandered the place. The fruit trees alongside the big house had grown. She and Donna would be canning peaches and pears together. The plums would make good prunes and jam. Plenty of apples for

Donna's growing children and a few neighbor kids to pluck and eat. And there would be lots of oranges and lemons, too.

Now that Donna tended the chickens and rabbits and kept up the vegetable garden, Marta had little work to do. She'd done laundry yesterday and baked bread this morning, enough for herself and the Martins. She could always spend the rest of the afternoon finishing up that five-thousand-piece puzzle Bernhard and Elizabeth had given her for Christmas last year. Bernhard had laughed and said that ought to keep her busy and out of Hitch Martin's hair for a while. She calculated how many hours she'd already spent on it and groaned. All that work for what? To break it up when she finished, put it back in the box, and give it away to someone else with time on their hands.

God, help me. I do not want to spend my life working puzzles and watching game shows. Time enough for that when I'm really old. At eighty-five or ninety.

The telephone rang.

Marta let the screen door slam behind her. She answered on the fourth ring.

"It's Trip, Mama."

She knew by his voice he hadn't called with good news. "Hildemara's sick again, isn't she?" She eased herself onto a kitchen chair. Maybe there had been a reason she'd been thinking so much about her eldest daughter lately.

"She's back in the hospital."

"She should start getting better then."

"She's been there two months and no improvement."

Two months! "And you're just telling me about it now?"

"Hildie thought she'd be home in a few weeks. She didn't want to worry you. We both hoped . . ." He fell silent again.

Lies, all of it, but Marta could imagine the worry on his face and calmed herself. "How are you managing alone with the children?"

"A neighbor lady takes care of them while I'm at work."

A neighbor lady. Well, wasn't that just grand. Hildemara and Trip would rather have a stranger taking care of their children than call her for help. How had this happened? Marta rested her elbows on the table. Holding the phone in one hand, she rubbed her forehead with the other. She could feel a headache coming on. She'd better speak before she couldn't. "She needs time, I suppose."

"Time." His voice choked up. "All she does is worry about hospital bills and leaving me in debt." He cleared his throat. "She says if she's going to die, she wants to die at home."

Marta felt the heat rise up inside her. So Hildemara had given up again. "You remind her she has a husband and two children to live for. She's not done with this life yet."

"It's worse this time. Wanting to live isn't always enough."

It seemed Hildemara wasn't the only one who had given up. Marta thought of her mother. Had she wanted to live? Or had she given up, too? Had she become so tired of the struggle to hold on to life, even for Elise, that she gave up?

"We could use your help, Mama."

"If you're asking me to come up and help bury her, the answer is no."

He drew in a sharp breath and swore. His tone hardened. "Hildie said you wouldn't help her."

The words stabbed deep. Marta wanted to say she'd helped Hildemara more than the girl would ever understand, but that wouldn't help Trip handle what was happening or make Hildemara get better.

Squaring her shoulders, Marta scraped her chair back and stood. "If my daughter can hold on so tight to old grievances, with God's help, she can hold on to life, too, Trip Arundel."

"I shouldn't have called." He sounded defeated.

"No. You should've called sooner! The trouble is I can't do anything right this minute." She had things to settle, and she'd have to work quickly. She and Hitch Martin had made a gentleman's agreement. Maybe it was time to put things into writing. She'd need to talk to Hitch first and then a lawyer. She wanted to make certain things were spelled out good and properly so both she and the Martins benefited.

"I'm sorry," Trip mumbled, voice tear-soaked.

Her son-in-law sounded so tired, so out of hope, Marta felt the sorrow rise up in her. Would she lose her daughter after all? Would she have to watch Hildemara suffer as Mama had, gasping for breath, coughing up blood into a handkerchief?

"We're talking now. And we're going to pray hard and get others praying with us. I've got a whole group of women with plenty of time for that kind of work. Come down to Murietta, Trip. I'll have to get busy and sort out a few things here. But you come. Do you hear me?"

"Yes, ma'am."

"Good. We can sit under the bay tree and talk about what I can and can't do."

Trip said he'd drive down with the children on Saturday.

❄ ❄ ❄

Marta sat down and wrote a list in her journal. First things first. *Talk to Hitch and Donna about taking over the ranch.* Hitch had said today he'd like to have a place of his own someday. Running this place in her absence would move him toward that goal. They'd need a legal contract to protect both of them. Charles Landau had a good reputation as a lawyer. She had accounts at the hardware store and feed and grain. She'd add Hitch to them so he could get what he needed without having to clear everything through her. She needed to copy the ranch maintenance schedule from her journal and give that to Hitch as well, though he seemed to know it already. Niclas had wanted to be sure she knew what needed to be done and when throughout the year.

Marta spent all day thinking over ranch business and things she'd need to get settled. Concerns buzzed like flies in her head, and she swatted them with prayers. Finally exhausted, Marta went to bed, but couldn't sleep. She'd talk to Hitch and Donna first thing in the morning, then go to town, set up an appointment with Charles Landau, and take care of the store accounts. Annoyed, she told herself to let go of it all and get some sleep.

Hildemara hadn't wanted Trip to call. *"Hildie said you wouldn't help her."* Did her daughter really believe that?

Lying in the darkening room, Marta weighed her actions from the past. She prayed God would help her see through Hildemara's eyes, and as she did, she wondered. *Does Hildemara Rose even know how much I love her?*

If only she'd been a gentler person, like Mama, one given to prayer and trusting in God from the beginning no matter how bad the circumstances. Life with Marta's father had been dire indeed. Nothing pleased the man. And yet, Mama had treated him with loving respect. She worked hard, never complained, never gave in to despair, and continued to love him, even at his worst. Marta saw how she had made her mother's life even more difficult. Hot-tempered, stubborn, willful, she had never been an easy child. She'd fought her father, refusing to be cowed, even when he beat her. How many times had Mama been in the middle, pleading, trying to protect?

Mama had only hurt her once. *"You are more like your father than you are like me."*

Marta had been offended at the time, but she should've listened. She should've been warned! Harsh words, fierce anger, a desire to achieve her goals at all cost—hadn't she inherited all that from Papa? Mama hadn't meant to hurt her. She had only wanted Marta to see her father in another way, without hatred and condemnation.

Did Hildemara look upon her the same way? Did her daughter see her as unbending, never satisfied with Hildemara's efforts, always looking for faults, unfeeling, unable to love? If Hildemara didn't feel she could ask for help, didn't that say it all?

How could such misunderstanding have grown between them?

Yes, Marta conceded, she had hurt her daughter at times, but to make her strong, not to tear her down. Had she been so determined to make Hildemara rise up and fight back that she had become as intractable, cruel, and heartless as her own father? God forbid!

But she saw clearly how she had been harder on Hildemara than the others. She had done it out of love. She had done it to save Hildemara from Elise's fate. She didn't want her girl growing up frightened of the world, hiding away inside a house controlled by a tyrant, utterly dependent on her mother.

And Hildemara hadn't.

Marta had hated her father. She realized now she'd never forgiven him. When he wired for her to come back, she had burned his message and wished him in hell. How dare she hope for forgiveness from Hildemara if she couldn't forgive her own father?

Pain clutched at Marta so fiercely, she sat up and hunched over.

She had never used her fists on Hildemara, or whipped her with a strap until she bled, the way her father had. She never called her ugly or told her she was stupid. She'd never told her she had no right to go to school, that education was wasted on her. She'd never made Hildemara work and then taken away her wages. Despised and rejected, Marta had fought back, lashing out in fury against her father for trying to bury her spirit beneath the avalanche of his own disappointments.

And Mama had held her and whispered words of encouragement. Mama had held her head up so she could breathe. She'd sent Marta away because she knew, if she remained, she'd become exactly like him: discontent, selfish, cruel, blaming others for what hadn't turned out well in his life.

She'd always been Papa's scapegoat.

As you made him yours.

Getting up, Marta went to the window and looked out on the moon-cast yard, the closed barn doors, the white-veiled almond trees.

Would she have left Switzerland and set out on her own journey if not for her father? She'd always credited Mama for her freedom, but Papa played a part, too. She'd been the least favored child. Hermann, firstborn son; Elise, so beautiful, like an angel.

She could see now how she had treated her own children differently. She'd taken pride in Bernhard as her firstborn son. Clotilde thrived, possessed from birth of an independent spirit. Nothing would hold that girl down. And Rikka, with her ethereal beauty and childlike delight in God's creation, had been like a star fallen from the heavens, not quite of this world. Rikka knew no fear. She would flit and float through life, delighting in the wonder of it, seeing shadows, but ignoring them.

And where had Hildemara fit in?

Hildemara, the smallest, the least hearty, the most dependent, had struggled from the beginning—to live, to grow, later to find a dream, to build her own life, to thrive. And now, she must struggle to survive. If she didn't have the courage to do that on her own, Marta must find a way to give it to her.

A flash of memory came of Hildemara racing home, terrified after Mr. Kimball had tried to rape her. But it occurred to Marta now, her daughter had kicked free of a grown man stronger than Niclas. She had been smart enough to run. Hildemara had shown real spunk that day, and at other times, too. She'd gone out and gotten herself a job. She'd said no to college and gone off to nurses' training. She'd followed Trip from one base to another, finding housing in strange cities, making new friends. She'd crossed the country by herself and come home to help Bernhard and Elizabeth hold on to the Musashis' land despite threats and fire and bricks through their windows.

My daughter has courage, Lord!

Despite appearances, and though Marta loathed to admit it, she'd always favored Hildemara a little above the others. From the moment her daughter came into the world, Marta had bonded fast to her. *"She looks like her mother,"* Niclas had said, unwittingly setting things in motion. All the cruel words her father had said about her appearance rose up inside her when she saw Hildemara Rose was plain. And like Elise, she was frail.

But she wouldn't stay that way. Marta decided that first frightening week she wouldn't cripple Hildemara Rose the way Mama had crippled Elise.

Now she wondered if she hadn't pushed Hildemara too hard, and in doing so, pushed her away.

Oh, Lord, can I bring her close again?

Hildemara had Mama's constitution. And now, it seemed she had Mama's disease. Would she share Mama's fate as well?

Please, Lord, give me time.

She covered her face and prayed. *Oh, God, I wish I'd been more like Mama with her and less like Papa. Maybe I could've made Hildemara strong without wounding her. But I can't go back now and undo the past. Hildemara Rose has no faith in me, no understanding. And that's my fault, not hers. Does she understand I'm proud of her and her accomplishments? Does she know me at all?*

She can.

Marta lowered her hands, drew back the curtains, and looked up at the stars. "Jesus," she whispered, "will she be willing to meet me halfway?"

What does that matter?

Marta bowed her head. It was just her pride butting in again.

Hildemara had worked hard and done well. She'd had her moments of despair when she'd wanted to give up, but she'd grasped hold when hope was offered and rose again. She wasn't Elise. She might be depressed, but she wouldn't give up. Not if Marta had anything to say about it.

Hildemara might be quieter than Bernhard, who thought he could tackle the world, less self-possessed than fiery Clotilde with her quest for fame and fortune, not as intuitive and gifted as Rikka, who saw the world through angel eyes. Nevertheless, Hildemara had spunk. She had her own special gifts.

Marta lifted her chin again.

My daughter has a servant's heart that should please You, Lord. Like Your Son, she's meek, but no coward. She might be a broken reed now with the cold wind of death in her face, but You won't allow her spirit to be crushed. You said it and I believe it. But give me time with her, Lord. I beg You. Help me mend my relationship with her. You know how I've fought against being a servant all my life. I confess it. I've always hated the very idea of it!

A gentle breeze drifted in through the open window, as though God whispered to her. Marta wiped tears from her cheeks.

"Lord," she whispered back, "teach me how to serve my daughter."

❄ ❄ ❄

Marta got up early the next morning and prayed. She went out the side door toward the garden, leaving her journal open on the kitchen table. Walking around to the front of the big house, she knocked on the front door. When Donna opened the door, Marta asked to speak to her and Hitch together about something important. They both looked nervous as they invited her to sit at their table and share a cup of fresh coffee. Marta told them about Hildemara and that she had been thinking about the ranch and making some changes. Hitch's expression fell.

Donna gave him a sorry look and then offered a pained smile to Marta. "With your husband passing on and all, and your daughter needing you, it's understandable you'd want to sell."

"I'm not selling. I'd like to offer you a contract to run the place. You tell me what you want. I'll tell you what I need. And we'll have Charles Landau put it all in writing so there will be no question about it."

Hitch's head came up. "You're not selling?"

"That's what I said." She gave Donna a teasing look. "Better see that he cleans his ears." She looked at Hitch again. "It may come to that, but if it does, you'll get first shot at buying it. If you want it, that is."

"We don't have the money," he said glumly.

"Knowing how hard you work, I might even be willing to hold the paper rather than have some banker come out the winner in the deal." She looked between the two of them. "So?"

"Yes!" Hitch grinned.

"Please," Donna added, face aglow.

That settled, Marta drove to town to take care of the rest of the details.

Then, on impulse, she drove to Merced and went shopping.

❄ ❄ ❄

She wrote to Rosie that night and told her about Hildemara.

I started thinking about Lady Daisy and our afternoons at Kew and tea in the conservatory. I think it's about time I shared some of these experiences with Hildemara Rose. So I went to Merced and looked through all the stores and couldn't find anything as fine as what I wanted.

After hours of searching, I was discouraged. Actually, I was annoyed. I ended up in a little shop, but one look around and I was ready to walk out the front door. Fortunately, the proprietor cut me off. Gertrude! Swiss, from Bern! We talked for an hour.

I'd completely forgotten why I'd come to Merced in the first place until we both noticed the time. She needed to close the shop, and I needed to drive home to Murietta. Before leaving, I finally got around to telling her what I'd been looking for and why. G went into her back room and came out with an old, dusty box filled with dishes. She said she'd forgotten all about them until that very moment.

I am now the proud owner of a Royal Albert Lady Carlyle tea service—four plates, four teacups, and saucers! G also sold me some dainty spoons and forks, well worth every dollar she extracted from me. I will make all the wonderful sweets and savories for Hildemara Rose that I once served to Lady Daisy. I will pour India tea and lace it with milk and conversation.

God willing, I will win back my daughter.

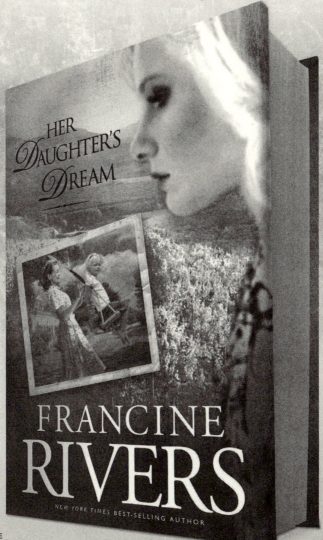

A Note from the Author

Dear Reader,

Since I became a Christian, my stories
have begun with struggles I'm having in
my own faith walk, or issues that I haven't
worked out. That's how this two-book
series started. I wanted to explore what
caused the rift between my grandma and
my mom during the last years of my
grandmother's life. Was it a simple misunderstanding that they never had time
to work out? or something deeper that
had grown over the years?

Many of the events of this story were
inspired by family history that I researched
and events I read about in my mother's
journals or experienced in my own life.
For instance, when I was three, my
mother had tuberculosis, just like Hildie
did. Dad brought her home from the

sanatorium and Grandma Wulff came to live with us and help out. It was difficult for everyone. A child doesn't understand communicable disease. For a long time, I didn't think my mother loved me. She never held or kissed me. She kept her distance to protect her children, but it took years before I understood what felt like rejection was actually evidence of sacrificial love.

Steffisburg, Switzerland

While thinking over the past, my husband, Rick, and I decided to take a trip to Switzerland, my grandmother's homeland. Several years earlier, we had gone on a heritage trip to Sweden to meet many of Rick's relatives on his mother's side. I knew I wouldn't have the same opportunity in Switzerland, but wanted to see the countryside with which my grandmother would have been familiar. We visited Bern, where my grandmother went to housekeeping school, and Interlaken, where she worked in a hotel restaurant. When I mentioned to the tour guide that my grandmother had come from the small town of Steffisburg near Thun, she and the bus driver decided to surprise us. Taking an alternate route, they drove into Steffisburg and parked across the street from the centuries-old Lutheran church my grandmother's family must have attended. Rick and I stood in front of the

The Wulff siblings

Francine's parents, the Kings

Steffisburg map for a picture before wandering the church grounds and sitting in the sanctuary. We walked up and down the main street, taking lots of pictures. It was a very precious moment for me. On the way out of town, we caught a glimpse of Thun Castle, another place my grandmother mentioned.

Going through family pictures, I came across several of my mom and her siblings. The one above is my favorite. Mom is second from the left, giggling. Sig was the eldest, then came Mom, Margaret, and Elsie. The picture was taken on the farm in the Central Valley where Grandma and Grandpa had almond trees and grapevines. They dried grapes to make raisins. When my brother and I were young, we often spent a few weeks every summer on the farm, romping and playing and swimming in the irrigation ditches that ran along the back side of the property.

Mom went away to Fresno for nurses' training, then worked at Alta Bates Hospital in Berkeley. My father worked part-time as an orderly. He told me with some amusement that he would go to Mom's ward and ask for an aspirin. Nurses were not to date orderlies, but Dad eventually won Mom over. Not long after they were married,

King family vacation; "Marta" on right

he was called off to war and served as a medic in the European theater. He was in the third wave into Normandy and fought in Germany during the final days of World War II.

My parents enjoyed camping and wanted my brother and me to see as much of our country as possible. Every year, they saved vacation time and took us off on a trip to visit as many national parks as they could squeeze into two weeks. They often invited Grandma Wulff to come along. When my brother and I would doze in the backseat, Grandma or Mom would prod us. "Wake up, sleepyhead. Look out the window! You may never see this part of the country again." Every few years, we made the trip from Pleasanton, California, back to Colorado Springs, my father's hometown, to visit Grandma and Grandpa King. The photo above is one of the rare pictures of my family with both of my grandmothers. Unfortunately, Grandma King died when I was six.

I am blessed to have many wonderful family memories, many of which include Grandma Wulff. I knew there were times of stress and tension between my parents and Grandma, but all families have them. Most work through them. Sometimes minor disagreements can escalate when things aren't resolved.

No one but God can see into the human heart. We can't even fully see into our own. My mother and my grandmother were both strong Christians. They both served others all their lives. Both were admirable women of strong character whom I loved dearly. I still love them and miss them both. I choose to believe my grandmother forgave my mom at the end for whatever hurt lay between them. I choose to believe she simply did not have the time or voice to say it. I know my mother loved her to the end of her own life.

This book has been a three-year quest to feel at peace about the hurt between Mom and Grandma, the possible causes, the ways they might have misunderstood one another, how they might have been reconciled. Jesus teaches us to love one another, but sometimes love doesn't come packed the way we want. Sometimes fear has to be set aside so we can share the past hurts that have shaped our lives, so we can dwell in freedom with one another. And sometimes we don't recognize love when it is offered.

Someday when I pass from this life to the next, I hope Mom and Grandma will both be standing with Jesus and welcoming me home— just as I will be waiting when my own beloved daughter arrives—and her daughter after her and all the generations yet to come.

Francine Rivers

Discussion Guide

1. Marta certainly had a difficult childhood. What factors shaped her the most, for better or worse? How do those influences shape the woman she becomes?

2. How does Marta's relationship with her father shape her early beliefs about God and His expectations? How is it different from the way Mama sees God? What seems to make the biggest impression on the way Marta views God? Does that change throughout the story? If so, what causes that change?

3. At the end of chapter 4, Marta's mother gave her a blessing when she left home to make her way in the world. In what ways, verbal or otherwise, did your parents give you their blessing? If they didn't, what do you wish they had said to you? In what ways did you—or do you hope to someday—do the same for your own children?

4. It has been said that women often marry a version of their father. How is Niclas like and unlike Marta's father? In what

ways is Niclas both passive and aggressive? Marta sometimes seems to harbor resentment toward Niclas. Is that fair?

5. Marta has a hard time trusting Niclas because of the way her father treated her mother. How do you think that makes Niclas feel? In what ways—good or bad—has your family of origin affected your marriage or close friendships?

6. Niclas asks Marta to sell the boardinghouse she bought as the fulfillment of a lifelong dream. Is that an appropriate request? What do you think of the way Niclas makes the decision and communicates it to Marta? If you were Marta, what would you have done in that situation? Have you faced a similar decision in your marriage or family?

7. Marta sometimes makes it difficult for Niclas to be the head of their household. Does Marta view herself as a helpmate to Niclas? Do you think he sees her in that way? How is he able to love Marta despite her sometimes-prickly nature?

8. Why does Marta never tell Niclas—or anyone else in her family—that she loves them? How does Marta best show and receive love?

9. In many ways, Marta is like the woman described in Proverbs 31. Which of the qualities described in that passage do you see in her? Which ones is she missing?

10. After rescuing Elise from the Meyers in chapter 5, Marta tells her friend, "I swear before God, Rosie, if I'm ever fortunate enough to have a daughter, I'll make sure she's strong enough to stand up for herself!" How do Marta's family dynamics come into play later in life when she has children of her own?

11. Marta loves Hildemara deeply. Yet of all her children, Hildemara probably feels the least loved. Why is that? Is treating children *differently* the same as *favoring* one over another? What challenges make it difficult to raise all the kids in a family exactly the same? How hard should parents strive to do so?

12. Have you ever felt, as Hildemara did, that others in your family have unfairly received a greater share of love, financial provision, or some other valuable resource? How did you respond? What advice would you give someone in this situation?

13. After Hildemara's incident with her teacher Mrs. Ransom, Hildemara tells her father that she prayed and prayed, but her prayers didn't change the situation. Niclas replies, "Prayers changed you, Hildemara." What does he mean by that? Have you ever had a similar experience?

14. Why is Marta so averse to Hildemara's decision to attend nursing school? Does she ever change her mind about Hildemara's chosen profession?

15. For several months, Hildemara keeps Trip at arm's length. Why do you think she does that? What makes her finally admit her love for him?

16. Trip, like many men of his generation, has tragic, life-altering experiences in World War II. Have you heard stories from or about men in your own family who were similarly affected? Have any of your loved ones been involved in more recent wars? How has war affected your family?

17. Tuberculosis is much rarer today than it was in Marta's and Hildemara's lifetimes. Yet life-threatening and chronic illnesses have never been more prevalent. How has your family been impacted by serious illness? Discuss the strain illness can place on family dynamics, regardless of the "relational health" a family may have at the outset.

18. If you could change one thing about the way you were parented, what would it be? And if you have children, is there anything you wish you could change about the way you've parented them? What is one step you could take in that direction?

19. At the end of this book Marta is determined, with God's help, to make a fresh start with Hildemara. Do you think she will succeed? Why or why not? How do you think Hildemara will respond? Is there hope for this relationship?

20. If you could sit down with Marta and Hildemara, what would you like to tell each of them? Is there someone in your family you need to talk with about mistakes or misperceptions from the past that are still affecting you today? If you have unresolved issues with a loved one who has passed away, who might you talk with to try to reach some closure for yourself?

About the Author

New York Times best-selling author Francine Rivers began her literary career at the University of Nevada, Reno, where she graduated with a bachelor of arts degree in English and journalism. From 1976 to 1985, she had a successful writing career in the general market, and her books were highly acclaimed by readers and reviewers. Although raised in a religious home, Francine did not truly encounter Christ until later in life, when she was already a wife, a mother of three, and an established romance novelist.

Shortly after becoming a born-again Christian in 1986, Francine wrote *Redeeming Love* as her statement of faith. First published by Bantam Books, and then rereleased by Multnomah Publishers in the mid-1990s, this retelling of the biblical story of Gomer and Hosea, set during the time of the California Gold Rush, is now considered by many to be a classic work of Christian fiction. *Redeeming Love* continues to be one of the Christian Booksellers Association's top-selling titles, and it has held a spot on the Christian best-seller list for nearly a decade.

Since *Redeeming Love*, Francine has published numerous novels with Christian themes—all best sellers—and she has continued to win both industry acclaim and reader loyalty around the globe. Her Christian novels have been awarded or nominated for numerous honors, including the RITA Award, the Christy Award, the ECPA Gold Medallion, and the Holt Medallion in Honor of Outstanding Literary Talent. In 1997, after winning her third RITA Award for inspirational fiction, Francine was inducted into the Romance Writers of America's Hall of Fame. Francine's novels have been translated into more than twenty different languages, and she enjoys best-seller status in many foreign countries, including Germany, the Netherlands, and South Africa.

Francine and her husband, Rick, live in northern California and enjoy time spent with their three grown children and taking every opportunity to spoil their grandchildren. Francine uses her writing to draw closer to the Lord, and she desires that through her work she might worship and praise Jesus for all He has done and is doing in her life.

Visit her Web site at www.francinerivers.com.

BOOKS BY BELOVED AUTHOR
FRANCINE RIVERS

The Mark of the Lion series
(available individually or as a boxed set)
A Voice in the Wind
An Echo in the Darkness
As Sure as the Dawn

A Lineage of Grace series
(available individually or in an anthology)
Unveiled
Unashamed
Unshaken
Unspoken
Unafraid

Sons of Encouragement series
(available individually or in an anthology)
The Priest
The Warrior
The Prince
The Prophet
The Scribe

Marta's Legacy series
Her Mother's Hope
Her Daughter's Dream

Children's Titles
The Shoe Box
Bible Stories for Growing Kids
(coauthored with Shannon
Rivers Coibion)

Stand-alone Titles
Redeeming Love
The Atonement Child
The Scarlet Thread
The Last Sin Eater
Leota's Garden
And the Shofar Blew
The Shoe Box (a Christmas novella)

www.francinerivers.com

CP0098

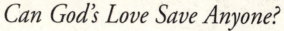
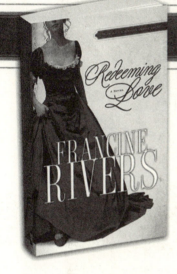